DUKES OF RUIN

THE ROYALS OF FORSYTH U

ANGEL LAWSON

SAMANTHA RUE

FOREWORD

Readers!

First up: Have you read the first part of this series, Lords? If yes, continue. If no... well, you may want to. This book is about the Dukes, one of the fraternities in the Royals of Forsyth series. It follows a specific harem and a specific storyline. BUT! Reading Lords first will be helpful to understand the players, their motives and backgrounds.

Second: Friends and family should excuse themselves right now. For serious. No really. We'll take a minute while you exit the room. Thanks.

Third, if you get squeamish about dark romance content that makes you uncomfortable in ANY WAY DO NOT READ THIS BOOK (and then go complain all over the internets that no one told you, like some kind of book police. Because here it is, we're telling you.)

But, if you're here on purpose, amazing! That means you know what you're getting into. Will this book be as dark as the Lords? God, we have no idea. We aren't here for shock value. We're all about the angst, trauma, and desperation and Dukes is packed with it. Everyone pull on their big girl or big boy panties and get ready.

For real T/W: non/dub, self-harm, suicide attempt, captivity, plus a shit-ton of mindfuckery and emotional manipulation.

For the full list go to our website, where you can also find a free prequel to this story.

Enjoy!

Angel & Sam

Join our facebook group, Angel's Antics to connect with authors, readers, and all the good stuff.

ANGEL'S ANTICS
READER GROUP

LORDS

KILLIAN PAYNE
KING

STORY AUSTIN
LADY / QUEEN

DIMITRI RATHBONE
LORD

TRISTIAN MERCER
LORD

POSEY PAYNE
IMPRISONED

DANIEL PAYNE
DEAD AS FUCK

MRS. CRANE
BAMF

AUGUSTINE
MADAM

DUKES

SAUL CARTWRIGHT
KING

NICK BRUIN
DUKE

SY PERILINI
DUKE

REMY MADDOX
DUKE

LAVINIA LUCIA
DUCHESS

SARAH
FORMER DUCHESS/ MOM

DAVIS BRUIN
FORMER DUKE / POPS

MANNY PERILINI
FORMER DUKE / DAD

MAMA B
MANAGER

VERITY
CUTSLUT

CUTSLUTS
GYM FANGIRLS

COUNTS

LIONEL LUCIA
KING

BRUNO PEREZ
COUNT

LARS
COUNT

SUTTON
COUNTESS

LETICIA LUCIA
DAUGHTER / MISSING

LAVINIA LUCIA
DAUGHTER / SOLD

CASH MALLIS
FRIENDLY NEIGHBORHOOD DRUG GUY

PROLOGUE

Lavinia

"Remember," Anthony says, sweeping his thumb across my cheek, *"as long as we're together we can do anything."*

I absorb the final words and then toss the paperback on the bed, pushing my fingers into my eyes. I've been following the sexy exploits of Anthony and Beth, former enemies, eventual lovers, stuck in Victorian England. The books, much like these walls, are fucking killing me, but I'm not in the position to be picky.

I've lost count of how many days I've been here. A few weeks? A month? Two months? One minute bleeds into the next in an unstoppable march, a marriage of days, and a chain of monotony that makes my muscles tense in anticipation of...

Nothing.

Absolutely fucking nothing.

It's been more than enough time to read the stack of trashy romance novels Auggy brought me—I'd never admit this, but some more than once. I probably should have left scratch marks on the wall, noting the passing days the way they do in prison. I guess when they first brought me here; I didn't realize I'd need to keep track. Now I'm just floating along like a restless, electric ghost, desperate for somewhere to put all this static that's been building in my veins.

I take a few moments to indulge in the phosphenes exploding behind my eyelids. The flash of stars helps me imagine being in space, a phantom among the cosmos, tracking an orbit around the sun. That's all time is, anyway: an involuntary trip around a dying star.

God, I'd give my left tit for a soda.

Sighing, I ease the pressure on my eyes, letting them open. It's evening, that much I know from the muted light beyond my sole window, and the build of the bustle outside the door of my living suite. The room was nicer when I first arrived, with plenty of room for a sofa and armchair, a large bathroom, and a walk-in closet that's lost on someone with nothing but a few pairs of shorts and shirts. That, plus the artwork and mirrors on the walls, the lush furniture, and clean carpet, are nice upgrades from the shitty hotel they had me in last year. Daniel Payne, the previous King of South Side and owner of this fine establishment, definitely knew how to treat his girls. I guess that's what happens when you marry a former prostitute. You take her advice.

And then you take her bullet.

Yeah, it used to be fancy. A real fucking retreat. A prison with gold-colored frippery. They should have known better than to leave me here. My second night, I smashed one of the glass frames and hid a shard beneath my pillow. The waiting was the easy part— time, time, time—and the first time they sent in one of those whores to dress me up, I slashed her goddamn throat.

That was the hard part.

I sorely underestimated how hard it is to cut a throat. There are a lot of tendons and muscles up in there, and it didn't even matter that I failed to hit anything vital enough to kill her. It was messy and excessively gross, and I probably wouldn't try it again.

But it was enough to get the room cleared of anything that

could be considered a weapon. Smart move on their part. If I had it my way, I'd carve a bloody goddamn swath through this place, gross or not.

The Velvet Hideaway. Real subtle branding there. I shouldn't be surprised. Daniel Payne might have run South Side, but he never struck me as the creative type. Why play coy with the name of your brothel when you own this whole fucking town? Might as well have named it Whores R' Us. *Where a perv can be a perv!*

Now, only Auggy will deal with me, always bitchy and cutting when she does. In another lifetime, maybe we would have even been friends, but since she's the twat who locks my door, Augustine can go fuck herself. The looks she gives me are always a mixture of irritated and sympathetic. She may not have dreamed of being a Madam when she was a kid, but it's sure as fuck a better position than slave.

Because that's what I am.

I'm a slave.

There's no dressing it up. I can't leave. No access to a phone or computer. There are no visitors, no weapons, and no hopes of getting out. My room is in the basement, and as if the pathetic, squat little egress window above my dresser isn't sad enough, it's also barred, caging me in.

Unbidden, a menacing voice floats through my mind.

"Little Bird."

Shuddering, I spring from the bed and begin pacing, wall-to-wall, my four-hundred square feet of prison. If he were here—if Nick could see me—he'd make a joke out of it. Something real obnoxious about a panicked bird flinging herself against the bars of her cage. That's what he calls me. His Little Bird. Wings clipped, thrown in a cage, trapped as I hurl myself around the confines of my prison...

But I can't help it. Baring my teeth, I pound my fist against the walls, wishing I could bore straight through. I've tried begging before—*"I won't go anywhere, just let me out."*—but it never works. No one's listening, and even if they were, they wouldn't care. No one here ever does. So I rattle the bars of my cage by pounding my fists into the walls, and then I race around the room to convince myself it hasn't gotten smaller between one panicked heartbeat and the next.

I'm not stupid.

I know it's hopeless.

No one's coming to save me. There was a time, in the beginning, when I used to imagine my father sweeping in to say I've learned my lesson. He'd give me that long, haughty, disappointed look, as if I've failed him in every conceivable way—*fact*—but he'd still let me go. It was a nice dream, for a hot minute.

Desperate for a distraction, I sort the books on the bed, searching for one I haven't read. There's one with a shirtless pirate that I've been avoiding. The man on the cover has a broad chest and piercingly blue eyes, and whenever I look at it, I think of storm clouds and thorns.

Little Bird...

My muscles tighten at the memory of Nick's voice. It's been a long while since he came here, which is both a blessing and a curse. It's never good when he shows up, but the longer he doesn't, the more the dread about his impending arrival builds. It's better to just get it over with, to bear his intense, creepy stare and filthy words for an hour, and then be free of it for a week or two.

I've just picked the book up again when I hear a noise outside my barred window.

There are a lot of sounds at the Hideaway. Music. Raised voices. Laughter. Moans. Grunts. Shrieks of faked pleasure. They're not always fun sounds. There's also the occasional bar fight. At least once a week, the police show up, lights flashing outside my window, carrying out a John who took a few too many liberties with one of the girls. Twice an ambulance has come.

I'm attuned to each sound by now, constantly awaiting the turn of that knob.

I wait a beat, but hear nothing else, so I settle back in against the pillows. I open the pirate book in an attempt to calm the disquiet writhing beneath my flesh. It's a dumb reason to avoid it, thinking the man on the cover looks like Nick. The most odious thing about him is how deceptively he's been nicknamed around these parts. *Pretty*. What a shit word to describe such a beautifully rotten person.

The pages have that musty scent of an old bookstore, and inside is the penciled in price of twenty-five cents. I find that I can't be bothered with it, though. My eyes grow heavy, attention waning, and it's a comfort to close the book and set it aside. To turn off the light. To grasp clumsily for the truest sense of freedom I'm afforded in this fucked up place.

Sleep.

SHATTERING GLASS WAKES ME, kicking my heart into gear, until I remember where I am. *What* I am. I refuse to fully rouse and deal with the midnight drama of the brothel. I roll onto my stomach, cheek against my pillow, and will myself to slip back under. It's warm here, in this place where time is without substance or form. So I'm not exactly sure what makes my eyelids rise. Maybe it's the strange breeze against my back, or the sudden loss of static in the air, like something is blocking it out.

The column of shadow in front of my dresser is so still that it doesn't even look like anything at first. It looks like furniture. A statue. A stone pillar that's been a part of this place's foundation long before I closed my eyes, even though I intrinsically know it doesn't belong. The sheer curtain covering the egress window above billows around it, caressing the silhouette's shoulder. I can almost believe it's part of a slow, prophetic dream.

Then, it moves closer.

A gasp catches in my throat.

Before I can even make head or tails out of the figure across the room, a heavy weight lands on my back, smashing me into the mattress. It knocks the air from my lungs, which escapes in a rattle as I thrash, heartbeat kicking into gear.

The weight gets heavier right before a hand covers my mouth, fingertips digging painfully into the soft give of my cheeks.

The person leans over me to speak into my ear. "Settle down," says the deranged voice, "or I'll gut you like a fucking fish." I pant through my nose, wide eyes pinging around the scant parts of the room I can see. The only thing I can make out is the harsh, excited breaths of the maniac pinning me down. The low timbre of his voice. The scent of him, spice and musk, as he breathes into my ear. "Nod if you understand," the maniac demands, his weight too constricting, too confining.

I give a rapid, stilted nod, blinking into the dark to get my bearings. I'd probably agree to anything if it meant getting the weight off me—if it meant being able to move and breathe and *be*.

But he doesn't leave. His thumb pinches into my cheek and he says, "If you scream, that's going to make us mad. You don't want to make us mad, do you?"

I try to shake my head, but the twist of my neck and the pillow against my cheeks restricts me from managing much more than a twitch.

The maniac's other hand runs down my bare arm, rough skin skating down to my hip. My muscles seize when his palm finds the curve of my ass, fingers digging into the flesh. "That's a good girl. He wasn't lying, was he? You're a sweet little thing. Ultramarine? No—cyanine blue." He seems to be muttering more to himself than me. "Blonde hair, nice skin, aluminum eyes. Yeah, we've got this."

I suck air in through my nose and try to move my hand, but he reacts swiftly, yanking my arm behind me. He captures the wrist that's not trapped beneath me already in a steel grip, letting out a gritty laugh. "Heard you were a fighter. Normally, that would be a fun time, but cyanine blue...that can get out of hand. If you want to get out of this, do what you're told."

"Fuck's sake," a cold, lurking voice from the end of the bed mutters. "Stop your batshit color babbling and fuck her already. I've got shit to do."

"It's important!" Maniac snaps. "I'd never stick my dick in primary magenta."

I really do thrash then, an angry, distressed noise clawing from my throat as I try to break free. There's a reason I've been holed away inside a whorehouse. I found it a bit funny at first that my father handed me over to the Kings because of it. Would I be the Baron's new virgin sacrifice, or the Princes' new virgin mother? Oh, but neither of those was quite severe enough, so it had to be the Lords. Daniel's shiny new virgin moneymaker.

Point is, I've always known what I'm here to do: Spread my legs and grimace in pain as some nameless piece of shit forces his way inside. And then, maybe afterward, they'd let me go.

But this isn't the way it was meant to happen.

My struggle is an almost comical attempt. The maniac has a knee or something planted into the small of my back, and he laughs as I buck, trying desperately to gain a foothold. "Classic cyanine."

"Hey, now," a third voice, softer this time, appears in front of me. The shadowy figure crouches beside the head of my bed, face obscured by black. My eyes widen as I take him in, featureless and looming, but his only reaction to my wild, useless jerks is to reach out and stroke a knuckle down the curve of my jaw, nudging his partner's hand away from my mouth. His voice is a coarse, bleak whisper. "It'll be okay. This is for your own good."

My brain slowly kicks into gear. *Three guys.*

Maniac, holding me down.

Lurker, at the foot of the bed.

Creep, brushing the pad of his thumb over my lip.

What the hell do they want?

You already know, Lav, a tiny voice tells me. When your father is Lionel Lucia, King of the Counts, it's a safe bet that it's always about him. Even locked away like a disorderly puppy, I'm still nothing more than a pawn in his game.

My eyes finally acclimate to the dark. The faint light coming in from the open window illuminates enough to make my heartbeat lurch. Creep is dressed in black, a mask pulled down over his head. There are two holes for each of his unsettling blue eyes, but nothing more.

"Listen," I rush out, breathless from the struggle. "If this is about my dad, then you're shit out of luck. He doesn't give a fuck about me. He's the reason I'm in this pussy trap in the first place. Hurting me means nothing to him."

The man holding me down—Maniac—lets out this low, ominous scoff. "You're thinking way too small, Miss Lucia." I hear in his voice that he turns his head, speaking to Lurker, the man at the foot of my bed. "Get her ankles."

In a flurry of movement that's too quick to counter, they flip me to my back. Lurker's hands capture my ankles before I can lash out —not that I don't still try. The muscles in my thigh burn with the force of my kick, which catches him right in the stomach. He releases a punch of surprised breath, but his reaction is lightning-quick.

Lurker hisses, "You fucking bitch!" and then wrenches me by the ankles with a powerful yank, making me slide to the end of the bed. I'm so caught up in the sharpness of the gesture—the pain of something in my ankle tearing—that I don't even realize he's pulling his hand back.

His open palm meets my face with a loud, jarring crack that sends me flopping sideways to the mattress. It doesn't matter that it wasn't a fist. My ears still ring with the force of it, the left side of my face a sweltering mess of sting and ache. From the sudden sluggishness of my brain, I'm guessing he didn't even bother holding back.

It's been a long time since I've been slapped like that. Not just out of anger, but out of a burning, white-hot hatred. I used to know how to brace myself for it, but it's been years since my father's looked down at me with that glint of violence in his eyes.

Now, I blink against the stars, only idly registering the scuffle happening nearby. There's a grunt, and then the sound of bone on bone. Punching.

"You motherfucker!" Creep is snarling. "What did I fucking tell you the plan was? No one touches her!"

Lurker bites back, "She had it coming!"

Beyond the sounds of their quiet brawl, Maniac, still on the bed, is already wrestling me back down into the mattress. "Enough of this bullshit," he huffs, reaching for my shirt. He yanks it over my breasts before tearing it over my head. And now that I can see him, I realize he's dressed just like the others. Masked. Obscured. But his two narrowed eyes are visible, and they're feral, bloodshot, and piercingly green. He's not as physically imposing as Creep, but the energy rolling off of him is electric, accentuating the compact muscles I see shifting beneath his long-sleeved black Henley.

He pants out, "Let's get this over with, huh?" and pulls at my shorts.

I'm still reeling from the slap, and it sounds like the other intruders are still fighting about it. That makes it easy to slide my hand beneath my pillow as I squirm ineffectually away. "Wait," I slur out, tasting blood in my mouth as I attempt to buy some time. I feel their rage building around me like a toxic cloud. The anger. They could be drunk or even high. There's a frenetic buzz in the room that's never good.

"Yeah, yeah, yeah," Maniac breathes, manic eyes fixed to my breasts. "You've got some nice tits here, cyanine. You and I can make this quick. We'd move good together, I bet. You shouldn't worry so much." I can practically hear the demented grin he's wearing under that mask, so it's no surprise when he reaches for his fly, popping the button.

My eyes slowly come into focus, seeing the other two grappling further into the room. They're so distracted that I doubt they even realize this one's shoving his black jeans down his hips.

They're also too distracted to see me take my chance—maybe my *only* chance. Pulling my hand from beneath the pillow, I strike out fast, slashing the shard of glass I have clutched in my hand across his lower belly.

They didn't get everything when they cleared out the room.

He makes a startled noise and hurls himself away, yelping, "Son of a fucking *cunt*! She cut me!" Even though there's outrage in the words, he sounds strangely delighted about it. "Holy shit, cadmium red like a motherfucker. Nice work, Lucia."

This gets the others' attention. They turn just in time to see the blood bubbling out from between Maniac's fingers.

"Shit," Lurker mutters, but Creep is suddenly storming toward us.

"What the fuck?" he spits, bearing down on Maniac as I scramble up the bed. "I told you before! She's *mine*!"

Lurker gestures to the gash. "Are you happy now? This is going to need stitches."

The slice I cut into him stretches from his navel to his hip. Blood oozes from it, but unfortunately it's not deep. When he looks up, he just lets out a quiet, sinister laugh. "Oh, I've had worse. But tit for tat, girl. You leave a mark on me, and I'm going to leave one back. Look! You bisected one of my favorite pieces." He must be talking about the tattoo spanning his lower belly. I can't make out much more than the dark edges of it.

"No," Creep says, shoving him away. "I found her. I came up with the plan, and I got you in here. She's *mine*."

Lurker growls, "We're running out of time."

Creep mutters, "Fuck this." He fishes a phone from his pocket, thrusting it at Lurker. Then he turns his blue eyes to me. "I'm not here to hurt you. You can make this difficult, or you can make it easy, but it's not going to change a goddamn thing."

I'm still clutching the bloody shard in my fist, the throb in my cheek igniting fury in my veins. "If you want your dick cut off," I say, giving him a bloody smile, "then go ahead and try me."

His chest expands and contracts with hard, angry breaths. "You want it rough? *Fine*." He claws at his belt, the sounds of the buckle clinking metal on metal, making my muscles tense. "But one way or another, this is your last night as a virgin. Start the recording." He growls the last part to Lurker as his fingers pop his fly.

Unthinkingly, I drop my fist and the shard of glass with it, incredulous laughter bubbling up my throat. "You're here for my *virginity*?" I don't try to hold in my peal of laughter, even when it makes the three of them go rigid with the sheer volume of it. "Oh my god, are you people really *this* predictable?" That's some premium goddamn *Royal* speak—just like the Kings and Counts I've spent my life around. But these men aren't wearing rings, and real Royals don't sneak around. They walk through the front door and take what they want. These men are renegades—assholes who know just enough to understand what's valuable, but not wise enough to understand what a façade it all is.

Virginity.

What a crock of shit.

"You realize virginity's just an artificial construct, right?" I ask, feeling sore and belligerent. "It doesn't mean anything! Pussies don't have a fucking safety seal!"

Maniac just shrugs. "Doesn't matter. It means something to them, so we're going to take it."

This makes me pause, chest heaving from adrenaline. "Them?" I take a guess. "The Kings?"

Maniac looks up from his sluggishly bleeding wound to say, "Of course, the Kings. We're here to ruin their new toy."

He probably means it to sound menacing. It's not that it doesn't. These three aren't Royalty, but they know the inner workings of it. If anything, that makes them more dangerous. It means they aren't following a clearly defined protocol. It means they could kill me. It means I can't anticipate their next move. But it also means a way out.

I toss the shard of glass on the floor. "Fine."

Creep freezes halfway through lowering his zipper. "*Fine*?"

Stiffly, I lay back on the bed, trying to will myself into accepting this. "Go ahead and fuck me. I'll let you."

There's a long beat of silence, nothing but the distant sounds of

Hideaway life penetrating the tension. Lurker breaks it by releasing a sharp scoff. "I fucking told you all these bitches were whores."

"Nah, no." Maniac is smarter, shaking his head. "It's a trap. This is *vintage* cyanine tactics, you guys."

Lurker hisses, "Would you shut the fuck up about the paint colors! I'm cramming your meds down your throat the second we get home, I swear to fucking god..."

"No trap," I insist, letting my thighs fall apart. "If you plan on sending that video to the Kings, then go ahead. Show them how worthless I am."

That may be the only thing that gets me out of this hellhole.

They glance at one another, two sets of matching blue eyes against a third pair of green. The guy with the phone holds it up and nods. "Do it."

Still, Creep seems to take Maniac's advice. He jerks his chin and says, "Does he need to hold you down?"

I swallow the lump in my throat, resenting the tremble in my thighs. "I won't fight you."

He stares at me like he's waiting for a sign that I'm lying, and he's smart too. But when I do nothing but lie there, resigned to my fate, he lowers his zipper the rest of the way.

And then he takes his cock out of his pants.

It's too dark to make out more than the intimidating jut of it, thick and long, but I catch the cut of his hip bones too as he plants a knee on the foot of the bed. I wish I could say I felt nothing but utter revulsion. Oh, it's there, but the sight of his cock, the adrenaline, the toned cut of his hips... it penetrates the fog of disgust in the fashion of a woman seeing an attractive man.

As promised, I don't fight as he muscles his way up the bed to me, hands gripping my knees and pushing them apart to make space for his thighs. The denim of his jeans is scratchy against my bare skin, and it doesn't matter that some deep, fundamental part of my libido is stretching itself awake. I'm so rigid that my bones ache.

Sitting back on his heels, his eyes ascend my naked body,

climbing my legs, traveling over my thighs, pausing at the apex, locked on my pussy, and then rising to my stomach and breasts. It makes me stiffer, muscles aching with the tension of moving away from him without actually *moving*.

"Fuck," he sighs, reaching out to cup my breast in a large, hot palm. "Look at you."

I wrench my head to the side, averting my eyes. "Just do it," I grind out, flinching when he flicks my nipple.

I feel more than see him lean over me, a fist pressed into the mattress as he hovers, watching. "Look at me." I squeeze my eyes closed, face turned away. Even so, I know he sees my angry grimace, can feel my flinch at the brush of his knuckles over my sore jaw. "That's going to leave a mark." He doesn't sound happy about it.

The tip of his cock drags against my inner thigh, causing me to shudder. "Get on with it!"

Still, he takes his time, sliding his hand down my body, as if he's mapping every single one of my curves. "Need to make you wet," Creep says, voice husky and rough as his hand ascends, dipping between my thighs.

I didn't think I could get any more tense, but the first touch of his fingers down the slit of my folds makes me lock up in revulsion. Part of it is because of the touch—invasive, wrong, forceful—but a bigger part—the much, *much* worse part...

He freezes, fingers poised just outside my entrance. Quietly, *arrogantly*, he whispers, "Or maybe I don't."

I bite down on a sound when he replaces his fingers with the head of his dick, running it through the slickness that's gathered in my folds. His breaths are hot and loud, so close to my ear as he hovers above me.

"Look at me," he says again, but this time, he doesn't take no for an answer. He grabs my chin, yanking my head toward him. His stare through the mask is just as hard and unforgiving as the press of his dick against my entrance. "Watch me make this pussy mine."

I gasp at the invasion.

That's exactly what it is—unwelcome, violating, aggressive. He enters me without any fanfare at all, filling me with one powerful, violent shove of his hips. His hand flies up to the top of my head, fisting in my hair as he pushes me in counterpoint to it, eyes flashing in anger when my heels slide against the sheets in an attempt to scurry away.

"Stop!" he growls, pinning me with his hips.

I think I mean to tell him to go fuck himself, but what comes out is a plaintive gasp. "It hurts." I don't mean to say it. The last thing I want to give these assholes is the satisfaction.

From the edge of the bed, Maniac hums. "I bet it does, little girl. Hung, isn't he?" From my periphery, I can see him squeezing his crotch.

But Creep isn't swayed into gentleness at my declaration. He tightens his fist in my hair and surges into me, punching his dick against my cervix. The second my mouth opens in a sharp cry, Maniac is there to clamp his hand over it.

"Keep your fucking mouth shut," he snaps, tone switching from malicious delight to stony anger so fast that I can't even keep up. His hand is slippery, and it isn't until the metallic tang fills my mouth that I realize it's covered in blood.

"So fucking tight," Creep mutters through his clenched teeth. He fucks into me with slow but brutal thrusts, those blue eyes never leaving mine. "How does it feel?" he asks, ignoring the swell of my throat—my shout trapped by the other man's palm—as he digs into me. "Tell me how it feels to know this pussy belongs to me now."

All I feel is trapped. Trapped beneath his body, beneath the palm clamped over my face, beneath the lens of the phone, Lurker is pointing at us. His hips are crushing me, unyielding as he hammers me with tight, back-curling thrusts. I fix my gaze to the flexing point of his shoulder, unwilling to see the sweat darkening the fabric of his mask.

I still feel it, though.

When he leans down to press his face against my cheek, it's damp with it. Sweat. Breath. Saliva. It makes my stomach flip and churn, and when I whip my head to the side to avoid it, Lurker lets me, finally freeing my mouth from his grip.

"Goddamn," he says, hovering somewhere close. Vaguely, it registers that he sounds impressed. "You're really giving it to her."

Creep... it's like he doesn't even hear him. It's like the other two aren't even in the room. He wedges a hand under my cheek and forces me to turn to him.

And then he kisses me.

It's not really a kiss, impeded by the fabric of the mask, but I can tell that's what he wants. I can feel the hard jabs of breath through it, and even when I try to turn away, he won't let me, covering my mouth with something I might call passion on someone less unhinged.

"You're so fucking beautiful," he's saying, voice full of harsh sandpaper grit. "Always knew I'd make you mine. Been watching you for so long, baby."

I make a tight, disgusted sound against his mouth, and I can't even help it then. I push at his shoulders, desperate to get him off. I've spent the last year surrounded by creeps, maniacs, and lurkers. Who even knows which one this guy is? None of them are good.

He responds by grabbing my wrists, which settles all of his weight on my chest, stealing the last of my breath. He pins them high above my head, but it works.

He lets me turn away, jaw flying open as I gasp in wild gulps of blood-scented air.

It's easier then. When he accepts it. When he lets me lie here, limp and breathless as he uses me. When he holds my wrists down and rests his mouth against my jaw, panting as the bed creaks with the force of his hips. He never really pulls out. He keeps his dick so far inside that he has to drive me into the mattress for any sense of friction. Each excruciating thrust makes my chest swell, like something is growing inside of me and I don't have room for it.

And then *he's* the one who starts swelling.

If I didn't feel it—his dick getting harder, bigger—then I'd be able to hear it in the short, ragged grunts that tear from his chest.

Suddenly, it occurs to me what's going to happen.

"No," I gasp, planting my heels against the bed. I push and buck, trying to free my wrists with useless tugs. "Don't! Please don't!"

His response is immediate. "Hold her," he grunts.

Maniac rushes over, knees pressing into the mattress on either side of my head as he wrenches my arms up.

"I'll scream!" I warn, heart hammering just as hard as his dick. "I'll scream, I'll cut your goddamn throat, you mother-fucking—!" My words get caught in my throat when my neck snaps up, and I actually see it. His body moving between my legs. His black jeans have worked their way down his hips, giving me a clear view of the upper muscles in his ass, working, *flexing*, to force his body into mine. The sight of it is briefly mesmerizing, as if I've just fallen headfirst into an experience I'm somehow shocked by.

When he slams into me with a deep, agonized rumble, I know I'm too late.

He wraps his fingers around my throat, slamming me back to the bed as he comes with a gnarled growl. I can feel it inside, a pulsating rush of warmth that makes every cell of my being recoil. The thought of him leaving a piece of himself inside me is so repulsive that a wave of nausea rushes through me.

"You son of a bitch," I croak, his fingers still pressing against my throat. I try to get my feet under him for a kick, but all I can manage are weak, useless thuds against his legs.

He hovers above me, panting like a dog as he rears up, head tipped back. "Fuck, I needed that."

"Get off!" I thrash and buck, but even though he looks boneless from the orgasm, he easily wrestles my legs down, sliding back to let his dick slip free.

"You ready?" He glances over his shoulder at Lurker, who's still holding the phone. "Come closer."

Lurker gets on the bed, edging close as Creep yanks my thighs wide, a palm shoving each side open. Lurker's eyes pinch with whatever expression he's making under that mask. "Fucking disgusting," he says.

My veins erupt with wildfire as I watch them inspect my pussy, Creep shoving my knees up for a better angle. There's a long silence, and then Lurker's muttered curse. "Isn't there supposed to be blood?"

Creep digs a finger into my hole, his voice a mixture of incredulous and annoyed. "You saw how hard I fucked her. She should be fucking gushing! *Goddamn it.*"

They're so caught up in their own disappointment that they don't even realize my legs are free. It gives me the opportunity to slam my foot right into Creep's collarbone, sending him snapping back.

Before the pained sound can even escape his throat, I yell, "Because I'm not a virgin, you fucking morons!"

Lurker drops his phone to wrestle my legs down, a snarl ripping from his chest. "Getting real sick of your shit." His grip is savage, bruising, and forces a whimper from me.

"What the fuck," Creep growls, holding his shoulder, "are you talking about?"

"My virginity," I answer, glaring daggers into his blue eyes. "I haven't been a virgin since junior year of high school."

"Bullshit," Maniac says, tightening his grip on my wrists. "The Kings were keeping you here because—"

"Because they think I'm lying!" I spit, wishing I could close my legs. "I tried telling them, but they wouldn't listen to me. Turns out, they believe my goddamn father over me." Breathless, I collapse into the bed, the corner of my mouth lifting. "But now, they will."

It's a relief.

Even with the cost, the pain, the disgust I feel at letting this masked intruder violate me, it's still a relief to know I've won. Surely, they won't want me now.

"Shit," Maniac hisses, tossing my wrists away. "This bitch fucking played us. What did I tell you?" He jabs a forefinger into his temple. "Cyanine tactics!"

Creep's surly voice rings out. "Who cares? We have the video. It's proof she's not a virgin. Let's get the fuck out of here."

Lurker pushes his fist into Creep's shoulder, right where I kicked him. "That wasn't the objective! We had to take her virginity to secure our place—"

"All three of us," Maniac clarifies, pacing beside the bed.

"You fucked this up!" Lurker goes to hit him again, but Creep dodges it, shoving him back. It doesn't matter. He's focused on me again. "You're a dirty slut, just like every whore in this place."

"We can still fix this." Creep takes a deep breath. "We can still win. Not all virgins bleed."

"Oh, fuck this." Maniac stops pacing and gets back on the bed, shoving them out of the way. When he lifts his shirt, I don't even know what I'm expecting. Definitely not for him to swipe two fingers over the gash on his stomach, and then bury them—dripping with his blood—right inside me.

"What the—!" I scramble away, but he follows me up the bed, thrusting his bloody fingers in and out of me.

"Stay fucking still!" he orders. The others are there by then, anyway. Creep holds me down by a shoulder as Lurker presses a knee into my thigh. When he pulls his fingers out, he and Lurker inspect me again, spreading me open. "We need more cum," Maniac decides. His pants are already unfastened, so it feels like he pulls his dick out faster than I can process.

Creep bolts upright. "Don't you fucking dare put your dick in her," he says, voice threatening.

"I won't! Chill the fuck out." Maniac starts stroking himself, eyes darting from my face to my pussy. My own eyes are fixed on the movement of his hand—the way his own blood is slicking the way.

In a moment of stunned disbelief, I realize, "You're demented."

He just jerks off faster. "Don't worry, little girl. This won't take long. Your pussy's really hot like this, you know. All swollen and used up. So many pretty colors..." It sounds like he licks his lips, eyes flashing at whatever he sees on my face. "If my buddy here wouldn't get so bent out of shape about it, I'd fuck you just like this. Give you some more of my red. I'd make you like it."

True to his word, it only takes a couple dozen of those short, pointed strokes before he pitches forward, hand holding my hip. He presses the head of his bloody cock into my folds, shoulders curling as he erupts. The slick sensation of him coming mingles with the punch of breath he releases, his fingers digging painfully into my hipbone.

When he pulls away, my inner thighs are stained with his blood.

"You next," he tells Lurker, stuffing his cock back into his boxers.

"Hold this," he bites out, thrusting the phone at him. He shoves his sleeves up, revealing brown, muscular forearms, before unbuttoning his own pants. This one hesitates before whipping it out, though I'm not sure why. From the bulge of his crotch, he's clearly hard. *Sick fucks.* He says his next words to Creep, low and dangerous. "If she says anything, I'm going to shove that fucking pillow over her face."

"Just do it!" he replies, pushing down on my shoulders.

Lurker obeys, but he's all slow and hesitant about it, reaching into his pants and giving his dick a few strokes within the confines. When he finally does pull it out, it's like all the air gets knocked from my lungs.

"Oh, fuck no." I fight against their hold, but it's like knocking up against steel.

"It's not going in," Creep assures, watching as the man between my legs starts jerking his freak of a cock.

"Shame," Maniac says, pressing a palm to his bloody wound. "I bet she would have bled if it were him."

It's the only comment tonight I find myself agreeing with. Lurker's cock is grotesquely gargantuan—like something out of a freak show. He hunches inward as he pleasures himself, almost like he's trying to hide it away, but it's the equivalent of putting a throw blanket over a bus. It's long and veiny and thick enough that it'd almost certainly tear me open.

I cower away from it.

He surges with anger, yanking me back. "Stop being a bitch and take it!" He leaves his hand clamped around my thigh, fingers digging into the soft flesh. He squeezes so hard that I can see the corded muscles in his forearms strain with the force.

"Ah!" I cry out, back arching in my attempt to break free, but it just makes him squeeze harder, a soft noise emerging from his throat.

Maniac helps by holding my other leg open, spurring his friend on. "Yeah, man, come on. Squirt all over this pretty pussy. Little slut like this? She deserves it, doesn't she?"

He makes a short gasp, nudging nearer. "Close..."

"When was the last time you got some, anyway?" Maniac asks, looking every bit the devil on his shoulder. "I've never seen you with a chick. Imagine what it'd be like to cram your dick into that hole. Imagine how tight it'd be." Lower, he urges, "Imagine how loud she'd scream."

Lurker lurches up, cock in his fist, and shoves it right up against me before he comes. His shoulders heave as he empties himself into my folds, a growl ripping from his chest. "Get the phone, get the phone." Apparently not one for the afterglow, he pulls back, allowing the other two to spread me wide, phone pointed right between my legs.

A block of dread drops in my stomach at the realization that nothing the Kings had in mind for me could possibly be as humiliating, as dehumanizing, as fucking undignified as *this*: The three of them huddled around my vagina, recording the image of their spunk and blood dripping to the mattress.

"Got it," Lurker says, still a touch breathless as he springs from the bed. He marches to the dresser and picks something up—a black leather bag—and throws it to Maniac, adding, "Do your thing and let's roll."

"Careful," Maniac snipes, setting the bag on the bed. "I need a

sterile environment, you fucker. *Sterile.* Titanium fucking white."
He mutters nonsensically as he rifles through the bag.

I look between them, feeling sick with embarrassment and useless anger. "What *now*?"

Creep just flips me over and every nerve in my body tenses when he says, "Don't move."

Maniac straddles my backside, sweeping my hair away from the skin of my back. But it's a long moment before anything happens. The other two move around, acting when he demands something. "Wet cloth." And then, "Find an outlet. Plug this in." And then, "Hold this *still*."

There's a click, and then the sharp, acrid smell of alcohol, a shock of cold against my shoulder blade.

And then, there's the sudden buzz I'd know anywhere.

Tattoo gun.

"It's loud!" Lurker hisses, standing close.

But Maniac doesn't care. I can feel him hunching over me, and suddenly all that frantic energy that's been radiating off his body disappears. He goes so still, *so focused*, that it lulls me into the coming numbness.

The first touch of the needle against my skin doesn't even make me flinch. I think somewhere, buried deep in my brain, is the urge to resist. To fight. To throw him off and run away. But he and Creep are holding me down, and anyway, there's nowhere to go. I lose the motivation to do much more than stare unseeingly at the soiled bed sheets.

I can't make out what he draws, too numb to follow the sharp, hot sensation of the needle piercing my skin, but I know that he's methodical, taking his time as he leans over me, putting his mark into me. I know that it's small, maybe two or three inches in diameter.

It could be ten minutes later that the buzzing stops or it could be hours.

"See? I said I'd leave a mark," Maniac says, lips brushing the shell of my ear.

His weight leaves. I hear him and the others packing the supplies back into that bag, ignoring me like discarded trash. I sense them walking toward the dresser and using it to lever themselves out the narrow egress window. I watch them, that broken window being the only part of the room in my line of sight, and I don't bother rolling over or getting up. Some part of me is firm in the belief that if I stay here—if I stay as still as possible—that none of this will have happened. Moving will mean that I'll feel it. Between my legs. In my jaw. Around my ankle. In the permanence of the ink on my shoulder blade.

Creep is the last to climb the dresser to the window. He lingers beside my bed, and it's just like when I first woke up. A pillar of shadow. A part of the foundation. He stares at my used body, defeated and defaced, and then pulls something from his pocket, setting it carefully onto the nightstand.

A can of soda.

He waits, like he's hoping I'll react. Perhaps he expects gratitude. A smile and a thanks. I suppose all whores deserve a payment.

When I do nothing but stare expressionlessly at it, he puffs out this hard, annoyed breath, and then pulls something else from his pocket. "You're welcome." He tosses it onto the bed right beside my shoulder. It's a small box, white and purple, with text on the front.

Plan B.

"I told you that you'd be mine someday," he says, walking backward, "Little Bird."

And then he's gone, climbing out of the window in one lithe move.

But I'm left staring unblinkingly in his wake, finally putting the voice to the unsettling blue eyes. *Pretty Nick*, my handler for the Kings.

I stay like that for some stretch.

Time.

It's never meant less to me than it does right now.

My body sleeps, but my mind never does. I stare at the window

—the flutter of the curtain—and let my flesh drink its fill of rest. I lock my thoughts into safe things. The way those books smelled before. The texture of the pages beneath my fingers. The weight and shape of them. Carding through their thickness. I think of the sky, and how long it's been since I've seen it. The stars. The moon. The sunrise.

I think of birds and the flutter of wings, and then I cry.

I'm not proud of it.

In fact, I spend the whole time resenting the shit out of each tear that tracks its way to the mattress. I can hear my father's voice in my mind, telling me that it's weak. Lucias don't cry—we strike with venom and the points of our fangs. That's probably what burns me most. The blows were bad, and the sex was worse, but the fact that it's driven me to tears?

That's what makes me want to kill Nick.

The sun has long ago come up by the time I twitch my fingers, allowing my muscles and bones to slowly awaken, coming back to life. I know my body isn't ready to face it. The ache between my legs. The sting in my cheek. The pang in my ankle. It's just that I need to know.

Hobbling to the bathroom is a series of challenges involving excessive wincing and the avoidance of the blood and semen that's dried on my thighs. But the moment I do, I turn my back to the mirror, finally seeing the message Maniac had inked into my skin.

A bear.

Not just any bear.

Everyone in Forsyth has seen the Brass Bruin, in one form or another. This wasn't some mere attack in the dead of night. The Maniac, the Lurker, *Nick*...

They've declared war.

With any luck, I'll soon be in the position to give them one.

1

Nick

"Proper planning prevents poor performance."

That's what Daniel Payne always used to say to us. His foot soldiers. His captive audience. His little wily murder pets.

Guy was an arrogant son of a bitch, but sometimes he was right. It doesn't matter why I started working for him or why I eventually turned. The King of South Side always had a lesson to give, and a lot of people wouldn't want to hear it, but if you could get past the megalomania and greed, he made some damn good points. They just weren't always constructively solvent. That's the brilliance of it. Daniel needed us smart enough to be useful, but stupid enough to not realize it.

A lesser man might have seen Daniel as a passable father figure, but fuck that. I've already got two of those, and both of them are a hell of a lot smarter than the King of Payne.

Case in point, my real dads are still alive.

Daniel Payne has been dead for six months, but I can still see him everywhere, tagged around this city like bold graffiti. He's in the skyline, the silhouette of buildings he'd financed rising over the horizon at dawn. He's beneath our feet, the network of sewers he had gutted and reclaimed, making for the perfect intercity smuggling maze. He's in the air, the permeating scent of car exhaust and the putrid waste treatment plant keeping anyone too important at arm's length. He's in the people—the dealers he regulated and the junkies they feed.

Mostly, he's here.

Killian Payne's truck is in the brothel's driveway when I arrive, the front wheel halfway up the sidewalk. He'd parked in a hurry, rushing over when he got the call, no doubt.

While he was learning what happened in the basement of the Velvet Hideaway, I was busy scrubbing the blood off my hands and the scent of pussy from my cock. Nothing I do can diminish the adrenaline running through my system. It's not just the thrill of finally getting what I've wanted after all this time, although... yeah.

Won't lie, my balls are still zinging from that fat load I'd buried into Lavinia's pussy.

It's not really what I'd wanted, anyway. Good pussy, for sure. The sight of her beneath me, taking my cock as I drove into her, was unquestionably inevitable. Lavinia Lucia's been mine since the first moment I laid eyes on her; it's just that no one's bothered to see it yet.

The real thrill is that everything is in motion now. I can feel the cogs turning as I leisurely stalk up the drive, the satisfying dive of that first domino, knocking into the next. People underestimate a lot about me, but none so much as my patience.

I stroll into the brothel with a casual, bored swagger, as if I hadn't been the one breaking into the basement mere hours ago. One of Daniel's best lessons is the art of showing people exactly what they're expecting. It makes them complacent. Makes them feel smart. Makes them think they've got you all figured out.

In the main room, a few girls are huddled around, speaking in whispers, eyeing me balefully as I cross the room. The whole atmosphere is heavy and solemn, and even the building itself feels like it's hunching in on itself, hurt. Auggy, the Hideaway's madam, stands near the basement door in a robe with her arms wrapped around her slender, womanly body. A thin wisp of smoke tendrils from the end of her cigarette as she tracks my approach.

"Hey," I say, pushing my damp hair off my forehead. "I got a call. What's going on?"

"There was a break-in last night," she says, looking away. The heel of her right foot is bouncing nervously, even though her face is flawlessly composed. "The Kings' asset was targeted."

Asset. AKA: Lavinia Lucia. Daughter of Lionel, King to the Counts. Royalty, but not. Valuable, but only just. She's been holed up in the basement of the brothel for a while now. I should know. I've been the one handling her.

My voice emerges carefully. "Is she okay?"

"I went in this morning to drop off some breakfast and found her..." She takes a long drag of the cigarette, something delicate shuddering across her features. "She's a mess, but okay. I mean... alive." She shrugs. "Go look for yourself."

I nod and head down the stairs, stomping but not rushed. It'll be what he expects.

This house was custom-built by a rapper who got in trouble with the IRS. The bottom floor is a suite he built for his mother, complete with all the amenities. Lavinia has been living down here in service of Daniel, but now that he's dead, she's as good as a can of soup that's missing its label, all tucked away and forgotten in the pantry. Killian, being Daniel's son and heir, has been trying to figure out what to do with this part of his 'inheritance'.

I knock on the door, and a moment later, it swings open. My eyes go to Killian, but only because he's so big. Imposing motherfucker. Covered in ink, the quarterback was in line for first draft with the NFL before he decided to take his father's crown of trash.

I drag my eyes away from him over to the mess. The glass on the dresser and floor sparkles in the low light coming in from the broken window above. The bedside table has been overturned, as well as the armchair in the sitting area. The sheets on the bed are twisted, patches smeared with blood that's dried into a ruddy brown color.

Fuck, it's like a bomb went off in here.

The can of soda I left her is still on the bedside table.

But the Plan-B box isn't.

I take her in last, putting it off as long as possible. It's not that I feel bad, because I don't. She got her swings in. Aside from the purple welt on one cheek, her face is pale, her blond hair as wild as her eyes. She stares at me, cold and hard. Girl fought back something nasty, looking more like a victor than a victim. But it's just like I said. It was for her own good. She'll be thanking me for it, come next week.

But there's this little inkling of dread swirling around my head, and I don't fucking like it. It really *had* been sloppy to tell her who I was—and I basically had. *Little Bird.* I'm the only one who calls her that. If she told Killian, he'd pull out that gun peeking from his waistband and bury a bullet into my skull, and that would be his right.

But I know the second we lock eyes, she hasn't said a thing.

Lavinia's had a few lessons herself.

"What the hell happened here?" I ask, keeping an eye on her. The flare of anger that hardens my features isn't even entirely fake. Fucking Sy, hauling off and slapping her like that. My brother is a lot of things, but even-tempered has never been one of them.

"I have no fucking idea." Killian's wearing sweats and a Forsyth practice jersey. This one little patch of his hair is standing straight up, and he's wearing two different-colored socks. I showered the pussy off me, but he obviously didn't have a chance to. He looks like he just woke up. I know him well enough to understand that if he had to leave his Lady's bed, he's agitated. "It's not her blood. I had Mrs. Crane check, but..." he glances over at her, grimaces and gestures for me to follow him into the hallway. He pulls the door closed, but not all the way, eyes still sleep puffy despite their wildness. He's keeping an eye on her, too. I can physically see him brace for my reaction when he quietly rumbles, "It looks like she was raped."

He watches me. I haven't been discreet about my interest in her. Rath knows—it's why I made the deal with them about turning on Daniel. It's why Killian called me here at the ass-crack of dawn. They probably think that's sloppy of me, showing how much I want her.

It's what they expect of me.

"Someone touched her?" I ask, a clear, lethal edge to my voice. "They hurt her?" I call up that quiet, blazing rage that swelled in my chest when I saw Sy's palm print on her cheek, letting it drive me. "Tell me who." I reach for my own gun, but his hand stops me.

He rubs the back of his neck. "Again, it's not her blood. Looks like she got one of them pretty good. I don't think she needs a knight in shining armor here."

Remy. When I left, Bianca was stitching him up—her last task as Duchess before moving on. Lavinia sliced his abdomen with a piece of dirty glass, but he had it coming. Even Remy knew that much. He was still laughing about it, even when we got back to campus. Crazy fucker.

"They marked her, though." His eyes hold mine, narrowing. "With a bear."

"A Bear," I repeat, wrapping my fingers around my gun. "You mean a bruin."

"Nick," he starts, but I cut him off.

It's what he'd expect.

"Someone's sending me a message," I lie, shrugging off his grip to pull out my gun. "Tell me who."

He gives me a warning look. "The message isn't for you. Saul Cartwright has it out for me. Has for months now. The Dukes have graduated, so I'm guessing this was his last hurrah for them." His jaw tenses. "This is payback."

Baby Payne doesn't even realize how spot on he is. Saul really *had* given this task to the Dukes. But the graduating Dukes are gone, and to become a Duke, you have to prove your commitment to the belfry.

There are new Dukes now.

I pull myself to my full height, letting my rage show. "You're telling me Lucia's daughter was raped because of some fucked up frat rivalry bullshit?" Saying it like that, it really does sound convincing.

"I know what it is," Killian says, sparing the cracked door a lingering glance. "It's a power move. Saul's getting in two punches with one fist. Dukes and Counts, just like that." He grunts. "Yeah, if I wasn't so pissed about it, I'd be impressed."

"Doing that under your roof, and then leaving their mark, is a pretty bold goddamn move." Best to leave some skepticism in my voice, even though I'm tucking my gun away. I glance back into the room. Lavinia is still in the chair, watching us closely.

"If you're worried about her, I wouldn't. She's tough," Killian says, but he doesn't even know the half of it.

I think about how she fought me. I mean, she *agreed* to have sex with me, even if it was just to get back at her father and get out of here. But holy shit, she fought it. Tooth and nail. Blood and tears. And all of it just made her pussy tighter. *Fuck.* I shift, not wanting to get hard in the middle of all this.

"Too tough," he adds, running a hand down his worn face. "She's too risky for the pit. I have no idea what my father was thinking."

"He was thinking she was a virgin," I say, pitching my voice low, annoyed. "I know what the Kings kink on. But now that her cherry is popped, that angle is useless. She's lost her value, and she's too dangerous to put on the floor with the other girls." Killian nods along, going right where I'm leading him. But there's more to this.

"Story is going to fucking kill me," he groans. His Lady is annoyingly vocal about not being into the flesh trade. I know from my glimpses into their life with Rath that having this girl locked up was already causing problems at home. Yeah, Story finding out about Lavinia getting raw-dogged on his watch? My man is about to experience a sudden dry spell.

I lift my chin. "You know why Lionel gave her up, right?"

He looks at me, surprised. "No. I figured it was a debt of some kind. I'm not exactly a stranger to messed up family drama."

I shake my head. "Some shit went down between her and her big sister. Lionel's been all fucked up over it. I guess she's missing or something."

Killian frowns. "Missing?"

God, he's been out of it—focused on football, family, and his Lady. That only makes this easier for me. "Point is, if you can't find some use for her, Daddy's going to come collect for himself."

I can already see him looking annoyed at the prospect of Lionel sweeping in here to drag her away. For someone intimately familiar with family drama, Killian Payne sure as shit doesn't want to deal with someone else's. "So let him," he stresses. "I'm not a goddamn daycare for wayward girls. If Lionel wants to punish her, let him do it."

"Excuse me?" I say, low and lethal.

Killian angrily explains, "I've got Saul Cartwright's throbbing grudge-boner to worry about. I don't have the time or energy to referee this shit. I need to figure out how to get Saul out for good."

I have to play this next part very carefully. "And how are you going to deal with him?" I wonder, sneering. "Dethroning a King is easier said than done."

He seems to think this through, and I can see the gears turning. One domino falling into the next. It's not a difficult idea to plant into his head. He's been bugging me about it since he became King. "Nick," he says, leveling me with a look. "You're a Bruin."

That's the thing about Royalty. It's always about legacy and blood, at the end of the day. My great grandfather was King. My grandfather was a King. My father was a King. Bruins have led the Dukes for generations.

Until my father abdicated his crown, giving it to Saul.

Killian gives me a meaningful look. "That means you can challenge his claim."

"I've already told you," I say, looking away, "I don't want it." It's not even a lie. I don't want to be King. I'd rather flicker out into nothing than rule the pile of trash that comprises Delta Kappa Sigma and the West Side.

"Oh, you will," he insists, reaching out to push the door open. His gaze doesn't leave mine, even as my eyes fall on Lavinia's searing glare. "Because she'll be your Duchess."

There it is.

The crash of the domino.

The spin of the cog.

The culmination of my machinations.

Proper planning prevents poor performance.

2

Lavinia

The first time I met Nick Bruin, I was being shoved to the pavement by my father's hand.

I still remember the sting of gravel cutting into the heels of my palms and the points of my knees. It hurt, but the feel of the night air cutting across my skin was possibly the best thing I've ever experienced. To be outside, to smell the exhaust of their cars, the ability to move for the first time in days. I remember looking at his feet—Pretty Nick, not to be confused with the Ugly one—the scuffed toes of his boots, the glowing ember of a cigarette butt as he listlessly discarded it, the weight of his eyes on the back of my neck as I panted into the blacktop.

It was a nondescript parking lot somewhere off the Avenue. Dark. Deserted. The headlights of two cars were all that illuminated the lot; my father's sleek sedan and Daniel Payne's imposing SUV.

"Take her," my father growled. "You know the deal. Use her how you like."

There was a pause, and then Daniel Payne's voice. "Are you sure she's—"

"Yes, yes," my dad said impatiently. "Trust me. No one would want her. She's fresh meat."

"I'm not—" My breath escaped me in a pained wheeze as my father buried his foot into my side.

"If you're not fessing up to what you've done to Leticia, then I don't want to hear a single word coming out of your fucking mouth," he hissed.

It was Pretty Nick who lifted me to my feet. It'd be stupid to describe his attention as gentle, but after three days under the whirling inferno of Lionel Lucia's wrath, it sure as hell felt like it. I didn't even mind him shoving me into the backseat of the SUV, not fighting when he bound my wrists or closed the door, cloaking the two of us in a frenetic, uncomfortably intimate silence.

Outside, between the beams of headlights, the two Kings made their negotiations. Flesh for a swift reprisal. Later, I'd learn my dad was explaining to Daniel how I'd lie. That I'd say I wasn't a virgin. That it was just a ruse to get out of my punishment. That he knows for a fact no one's ever had me.

But inside, it was just the two of us, quiet and still, and here's the kicker.

I started crying.

I can probably count on one hand the amount of times I've cried, and this was one of them. It wasn't the prospect of being Daniel's new toy. I hadn't even had time to process that yet. It wasn't even the pain in my side; the bruises circling my throat, or the throb in my knuckles and knees from thrashing against the solid wood of the chest my father had me locked in.

It was *relief*. I was just so goddamn glad to be *free* that it all came crashing out into a whispered hitch of a sob.

And then Nick turned away—just a small pivot of his head to look out the window—and let out this long, unimpressed sigh. "Jesus, you Royal twats are some of the weakest bitches I've ever met."

I remember my sob being stolen away in a sharp inhalation. I remember tensing and shifting, turning my back to the opposite door. I remember the sound he made when the heel of my shoe made contact with his jaw. I remember the crunch of the window breaking and the flurry of his hands, the weight of his body as he wrestled me down, expression impassive except for a small, irritated crease dividing his strong brow line.

Point being, I keep my mouth shut for a reason. Sure, I could tell the Lords about Nick being the one to break into my cell at the Velvet Hideaway. I could watch the new Payne get revenge, all the Kings gathered 'round to place their bullets and blades into Pretty Nick's hard stack of flesh. I bet they'd even let me watch as they snuffed the light out of his blue eyes. My father would be there— Perez too, no doubt—and then they'd re-negotiate about where to hold me until...

Well, until they won't need to anymore.

Fuck *that*.

If Lionel Lucia taught me anything, it's that secrets have power. Leverage is currency. Knowledge may be the only thing that will keep me alive.

THERE'S ALWAYS A STRANGE, electric optimism to being shuffled from one pair of hands to another. The night my father gave me to the Kings, the day Daniel moved me to the Hideaway—these were opportunities. I see this one for what it is.

In the afternoon, tight-lipped contractors come to repair the broken window. Cleaners arrive for the soiled laundry and bed sheets, taking away all the evidence. Then Auggy and a couple of her fellow whores do another round of checking my suite for weapons. But it's not like it used to be. Where they once regarded me with irritated, suspicious demeanors, now they avoid looking at me altogether. They tiptoe and whisper, rummaging through my drawers so gently that it's almost like they'd rather not bother. It casts the room into a solemn, grim silence that makes my teeth gnash.

I bristle at their pity the longer nothing happens. Day after day, the sun rises and sets, and no one comes for me. Auggy leaves me food, morning and night, but even though she gives the perfectly-made bed a quick glance, she doesn't speak.

It goes on like this for a long while. Days, weeks—who knows? The only notable blip in time is when my period comes, confirming that Nick's Plan B actually worked.

At least I have that going for me.

After a while of this, I start to think maybe I hallucinated the conversation between Killian and Nick—the one about me becoming the new Duchess. Maybe I confused one of my books with real life, mixing up tawdry romances with my current situation. Trauma does crazy shit to the brain. I should know; I've had a lifetime of it as Lionel Lucia's least favorite daughter. There are nights I still wake up convinced that I'm trapped in the chest, legs flailing instinctively against a barrier that doesn't exist. And then there are nights I wake up unable to move at all, paralyzed by an inevitable certainty that I never left.

You can take the girl out of the chest...

It's just the stasis that gets me. I spend it pacing the length of the room, over and over, wound so tight with the need to get out that it could choke me. It was bad enough even before they came, but everywhere I step, everywhere I look, is a memory of that night. Their shadowy figures. Their low, gruff voices. The pinch of their grips, the ache of their touch, the sting of their needle. I think Auggy and the others assume I'm sleeping in the armchair by the door, or the floor by the closet, but the reality is a lot more embarrassing.

I sleep in the daytime, inside the cold, hard tub, with the door to the bathroom locked tight.

It's my destiny.

Trading one box for another.

When it finally happens, I'm not expecting it.

Noise outside the door makes me bolt upright. The light from the newly barred window indicates it's too early for dinner, so when old Ms. Crane walks in—carrying a large paper bag, not a tray of food—every cell of my body wakes to life.

It's never good when the old bat comes down herself instead of sending one of the other girls. If Auggy is the brothel's madam, Ms. Crane is the stubborn wart that won't go away—or the manager, as she prefers to be called. She's basically a den mother to the fucked-up Lords. If they're mean, she's half the reason.

"Smells like a goddamn kennel down here," she says in her rough, raspy voice. Her eyes take in the space, shrewd and calculating. "Christ, have you been *sulking*?"

"Sulking?" I repeat, narrowing my eyes. "*No*, not me. I've been using all the free time of being locked in a fucking basement to solve the worldwide hunger crisis." I offer her a sharp-edged grin. "After all, what could I possibly have to *sulk* about?"

Ms. Crane gives me a harsh scoff. "You think you're the first girl here to get raped? You're probably not even the first this month. You've got three hots and a cot, Goldilocks. At least you don't have to go to a corner to work off the loss of expense." Bitterly, she adds, "Hell, I had to marry mine."

I stare at her in disbelief, but even though I sneer, "Yeah, my violent sexual assault was a real lucky break," only half of the searing anger in my chest is directed at her.

This sickness of this city—or my awareness of it—grows every day.

She ignores the comment and sniffs. "When was the last time you bathed?"

I give an indolent shrug. "Hell if I know. At one point, the bathtub became less of a shower and more of that 'cot' you seem to think so highly of."

"Well, it's time. Go wash up." She shoots me a look, unfazed by the thought of me sleeping in the tub. "And you better scrub that pussy until it sparkles."

"Why?" I ask, lifting my chin.

Haughtily, she replies, "Because I said so."

I go rigid, knowing this is it. My life feels like a series of befores and afters. After I was put into the chest. Before Leticia disappeared. After my father gave me over to Daniel. Before being moved to the Hideaway. After the...

Rape, my thoughts scream, even though I can't even claim it as one.

Either way, I've learned to recognize the moments, to see the seams between a before and an after, and I can feel it now. That nervous crackle in the air, the impatient look from the old crone, the way my eyes zero in on that door, hungry for escape from yet another box.

I nod at the bag she's holding. The logo on the side is from a shop I might not be personally familiar with, but it's well known that the Avenue girls keep it in business. "Sending me on a date? You don't exactly look like a fairy godmother."

"I left my wand in the carriage." She tosses the bag on the end of the bed, and I stare at it. "New clothes for transfer day. Can't have you walking out of here looking like a wet blanket. Bad for business."

Transfer.

Not release.

"Lucky me," I mutter, standing and picking up the bag. Inside, the clothing is all black. Some kind of shredded cotton trying to pass for a shirt, along with black pleather leggings. "Oh goody, whore clothes."

"Sorry it's not a ball gown, Cinderella," she snaps, looking annoyed, "but if I were you, I wouldn't look a gift horse in the mouth."

I hold up the clothes. "You think this is a gift?"

"I think you don't want to live down here the rest of your life, and this is your only choice. You had something worth half a shit." Her eyes drop down to my crotch. "You lost it."

My erstwhile virginity, no doubt.

"I didn't lose anything. It was *taken*, and on *your* watch." It's a lie, but she doesn't know that.

Except when I meet her gaze, she's raising an eyebrow. "Maybe the jolly green jackoffs who come in and out of here buy that horseshit, but I don't. Look at you. You probably lost that cherry to the first wet-lipped maggot who humped your thigh." She gives me a long, considering look. "Not because you were easy. Curious, more like. I bet you sent that sucker back home with a limp, didn't you?" She lets out a low, raspy laugh. "Yeah, one of my boys told me about you. Called you a bruiser, and he wasn't lying. God only knows what Daniel was thinking."

My lips smash together with the restraint of not answering.

She's not wrong.

About any of it.

When she speaks again, her voice is slightly less harsh. "I've seen a lot of pussy in my time, girl. I can spot the types from a mile away. The hard hustlers, the bitches with claws, the delicate little dolls who'd break down if a man breathed on her too hard…" She shakes her head, staring me down. "You're not the right kind of girl for this business. If Killian kept you, put you to work upstairs, you'd be dead or in jail in a week, and we both know it." She nods to the bag in my hand. "This'll be a better fit for you."

I give a sharp, bitter laugh. "Serving three fuckboys who are caught up in fake royal titles? Yeah, I'm really moving on up in the world."

She doesn't look surprised that I know where I'm going. "It's up to you what you make of it."

I could tell her right now that Nick was the one who attacked me. Maybe it'd wipe that smarmy, impatient look from her expression if she realized what she was sending me to. Then again, maybe it wouldn't. Maybe she'd tell me I'm still coming out on top.

"You're something else, you know." I tilt my head, regarding her with calculating eyes. She thinks she has *me* pegged? "I wonder how many girls you've ruined with that bullshit you're slinging." Her eyes narrow as I casually stalk forward. "I bet you tell yourself you're just toughening them up, preparing them for the harsh, cold reality of the world. You're not a villain here. You're just a gold star victim. You've perfected it. Nothing bothers you anymore. Some girl gets raped and beaten, she should just pull herself up, pretend it never happened, and be grateful it wasn't worse. Oh, yeah, you're doing them a service," I mock, grinning at the flash of anger in her eyes. "You're not a friend to these girls. You're a traitor. I have more respect for the shit-stains who held me down and fucked me." I hold up the bag. "At least they never dressed it up."

She gives me a bored look. "I could give a rat's flaming fuck about gaining your respect. If I coddled every girl who got bad-touched, I wouldn't have time for anything else."

"Of course, you use your time so much more constructively."

Her eyes bore into mine, flaring indignantly. "Now it's time for you to do the same." She jerks her thumb toward the ceiling. "This is an opportunity that no one else in this pussy trap will ever see. You may have to spread your legs for them, suck their dicks, cook their food, and wash their clothes. So what? Any one of my girls would give their left tit for a chance at a Royal position." When she goes to yank open the door, Auggy is standing there with a duffel bag, waiting. "Get her cleaned up and presentable," Ms. Crane says to her, throwing me a dirty look. "They're coming for you at dinner. I don't give a fuck where you go, so long as you're not soiling my sheets anymore." She leaves, slamming the door behind her as Augustine regards me.

After a moment of suspended silence, she tips her chin up, looking down her nose at me. "You're wrong about her. Ms. Crane isn't a traitor. She's saved more girls from the street than you probably ever deigned to think about in that big fuck-you mansion you grew up in."

I meet her glare, but I can't call up any heat for it. "You don't know anything about how I grew up."

Arching an eyebrow, she says, "I'm betting you never went hungry."

"Then, again," I repeat, emphasizing, "you don't know *anything* about how I grew up. Hunger was nothing." Better to feel my stomach cramp with starvation than to be forced into six square feet of hell. She has no idea what lengths my father will go to get what he wants.

"Whatever," she sighs, stalking past me to the bathroom. "Let's get this over with."

If I thought a rigorous shower was all I'd be getting, then I'm sorely mistaken.

"You're fucking with me," I say twenty minutes later, hair dripping as I survey the counter of my bathroom.

Auggy snaps a pair of latex gloves against her wrists. "Don't worry. I wax all our girls myself. I know what I'm doing."

"I'm not letting you near my twat with hot wax."

She brandishes a flat, wooden spatula-thing and counters, "If we do it now, they won't have to do it themselves later."

I blink at her. "You can't seriously mean—"

"Oh, I very much mean." She nods to the pile of blankets laid out on the floor. "There's a reason you ride into battle hairless. Never give them something to pull." I must be experiencing some form of conditioned psychosis, because that's so close to being profound that I find myself getting my body hair ripped out for the next half hour. "Everything from the waist down," Auggy notes, slathering wax on my shins.

I can't even remember the last time I was able to shave my legs —let alone my cunt—so each rip of the paper hurts like a son of a bitch, making me growl, slapping the floor in useless anger with each strip.

She pointedly ignores this. "You're lucky to be so blonde, you know. It's almost white. My hair's so dark, I can see it growing back after a week, but I bet this lasts a month or more." She runs a finger over an angry, red patch of skin. "Sensitive, though. Your skin's too fair. You bruise easily, don't you? Some of them like that." The look she gives me is full of significance as she grabs the next strip plastered at the crux of my inner thigh. "Those are the ones to watch out for."

Rip.

"Son of a motherfuck!" I screech.

After that, she plucks my eyebrows, moisturizes my face, and then spends a long time combing the tangles from my hair, looking unbothered by the verbal abuse I hurl at her along the way.

"How much do men pay for this?" I sneer, head snapping back forth with each pass of the comb. "Am I getting the sadistic whore premium?"

"I think I'm going to miss you," she says, smiling at a knot. "Coming down here every day to feed you? It's kind of like having a really mean pet you can't bring yourself to put down."

"Fuck you." I stare sightlessly into her bag of horrors. There are all kinds of things in there; curling irons and makeup and hair dyes. It's the kind of shit my sister would know her way around. Leticia would spend hours getting ready in the mornings, always berating me for rolling out of bed, throwing my hair up into something sloppy, and applying nothing more than a layer of lipstick. I always suspected she was jealous. Now I know.

Auggy touches her chest. "Aw, see? My days just won't be the same without you snapping at me." Gradually, her smile disappears, voice carrying a more serious tone. "It doesn't have to be so bad. Ms. Crane was right. Give them what they want, and I bet they'll treat you like a queen. Not all Royals are monsters. Just look at the Lady. She's got a cushy life and three strapping, powerful men who love her like crazy."

I meet her gaze in the mirror, not missing the thread of envy in her voice. "You wish it were you." Truthfully, I pity Augustine. I wonder how many men she services in an average week. How many abusive assholes she has to smile at? How many dicks she has to take inside herself just to earn her place beneath the Lords' ruling fists?

I don't ask.

Instead, I jerk my chin at her bag, throbbing all over in a strangely familiar way. "That hair dye in there," I wonder, reframing this into just the thing she'd described before. A battle I'm riding into. Canon fire and hand grenades.

This isn't vanity.

It's war paint.

"You have anything in a blue?" I ask.

Augustine's red mouth lifts into a smirk. "That's my girl."

3

Lavinia

The man driving the truck is familiar. His lip piercings glint as we pass the bodegas, the occasional streetlight casting an ugly glow over the warehouse district in the West End. Dimitri Rathbone, or Rath, is well known in Royal circles for being both a Lord and Killian Payne's best friend. Now that Killian is a King, I don't know what that makes Rath and the third Lord, Tristian Mercer. Powerful, I guess.

He's not alone. A nameless soldier sits in the front seat next to him, pushing buttons on the radio, flipping from one station to the other. Rath's hand snaps out. In a low tone, he warns, "Stop fucking with the music, Bruce."

"Sorry," the guy says, realizing he overstepped. He glances back at me, forehead creasing. "Seems like overkill—tying her up like that?"

My wrists are bound behind my back with an industrial strength zip-tie. Truthfully, it doesn't bother me much. I'm very experienced in the art of having to contort. Give me three minutes alone back here, and I can wriggle through with my legs to bring my hands to my front. Ten more minutes and I could easily gnaw through them.

"Don't underestimate her," Rath says, flicking me a look in the rearview. "She's lucky I didn't hog-tie her. Bitch kicks like a mule."

I give him a wolfish grin. "Good to see you again, Rath. We should hang out more often. It's been a while since I got a good one in. How's your collarbone?"

His eyes flash back at me in irritation. "Or gag her."

The truck passes the front of a familiar building—the Dukes' gym. I've been to a fight or two down here before, back in high school. I even snuck into a Screw Year's Eve once. I lift my chin at the gym sign. "I'm not sure how this cheap pleather is going to perform in a Jell-O match, bud."

He turns down the alley and slams on the brakes. "Good thing you're not wrestling then."

"Then what am I doing here?" I ask, as the other guy wrenches the truck door open and grabs my shoulder. I'd like to keep up the catty repartee I've got going on with this Rath fucker, but the truth is, I'm starting to get annoyed and uneasy. "What is this?"

No one answers.

Instead, they march me, a hand gripping each of my upper arms, through the backdoor. I catch a glimpse of a flyer taped to the wall—*Friday Night Fury*—and the hairs on the back of my neck stand on end. I know what happens at Friday Night Fury. Two Royals get in the ring. One walks away with the prize.

To the Victor go the Spoils.

That's the Duke's motto.

The back hallway is long and bare, other than old flyers mounted to the wall, a timeline of past fights. It smells like cigars and old ball sweat. Rath opens a door and leads us up a flight of stairs until we get to the landing at the top. The pulsing beat of music and loud voices bear down on me. Above us is the riser to an empty loft, but the rainbow colored glow of lights draws my attention to the mass of bodies below. There's another loft on the opposite side of the warehouse, and there are people up there. An announcer, I'm guessing. A judge or three. Probably some bookies. The West Side does love their gambling.

Apprehension builds in my stomach. I hate my family, but I can't deny my programming. I was raised a Count, which means never going into something blind. These past two years haven't beaten it out of me, and I doubt anything ever will.

I'm so busy surveying the empty loft above that I completely miss their grips changing, the shuffle of feet, and the snick of a box opening. I *don't* miss the sudden pressure against the skin behind my ear, or the three seconds of piercing, stinging pain.

Rath grunts as I thrash away, clamping his arms around my middle. "Stay still!"

"What the fuck?!" I screech. I have this whole plan that involves lifting my knees, letting Rath hold my weight, and kicking back into his shins like the mule he thinks I am.

But then the other guy jabs me hard in the same spot—quick— and ducks away. "It's done, she's tagged."

Rath flings me away before my heels can make contact, glaring down at me. "You're going to go in there, sit quietly, and wait for the match to be over. By the end of the night, you won't be my problem anymore."

"How does your Lady feel about that?" I throw out, teeth clenched against the throb in my neck. As the other guy presses an adhesive-backed bandage to the wound, I coldly wonder, "She's cool with you using a human being as chattel in some stupid dick measuring contest? Tagging them like cattle?"

The corner of his lips lift into a dark smirk. "My girl's got the same tracker. She likes it."

My mouth tightens. "Of course she does. All these bitches around here drink your Kool-Aid, don't they?"

His eyes flicker with a threatening light. "Watch how you're talking about our Lady. If it wasn't for her, we would have paid the Barons to dispose of you months ago." He shakes his head, teeth catching on a lip ring. "You know how this works. You're a Lucia. As much as we hate your father, it's obvious you hate him more. You can either use that to your advantage or piss someone off enough to end up dead in a ditch somewhere tomorrow. I couldn't really care less which."

Without thinking, I lunge forward, hurling a thick wad of spit into his face. "Go fuck yourself."

There's a moment where his eyes close, nostrils flaring, and then he lifts the hem of his shirt, wiping his cheek with a grimace. "See?" he says to the other guy, jaw clenched. "Try to be nice and offer a little advice and all you get is lip. Next time I'm bringing a gag." After a beat, he hotly adds, "Actually, fuck this. There is no next time. You're not a thorn in my side anymore. Thank Christ."

He shoves me forward, except it's less of a shove and more of a palm-punch, sending me stumbling over the steel lip. I brace myself for the fall, but it never comes. I crash into the metal railing instead, landing painfully against my sternum. Before I even have a chance to catch my breath, my hands are freed. I turn to react, but the gleam of light off Rath's blade makes me pause. Faster than I can process, the other guy steps forward and cuffs one of my wrists to the railing.

Fuck.

"You're seriously chaining me up here like a dog?"

If there had been any understanding in Rath's eyes before, it's gone now, replaced by a stony sneer. "What does Nick call you? Little Bird? You're lucky it's not a cage."

A moment later, they're gone, and I yank against the restraints. I can gnaw my way out of a zip-tie, but the cuff and chain are solid metal, clanking noisily against the railing as I tug. All I get for my efforts is a sore wrist.

Fucking motherfuckers.

The sound from below draws me away from my situation, and I peer through the plexiglass, pressing a palm to the burning ache on my neck. The crowd is huge—maybe even bigger than New Year's Eve. But the Royal frats love their theatrics. Normal fraternities indulge in their keggers and football games, and sure, the Royal houses of Forsyth do that too, but that's never been enough. These sons of bitches are more like cults, criminal enterprises, and sadistic circlejerks. The deeper you dig, the more trouble you find.

They're all grand displays or ridiculous vendettas, each in line with their frat's founding agenda. The Lords covet land and possession: women, vehicles, property, and territory. The Princes are obsessed with their golden fucking heir and maintaining a pure, untainted royal line. The Barons get off on being the shadow behind the machine, with their secrets, leverage, and centuries-old traditions. The Dukes make a big show of ruling Forsyth with their fists, but everyone knows they run the gun trade in this town, keeping places like the Avenue flush in firepower.

But my people, the Counts, are all about the flash and posturing. They're drug dealers, car thieves, and sex traffickers. No, black market, backroom dealings are below my father. He has contacts all over the world, funneling narcotics into South Side, using the Counts to push the shitty stuff on the streets and the better, pricier dope on campus. The way I was moved from motel to motel before being settled at the Hideaway wasn't a surprise. Kidnapping is in the Counts' wheelhouse. Perez, the lead Count and my father's number one fuckboy, learned his signature move from my father. You'd think the little prick wouldn't want me, considering the mess I've put him in, but power is power. He needs a Lucia daughter to become King of the Counts.

And my sister is gone.

Which is why, when I see the ring below, everything starts to click into place. Bruno Perez is taking a few warm-up swings in one corner, shirtless and tall, his hair slicked back out of his face. Even from all the way up here, there's no missing him. He's not the most attractive man in the Royal sphere by any stretch, but from the way he holds himself, he probably thinks so. The line of his nose is arrogant, and when he turns to say something to one of his fellow Counts, I can easily make out a scar someone's given him, slashed across his jaw.

The Counts have their own hierarchy—how to ascend from one level to the next. My father has held his position as King for a long time, and he's in no rush to hand it over. He sired no males to continue the line, so the best way for him to keep control is by marrying off his daughter to the most trusted and high-ranking soldier; Bruno Perez. This breaks from tradition, since Leticia wasn't a Countess—god forbid. Lionel would never allow that. No, he'd just arrange for her to marry a disgusting drug-running sex-trafficker to hold onto his power just a little bit longer.

Unfortunately, with my sister missing, that has thrown a big fucking wrinkle into the system.

On the other side of the ring is an unmistakably imposing, ink-covered body. Whereas Perez is warming up, this one seems content to lounge back against the corner, his arm and shoulder muscles flexing as he casually wraps one of his fists. Behind him, a massive guy is on the other side of the rope, brows crouched low as he speaks into his ear. But the fighter isn't looking at him.

He's looking straight at me.

Pretty Nick.

Being under the heat of his gaze is enough to make bile rise into the back of my throat. The half-lidded, cocky grin that's plastered on his face doesn't even twitch when I flinch back, expression twisting in disgust.

Suddenly, I know exactly what this is.

Winner-takes-all.

Nick has spent the last two years running with the Lords—not his royal family, The Dukes. Not until that night he broke into the Hideaway and staked his claim. The Royals all have discrete ways of earning their titles. The video must have been enough to get him in the door, but Saul, their King, will want more. Blood—be it Nick's or Perez's. He has to win this fight—win *me*—just like he and Killian planned. That's how the Dukes work. Nothing won, nothing gained.

I try to look away from Nick's demented gaze, but then there's Perez, staring back at me with a vicious smirk. He bends his neck to meet my eyes, holding up two fingers and flicking his tongue between the V suggestively. My grip tightens around the railing, strangling it, wishing it were his throat. Apparently Nick wouldn't mind strangling him a bit, too. He's glaring daggers into the side of Perez's head, fist curling as he bites off the strand of tape from the roll.

The bell rings below and a loud voice blasts through the speakers, "Welcome to Friday Night Fury!" The crowd roars, and I can tell they've had time to publicize the fight, because the room is visibly split between vipers and bears. "Will there be a Bruin in the belfry for the first time in twenty years? Tonight is the unexpected return of a Duke legacy—the prodigal son—stepping into the ring to claim his title! Pretty Nick Bruuuuiiiinnn!"

I used to have this idea of Nick. Once, I thought of him as a barely sapient trigger finger. Daniel's little lapdog. A pair of fists in search of someone to guide them.

I know the second our eyes meet that I was wrong.

Nick sends me a smirk before looking out over the crowd, and the flex of his jacked-up biceps and well-cut abdomen probably isn't even meant to be showboaty. He just moves like that, stalking and fierce, the perfect Duke visage. The pretty features of his face are accentuated by the tattoo inked beside his eye—237, the Forsyth penal code for mayhem—but beneath that chiseled veneer is the silent, festering wrath of a Bruin. His stare out over the crowd is a twisted, arrogant thing, as if this whole event is his symphony and he's the conductor.

It makes me want to vomit.

"Tell me how it feels to know this pussy belongs to me now."

"But the Duke heir can't claim his throne without winning this fight. He's not the only one with a score to settle!" The sound of boos and cheers mingle as Perez's name is announced. Sutton, the Countess, gives him a dramatic kiss, but he shrugs her off. His ugly, scarred face lifts up, proud and boastful. There was a time I used to think he and Leticia were made for each other. They were never actually together, but everyone knew who the eldest Lucia daughter was sworn to marry, and the thing is, they fit. Both vain and snotty, obsessed with pleasing my father, cold and too proud. I used to be so amused at the thought of it. Never before have two people been so deserving of one another.

The thought of Perez winning me makes my stomach turn, but I can face the truth. The only way I win here is if he and Nick kill one another in the ring.

"Let the fury begin!"

The bell rings and the two men approach one another, bumping fists in a comical display of sportsmanship. Duke fights are notoriously no holds barred. Having a judge at all is basically a joke, and from the loose bounce of Nick's shoulders—a sharp laugh—he knows it. I lean over the edge of the railing, getting a long look at the VIP area just underneath where I'm linked to the rail. It's a small boxed-off section with a primo view of the upcoming carnage, and my blood turns to ice at the sight of the attendees.

The Kings.

I recognize them all. Why wouldn't I? They're each like some gnarled version of family, a collection of creepy uncles you try to avoid at a holiday dinner. It's how I know Nick Bruin is far more conniving than I gave him credit for. This is a show. He's making a spectacle of being initiated, because what better prize is there than taking a rival King's daughter as their Duchess? It's ridiculous, a little incestuous, and infuriatingly orchestrated. In short, perfectly Royal.

In the middle of the pack is Saul Cartwright, King of the Dukes. Even from a distance, I can see the strain around his eyes as he claps. This match is more important than most here would even realize. Any new round of Dukes means a potential threat to his title, but when one of those Dukes is a Bruin, it's basically playing the King equivalent of Russian roulette. Out of every guy in this school, only one of them is guaranteed a spot in the Dukes' belfry, and he's right there, circling Perez in the ring.

Beside Saul is the King of the Barons. He's dressed in a black, well-fitting suit, face veiled by his ominous, bronze horned mask. It's a bit of a farce. Anyone who's anyone knows Clive Kayes is King of the Barons, they've just never seen him unmasked in that specific capacity. But nothing gets a Baron's dick harder than the thought of becoming invisible.

This might be the most official meeting of the Kings I've ever had the displeasure of attending. Ashby, King of the Princes, is there, dressed in his fine, white suit. Killian Payne sits beside him, looking less like a frat boy and more like the slick, sleazy businessman his father had raised him to be. He's obviously not playing dress up anymore, but he sits on the edge, like he's trying to separate himself from the group of men who are decades older. Tristian and Rath flank him, and it gives off a strange vibe. How many more of the current Kings will be toppled, I wonder, as their children come of age?

But even as I assess them, there's one man I keep coming back to.

My father.

He sits with his back straight, and his eyes focused on the match. He looks stoic as ever—artfully disaffected. But no one knows Lionel Lucia like I do. There's a fire raging in his eyes, and it's hot enough to scorch. It's present in the tension around his jaw. The way his hand clutches the arm of his chair. The brief, deceptively casual glances he keeps shooting to Killian. There's a face I've had to wear for years now—one that never shows fear. But I won't deny that the thought of Perez winning—of being under my father's thumb again—makes something inside of me turn to ash.

In the ring, Perez and Nick circle one another, waiting for the first punch. Perez, notoriously impatient, takes the swing, giving Nick the chance to hop out of the way and land his own blow.

I straighten my back nervously.

Right into a hard wall of body.

Two arms trap me in, hands clamping over mine on the railing. "Don't worry, little snake," a familiar voice whispers in my ear. "Nick is going to win. He's good at that—doing whatever it takes. He's a fucking animal when he wants to be, but when he *needs* to be?" The guy lets out a gentle whistle. "Oh, he'll rip off Perez's arms.

He can keep them as trophies and hang them over his bed. That's our Pretty Nick, *armed* and dangerous."

I twist my neck at the sound of his sinister laugh, catching a glimpse of shocking blonde hair and a thin, angular jaw. I don't recognize his face, but I know him.

I know his voice. I've heard it whisper dark, dirty things in my ear.

I know his eyes. I still see them in my dreams, piercing and feral.

I know his scent, that expensive cologne that still bitters the back of my throat.

Maniac.

Hot, panicked anger courses through me, and even with the loud jeers and chants below, the fight is forgotten.

My body, clenched tight, recoils. "You've got some balls showing your face to me, you son of a bitch."

He tilts his head, getting a better look at me. "I didn't even know it was you at first. You used to be Lavinia Lucia, but now you're something else. Your hair..." He lifts a hand to touch it, green eyes zeroed in on the pale lock of blue. "You changed your colors." I lash out with my free hand to strike, but even if the chain weren't holding me back, he reacts lightning fast, catching my wrist with a tisk. "Come on, now. You're a guest in *my* house tonight."

That's when I see the letters tattooed across his knuckles.

D-U-K-E

Fuck, I'm an idiot.

Three attackers.

Three Dukes.

"You never cared about fucking over the Kings with that video," I realize, images of that night flashing through my head. "That was your initiation. Your *real* initiation." Jesus Christ, as if holding that night inside me like a creeping sickness wasn't bad enough, knowing that it was just some stupid ploy to further the Royal status quo makes my knees feel like they want to give out.

He hums, sounding bored. "Our King chose the objective, and

we pulled it off without a hitch. Our boy wants the ring, though. It might be his by rights, but he has to win a fight to get it." Maniac pushes aside the strap of my top, rubbing a thumb over a patch of skin on my shoulder. "Healed nicely," he mutters, voice rough and distracted. "Your skin is fucking amazing. Soft. Smooth. So evenly toned." It occurs to me he's inspecting the mark he left. The ink. The tattoo.

The Brass Bruin.

I swallow over the hard lump in my throat. "What do you want?"

His hips brush against my ass. There's no mistaking the hard press of his cock as he seems to shake himself out of it. "Just surprised to see you out of your cage, is all. Once again you've been left unattended." He pushes the hair off my neck, fingering the bandage. "These Royals don't keep an eye on you like they should, Vinny. It's almost like they don't think you're worth protecting."

His touch makes my skin crawl just as much as the nickname— Vinny. My sister used to call me that. I try to shrug him off, muscles clenched. "Or maybe they think I'm a little too good at protecting myself. Ever think of that?"

"You know what I'm thinking of?" he asks, those fingertips playing with the skin at the base of my neck. "Cause and effect. Like maybe we fucked you good, took away their golden ticket, and now they're finally ready to start using you." I feel his mouth hover over my neck, a damp exhalation. "I'm thinking you're here because those dusty old fucks down there are going to pass you around like a Frisbee tonight."

There's a thread of something in his voice, some awkward marriage of amusement and awe, almost like he's speaking more to himself than me. But I can't really untangle it, because I'm too busy being massively fucking confused.

This motherfucker has no clue that I'm the prize.

My shocked stupor is quickly shattered when he drops his hand, plucking at the waist of my leggings with an unmistakable intent.

I thrash forward, hissing, "What the *fuck*?!"

He surges against my back, pinning me. "Nice pussy like yours getting all used up on geriatric King dick? Such a waste. They'll fill you up with five flavors of rot." He pauses, head tilting. "Well, four, assuming your daddy doesn't want a taste, but he *is* a Count. I don't think anyone would be surprised. Three, if Payne is faithful to his Lady—six, if he isn't." He wrestles me against the railing, nodding at the VIP area below us. "This is basic arithmetic here. You'll be full of numbers and stink by morning. If I want to get mine— maybe I do, maybe I don't—then I should take it here. Fuck you right now while everyone's watching the fight."

Ignoring my ineffectual attempt at twisting away, his hand slides between the fabric and my skin. When he forces my cheeks apart, body trapping mine against the rail, his finger doesn't stop until he gets to the puckered hole.

I freeze, chest heaving. "Don't." It's as much a plea as it is a warning.

"Let me in—like you let him in." There's a shift of his shoulder and then he's curving his finger inward, toying with the tight ring of my asshole. "Relax, Vinny," he breathes, pushing, *invading*, making it sting. My body reacts by clamping up tight, the violation painful and humiliating. "Don't tell anyone, but it's sort of been fucking with me." He speaks low and casual, as if he's not restraining me with one arm and fingering my ass with the other. "I don't normally like putting ink on girls. It's different with guys. Just a job, right? But tagging a girl is so fucking heavy. Knowing she's going to carry around a piece of me for the rest of her life?" His exhale bounces against my skin with a shudder. "Makes me want to rip her skin off just as much as it makes my dick hard. Too confusing. You're a Count. You understand." His whisper is full of unshed laughter. "Don't tell the Lords, though. They wouldn't."

The crowd cheers and stomps below, and I let it take me, shifting every possible bit of my consciousness. It's the only way I can run.

For now.

I look down and see Perez swaying on his feet, but he's gaining his wits, feet crossing as he circles his opponent. Nick's so unconcerned that he actually looks away, his eyes darting up to me. They freeze on Maniac, whose arm is still curled around my middle, but Nick's not stupid. He looks right back at Perez, muscles coiling as he throws another punch.

Maniac forces his finger deeper, unconcerned by Nick's brief stare. "Your pussy looked so pretty covered in my cum and blood, though. Maybe I do want it." He takes on a pensive tone, ignoring the sharp, pained sound I make. "It's all translucent, Vinny. You wouldn't... you wouldn't even fucking believe. Like, the universe, it's just wax paper sometimes. Like the light gets through, but everything's all fucking... indefinable. Do you know what I mean, Vinny? I can't find your edges. Which is weird, right? Because last time... last time, you were so sharp."

Astonished, I realize, "You're a fucking lunatic."

He stills and I can feel the muscles in his torso coil. That's all the warning I get before his free hand grabs my neck, squeezing tight. "I'm *not* crazy!" It's delivered in a hiss of spittle against the curve of my cheek, making me flinch.

But he is. I can see it in the way his eyes spark dangerously. Feel it in the energy rolling off him. Taste it in the heat of his panted breaths.

Just like that, he's shown me his weakness.

"You can chill the fuck out and watch your buddy fight," I say, my voice a wheeze under the pressure of his grip, "or you can distract him enough for Perez to get the upper hand. All the same to me."

Both of us look down just in time to see two things.

Nick is staring right at us.

Perez slams his fist into his temple.

Jaw ticking, Maniac pulls his hand out of my pants, backing off. He shows his palms to Nick, but his friend isn't looking anymore, busy shaking off the blow.

Checkmate, psycho.

"Fine." Even though he curls his hands into fists, Maniac settles against the railing beside me, his green eyes fixed on the fight. "Take the Kings and all their rot."

Struggling to calm my pulse, I watch Nick as he gets his footing back, spitting a wad of blood on the mat. He holds his fists loose and a touch limp as he circles, looking thrown off. A few weeks ago, I might have bought the act, but now I see it for what it is. He's making the punch he took work for him, instilling Perez with a false sense of confidence, giving Nick the opportunity to toy with him a bit.

Perez takes a swipe that misses Nick's kidney by mere centimeters, sending Perez stumbling forward with the momentum. Nick deflects to the side so fast that Perez is still hunched when Nick buries a knee into his side. Perez tries to grapple his legs, but Nick isn't thrown off at all. He hops back, waits for Perez to straighten, and then slams his fist so powerfully into his jaw, it's practically a visible wave through the crowd's reaction.

Perez stumbles and then falls to a knee, fist pressed to the ground to keep him upright. Nick circles around him like a lion— no, like a *Bruin*—as if he's trying to decide the best way to finish him off. He glistens with sweat, the muscular line of his forearms chiseled perfection. He's a finely tuned machine here, moving with efficient purpose. The crowd holds their breath as he grabs a thick fistful of Perez's hair, yanking his head back in a move that looks just as jarring as it probably feels.

But Perez's dazed eyes aren't looking at Nick.

They roll toward my father.

Lionel Lucia always wanted a son. I've heard it so often that it's almost as much a part of me as the color of my hair or the birthmark on my ankle. It's why my father could never love me. I've always been an 'except'. I'm a Lucia, except I'm not good enough. I'm his daughter, except I'm not compliant enough. I'm a woman, except I'm not pretty enough.

Perez is everything my father ever wanted in a second child. Calculating and ruthless, just like Leticia. I think there was a time it galled me to know it, as if some part of me still ached to feel accepted and wanted.

That's long gone now.

I can tell, because when my father meets Perez's gaze and gives him a single, definitive nod, an understanding passes between them. A connection I could never form.

And all I feel is alarmed.

There's a flash of silver from Perez's ankle, and my reaction is to belt out a loud, instinctive, "Look out!" It echoes across the arena, but the only person I watch my voice carry to is Nick.

Somehow, he doesn't even need to glance at me. His eyes go instantly to Perez's hand, and when his foot comes down on it, crushing his fingers under the sole of his shoe, the resulting scream is loud enough to drown out the sound of my rushing heartbeat. Slowly, Nick bends to pry the metal from his grip, giving the blade a skilled spin through the air.

He reaches down to grab Perez's fingers—the same two he'd raised to his mouth before—and settles his icy gaze on my father. I can only just make out the words he speaks through a toothy, blood-stained grin. "Killer was right. This *is* fun."

Then he cuts off his forefinger.

The gasp that falls over the crowd is louder than Perez's shriek as Nick saws deftly through his bone, muscled shoulder jerking as he rips it away. The shockwave hits me even from all the way up here, sending me jerking back in shock.

My father is halfway out of his seat, but it's the Baron King who reaches out, placing a calm hand on his shoulder. He gives a single, slow shake of his masked head, and my father falls back into his seat, jaw tight.

Nick only gives the severed finger a brief look, but it's demented. You'd think he was inspecting a flower he just plucked from a garden. I half expect him to smell it.

Instead, Nick drops Perez much like he drops the knife, tossed to the ground like discarded trash as they announce his win from the opposite loft. Nick lifts his chin, but where a Duke would usually do a boastful, proud lap around the ring, Nick doesn't bother.

He glances up, catching my eyes, and raises the finger into the air.

Smirking, he bends it into a little mocking wave as the announcer closes the fight.

"To the Victor go the Spoils."

4

Sy

By the end of the fight, my palms hurt from fisting my hands so tightly. It's the worst, watching someone else in the ring, knowing that I can't jump in and feel the pressure of their bone against my knuckles. And fuck, do I want it. How long has it been since I really got to let loose on someone deserving? Not since spring. It becomes an ache, like I'm holding back an urge that's primal and animalistic, and it wounds something inside of me to deny it.

Pops has always said I've got his Bruin blood thirst, and even though it's spoken in that light, playful way, I can tell he worries. I'm not a Bruin—not his flesh and blood—but I might as well be.

Dad says I'm just 'balancing', since, fights aside, I'm usually the level-headed one of the bunch. "Everyone," he likes to say, "has a demon inside of them. Push it down too long and it'll claw its way up."

Mom just says I have an impulse control disorder.

None of them are wrong.

It's been a long time since my parents have gotten that call. Me in the principal's office, staring down the barrel of an expulsion. Me in the Sheriff's station, staring down the barrel of an aggravated assault charge. It's been years now, but I know each of them is always dreading the next, how bad it'll be now that I'm actually trained and dangerous.

Speaking of which, it's been twenty minutes since the last text from my pops, so I'm fully expecting it when my phone dings with another notification.

Pops: *What am I supposed to tell your mother*

Pops: *Did either of you think of that?*

I don't answer, because this isn't a discussion worth having over text. Davis Bruin might be Nick's biological father, but they haven't spoken since last Thanksgiving, almost nine months ago. Just one more reason to be pissed off at my brother, leaving the fallout on my shoulders while I follow him into the gym's back room.

Nick should have told our parents himself, weeks ago. I've been preparing them since my first year at Forsyth, pledging with DKS, making it clear that I planned to become a Duke. That was bad enough. Dad didn't speak to me for a month. Pops wouldn't *stop* talking. Mom did her usual song and dance of trying to psychoana-lyze why I'd ever want to be part of an institution that's demon-strably toxic.

But Nick just struts in here, takes down Perez, lands the ring, and hasn't had to hear two fucking words about it.

Classic Nick.

Ever since I pledged to Delta Kappa Sigma, the Dukes' origin frat, I've learned how to control the festering violence clawing to break free. I train three days a week, pouring all my energy into the discipline, the art, the sophistication of brutality. When you pummel a guy in a bar, it's assault. When you do it in a ring, it's a sport. Funny. It's probably why my parents stopped voicing their disapproval about me being in DKS, becoming a Duke. The phone calls stopped. Instead of being told I was a problem, I began being hailed as a victor. I guess, to them, it's better to be a Duke than to be rotting in prison. Remy's family bailed me out once. I can't count on it again.

Nick, however, doesn't have a worthwhile excuse.

He's fucked.

"You're telling them," I warn him, looking over my shoulder to see the procession of Kings in the distance, coming our way. "Dad and Pops. Mom, too. I'm not smoothing over that steaming pile of dog shit."

Nick wipes a towel over his face, collecting sweat and blood. "Never asked you to."

"Never said you did," I counter, propping the door open for the train coming our way. "But that's always how it works out, isn't it?"

Nick rolls his eyes, dropping onto a bench to dig into his bag. "Christ, can a guy not bask in his victory for ten minutes?"

Crossing my arms, I expect the first person to enter to be Saul.

Instead, it's Remy, having ducked around them at some point.

He's got his black DKS hoodie raised, blond hair peeking out at messy angles, and his mouth is tipped into a smirk. "Nice upper-cut," he says to Nick, holding his fist out. "Rocked his shit. That little bitch can't cash a check."

Nick bumps it with his own, but I don't miss the flash of animosity in his eyes. "What the fuck were *you* doing?"

Remy stuffs his fists in his pockets, shrugging, but he's wearing this devious little grin. "Just fingering her ass a little. No big."

Nick goes stony and silent in a way that usually precedes him storming off like a moody fuck, but before he can, the Kings start sweeping in. Nick pushes to his feet, hair damp with sweat, split lip still trickling blood.

"Looks like we've got a new Duke," Saul says, giving Nick's hand a shake that's, I'm guessing, just the hostile side of firm. Having me earn a spot was bad enough, but Nick? He's the real legacy. The Bruin that carries not just the blood, but the worth. It's not like I didn't grow up hearing about that all the time. We share the same mother—*not father*—and that's the kind of thing that matters to these people.

Killian, King of the Lords, shakes his hand next, saying, "Good shit out there, Bruin. Gave us a show." I narrow my eyes at the look that passes between them. It's full of an understanding that makes my insides flare up.

"Of course he did," I snap. "He could have had his ass to the mat in two minutes flat. He's my brother, isn't he?"

The other two Lords, Tristian and Rath enter next, and at first, I don't even notice the girl they're dragging between them. Mostly, I'm just remembering that these fools and Killian Payne's old man have been using my brother like an expendable felon for the last two years. I think I might despise them, except it's all muddled beneath how pissed off I am at Nick for turning his back on his own. After what happened to Tate, none of us were the same.

But Nick's the only one who ran away.

Ashby, King of the Princes, is next into the room. It's a surprise to everyone when he offers Nick his hand, too. "So these are the new fists of Forsyth. It'll be nice to see a Bruin in the belfry again." It's an oddly friendly gesture, so it's understandable that Nick pauses before shaking. Ashby ignores Saul's pointed look, adding, "Saw some shades of your old man out there. Back in our day, it wasn't a real Bruin fight until the other guy's blood and piss were staining the mat."

"I saw the mat," Killian says in a dry voice. "Trust me; it was a real Bruin fight."

I finally get a good look at the girl his boys are toting to the corner. My neck snaps in her direction when it hits me. Her hair's different, but just as stringy and limp as it had been that night, two weeks ago. Her mouth is covered in a thick strip of duct tape, but I know what the lips beneath it look like. Her pale skin peeks out of the whorish shirt she's wearing, reminding me of the mark Remy left.

The mark *we* left.

It takes me like a tidal wave, pulling me under as I sink into the memory of her pussy, creamed with my cum. I've replayed that video a dozen times. Two dozen. Maybe even three. I thought I'd lost my taste for porn years ago, but apparently when it's my own dick making an appearance, my freak of a cock perks to attention. That first week, it was practically all I could think about. What it might have been like, burying my cock into her, tearing her open on me, shooting my load deep inside.

"Oh fuck, no," she said when she saw my cock that night. The look of terror and disgust etched in her features. I don't need some little whore to tell me I'm a freak. She's lucky I didn't shove it down her throat and let her choke.

When I rise from the fog of sudden, sickening lust, I realize her eyes are glued to mine.

She's frozen as she glares at me.

I shift uncomfortably, tearing my eyes away as my jaw tightens. Fucking bitch, making me feel... *this.* That tight, feral wildness in my chest. The one I've been pushing down for years now. The urge to fight and fuck, so tightly connected in my psyche that it's impossible to untangle them, have merged into one indefinable demon, threatening to claw its way up and up.

She has no right to get inside my head like this.

She has no right.

"To the victor go the spoils," Saul adds, opening a square mahogany box. An identical ring to the one on Saul's finger—the one that should be on Pops'—is waiting within.

The fight was a pointless production. Pretense, most likely. All three of us passed his initiation by violating the Count whore. Highest point score in any Duke's challenge yet. But people would ask questions, wonder what the talk was. Saul places the ring on Nick's finger, pushing it over his bloody knuckles.

Nick doesn't even give the ring a second glance, already bored by it. Instead, he moves his attention to the two Kings by the door. The ones who didn't offer him a handshake. The Baron and the Count. There's a strange crackle in the air, and from the slow, tense look Remy slides my way, I can tell he feels it too. The build of static before a lightning strike. Probably has something to do with the way the Lords are staring Lionel down. Like they're waiting.

I force myself to breathe, batting down the hot, creeping hope that all of this comes to blows so I can get one in. Remy isn't even looking at them, eyes locked on me, ready to hold me back if it comes to it. Just like old times.

The crack comes a moment later, when Lionel storms across the distance between him and his daughter. "Don't think this means your punishment is over," he spits, barreling at her.

Nick steps out to block him, shifting his shoulders in a way Remy and I both recognize. Instinctually, we react the way we always have. It doesn't matter that we have no fucking clue what's going down here. That we don't really understand the fire in Lucia's eyes. That the other Kings are watching and measuring us up.

We've always been six fists.

And mine are itching.

"She's not yours to talk to anymore," Nick says, stepping into Lucia's space. He raises his chin, arrogant as ever, as he spreads his arms. "To the victor go the spoils."

Lionel's coiled tight, almost as if—and the thought very nearly makes me laugh—he wants to take a shot. Killian and his boys are right behind, seeming like they're prepared to pull him away. But they don't need to bother. Lucia lets out a low, scornful chuckle. "You don't scare me, little boy. You think you can ruin her?" He gives his daughter a long, seething stare. "Not before she ruins you." Walking back two steps, he angrily adjusts his blazer. "But you're welcome to try."

Lucia storms out, and one by one, the other Kings follow. Baron. Prince. Duke. Lord.

But Rath lags behind, turning to say, "My advice? Leave the tape on until completely necessary."

Nick doesn't stand down until they're all gone, and even then, he just goes back to the bench, unwinding the tape from his knuckles.

Remy gestures limply at the door, calling out, "Excuse me! You forgot your Count Trashula!"

"What the fuck," I ask, looking at the girl, "was that about?"

She's still got that prissy look on her face, like we're all beneath her, and she's above this. I've never known such a haughty whore. I guess that comes with being the daughter of a King, even if he's a corrupt bastard.

"She's ours now," Nick says, deceptively casual as he raises his gaze to hers.

Looking distinctly unimpressed, she makes a sharp, muffled sound from beneath the tape. If I were pressed to speculate, I'd guess she tells him to go fuck himself.

My eyes whip between them. "What the hell are you talking about?"

"As of ten minutes ago, we're officially Dukes. We need a Duchess." He raises a hand, as if he's introducing us. "Here she is. You're welcome."

Nick has always been unpredictable. For instance, I never thought he'd handle the death of one of our best friends by defecting to Daniel fucking Payne. I never thought he'd spend three years being his attack show-poodle. And I never thought he'd show up at the DKS doorstep wanting to claim the title. It meant enrolling in school, joining the frat, taking a lot of tedious steps that Remy and I have been chipping away at for years.

But as impulsive and hard headed as Nick can be, he's also patient. Strategic. Disciplined. Worst of all, he's smart.

Smarter than most people would suspect.

"No." My answer brooks no argument.

"Yes." Neither does Nick's.

Face screwed up into a baffled expression, Remy cuts in. "There's a whole goddamn pool of cutsluts to choose from. Why the hell would we take on—" He flings a hand in her direction. "Count trash! She's Count trash, Nicky. Fuck this bitch."

Nick's gaze is fixed to his phone—a message from our parents, most likely. "She's not Count trash. She's our Duchess. The deal's been made."

I stalk forward to yank the phone from his hands. "She's not pre-med. She's not a student. And most importantly, she's not in the increasingly small sum of bitches I want near me."

Remy agrees. "I had plans for the Duchess this year, and none of them included having to duct tape her fucking mouth shut." When another muffled sound comes from the corner, Remy whips around to glare at her. "Though if it were, I would have done a better job."

"What happened to Verity?" I say, trying to reason. "She was the obvious pick."

But at this, Remy pauses, tilting his head at me curiously. "You wanted Verity? But she's so..." He pulls a face. "Breakable."

"I didn't want Verity," I insist, fists curling. "I didn't want a Duchess period, but since we have to have one, you can't just unilaterally decide who she'll be." I seriously consider adding to that cut on his lip. "We don't want her."

Nick rises to his feet, meeting me not unlike he'd met Lionel Lucia moments before. He holds up his fist, which, like Remy, now has 'DUKE' tattooed across the knuckles. But he's not showing me the letters.

He's showing me the ring. "*I* want her."

I hold his stare, as deep and long as the chasm he put between us by dipping out all those years ago. "So that's how it's going to be. Pulling rank on us?"

"For this." Nick drops his fist, glancing at the girl. "Don't act like you aren't down. Look at her." He jerks his chin and when I turn, there's napalm in her eyes, fixed directly on my brother. You wouldn't know it, looking at Nick. He's all razor-sharp smirk and leering eyes. "She's the daughter of a King. We have the chance to conquer the unconquerable."

I stare her down, lip curling. "She's not worth the effort."

Nick scoffs, burying a punch into my shoulder. "Stop acting like you haven't been locking yourself up in your room to replay that video for the last two weeks." He jabs a finger into his temple. "You get that psycho look in your eye every time someone gets your dick hard."

I punch his shoulder right back. "And you must think I'm an idiot to believe you can handle sharing. This isn't about us getting a Duchess. This is you getting your own toy."

Remy scrubs his fingers through his hair, looking tired. "He's right. The Duchess is supposed to belong to all of us. I can smell it on you, man. She's got her fucking venom in your blood." He shakes his head. "You're too attached."

But Nick just laughs, low and dark, as he looks at her. "Oh, I can share her. Trust me."

That's easier said than done. I used to know this guy like the back of my hand, but now? Nick isn't just coming to play. He's playing to win.

But if she isn't the prize, then what is?

5

Lavinia

I don't know when it started raining.

There's a palpable tension in the car on the way home and even I know better than to stoke it—not that I could. The windshield wipers fill the space with a rapid rhythm that's intercepted by the static of the rain hitting the roof of the car. But even louder than that is the silence.

Lurker is absolutely fucking *livid*. It seethes under his skin, like maybe if I looked hard enough, I could see it coming off him in refracted waves. His jaw has been clamped tight since I first saw him in that room with the Kings. Now that I look, I can see the family resemblance. It's in the eyes, the structure of their faces, their builds.

I'm used to big, angry men, but my father is a Count. We keep that shit simmering inside and strike when it can do optimal damage. The Dukes are just like their house sigil. Bears lumbering angrily around, no finesse or subtlety. Lurker—Sy—has it rolling off him, entirely unconcerned about who sees it. It's weak. Too visible. Shows people your softest area.

It makes me antsy, but my hands are bound, as well as my feet. My mouth is still covered with tape, so I guess they're taking Rath's advice, the fucker. Instinctively, I scan the interior of the car for any way out, but my heart's not in it. It's dark out, we're deep in the West End, and even if I did get away by jumping out of a speeding car, who's going to help me? These guys own this area.

No.

I'm not a bear, I'm a viper. What I need is patience. A plan. Leverage.

The Royals are trading me back and forth because I have value, even if it's no longer my virginity. Seeing the look on my father's face when his house took that 'L' tonight makes whatever comes next a little more bearable. Funny to think about. A few years ago, he wouldn't have cared who had me. But he's the biggest Count there is, and if he showed his hand, coming at me like that, then I'm no idiot. It was on purpose. He wants everyone to know I'm his weakness, because it makes me a target.

Tap, tap, tappity, tap.

Fuck, even if I did find a way to escape, the crazy one is right next to me, with those wiry, fast arms and ink-covered fingers that are currently occupied in tapping an erratic beat against the window. I can't get a handle on this guy. He's hot one minute, cold the next. He's wearing a worn hoodie, the Delta Kappa Sigma symbols emblazoned on the front, but he's also in a pair of jeans that I know for a fact run in the high hundreds. His sneakers are just as expensive—designer crap—but the laces are loose and dragging in the street. God, and his rich cologne is still hot in my nose. This guy comes from money and looks like it, without even trying.

And he'd probably grab me before I made it halfway out the door.

Tap, tap, tappity, tap.

"Jesus Christ, Remy," the one driving snaps, making me jump. "Give it a fucking break."

The tapping abruptly stops and Maniac—apparently Remy— stares at his fingers for a long moment before dropping his hand.

Lurker lets out a hard breath. "Thank you."

Nick's been unabashedly watching me in the rearview mirror this whole time, eyes dark and unreadable. Now, he finally speaks. "Don't mind Sy here," he says, turning his head just enough for a passing streetlamp to illuminate the sharp cut of his jaw. "Nothing gets him prickly like a nice piece of ass."

Sy's fingers audibly tighten around the steering wheel. "So help me god, if you don't shut the fuck up..."

Nick turns back, grinning. "See? If he's this bitchy, you must really get his motor revving. He doesn't like being reminded he's not a robot."

In the distance, I see the dark outline of our destination: the clock tower. The tower's been the Duke's home base since the day DKS was established, a gift deeded over from a Forsyth University benefactor to protect the historic architecture from being razed. It's tall enough to be seen even off campus, but even though it's old, it bears the timeless intricacies of its era. The baroque stonework. The aged, bronze bell at the tippy top. The bear-faced gargoyles that stare out like sentries from each of the four corners.

According to my father, the Royalty all started innocently—a social club for the male students at the university. Someone had the bright idea to base it on a Royal system, calling themselves Lords and Counts and all that snobbish bullshit. I guess guys have always needed to measure their dicks. In any culture, there is no higher figure than king, and Forsyth is no different.

The difference is that, back then, it wasn't about running drugs, selling guns, or hustling flesh. The OGs were academics, just a bunch of rich nerds looking for a way to bond groups of students in an effort to keep them focused, network, and build the community. Unfortunately, the small town that surrounds the University went from quaint and safe to abandoned and derelict in a few short decades. It felt the aftershocks of the 1970s. High gas prices. Soldiers that returned home villains instead of heroes. Businesses closed, and factories—the warehouses that line the city—shut down for good. Sure, the University and suburbs where I grew up survived, but not the downtown. Not the Avenue. Slowly the streets became overrun with crime, ruled by thugs, and the Royals at the time didn't banish the decline, they embraced the anarchy of it. They claimed territory, recruited foot soldiers, created enterprises, established *rule.*

The car comes to a stop at the base of the tower, and I crane my neck up at the tall, statuesque building, trying to see the clock face in the dark. I know it's broken. It probably hasn't even worked in my father's lifetime, let alone mine. I make out the frozen hands, 7:23, marking that as the moment I enter their world.

The day I truly become a slave.

Nick is the one to cut the ties binding my ankles before ordering me from the SUV.

When we enter the tower, there's an elevator by the entrance and I go stiff at the sight of it. Maybe I could last the ride up —*maybe*—if I were alone, and the ascent was quick, but all four of us crammed into that metal box?

I'll die.

I just know I will.

To my relief, all three of them ignore it. Broken, probably, like everything else in this place. The stairwell they herd me to is dark and has an odd smell, a mixture of dirt and damp, but the steps are solid beneath my feet as we rise.

And turn.

And rise.

And turn.

And rise.

Life at the Velvet Hideaway didn't afford much space for cardio, and I count ten stories as we go up before Sy sneeringly says, "That's right, princess. Dukes need the exercise. Get used to it."

I shoot him a withering glare, second guessing my assumption about the elevator being broken.

Fucking masochists.

Better that they not know I'd rather take a million flights of stairs than be crammed into another box. It's been two years since I've had that particular brand of punishment, and I'm in no hurry to show my cards. By the time we finally reach a door, I'm huffing through my nose, calves burning in protest. The first room we pass through smells like stale beer and weed. The walls are decorated with faded and torn banners, DKS iconography, and a cracked, framed print of Muhammad Ali. There's a big screen TV on one wall and the long, flat surface of a bar spanning another. Half-empty bottles of booze line the shelves behind it. I wrinkle my nose at both the smell and scene. These must be the crumbling dregs of the West End's frat party scene.

Suddenly the Velvet Hideaway isn't looking so shabby.

"Go," Sy grunts, pushing me toward another long, narrow staircase. Remy runs ahead, feet echoing on the steps. Unlike the other stairs, these are made of metal. Iron, maybe. I stumble up the first riser, but strong hands stop me from actually falling. My skin recoils, remembering the last time Nick touched me. Thankfully, once I'm upright, he releases me.

At the top of the staircase, we spill into the tower's main chamber. It's a square, cavernous area with ceilings that must be at least thirty, maybe even forty feet high. The look of the space is a mixture of antiquated stone, retro plaster, and rusty industrial, with ductwork and pipes running up along the massive wooden beams. I can spot a kitchen near the back, a drab dining area, a lounge space with two couches, and lighting that roughly resembles that of a dank murder basement.

It's like someone took a cathedral and renovated it to be...

Well, a frat house.

But what really draws my eyes is the colossal clock face.

It's just as breathtaking as I've always heard, taking up nearly the whole wall, corner to corner. One of its massive roman numerals could easily cover my entire torso. It's cordoned off from the room by a raised loft. A rickety-looking staircase in the corner spirals up to the platform, which sits above a long row of tall, gothic-styled observation windows.

It's no wonder someone gifted this place to the Dukes instead of seeing it torn down. Even in the midst of the ratty couches and faded area rugs, the craftsmanship outshines the filth. I note the doors along the interior walls—additions that were made farther into the industrial revolution than the tower itself, no doubt.

"Welcome home, Little Bird," Nick says, spreading his arms in a mocking gesture.

"I have a question," Sy asks, tossing his keys in a bowl on the kitchen bar. "Where exactly do you plan on her staying?"

Nick's forehead creases. "Staying?"

"Sleeping," Sy condescendingly enunciates. "The place where she goes to *not* be around me. Or did you not even think through something as simple as that?"

Nick scoffs, giving Remy a weary look. "I think my brother is confused as to what a Duchess is. Maybe you can explain it to him."

Remy falls onto the couch and kicks a foot up, looking almost as tired as I feel. "The Duchess doesn't get a bedroom. She doesn't need a bedroom." He lifts his gaze in my direction, head tilting as he assesses me. "She sleeps with her Dukes. Duh."

My protest emerges in the form of narrowed eyes and a snarled grunt.

"Fuck *that*." Sy flings a hand toward me. "I'm not sleeping with some skanky North Side whore. Are you out of your goddamn mind?! She'll fucking shank us!"

Nick fixes him with a long, threatening gaze. "She's not a whore. She's our Duchess, like it or not."

Sy begins pacing. "God, you're an idiot. Do you know that? Probably not. Too busy thinking with your dick to use the last brain cell you brought back from South Side. Fuck!" Sy slams his fist on the counter. "I knew bringing you back in was a bad idea. You're going to ruin everything we've worked for!"

They argue, voices rising, chests puffed, hands flying around. I don't care. Cracks are good. The more they focus on one another, the better it is for me. I scan the room for anything I can use. Weapons, escape routes, hiding spots. Being this high up is a problem. One way in, one way out.

"Stop!" Remy explodes, shooting up from his seat. The guys snap their attention over to him. "We've got two semesters ahead of us here, and I'm not living with two ticking cum-bombs until it's over. If you want to throw tantrums like we're back in middle school, then fine. She can stay in my room." He turns to me, those crazed green eyes descending my body. "I don't mind sharing my bed. The two of us have unfinished business anyway."

Like a switch has been flipped, Nick's entire demeanor changes. "Like hell you are." His blue eyes hold Remy's. They contain less of a challenge and more of a warning. "She's sleeping with me."

"I knew you wouldn't share." Sy pinches his nose and sighs deeply. "Fucking knew it. This is just like you."

"You'll both get a turn," Nick insists, whipping his gaze to his brother. "I negotiated, fought, *and* won her. Tonight, she's mine."

I force back a shudder at the thread of darkness in his voice. Unbidden, I'm transported back to that night. I feel his touch, smell his skin, and see the possessive spark in his eyes. I hear his voice, a ragged rumble against my ear.

"Tell me how it feels to know this pussy belongs to me now."

Nick's room is practically empty.

There's a messily made bed, a box acting as a nightstand, and a desk lamp sitting on top of it. Unlike the other rooms, most of Nick's walls are made up of an old, mortared stone. There's an ancient iron ladder attached to the interior wall, and a tall opening at the top of it, leading out to the rafters that run through the main room. It's a reminder of what this room used to be—something functional to the workings of the clock, most likely. Aside from that, there's various detritus scattered about. A pile of clothes kicked to a corner. A gym bag, not unlike the one he's dumping on the foot of his bed. A pizza box.

And then there's me.

That's what he focuses on when he turns. The whole force of that dark, blue-eyed stare pins me in place as he stalks forward. I track him, trying to feel more like a predator than his prey, but the whole 'being bound and gagged' thing might ruin the effect.

He thumbs the corner of his mouth as he stops in front of me, eyes dropping to my throat. My wrists smart when I fidget, the plastic zip tie pinching my skin. I'm imagining all the things I'd like to do to him. Smash my foot into his smug face. Knee him in the balls. Cut off the fingers he's put inside me, just like he'd done to Perez.

Instead, I wait.

Patience.

He folds before I do, springing forward in a flurry of motion. He grabs the back of my hair and hauls me up against him, putting his mouth to my jaw. The solid wall of his body is the first warmth I've felt since Maniac forced his finger into my body. Nick, though...

He breathes in through his mouth like he's tasting me, spreading his wide palm on my lower back. "What'd I say?" he whispers, voice a gruff exhale against my ear. "Took some time, but I did it. No one will come for you now that they've given you to us." I feel his hand curl into a fist against my back. That, plus the rumble I feel against the swell of my own tits, must be the sad vestige of his restraint. Dragging his mouth over my jaw, a damp trail that makes me grimace, he pauses over the tape, letting out a quiet chuckle. "Almost forgot." He lets my hair go to scratch at a corner, grabbing it tight before ripping it away in one quick motion.

It stings like a son of a bitch, which is the only reason I make a sharp, pained sound. Nick tries to soothe it away by thumbing at my bottom lip, eyes trained on the soft part of my mouth. They go heavy-lidded and dazed-looking, zeroing in as his head cants to the side.

I've seen this kiss coming since he stepped into the ring.

Being still for so long makes the action feel like a loaded spring. I wrench my head back and slam it forward, the curve of my skull cracking against his nose.

"Shit!" Nick shouts, stumbling back, hands coming up to his face. "What the fuck was that for?"

I answer by lobbing a wad of spit at his head. "Take a guess, asshole!"

He straightens, eyes aflame as he lowers his palms, surveying the blood. "You could have broken my fucking nose!"

Could have?

I try to hide my disappointment with a venomous grin. "Well, if at first you don't succeed..."

He responds by barreling forward, wrapping his fingers around my throat only to march me backwards until my shoulders slam into the wall. "Try again," he growls, lunging down to press his bloody mouth to mine.

I turn away before he can.

His lips stutter against my cheek and freeze there. "What kind of bullshit thanks is this?"

Staring at the door, I fume, "The only kind your sorry ass deserves, honestly." There's a moment where I brace for the strike, because Nick is a Duke. He can't hide his anger. I can feel it vibrating in his grip—the struggle of holding back. He wants to crush and hurt. It's all a Bruin knows.

"What's your problem!" he snaps, wrenching my gaze to his. Those blue eyes narrow as he scrutinizes me. "Don't tell me you're still pissed about the Hideaway. I told you it was for your own good."

Incredulously, I reply, "You mean the part where you raped me?"

He gives a derisive scoff. "Rape? Hardly. You asked for it, Little Bird." He jerks his head toward the bed, where a laptop is sitting. "I have it on video and everything. You wanted it."

Something poisonous wells within me at the thought of them

having it. Watching it. Getting off to my darkest, sickest moment. I'm going to get out of here—that's a done deal—but I make a promise to myself.

Not until I destroy it.

"Does that make you feel better about it?" I wonder, only half curious as I unflinchingly hold his stare. "Do you lie to yourself to soothe your sad little ego as you jack off into your hand like the sack of shit you so clearly are?"

His nostrils flare, fingers tightening around my throat. "The next words that come out of your mouth better be 'thank you for rescuing me, Nick' and 'let me suck your fat cock to show my appreciation.'"

I strain against his grip, raising myself to my full height to sneer, "Fuck you, Nick. Put your cock anywhere near my mouth and I'm biting down until it comes off."

"What the fuck is your problem! I saved you!"

I fight the urge to grab his wrists. "You can't really be this deluded," I say, glaring at him. "You can't possibly have me tied up in your fucking tower, making plans to give your buddies a go at me, and think this was what I wanted."

Only it is.

I can see it in his eyes, all wild and furious. "I freed you."

Gaping, I raise my bound wrists, bumping his hip. "Maybe the concept of freedom has changed since being chained in a basement, but I'm pretty sure this isn't what it looks like."

"Then why," he asks, flexing his grip, "did you warn me about Perez and the knife?"

A strained laugh escapes my throat. "Oh, don't flatter yourself. That wasn't about you winning. It was about my father losing."

His eyes jump back and forth between mine, so close I can taste the tang of blood on his breath. "You're really not going to even thank me."

"No!"

There's another beat of silence, like he's waiting for me to admit it's all a joke, his face growing redder and redder by the second. "Do you have any idea of the things I've done to get you here?"

My own face must be red by now too, throat stinging with the crush of his grip. "I don't care."

I've never seen someone's eyes go truly black before. Not in color. Nick's eyes are as blue as ever, but his wide pupils are bottomless, transformed into something darker than death. "Fine." Suddenly, I'm being pulled toward the door, his fingers constricting my throat as he marches us through it, uncaring of the way I'm clawing at his forearms. "If being in my bed isn't freedom enough for you," he growls, giving me a rough shove through the main room, "then let me show you the alternative."

I'm too busy trying to gasp for air, struggling against his hold, to take note of where he's pulling me.

And then I hear the sound of metal on metal.

Scraping and sharp.

The elevator.

"No, wait!" My voice can barely form a wheeze under his grip, and the next thing I know, he's pushing me inside, the metal cage closing just as I bang into it. "Nick, wait!"

"I won you, Lavinia!" His fists slam violently into the metal, sending me scurrying back. "I *won* you!"

If I had any hope that he'd give me the gate, but leave the heavy outer door open, then I'm stupid. So fucking stupid. It never works out like that, does it? It's never a proper punishment until it's dark and closed in, leaving you all alone with nothing but your own torment.

He wrenches the outer door closed with a powerful jerk of his muscular arm, shrouding me in black.

It's been two years.

Two years since I've been closed up in the dark, surrounded by nothing but the hiss of my own panicked breaths. Two years since I found myself thrashing against the confines of a space too small. Two years since I had to feel the crushing weight of hysterical terror clawing its way out of my chest.

I stave it off for as long as I can, closing my eyes, pretending I'm somewhere else. It's the smells and sounds that get me, the way my breaths ricochet off the surface in front of me, beside me. It makes it impossible to truly get away. The words I've held onto inside my mind fluttering away like dust in the wind. The elevator is smaller than I thought—barely big enough for three. Every shift of my weight disturbs whatever fragile sense of mental escape I manage to muster, sending vicious creaks to slice through the silence.

The sweat comes first, making my clothes feel heavier, tighter. Then the nausea, my stomach roiling painfully as the tremors begin. The dizziness is next, made all the more disorienting by my complete inability to even see what's up or down. Then comes the tightness in my chest, as if a fist has been wrapped around my heart.

I doubt I last ten minutes.

It explodes out of me in a stampede of urgency, my jaw locked tight around a scream as I ram my shoulder against the gate. These have always been the worst—the thrashings. It's an instinct stronger than the will to breathe, driving me against the walls, my body struggling to find a way *out, out, out.*

The longer it goes on, the more it feels like my throat is closing up. Rationally, I know it isn't, but I lift my chin and I can't fucking *breathe.* Too dark, too hot, too small. I must spend hours like that, thrashing, then hyperventilating, then thrashing some more.

After that comes the doom—the certainty that I'm going to die here.

It gets easier then.

Not better.

Just... easier.

Sore and breathless, I collapse against the wall, sliding until I hit the floor in a tense, trembling heap.

What was the last thing I read?

I pull my panic back inside, determined to remember the words. I always remember what I read. It's the only thing I've ever been good at—flipping through the pages in my mind. Red cover.

Corners creased. Something Augustine gave to me. A tawdry romance novel. Happily ever after.

Closing my eyes, I remember.

"Remember," Anthony says, sweeping his thumb across my cheek, "as long as we're together we can do anything."

I'M NOT EXPECTING the shock of bright, piercing light when the door slides open. There's no way I haven't been here for twenty-four hours. It should be night. Only the light pouring in from the clock face across the room is muted and gray.

Late morning.

I'm up against the gate before the outer door even finishes closing, gulping cool air through the metal lattice. Nick stands in front of it, and for some reason, I get a sharp memory of something Remy said to me last night.

"The universe, it's just wax paper sometimes. Like the light gets through, but everything's all fucking... indefinable."

Nick is just like that; a blur of shape in an aggressive stance. Everything is hazy and I squint against the light, trying to find his edges. I know it's bad when Maniac's crazed ramblings begin making sense.

His fingers are the first things to come into definition, hooking through the gate as his arm hangs. Lazily, he leans his forehead against his wrist, indulging in a suspended stretch of silence. Observing me, I realize, feeling his eyes tracing the lines of my face. "Jesus Christ, Little Bird. You look like shit."

"Let me out," I mutter, exhausted down to my marrow. There's an ache in my shoulder from one of my thrashing fits that throbs in time to my pulse.

His face comes into focus next, dark eyes taking in the state of me. There's a frown etched into his forehead and his eyes are dark underneath. "Were you crying?" I'd expect the question to be mocking, but it's not. He says it very quietly.

His tone is troubled and horrifically tender.

My chin trembles as I lace my fingers through the lattice, repeating, "Let me out now." I shouldn't give this to him. It's a weapon for Nick to know that this metal box is my undoing. So I swallow it back and strengthen my spine, determined to walk out of it with my head held high.

Immediately, he's unlatching the gate and flinging it open, catching me around the waist as I all but stagger free from the thick, musty air. Winding an arm around me, Nick pulls me up against his broad, warm chest. He stands like that for a long moment, pressing my cheek to his shoulder as if I'm not as rigid as steel.

"Are you grateful now, Little Bird?" he asks, tucking a hand behind my neck. It's a wicked sort of embrace. The kind of forced closeness that makes my skin crawl. "No one was coming for you. No one cared what happened to you. No one but me. I came in there and claimed you before the Lords could sell you off to the highest bidder. Don't you understand?" He touches my cheek, coaxing my eyes to his. "I'm all you have. I'm all you *need*." Quieter, his eyes flick to my mouth when he roughly whispers, "I'm the only one who loves you."

I jolt back, nearly tripping over my numb legs, and crash into the wall beside the elevator. "You don't love me. That's crazy. You're *all* crazy!"

My words make his brows crouch low, arms going tense at his sides. And I'm guessing the shocked, repulsed tone they're spoken in doesn't help matters. He bears down on me, but the only place to run is back into the box. "I'm not crazy. I'm the only person in this whole goddamn town who knows exactly what I want and exactly how to get it."

I grit my teeth when he traps me with his body, his bare, tattooed chest hemming me in. "You won me," I concede, the words bitter on my tongue. "You won me as an object. Not as a person. You can't... *love* something like that. You don't even know me!"

"You're mine now. Body, mind, and soul. That's all I need to know." I swallow down a disgusted groan as he reaches out, touching my throat. The marks, I realize. The bruises he made with his fingers last night. His eyes zero in on them, and there's something sharp and displeased about his frown. "Jesus Christ, you've got me fucked up. None of this is going the way it was supposed to."

It's clear now that he expected my gratitude, and for a second, I consider playing into it. If I piss him off again, he'll stick me back in the elevator. That's what makes my gaze drop to his mouth—the question of whether or not I could do it. Can I bat my eyelashes and pretend? Get on my knees? Tell him how thankful I am?

I almost think I could if it means avoiding another night in that box.

But then he catches my eyes and I know he's seen it. The glance at his lips. The unspoken invitation. The unfettered tension whirring between our skin.

I twist just before his lips can land on mine, and this time, his hand comes up to slam into the wall beside my head. "Don't fucking test me, Lavinia!"

"If you want to rape me again," I whisper, staring sightlessly into the elevator, "then get on with it. I'm tired."

I never was good at pretending.

There's a long pause, but I can feel the fury and disbelief rolling off of him long before he hisses, "You ungrateful bitch." The second he lurches away, I slide down the wall, heart thumping wildly. "Here," he growls, reaching into a bag on a nearby armchair. I don't catch what he pulls out of it until it lands in my lap, pale and bloody. He thrusts a finger at it, sneering, "I got that for you."

"What the—" I jump up and away, letting the finger fall to the floor. "I didn't ask you to do that."

"You didn't have to. Perez made that gesture as a sign of dominance. Of what he wants to do to the thing that belongs to *me*," he says, like it's the most normal, rational, *sane* thing in the world. *The thing.* "In return, I showed him exactly what happens to anyone that tries to fuck with my things."

The finger lays there, pale and grotesque. It's a symbol of what this man will do—how far he'll go to protect the things he believes are his.

It took me a while to see it, to understand it, but Pretty Nick Bruin isn't just a frat boy with dreams of being a leader. He's like all the other Kings out there. Ruthless. Dangerous. Relentless.

I should know. I grew up with one.

6

Remy

I pause before my marker touches the wall.

Annoying.

Back in my student housing—hell, even back at home—I had a habit of drawing on my walls. I always painted over it eventually, giving me a nice, fresh canvas to start over with. I always left it wiped clean too, but I always knew it was there. The places we sleep, wake, and fuck are imbued with a little part of us. I just make it visible. Being surrounded by the etchings of my soul is all that gets me through some days.

A voice comes from my right. "Are you going to write something?" Haley asks. Tan skin. Freckles here and there. Eyes like a gaping maw. Diarylide yellow. Too bright for me, thanks.

My eyes tighten as I assess the wall. *Write something.* Like I'm a fucking poet or whatever. Who just *writes* something? No, I'd had this vision of stars. Smoke. Black glass. Blonde hair. Red lips.

Stop.

My body remains perfectly still, but inside, I flinch. Shaking my head, I reconsider. Smoke. Black tendrils curling over the party, eager to wind between and around us, like the tower itself was taking us into her stone arms.

Shit would look sick as hell.

Huffing, I lean back and cap the marker. "No."

The three of us have only been living here for a few days. The first thing I did was walk into my room, assess the plaster and exposed stonework, and ask myself what I wanted.

The answer was 'nothing', and I wasn't the one saying it.

It was the tower.

This big, beautiful son of a bitch. Hard to make art on top of someone else's, and that's exactly what the West End clock tower is. It'd be profane to try. That first night, I'd tried to explain it to Sy. How the tower is silent, but it still speaks. It's inanimate, but still perceptive. It has memories. It has feelings. Can't say how, I can just tell. To put my mark on something is to claim it as my own. Trying to own the tower would be like trying to own the whole fucking cosmos.

Cosmos.

Stars. Black glass. Blonde hair. Red Lips. The rattle of bare, skeletal trees.

Stop.

"Turn it up!" I shout to the DJ, making a twisting motion. He knows what I want—the bass, not the volume. Something about the way it thrums in my blood and vibrates in my ribs feels transformative, like it's packing me into something tight and settled. I point to him with the black tip of my marker, yanking it up until I feel the happy zing. If I can't etch my soul into these walls, then maybe the pulse of all of us can.

He nods in approval, head bouncing to the beat, and I abandon the patch of wall to turn to Haley. "Beer."

One word. Simple. Not a request.

She runs to fetch it.

The DKS underlings restocked the bar hours ago, so it's still half full. We'd been waiting until Nick claimed his ring to really, properly celebrate. There's been this little voice in my mind saying it's not real. That happens a lot, though. Anything unexpected is suspect. Anything too expected is suspect. There's really a very narrow window of believability when it comes to what my brain can trust, and Nick becoming a Duke doesn't pass muster. It'd be easier if I could... just... fucking...

Stars. Smoke. Black glass. Blonde hair. Red Lips.

Stop.

My marker stops an inch from the wall.

Damn it.

"Here you go," I hear from behind me, feeling sharp nails drag down my back. I was wearing a shirt an hour ago, but I took it off because I couldn't feel the air. The air is part of the tower. The tower is part of Forsyth. Forsyth is a part of the world. The world is part of the universe.

Stars. Blonde hair. Black gl—

Stop!

Also, I was hot.

I turn and see Haley holding out a drink. She grins up at me, nails scratching along my abdomen, dipping beneath the waistband of my jeans. "So I guess congratulations are in order, Remy. The title looks good on you."

I take the drink and down half of it in one swallow. "I know."

She laughs, like she thinks I'm joking. I'm not. "It's crazy to think that after all this time together, you're finally a Duke."

I recognize the excited glint in her eye. It's familiar and expected. Like just because I've fucked around with Haley for a few years, she thinks she's become hot shit. Truth is, she's just another cutslut—a Duke groupie. She's bloodthirsty, loves fights, and gives epic head. But there are two dozen of them in this room, and they're just like her. They follow us from fight to fight, party to party, and bed to bed. They're good at being casual pussy, ready to do whatever we want at the snap of a finger. Get drinks, clean up, take it up the ass, you name it. No expectations. No commitment. Even more so now that I'm a Duke.

"I heard rising Dukes have to do some epic crazy shit to make it in," she muses, gliding her finger over the barely healed, puckered scar on my side. I bristle at the touch. "What was it?"

I glance down at her, past the heavy eye make-up, black bikini top and cutoff shorts, and remove her hand. "Business," I reply, taking a moment to assess the smooth, tan skin of her collarbone. "None of yours."

A design swirls in my head. I hold up the marker, still capped, and drag it distractedly over her skin. I rarely ink females. Too personal. Makes my skin itch. The Lady was an exception I made to clear Sy and Nick of their debt. The design was specific enough, anyway. I drew it, pricked it into her skin, but it wasn't mine.

The cutsluts are gagging for my needle, though.

They think they're subtle about it, but they're not. It's been that way since sophomore year, just a couple of them chasing me around, offering to be my canvas. I'd never tell anyone, but I wasn't actually good at it back then. Shit technique with a jank-ass kit. But a guy's gotta practice. Nick wasn't my first, but close to it, and he was always down for anything. Patches of skin never meant anything to him. He sees his ink as a forest.

Still, sometimes I get inspired. Girls are different from dudes. More delicate. Better curves. Softer skin. Every now and then, I'll be tracing invisible lines over their skin with the hard tip of my marker. I trail the one in my hand between her breasts, seeing the design clearly in my head. I'd give her some vines below her tits. Something feminine but brutal. You can't get that kind of contrast with guys, they won't let you. I get lost in the thought of it, pushing aside the triangle fabric, flicking the marker over her nipple as I expose the skin there. Her nipple peaks up and, without thinking, I bend, licking the hard pebble.

Her back arches, and hey. What the hell, I can fuck her right here get rid of this hard-on that's been building between my legs since last night. I heard Nick and the snake fighting in his room and almost went in there to hold her down, like last time. But I let it slide. Nick's got her venom in him and the only way to pull it out is to get to the source: this negotiation with Killian Payne, made behind our backs.

That doesn't mean I didn't beat off to the idea of having another go at her.

I grab Haley's wrist and place her hand on my cock. She grins up at me, ready and willing, and I fight back a cringe. Diarylide yellow. She has such a shallow, mirror-like soul.

Black glass. Stars. Red—

No.

"You make my eyes hurt," I tell her over the music, because sometimes I do that. Think things. Say them out loud.

I can see her wondering whether to take offense, ask for clarification, or take it as a compliment. She lands on the latter, smiling. "Thanks." Classic diarylide yellow. Toxic positivity.

Before I can decide whether or not to shatter her illusion, there's a shift in the room, like the energy is flowing away from me. It pulls me in its wake, drawing my attention to the stairs. Nick comes sweeping down like he's lived in this place his whole life. He's good at that. Belonging places. Or maybe just seeming it. Damon, a DKSer who used to room with me a couple years back, gives Nick's shoulder a firm shake as he boisterously congratulates his win.

But Nick doesn't care.

Not about the congratulations.

He's got the snake under his arm.

Counts, man. North Siders are the fucking worst. Look at this bitch. Sold into slavery, basically, and she's got that chin jutted out like she's fighting against the arm Nick has around her neck. My boy is stronger, though. He jerks her closer as he nods to some pledges, snatching a beer from the bar. Bear beats snake. He doesn't want all eyes on him. He wants to show off his prize: The blue-haired trophy beneath his arm. Lavinia motherfucking Lucia.

Like the other females in the room, she's showing a lot of skin, her flesh almost glowing against the dim light overhead. Her top is cropped, the straps made of crisscrossing lines. Nick's arm might be holding her shoulders firm, but when he turns her to greet a cutslut, the Bruin mark I'd inked into her is still visible. But the best part is that she's multiple shades of bruising, too. The knob of her shoulder is a fantastic, blooming blue. Her neck bears the obvious mark of a choking and I wonder how much of the mottled purple there is my own, having squeezed her throat during the fight. My cock twitches at the sight, and Haley's hand squeezes the bulge.

"I don't get it," she says, watching their entrance. "Who is this bitch, anyway?"

I watch as Nick pulls her across the room like a naughty dog. "Ours, apparently."

"She doesn't even want to be," she grumbles, tucking into my side. "What a waste of a Duchess position."

Snorting, I lift my bottle. "Careful. You sound jealous." The cutsluts are a lot of things, but they generally keep the envy in check.

She makes a show of shrugging it off. "Not even. I'm just not used to getting a call to bring clothes over for some random bitch."

"Call?" I watch idly as Nick parades her around the room. His hand slips free of her shoulder just to fall to the round, perky swell of her ass. He gives it an aggressive squeeze that makes her spine go rigid, and there's this flash in her eye that makes all my nerves spark to life in anticipation. I wait for her to snap, bare her fangs, and take a chunk of his throat.

But it doesn't happen.

Must be killing her.

Haley rambles, "Yeah, Sy called and asked for some clothes. Other stuff, too, like a toothbrush and... uh, woman things. You know." Haley is beyond blushing, but apparently I'm not. It makes her smirk. "He told me to assume I was stranded on an island and didn't want to—and I quote—stink up the place with my snobby, North Side cunt." She goes on and on. Haley always did talk too much. Do I really need to hear about Lucia's tampon needs? "The girls and I got some stuff together and sent it over. Shit we don't wear anymore. Verity donated some shoes and moisturizer. That's what she called it. 'Donating'. Isn't that hilarious? A Lucia being West End's charity case?" She throws her head back and laughs.

Well, no wonder the snake looks like a Cutslut.

I'd been unable to get a good view of her body that night at the Hideaway. The room was too dark; the mask was too obtrusive, and I'd be lying if I said I was the right kind of medicated for it. But I know what she feels like under those tiny black shorts. Her ass was firm, the sliver of skin between her cheeks warm. Vulnerable. Pure. Just like so much of her flesh.

I should have fucked her there and then.

Haley continues, "Actually, I think that's my top. It's hard to tell. It fits different on her."

"Because her tits are bigger than yours," I point out. "And her skin's better, too. Smoother. Softer."

Haley stiffens, but sucks back any retort. That's the other thing that's different. Cutsluts are compliant. The Count's daughter? Well, the scar on my stomach and the bruises all over her body tells that story.

Haley tries to laugh it off, curling her hand around my bicep as she leans into my chest. "Fuck this bitch, yeah? Take me up to the belfry." She bats her eyelashes. "I brought some shrooms, just to celebrate. Let's go trip our balls off and fuck."

I only give it a brief thought. "The top of the tower is probably the last place I want to have a bad trip." But it's not just the thought of accidentally jumping to my untimely and grisly death that makes it unappealing. It's that my eyes are tracking the snake, slithering across the room, and I'm getting all these...ideas. Scales and scales on that pristine skin, my fingers dancing the marker between my knuckles. In fact, "I don't think I'm going to fuck you anymore." I look at Haley, watching the way her face falls. "Nothing personal. You're fun and all. Just need some new skin." I touch her cheek to soften the blow, but I've never been good at that.

So I pull out a few crisp hundreds and tuck them into her stringy top, giving her tit a pat.

For a job well done.

I peel her off and walk away, finding Sy by the bar. His eyes are narrowed as he watches the spectacle. And that's exactly what it is. To the untrained eye, it might look like territorial pissing, but Sy and I both know better.

"What the fuck is he up to?" I ask.

He shrugs. "I don't know, but you know my brother. Never as dumb as that pretty face suggests." Well, that's the thorn of it. Nick set all this in motion without telling us, made deals without consulting us. With a goddamn King. Boredly, Sy muses, "It's probably multifaceted. Part gameplay, part leverage. But the way he acts around her is a bit..."

"Over the top psycho obsessive?" I wager.

Sy nods, raising his drink. "That's our Nicky. You know what I think?"

I lean back against the bar, watching as they get closer to where we're standing. From this vantage, I see the unfinished tattoo coiled around her calf. My fingers twitch and I roll the marker over my knuckles, building, seeing. "I'm probably going to regret this, but..." I tip back my beer and swallow. "What do you think?"

"I think he's trying to replace Tate."

I still feel the name—*Tate Tate Tate*—like a sucking chest wound. A blade in my side. An old injury that refuses to heal. It makes me twist inside, like my guts are fighting to get away from it.

Stars. Smoke. Black glass—

I blink long and slow, warning, "Don't."

To his credit, Sy does shoot me a dark, rueful look. "It's as much of a possibility as anything else."

"Nick is an asshole, but he knows as well as we do that Tate is irreplaceable." His brother walks by, flashing a smirk. The girl holds herself rigid, like she can't stand him touching her. Nick's hand slides possessively over her ass. I point to it. "*That* has nothing to do with Tate."

Reluctantly, Sy agrees, "This is some kind of psychosexual nonsense. I guess we'll find out eventually." But even as he says it, he looks annoyed. To him, there's nothing worse than sitting back and waiting for a problem to appear. Sy is way too Type A for that. "I'm going to go get ready for Monday," he mumbles, dropping his empty bottle and sweeping away.

I'd usually force him to stay—have some fun, pretend he doesn't hate half the people in here—but tonight, I let him run to his computer and textbooks. I haven't liked the set of his jaw lately. The way he looks so tense and keyed up all the time. It's been years since he's radiated this kind of energy. Red and gold and black.

Across the room, Nick has settled himself on an armchair, wide shoulders taking up the width of the space. Lavinia is perched on his lap—*Little Bird*, he calls her—hands balled into tight fists. One arm is cinched around her waist, like he knows she may run for it if he loosens his grip. The other hand is occupied with toying at the ends of her hair.

"Remy." He tips his bottle against mine in a toast when I approach, gesturing for me to take a seat. The girl watches me warily, those shrewd eyes assessing every move I make. But she's not fighting *him*, which is...interesting. I wonder what kind of leash he's got on her for this level of compliance. He notices me looking at all those beautiful bruises and tightens his grip around her waist. "Sit down. Have a drink."

I flick my eyes at Lavinia and then bend, whispering in Nick's ear. "My turn."

He freezes, meeting my gaze. "Excuse me?"

"Word around the establishment is that you're willing to share." I nod at the girl, who's even more rigid than Nick. "It's my turn to play with the prize."

Nick's jaw goes tight. "Maybe in a while, or—"

I make a sharp sound. "You may wear the ring, Bruin, but we gave you the opportunity. She's the spoils of war, and we're all victors. Don't be a stingy bitch."

The muscle in the back of his jaw tics, and his hand skates up her side, latching onto one of her full tits. Christ, he's like a little boy, refusing to share his toy. "I haven't fucked her yet." He says it with this hostile edge that's not hard to decipher.

"Then you can chill," I assure him, giving my marker a spin. "I'll save the first bang for you. Just need a fresh canvas."

What I need is to see how far down those bruises go. Excited to map them out, I stare her down, expecting her to shrink back or lash out. What I'm not expecting her to say is, "It's fine. I'll go." Nick swings his gaze to her, understandably suspicious, and she stares vacantly back. "Turns out being some meathead's slutty arm candy has a touch of humiliation that doesn't really suit me."

Snotty, but he lets her go when she stands, watching as she shudders his heat off her body. "If you don't behave?" He gives her a long, threatening look. "There will be punishments."

His warning makes her shoulders give a little shuddering hitch, and I like it.

I like the way she turns to me, regarding the middle of my chest. "I'll be good."

7

———

Lavinia

*W*ait *for an opportunity.*
Play nice.
Do what you have to.

The mantra slams around my head, but it's the opposite of my nature. I get through it by way of a healthy imagination. I think of what it'd be like to cut this fucker's balls off. Messy, I'm guessing, but probably satisfying. It helps keep the urgency writhing beneath my skin at bay for just a little while longer.

The sound of the party fades as Maniac takes me back upstairs. I know his name is Remy, but all I sense when I look at him is the wild eyes and erratic energy. 'Maniac' is more apt. Dude might be lucid tonight, but he violated me during the fight before he even realized I was one of the stakes at play. I'm well aware of that little bit of crazy he carries just beneath the surface, because I've got a little of my own.

I'd caught a glimpse of Nick's laptop this morning.

It's September 10th.

That gives me two weeks.

Fourteen days.

"Where are we going?" I ask, allowing my nerves to show through. I'm not thrilled about being alone with this guy, but he *must* be better than Nick. Aside from the constant looming threat of being locked in that elevator again, there's no getting one over on him—not easily. Nick was my handler for far too long. He watches me like a goddamn hawk.

Maniac doesn't answer, just whistles some creepy little tune as he twirls that marker between his fingers. We cross through the living space, past the kitchen, and into what I assume is his room. The instant I step over the threshold, I'm taking a mental inventory.

This is nothing like the rest of the tower.

The main room is a mash-up of what looks like discarded furniture that's been collected over the years. I understand it. No one wants to lug furniture up all those steps, and I know all too intimately that the elevator isn't big enough for anything elaborate. Nick's room is barren and cold, barely looking lived in.

But going into Remy's room is like stepping from South Side to North Side.

This one has electronics. A huge TV on one wall, a complicated computer system against another. It's a big room, but most of it is set up as a tidy, makeshift workspace. There's a wide drafting table splitting the area into two halves, sketch pads haphazardly scattered over the surface, along with cups full of paintbrushes and cubbies with a hundred different markers and tubes of pigment. A big, complicated-looking chair sits on one side of the drafting table, but the bed that's shoved against the wall on the other side, blankets rumpled, seems like an afterthought. Just like his designer jeans and shoes, this room reeks of money that's been spent by someone who paid no thought to it. I'm a Lucia. I know the signals. The ear pods that lay discarded on the bed. A takeout coffee cup seeping old liquid onto the nice table. Remy doesn't take care of his things.

All the better for me.

There's a tall mirror propped against the wall behind the chair, but what really draws my eye are the designs pinned everywhere. Some are vivid with color, electric blues and shocking reds, but some are oppressively gray and chaotic with darkness. In the sea of them, I can spot certain threads. Religious imagery, horror, anatomy, abstract designs that would take me hours to make heads or tails out of. All of them, however, are painfully intricate. Bold. Evocative. *Anarchic.*

My eyes pause for a long time on a row of canvases in particular. All of them are half-finished paintings of the night sky. There's nothing really unique about them, except the fact there are so many. They look like pieces of a thought, pushed together as if they could finish a puzzle that lacks edges.

In a frantic attempt to look at anything else, I turn and see *him.* Shirtless, worn jeans slung low on his hips, revealing the fine trail of hair tapering below his navel. He's inked with art just as elaborate as the designs gracing his walls. The image of the weeping Virgin Mary on his bicep, heart impaled by swords, catches my attention only briefly. Remy's not the bulging muscle type like Sy or even Nick. His body is that lean sort of perfection, fast and efficient, like a snake coiled to strike. Mostly, I see the half-healed slash I'd made, and it's with a detached sort of curiosity that I finally make out the tattoo I'd ruined. The words 'momento mori' are inked in an arch over his belly button, and below each side is a pair of guns in a cloud of smoke that fades into two distinct skulls. When he twists to turn on the light over the table, the scarring wound I'd made pulls the skull on his left side into an awkwardly distorted image, as if I'd just crossed that sucker out.

Good.

I've seen his cock, felt his hot cum against my skin, but I've also made this fucker bleed. I itch to pick at it. To tell him I'd take more, if I had the time. To say that I'd cross out all of his mementos, one by one, if I didn't have more important things to do.

I snap my jaw shut before I can.

Wait for an opportunity.

Play nice.

Do what you have to.

See, Rath? I can keep my mouth shut.

Prick.

"Take off your clothes."

I snap my gaze back to him, the smooth rumble of his voice just as jarring as the words. "What?"

He doesn't even look at me. "Strip. Bare." He slides the marker into his back pocket and walks over to the chair, fiddling with a lever beneath that makes it recline into a bed. It's then that I realize this isn't a chair. It's just a different kind of workbench. "I want to see what I'm working with."

I take this order calmly. I've accepted that he's going to fuck me. That's just a sacrifice I'll have to make. The more compliant I am, the less injured I'll get, the more of his guard he'll let down.

At least that's the plan.

I peel off my clothes, freeing myself from the twisted straps of the top, and pushing down the shorts that are so far up my ass it takes me a minute to dislodge them. Basically was already naked anyway, in the slut clothes Nick had brought for me. The lace panties go next, and I toss them all into a careless pile on the floor at my feet. Modesty is a virtue I've never thought much of, which was useful at the Hideaway. The whores would have made me pay for the luxury.

Even still, I have to force my hands down to my sides instead of covering myself. Not that I need to. It takes him forever to even acknowledge or look at me, distracted by flipping frantically through the pages of a sketchbook. After a minute or three, he stops on one, giving the page three decisive taps. He sets the sketchbook down on the desk, smoothes the page with a careful palm, and finally turns, taking me in.

His green eyes pin me like a bug, but it's not so much the staring that makes me want to squirm. It's the way his shoulders go lax, chest contracting with a slow exhale. It's the slackness of his mouth as his gaze rakes down my torso, over my tits, down my belly. It's the way he thumbs thoughtfully at his lip, head tilted, like he's trying to solve a long equation.

When he speaks, I'm certain he can see me flinch. "We can do this one of two ways."

This. I still have no fucking clue what *this* is.

"Okay."

"Depends on which one of you showed up today." His dark gaze zeroes in on my knees as he picks up another marker, spinning it. A nervous tic? A restless fixation? "Are you the good girl I saw upstairs with Nick? Or are you the bad girl I'm gonna have to tie down?" From the way the corner of his mouth twitches, I'm not sure which one he prefers.

But I don't waste the opportunity, flashing him an empty smirk. "I'll be a good girl." *You motherfucker.*

"We'll see," he says, giving the chair-bench a magnanimous pat.

It takes everything in me to comply—a bigger strength than I knew I possessed. I'm good at running away from problems, and I'm even better at kicking the ever-loving shit out of them. But this? Sliding my bare ass onto the cool vinyl, handing my body over to a maniac? My veins throb in resistance as I lay back, staring sightlessly into the ceiling.

Part of the vein-throbbing resistance may also be owed to my body, feeling as though it's been put through a meat grinder. I never did get used to this part of punishment. The ache that lasts for days afterward. The impulse to stretch my muscles, over and over. The hollow sensation in the pit of my chest, like my guts have been rubbed to numbness.

And then he flicks on an overhead light. It's so bright that it blinds me, putting every inch of my body on sterile, microscopic display. I squint against the glare, muscles going impossibly more rigid. This is starting to feel less like a possible tattoo and more like my kidneys are about to go missing.

"Not all flesh is the same," he says, running the capped marker down the length of my thigh. "Some people have smooth skin. Others are bumpier. Keratin and such. I don't mind it, but it's not ideal. You bruise easily." His face is a bare facsimile through the glare of the lamp, showing me nothing but the contemplative tilt of his head. "Is this all Nicky's work?" I realize then that he's tracing the bruises.

"Not all of them."

He mutters over me, like he doesn't even hear. "I sort of have a thing for freckles. Birthmarks. Scars." He trails the marker over my knee. The skin there is rough and raised—a trophy from the chest my father used to lock me in. "Those little human imperfections. It's like a galaxy of stars..." Something falls over his expression, eyes shuddering, and I get the impression he's gone somewhere faraway. He quickly shakes it off. "Everyone's skin is unique for the artist."

"For your tattoos," I stiffly clarify.

His eyes glaze over as he inspects my abdomen, trailing the marker around my belly button. "You've got a damn fine body, Lucia. Some people just see a flat surface to stick and poke, but I see the peaks and valleys. The curves. The angles." The marker ascends, pressing into the soft skin below my breast. "I look at a body like yours and I see a living, breathing canvas. A potential masterpiece."

My jaw tightens when he raises the marker, flicking it over my peaked nipple. "How many masterpieces have you created so far?"

The marker suddenly stops. "None."

I don't miss the tinge of disappointment in his tone, even though it makes no sense. He obviously inked himself, not to mention Nick. Probably half this frat has his designs covering their muscles.

Without explanation, he walks closer, startling me when he tucks a hand beneath the back of my neck, thumb digging into my jaw until I'm forced to arch my head back. He runs the marker up the center of my throat, right in the space where some targeted pressure could cut off my air supply. But somehow, nothing about it feels nearly as menacing as it should.

He's almost... *gentle* as his eyes follow the path.

He's mapping me, I realize. "I know what you're thinking." He speaks the words to my collarbones more than to me, looking absorbed in the drag of the marker. "You've got a storm of stars in your skin, and those bruises are really pretty. But I'm not going to tattoo you."

I swallow, regretting it when his eyes instantly jump to the motion. "You're not?"

He blinks, finally lifting that marker from my skin. "Sy's got this whole idea." He casually walks away, stopping at the middle of the bench. "I'm not really sure I agree with it, but I can relate. Something about holding onto certain parts of yourself." I have no idea what any of that means, and when his gaze rises to mine, he must see it. "I never ink bitches with my art," he explains.

I look away, letting the light blind me. "The tattoo on my back says otherwise."

He gives a low, derisive chuckle. "That's a tag—not art." Suddenly, he grabs my hip, shoving me onto my side. My body clenches up, but to my relief, he doesn't go for my exposed ass. He flicks the half-finished tattoo on my calf. "And neither is this. It doesn't fit the area at all. It has zero imagination. No passion. It's *soulless*. You pulled this shit out of a fucking binder and threw some money at a low-rent apprentice who just couldn't wait to get you out of his chair. Shit's embarrassing."

I twist to insist, "It's not done yet!"

He clutches my calf, fingers digging painfully into my skin. "This tattoo is fucking garbage." His eyes flash with the same wild, chaotic anger I see on his walls. "It's a whisper of a lie you didn't even bother to breathe any life into. Add some color and shading, it won't make a difference. This isn't art or even a brand. It's a performance. I can see it in your eyes, girl. You can't put a snake on top of scales."

"What are you even talking about?" I try to turn to my back, but he's already pulling the cap off the marker with his teeth, holding my leg down.

"Stay quiet and still for ten minutes," he says, face expressionless as he spits the cap onto the floor, "and I'll think about letting you leave this bench with the same amount of bruises you came onto it with."

A long, frustrated groan rips from my throat before I go limp.

Wait for an opportunity.

Play nice.

Do what you have to.

I look away when he puts the marker to my skin, the cool felt tip sketching against my flesh. Marker can be washed away. That's what I remind myself as he bends over me, re-shaping my snake tattoo into whatever he thinks is more fitting. It could be worse. It could be the edge of a knife or the heat of a brand. That's how Duchesses are usually marked—the Greek symbols of the DKS house signed into their flesh.

The most annoying thing is that he's not even wrong. I'd gotten the outline done during my junior year of high school. Homecoming night. While the other girls in my class were getting into limos and sucking off their dates, I was walking the Avenue in search of something I didn't quite understand yet. I just knew I wanted something permanent. Something I had complete control over. Something that hurt.

I walked into the first parlor I saw, flipped through their binders of cliché designs, and chose a serpent that didn't immediately repulse me.

But when the woman—not a guy—asked me what colors I wanted, I locked up. Suddenly, complete control seemed like the worst thing ever. So I walked out with an incomplete design, nothing but the outline of a serpent winding up my calf, devoid of life. I spent the next year telling everyone I intended to finish it, but the truth is, I never did. It's already a perfect depiction of what I am. An outline of a Lucia. The shape is there, but it has no substance or form. It's exactly what my father always wanted.

Empty space.

Maniac spends a long time filling it. The longer he draws on my skin, the more the tension seems to bleed away—from him or me. It's hard to tell. There's just something about the motion, about the calm rhythm, that makes it hard to *not* relax. I fight it for a while, but the exhaustion from the last two days creeps up on me like a shadow, holding me just as still as he'd ordered me to be. I hadn't slept in the elevator, even though I tried to. It's always easier when I can. I remember that much from my time back home.

I tuck my hands beneath my cheek and lay there, blinking heavily as my eyes travel back and forth between the designs on the wall. He might be a fucking psychopath, but *goddamn.*

He's really good.

It makes me take a furtive glance at him, watching wayward locks of platinum hair fall into his eyes as he tilts his head, wrist moving in elegant sweeps up my shin, my knee. It makes me wonder if brilliance requires a certain level of insanity. I think about the Lords and their King, so gifted on the football field that for Killian's first three years at Forsyth, you couldn't avoid seeing his face. Then there's the Rath bastard, blemished musical prodigy. The Princes, The Barons—even the Counts have had some celebrity. I doubt there's been a truly gifted male student in Forsyth who wasn't part of the Royalty.

Then again, maybe the Kings just court the cream of the crop.

I watch as he draws, allowing my gaze to wander to his own tattoos. Sometimes he'll swap out the marker for a finer point or a new color. This is a man who's all hard angles and wild brutality, but here, he's calm. Whatever frenetic energy usually surrounds him seems to be channeled into... *this.* The curl of his shoulder as he draws a long, swooping line up my thigh. The way his teeth sink gently into his lower lip, brow creasing in concentration as he chooses another marker. The darkness in his eyes remains, but the burn of them is gone. I think I'm so baffled by the transformation— so distracted by his fingertips on my skin—that I barely realize he's tipping me onto my back again.

And the marker is going higher.

It's been so long since I felt anything except anger and revulsion that I've forgotten what it feels like to be touched without aggression or spite or painful displays of power. With soft fingertips. With care. With...*passion*. It might be meant for the design more than me, but turns out, my body doesn't actually give a shit. It hits me as hard as a freight train and just as sudden—a white-hot bolt of *want* that settles like lava between my legs. I move my hand to cover my crotch, but he bats it away like an unruly fly.

It doesn't get any better when he pries my knees apart, bringing his design up my inner thigh. The marker keeps climbing and climbing, and the closer it gets to my center, the more my muscles lock up, nipples stiffening.

Unexpectedly, he stops.

The marker lifts from my skin.

Breathing harder than I'd like, I ask, "Are you done?"

He moves closer, eyes rising. "Your pussy's all red and irritated," he mutters, stroking the newly waxed skin with his finger. "Nick?"

"*No.*" A tremor runs through my body and I try to twist away. If he keeps touching me like this, my pussy won't be the only hot and irritated thing here. "They waxed it back at the whorehouse."

His fingers chase me while his other hand hauls me back. Again, he runs a soft, cool finger into the overheated flesh, gaze locked on my mound. "They made you smooth for me—us, I mean." My stomach flips, caught in the web between gentle touch and unwelcome invasion as his touch descends. It's just the adrenaline crash of the elevator fucking with my nerves, making them flare to life against my will. The second he brushes against my clit, I react with a sharp quake, a full-on tremor that runs along the fault lines of my body.

He slowly lets me go, only to grab my thigh and return to marking me. I exhale, relieved he's stopped. My body and mind are not on the same page. Out in the world, a guy like Remy would be my kryptonite. Not just his body, but his wild nature. It's the volatility, like sitting too close to a flame. The feral guys. The unabashedly horny assholes. I always did have awful taste. But here, I need my wits about me. Even if I have to let him fuck me, enjoying it is *not* on the table. It's a means to an end, an opportunity.

God, I wish he'd get it over with.

He picks up another marker, this one an inch thicker than the others. It has a wide tip that he uses to fill in spaces, and when he goes for a spot high on my inner thigh, I know he can feel the quiver in my muscles.

I know because I watch him go still again.

Slowly, his eyes climb to my pussy. It's almost believable as an innocent shift of his wrist when the thick tip of the marker brushes against my clit. But I know better. I instantly try to snap my knees together, but it doesn't stop him from pressing it between my outer lips, thrusting into the slit.

"I can smell it, you realize. Sweet, warm, wet pussy..." He wedges his free hand between my thighs, dragging in an obnoxious inhale. "Distracting and *annoying*. I already told Nicky I wouldn't." When he flicks his eyes to mine, he smirks. "What? Did you think I'd lie to my best friend? Your cunt's not that good." He breaks my gaze to watch the marker disappear into my slit. "*Probably* not that good."

I curl my hands into tight fists, fighting against his hand with my thigh muscles. "It's not."

But he's lost again. The same glaze that was in his eyes before has returned, lips parting as he pries my thighs apart. "But your body..." I know what's coming, but it doesn't make it any easier when the blunt end of the marker enters me. The more I squirm away, the deeper it goes. He watches it sink inside and says, "Bodies change when they're fighting and fucking. Muscles contracting. Skin going tight." He thrusts it deeper and I whip my head to the side, eyes clenched shut.

When I feel the pressure of his other hand on my clit, I beg through gritted teeth, "Don't."

"Why shouldn't I?" He rubs two fingers into my clit as he fucks me with the marker. "You're ours now. Ours to touch. Ours to look at." He takes a deep, sharp breath, voice dropping a couple of octaves. "God, you're fucking soaked. Don't you want to come? That's our job, you know. Keeping our Duchess satisfied. I'm not allowed to think of stars, but I can show you some." I answer by trying to thrash away, but all I get for my efforts is his hard palm slamming into my upper chest. "It's not too late to tie you down," he warns, and even though his voice is full of that wild energy I haven't been missing, his fingers are still rubbing a slow, decadent rhythm into my clit. "I want to see it and you're going to show me."

Wait for an opportunity.

Play nice.

Do what you have to.

I go lax, spreading my thighs for him.

He mutters a soft curse, and then, "That's right. Good girls are nice, too."

I fix my gaze to the drafting table, the glint of metal shining out at me from between the cubbies—*scissors*—and try to fade away, just like the elevator. I used to go to the river when I was a kid. Sometimes from the cliffs, it almost looks like an ocean. As if the other side of Forsyth is a world away and nothing could possibly touch you up there. That's what I used to think about, back when my father put me in the chest. Beneath the blind panic and urgency, I'd wrestle myself into the memory like an astral projection. I try to go there now, imagining the misty wind against my cheeks, the cries of the birds above and below, the cracks of thunder in the distance.

"Can you see the stars, Vinny?" Remy fucks me with one hand and coaxes my clit to life with his other. He lets out these low, pleased sounds as my body clenches and shakes, but I don't watch. I make myself an instrument for him. An object floating in a vast ocean, ebbing and flowing with the slow circles he's pressing into me. I become nothing. Blank. Lifeless.

When I come, I bite my lip hard enough to taste salt.

HOURS PASS.

That's how long it takes for the tower to grow still. The sounds of Nick and Sy returning upstairs and closing themselves in their rooms happened sometime after midnight. Remy fell asleep soon after dragging me over to his bed and telling me how unattractive he found girls who tossed and turned. I wait until long after his breath has evened out to ease upright, keeping my eyes on him the whole time.

I was still and compliant after he forced me to orgasm. Best to let him think he broke me, wore me down, fucked me up. That's why it had to be him. Nick would know better.

Thirteen days now.

I stare at his hands—at the tattooed fingers that spell DUKE— and refuse to reconcile what they did to me. I'm surviving. I'm a survivor. And I'm done being a prisoner to these bastards.

Duchess.

There are a million reasons that is the dumbest fucking idea I've ever heard. What kind of sick system puts men like these in power over anyone? Idiots, all of them. Flash them your cunt and lay still, and they think they've got you in the palm of their hands.

I place both feet on the floor, knowing I'll have to forego my shoes. The strappy silver heels they gave me will get me killed before they can catch me. I slowly rise, again watching Maniac for any sign of movement. I forego the panties and step right into the shorts, and then I take his hoodie from the hook on the door, slipping my arms inside without daring to zip it up. I tiptoe to the drafting table, to the cups and cubbies with various and sundry art supplies. The small pair of steel scissors is still tucked between the markers and the brushes, and I ease it loose in small, hesitant increments, holding my breath as a marker rolls from beside it.

Once they're free, I grip them tight and creep to the mirror behind the chair, crouching down. I sweep my hair from my neck and turn, struggling to make out the skin behind my ear. The scab helps. It's not big. Whatever they used to put the tracker in was sophisticated. Medical grade.

I open the scissors and press the blade to the tender skin, inhaling a bolstering breath before slicing into the flesh. I watch the blood bubble to the surface and then trickle down my neck before trying to feel for the implant. All the while, my eyes keep jumping across the room, so alert to any movement that a falling lock of my own hair almost makes me slice my ear clean off.

Breathing as quietly as I can, I get my fingernail into the wound, digging, searching. It doesn't take long to feel something foreign and hard. It's bigger than I'm expecting, but it's easy to move. Not attached. I pull the bottom of the hoodie up to my mouth and bite down on it before tugging the tracker free. The hole I made is too small, making me wince and growl as I force it through.

It makes a small, metallic sound when I drop it to the floor and I freeze, whipping around to watch Remy.

His foot twitches.

I wait a long moment before moving again, setting the scissors on the vinyl of the chair before rising to my feet. But he's out cold. Fucker fell asleep faster than I expected. I guess holding someone down until they cream on your art supplies takes a lot out of a person.

Whatever it was, it's not happening again, because I'm out of this fucking hellhole.

Once I get moving, it goes fast, like ripping off a Band-Aid. The plan is locked and loaded in my head. When I ease the door open, I'm relieved to find both of the other bedroom doors are closed. I tiptoe past them, veins zinging with adrenaline, and head for the kitchen. All I need to do is grab the SUV keys Sy stupidly leaves in an orange ceramic bowl.

Except when I get there, they're not in the goddamn bowl. I stare into it, all ugly and orange and infuriatingly *empty*, and just... breathe.

Think. Breathe. Look.

Where else would he keep them?

I scan the room, ignoring the thundering beat of my heart as I zip around the kitchen, the couches, and bury my hand into the two coats by the door. This should have gone smoothly. I'd deleted the video from Nick's laptop while he was taking a piss this morning. I played nice. I got away from him. I got through Maniac. I got the tracker out. Now the fucking keys aren't—

I spot them. Over on the small table by the door. *Victory, you shits.*

Grabbing the keys, I exhale and head for the door, but I find myself freezing at the elevator. It's between the entry to the staircase down and Nick's bedroom, looming like a physical threat. I know from banging around in there last night that none of the inner buttons are functional, but the outer ones might be. It could take me to the bottom floor before Nick even had the chance to cover half the flights of stairs. It'd be the smartest move.

But I just can't do it.

I dart my eyes to the rafters. The other side of the open passageway I'd seen in Nick's room looms high enough to be dangerous for anyone who'd think to walk the beams. It's dark, deserted, empty, but it reminds me that Nick is on the other side of the wall, sleeping.

I inch the door open quietly.

The metal steps to the party room are cold on my feet. This whole stone building is ten degrees cooler than it is outside, and my fucking booty shorts certainly don't help matters. I blindly zip the hoodie as I descend the pitch dark stairwell. The only windows are small cut-outs along the shaft, none providing much light. I use my hands and feet to guide the way.

Oh, and my nose. God, the stench rolling from the party room is enough to let me know I've reached that floor. This is where I have to be careful. Neon bar lights give the room an eerie glow just bright enough to see the patented Duke cutsluts are curled up on the couches. A frat boy is sleeping on the bar. I push down any urge to make an example out of him on my way out the door. There's a reason I didn't bury those scissors into Remy's throat upstairs. Revenge makes people sloppy, and that's not my motivation right now. Only escape.

Tiptoeing through puddles of beer and other waste, I head into the main stairwell and begin the long jog down the gazillion flights. I go faster than I should, but I find the rhythm of the steps and traverse them blindly. Impatiently.

At the bottom, I test the door. It's unlocked, at least from the inside, so I push it open. The first thing I do is take a gulp of sweet, crisp, freedom-laced air, but there's no time to bask. I haul ass to the SUV parked by the curb and don't bother pressing the key fob. I shove the key into the lock, open it manually, and close the heavy door as quietly as possible. Taking no time to celebrate, I adjust the seat so that my feet can reach the pedals and turn over the key, cranking the engine. The SUV roars to life and I'm panting in anticipation, mashing the brake and reaching to put it into drive.

Click.

I freeze, blood turning to ice.

There are certain sounds that are just unmistakable, and the cock of a gun's hammer?

That's number one.

I flick my eyes up at the rearview, heart lodged in my throat. "Nick, wait, just—"

The rest is cut off as a strong hand clamps around my neck, slamming me back into the seat. I smell his hot breath before I hear it, thick with the scent of beer and smoke. He jams the hard nose of his gun into the bloody flesh beneath my ear and seethes, "You think I'm an idiot, don't you?"

I struggle to speak, but his fingers dig into my throat, silencing me.

"You think I bought that little 'play nice' act you put on tonight? Right, because that's our Lavinia. So docile and submissive. Do you really think I'm that easy?" He pauses, and I know he wants a response. I shake my head as much as I can, but his voice is no less irate when he continues, "I rescue you, and you spit in my face. I try to give you a nice, warm, *safe* place to sleep, and what do you do? Try to run away from it." I make a small, urgent sound, but even though he loosens his grip, his nose jabs into my temple, voice acidic. "No one would treat you as good as me. Do you fucking hear me? If you'd stop being such a massive cunt for five minutes and *let me*, you'd see that. But you won't!"

I swallow and say, "I'm sor—"

He slams me back into the seat again, snarling. "Don't you fucking dare apologize. I know it's not real." He releases me with a growl, but the gun is still against my head. Calmly, he demands, "Give me the keys."

A series of actions runs through my head. I left the scissors upstairs like a dumbass, but the keys are sharp enough. I could stab him right now. Gouge out his eyes, puncture his eardrums. I slowly pull them out of the ignition, but before I can make a move, his hand circles mine, taking them easily from me.

He slides the gun down the back of my head, using it to push aside my hair. I feel the dueling sensation of metal versus his warm lips on my neck. I recoil from both. "Where would you even go, Lav? You have nothing. No money. No clothes. No possessions." I hear more than see him put the keys into his pocket. "I guess you could always go home to Daddy."

I stiffen and he chuckles softly.

"That's what I thought."

I burst, "You don't know how fucking easy you have it, do you? Running the streets, fighting, partying, fucking cutsluts!" I slam the heel of my palm into the steering wheel, screaming, "I don't have time for this!" I immediately regret the outburst when he draws back. I brace myself for the hit. Maybe it'll be his fist, but a bullet is just as likely.

Instead, he sniffs, the sounds of the gun being un-cocked loud enough to make me tremble. "And you have somewhere to be?"

I look into the rearview mirror, catching those cold blue eyes. "You might be a Bruin, but you didn't grow up in this game. Not the same way I did." I let my gaze wander to the streets of the West End, just as empty as the snake on my calf. "Even Killian wouldn't get it. Being the son of a King is a lot easier than being a daughter. Not that you'd know either of those."

"You're right." Nick holds my gaze in the mirror, face sharpened with shadow. "My father was a fool to give up the power."

"Your father gave you options. Freedom." My shoulders drop in defeat. "You don't know what it's like to be trapped."

"Well, lucky for you, you don't have to go back. I solved that for you." Brows crushed together in annoyance, he asks, "When are you going to get it, Lavinia? I saved you."

I give a cold, humorless laugh. "You can't be stupid enough to really believe that, which tells me you're deluded. I don't know which one is worse."

Lionel Lucia is ruthless and the deal he made with Daniel Payne isn't what he or the Lords think it is. Giving me up that easy? Yeah fucking right. This is just a single move on a chessboard, pieces scattered across the squares. We're all pawns. Me. Killian. Saul.

But none so much as Nick Bruin.

He thinks he's saved me, but all he's done is tighten the manacles around my wrist. I get out of the car by the barrel of a gun and feel that deep, inner numbness throbbing like a wound. "Nick." I close my eyes, a blackness roiling within me at the request I'm about to make. "Please don't put me back in that elevator."

A quiet comes from behind me, and I feel more than see his stare—a heaviness on the back of my sore neck that's accompanied by his own hand. "Where else can I possibly put you, Lavinia? I can't lay awake watching you all night."

Having known that'd be his answer all along, I peer up at the tower. If only life were like that broken clock, hands frozen, time stopped. But it's not.

I've already lost enough of it, and soon, I'll run out entirely.

8

Nick

I stare at my ceiling, teeth clenched against the sounds. My bed is big, but I'm only laying on one side of it, the other cold and vacant. It was supposed to be for her, and I turn my head now to stare at it, trying to imagine her on the pillow beside me, staring back. Maybe she'd shimmy up against my side, resting her cheek on my shoulder as I leaned down to kiss her. Maybe her hand would land on my belly, tickling the patch of skin above my boxers. Maybe she'd dip her fingers inside, grinding into my thigh as she touched me.

There's a scream, muffled through stone and metal, and the fantasy falls away like sand through my fingers.

My room is right up against the elevator shaft. Last night, I put in my earphones and blasted some music to drown her out, but when I pulled them off, three hours later, only to realize she was still going at it in there...

I found myself at my door, hand poised on the knob.

But I didn't crack.

I laid back down and listened to it as if I were teaching myself a lesson. I made the punishment. It was my responsibility to hear it. Refusing to turn away and ignore it, I laid awake, just like I am now, and let the sounds of her fight cut their way inside me, as sharp as barbed wire. Again, the question comes to me.

Is it really that fucking *bad*?

It's not like I'm Daniel, ready to put her in the Pit and let a few linebackers loose on her pussy. I rescued her from that. Killian would have sold her off, I'm sure of it. The flesh trade is an unspeakable hustle. People aren't bought to do their master's knitting. Most of the time it's sexual, and if a guy wants nothing more than a convenient hole to cram his dick into, he could get it for a lot cheaper than buying a slave. No, Lavinia probably would have been auctioned off to people who wanted to take her apart, piece by piece, organ by organ. But I never would have let that happen. Can't she fucking see what belonging to me means?

All I'm asking for is a little goddamn gratitude.

She gets quiet just after four in the morning. My muscles are all tensed, waiting for the next shriek, the next clang of her body against the metal, and I realize they've stopped.

I find myself back at my door, hand poised on the knob.

My resolve for this shit is growing weaker, and I press my ear to the wall, knowing she's on the other side. She's not dead. Maybe she's finally fallen asleep. God knows she didn't get any the last time I shoved her in there. If the constant sounds of her banging around weren't enough, I knew it the moment I pulled the doors open and saw her dark, hollowed eyes, shoulders curved in exhausted defeat.

The anemic light of dawn slithering in through the tall arched window behind my bed brings a certain kind of clarity with it. I can't fucking take another night of this. I'll fold—I know I will. I've got two semesters ahead of me, at least. I can't go to school if I'm up all night, waiting for her to book it. And if I can't go to school, then I can't be a Duke, and if I can't be a Duke...

Then she can't be my Duchess.

I scrub my tired eyes. It's been a while since I was pulling all-nighters for Daniel Payne. I'm rusty. I'm also aggravated and hungry, and I'm stewing over the conversation that set this all into motion, almost a year ago.

"I hear your Lady is going to be in the wrestling match," I said to Rath the first time we moved Lavinia.

"She wanted to do it," Rath replied, following to the motel room. *"She's really into the charity stuff with the South Side kids."*

"A little do-gooder, eh? The fuck's she doing shacked up with the lot of you?" I said it like a joke, but it wasn't. It didn't make sense. Their Lady, Story Austin, is all soft and sweet and timid, and the three of them are... well. Complete fucks.

He answered with a casual shrug. *"We're her Lords and she's our Lady. That's just how it's done."*

That small, otherwise forgettable discussion has been echoing in my head for hours, so when I finally lumber myself out of bed, more than one goal for the day is forming in my thoughts. I pull on my jeans, grab my gun and my phone, and stalk out into the main room, pausing outside the elevator doors.

Then I dial Rath's number.

He doesn't answer the first call, or the second, or even the third, but on the fourth, his throaty, threatening voice finally rings out. "Motherfucker, I know you aren't calling me at six in the morning on a weekend."

"You said this is how it's done," I hiss, pacing in a tight circle. "You said she's your Lady, and she fucks you because you're her Lord, and that's just how it is. Either Lucia never got that memo or you're leaving something out, because this bitch isn't budging. If she's not plotting a way to shiv us in our sleep, then she's trying to run away. What the *fuck*?!"

A sleepy-soft voice can be heard in the background, and then Rath saying, "Nothing, baby. Just Nick being a pain in my ass. Roll over to Tris, I'll be right back." After a moment, his voice comes clearer and even more annoyed, "If you got me out of bed because you can't handle your woman, then so help me God, Bruin, I'm going to drive over there and beat you to death with my fucking shoe."

"You misrepresented the situation!" I catch my voice before it can get too loud, seething silently.

"We did our part. We got her out of the Hideaway. We got her into your big, dick-shaped tower. What, do you want us to fuck her for you, too?"

I yank the phone away from my ear long enough to glare murderously at his name. "I want you to give me some goddamn ideas here." Mine obviously isn't working. Daniel kept her shut up tight with a lock and key, but I can't...

I can't fucking take the screams.

Unwilling to admit that to Rath, I add, "Else, I might just have to take her back."

There's a pause, so I know he understands what I'm saying. Killer has more than one reason to be glad she's not his problem anymore. She's unnecessary drama between the Kings. Plus, his Lady would flip her shit. A hard sigh crackles over the line.

"I don't fucking think so. You don't get to return her like a defective piece of clothing." There's a long pause. "Do you think Story was compliant when she first became our Lady?"

"She auditioned."

"Yeah, along with a bunch of other chicks who would have done anything we asked. Part of the fun is the challenge. She was a no-brainer, but that doesn't mean she fell in line. We had a contract. Legally binding. She had no choice but to do what we asked, and even then, every exchange was like pulling fucking teeth."

"So you broke her in," I say, mulling it over. "Forced her into compliance. How?"

"You could say we broke one another in. In our situation, everyone had needs to be met."

I shake my head. "Yeah, that's not going to work with Lavinia."

"Goddamn it, Bruin," he snaps. "Have you tried just leveling with her?"

I grit my teeth, pushing my hair back. "I know you've met this girl. Don't be obtuse. She acts like she's got somewhere to be. She can't be left alone, she doesn't take orders, and to top it off, she cut the fucking tracker out of her neck last night."

Another long sigh. "Fuck, then I don't know. Make a deal with her. I know how you're used to working, but these girls... you can't always brute force them, Bruin. Give her something worth staying for."

I freeze, perking up. "Bribe her, you mean?"

"I meant more like—"

But I roll over him. "Bribery, *fuck*. You're right." I've been approaching this like it's something new, but it's not. I've been bribing this bitch with candy since the first time I saw her after tossing her into that ratty motel room. She eyed the Snickers poking out of my pocket in that special Lavinia-patented way that made it clear she'd be willing to stab me for it. Now that the gears are turning, I add, "Maybe even a little good, old-fashioned extortion. Make her need it, like your Lady and that stalker fuck." Some of the tension in my chest melts away and I rub it, realizing how hungry I am. "Yeah, that could work. Good idea. Talk to you later." I hang up before he can answer, a plan brewing in my head.

She looks even worse than when I went to fetch her yesterday. Black and blue, skin ashen, dark bruises beneath each eye, shoulders drooping as she staggers to her feet. Her wrists are still bound in front of her from the trek back up the stairs last night, and she's still in Remy's hoodie. It's not the bruises that do it. It's not her posture—tired and full of defeat. It's the pain in her eyes when she finally looks at me through the gate that gives me the realization.

This is going to kill her.

I'm not entirely sure why. It's just a fucking elevator, and it's not even a particularly bad one. Old as fuck. Dark. Drafty. But it's clean, quiet, and safe. Part of me stupidly thought she'd find some security in it. If anyone opened this door, I'd know it. She's better off in there than anywhere else in this town. Doesn't she know what people around here want to do to her? Fuck, I've lived here for a month and even I've considered it might be a nice place to sleep.

I only get to catch a brief glimpse of it before she pulls herself to her full height, raising her chin in defiance. When I open the gate, she comes flying out, which I'm not expecting. She looks so battered and conquered that I wouldn't think her capable of darting around me, shooting me a hot glare.

She snaps, "I've had to pee for *hours!*"

At least the sight of her in the light of day gives me a second to properly appreciate what Remy was doing with her last night. The outline of the snake tattoo on her calf has been completely transformed into a three-headed dragon, winding around her leg and up her thigh. It disappears beneath the hem of the large sweatshirt that's swallowing up her small frame, but if I know Remy, its barbed tail is probably pointing right to her perfect cunt.

I stare dumbly as the door to the toilet slams closed.

She won't sleep with me, and she's damn sure not sleeping with Remy or Sy. Nothing about this is going the way I thought it would.

Hopefully, that's all about to change.

I listen to her piss through the door, arms crossed as I prepare myself for the coming discussion. Lavinia needs a firm hand. No one knows that better than me. But I don't have the time to break her—not enough to do it right. Her stream goes on for so long that I wince. That's another problem. I'm good at being told to ferry supplies to a slave, but I'm not as good at being responsible for one. I can't tell her when to eat, when to dress, when to piss. It just bolsters my resolve.

I listen to her flush, and then wash her hands, and by the time she finally swings the door open, I'm already half poised toward the kitchen, anxious to get this moving. "Come on," I say, grabbing her by the back of the hood and pushing her toward the table.

"I can fucking walk myself, thank you!" she sneers, trying to twist away. The effect is kind of dampened by the way she looks, wrists still bound in front of her, stumbling toward the kitchen table as I shove her to a chair. Her hair is a crazy mess of blue tangles, expression puckered and severe. She looks as menacing as an abused cabbage patch doll.

I nod to a chair at the old wooden table. "Sit." We stare at one another for the amount of time it takes for her to decide if she's going to comply. I urge, "If I were you, I wouldn't test me." Not dressed in Remy's borrowed zipped-up hoodie with nothing on underneath but those tight booty shorts. I'm doing my best here, but I can just as easily bend her over the bar as anything else.

There's a flicker of apprehension in her eyes that makes me suspect she thinks I'm talking about something else. Maybe she's afraid I'm going to throw her back into the elevator. My Little Bird and her rattling cage. Jesus. The thought alone drains me.

She aggressively slams her tight little body into the chair, glaring hot lava at me.

That's a good girl.

Even though she's tied up, I still sweep the room for sharp objects and make a big show of putting the knife block in the upper cabinet, over the stove. The move reveals the gun I have tucked in my waistband and that's on purpose, too. She needs to know I'm packing. I'm done playing games.

I open the refrigerator and stare inside. At my old place, I never had much in the way of fresh food. Daniel had me working crazy hours, so I mostly ate takeout. Mama B feeds the Dukes down at the gym once a week, so occasionally I'd stop in for that, being legacy and all. But things are different now. My brother keeps the refrigerator and pantry well stocked. He burns a shit ton of calories down at the gym and he likes to stay lean, which means the refrigerator is packed with protein like eggs, chicken, and steak, plus a ton of veggies. I give it all a baffled look. My culinary expertise begins and ends with microwaveable rice pouches.

Since I have another mouth to feed now, I grab the eggs, a red and green pepper, and a pack of bacon. I can make an omelet. Probably.

She's quiet while I grab a skillet and turn on the gas, letting it heat up while I crack the eggs in a bowl, but I feel her eyes on me. I chop up the peppers and mix all that shit together, but when I hold the bowl over the skillet, she lets out a venomous scoff.

"You need oil, Einstein." Her voice is a hoarse, thin rasp that grates against my insides.

I look up. "Oil?"

She rolls her eyes so hard that her head drops back. "Oil or butter. You need it in the bottom of the pan or it'll burn and stick and make this place smell worse than it already does." While I'm searching the kitchen for one of these things, she continues in her rough voice, "And you've got the heat up too high. Have you ever even used a stove before?" I find a green bottle of olive oil that I immediately begin pouring into the pan. In an exasperated tone, she adds, "That's too much, and it's still too—*and* there it goes."

The oil splatters against the hot pan surface and pops and crackles. I shove it to a back eye, burning spots of oil dotting my hands. "Goddamn it!"

"Well, if you'd fucking listen and use that walnut-sized brain of yours for something other than hitting people and—"

"Do you ever shut up?!" I turn down the heat, trying to ignore the frustration rolling down my spine. "Who the fuck are you, anyway? Martha Stewart?"

Our eyes meet over the distance and she bites out, "You're cooking eggs, Bruin. Not building a skyscraper. Pick up any basic cookbook or watch literally the most beginner-ass YouTube video, and the information's all there."

I give her a hard stare. Like I need to be lectured by this girl, an entitled Royal daughter who's probably never cooked a meal in her life. I've seen her father's house. Excuse me, *mansion*. I place the skillet back on the eye and pour the eggs in, ignoring her critical gaze as I let it heat and bubble. I make a pitiful attempt at flipping it in half and then start the bacon. For this, she manages to keep her opinions to herself—at least verbally.

I'm searching the fridge for something non-alcoholic to pour into two glasses when I hear the shuffle of feet behind me. When I turn, I come face to face with Remy, who's shirtless and sleep-mussed and annoyingly wide-eyed.

His face is eerily blank. "What's happening?"

"Breakfast," I answer, nodding at the stove. Which is... smoking. A little. I zip to the range and quickly take the omelet off the heat. Fuck. Isn't a Duchess supposed to do shit like this? Flustered, I note, "Wasn't expecting you up this early."

"I didn't sleep," he says, pointing the full force of that soul-sucking gaze onto Lavinia. "I just dreamed."

I give him a long-suffering look. "Jesus, Remy, I need you to be fucking present. She almost got away last night."

Tonelessly, he responds, "I heard screaming. And there's blood in my room."

It takes me a stretch of calculating to realize what he's talking about. "Yeah, she cut the fucking tracker out."

Lavinia keeps holding Remy's gaze, even though her shoulders curl uncomfortably. "Not like it was a sophisticated operation."

"Like I was saying about being present. You can't leave her unattended with anything sharp. You're lucky she didn't shank your ass." Something occurs to me, halfway between plucking the bacon out of the pan and cutting the gas. I turn to him, searching his face. "Wait, you had a dream? When did that start happening?"

Part of having been away for so long is accepting that I don't really know Remy and Sy anymore. It's only been a couple of years, but it's long enough to have lost grip on the threads that used to hold us together. Just after the news, Remy wasn't the same. Psychotic break, they said. Losing Tate wasn't easy for any of us, and his mind's always been a little fragile, but *Christ*.

It fucking broke him.

I didn't even have a chance to see him before I left for South Side. His dad must have admitted him into the mental clinic the second he got the news, because I never got to see his reaction. We never spoke or grieved about it together. His dad sent an obnoxiously elaborate floral display, but Remy wasn't even at the funeral, too busy getting pumped full of antipsychotics or whatever. He apparently got better with medication and treatment, but some things were lost forever, like his memory of that time period, and strangely, his ability to dream.

So when Remy answers, "Seven hours ago," a part of me feels shittily relieved. At least that's one thing I haven't missed.

"That's great, man." I try to give him a pat on the shoulder, but he's standing all rigidly limp. He doesn't even acknowledge it. I guess being around for a single milestone doesn't really erase the distance. I offer, "You should tell Sy about it. I bet he creams his pants over the smallest breakthrough."

"I can't." Remy, I realize, hasn't looked away from Lavinia since he walked into the kitchen. Carefully, I edge myself between them, watching as he visibly snaps out of whatever trance he'd been in. Finally, he looks me in the eye, face white as a sheet. "Do you have any idea how many stars there are?"

Squinting, I ask, "Like, observably, or...?"

"Don't knock on my door today, Nicky." And with that, he turns on his heel and leaves. I stare at the empty place where he was just standing, wondering if I should have said something different. Sy would know. But I'm just treading water.

"Fucking maniac," Lavinia mutters.

I whip around to snap, "Shut the fuck up. He's not a maniac. He's the best person in this whole fucked up town." I grab a plate from the cabinet and plop the *only slightly burned* omelet onto it, along with a handful of bacon.

"Oh, my bad," she says, voice mocking. "I must have had him confused with the guy who keeps sexually assaulting me. Mistaken identity, I suppose. Was that his twin?"

"*Eat.*" I slide the plate across the table to her.

She looks at the omelet. "I can't eat that."

"Why the fuck not?"

She raises her wrists, the zip tie firmly in place.

"Christ." I pick up the fork and cut off a piece of the omelet, holding it up to her mouth.

She gives me an unblinking stare. "You're fucking kidding me."

"Nope." I let the egg hang there. "Better hurry. It's getting cold."

"Let it." She lifts her chin. "You're not feeding me like a child."

"I'm feeding you like a bitch who doesn't know how to handle her own leash."

Her mouth twists into a bitter grin. "So like a prisoner."

I snort and shove the fork into my own mouth. Good enough. "Your words," I say over the food. "Your choice. I brought you here to be the Duchess. To love you. To fuck you. To make you safe and fucking happy. And here you are, fighting it every step of the way. You think I wouldn't rather have you in my bed than in that fucking elevator?" Shaking my head, I insist, "You're the one making this hard, Lavinia." I cut off another piece of the omelet and hold it up to her. "Don't make me do the airplane."

She eyes it for a long moment, then rears her head back and spits on it. *And* me.

I drop the fork and it hits the counter with a loud, metallic clatter. "You," I lean toward her, slamming my palms on the table, "are the most ungrateful bitch I've ever met!"

"Ungrateful?" Her voice is shrill, echoing off the high ceiling. "I'm a motherfucking slave, Bruin! I don't want to be your goddamn Duchess! I didn't ask for it, I just want to leave. Every minute I'm locked up in here—" She visibly bites her word back, eyes flashing angrily. "Stop trying to bullshit me into thinking you're doing me some amazing favor. You might not know better, but I sure as hell do. Deep down you have to know the truth." She pitches forward, eyes darkening. "You're not a fixer, Nick. The reason Daniel Payne wanted you? It's because ruining things is all you're good at." I'm usually pretty good about keeping my face in check, but something must get through, because she nods, leaning leisurely back in her chair. "That's right. Nick the fuck-up. Good at hurting and killing. Not much in the savior department. I bet your pal Rapey—sorry, I mean *Remy*—knows all about it, doesn't he? Yeah, I can tell when you look at him. I bet it takes something monumentally shitty to put a glimmer of guilt into Nick Bruin's eyes."

I'm calm as I sit back in my chair, carefully placing the fork back onto the plate. "This isn't going to work."

Her demeanor shifts instantly, back straightening as she stares into my eyes. "You're right. You should just let me go." The way she looks at me then pierces right into my gut. Soft. Pleading. "I'll keep my mouth shut about you. I won't tell anyone about..." Her gaze drops to the table, jaw tightening. "I won't tell anyone anything."

My eye twitches, a boulder of displeasure settling in my stomach. I worked my ass off to get this girl. I've fought, bled, *killed*. Killian Payne didn't ascend to King alone. Part of that was me. Just one domino in a long line that was supposed to get me here. "You're right. I'm not a fixer," I admit, holding her eyes. "But I'm also not a quitter."

Her shoulders crumble into a dejected curve. "Oh my fucking god, why?! I'm not..." She looks around, like she's lost. "There's nothing special about me. You don't want me, Nick!"

"You're wrong." The response is instinctual, fundamental. And the instant her mouth opens to protest, I reach over the table to grab her face, snapping it shut. "It doesn't matter why I want you. What matters is that I *have* you. You're Forsyth royalty now, like it or not. Do you have any fucking idea the things I've had to put into motion to get you under this goddamn belfry? Even if I wanted to let you go," I give her a hard, significant look, "*and I don't*—I'd have to pull it apart." I idly press my thumb into her plush bottom lip, imagining it wrapped around the digit. Sighing, I let her face go. "Anyway, you're going about this all wrong. Kind of disappointing. I thought you were smarter than this."

She sputters, and I'm relieved—so fucking relieved—to see some of that bright, hot indignation returning to her eyes. "What's that supposed to mean?"

I take the opportunity to shove a piece of bacon between her teeth. "Well, it's like you said. I'm a ruiner. A fighter. A killer. All this effort you're wasting to run away? It's like a mechanic throwing away his toolbox. Now," I take a bite of the omelet, not bothering to close my mouth as I chew, "I don't know what you're in such an annoying fucking rush to do, but something tells me it's probably more up my alley than yours. While you're here, you're practically untouchable." One of her cheeks scrunches up in disbelief, so I know she's understanding. "Use me."

She raises both wrists to take the bacon from her mouth. "Use you for *what*?"

I shrug. "Anything."

Her chest bounces with empty laughter. "What, like you'll kill my dad if I asked?"

I raise my eyes to hers, unwavering. "Yes." I watch her take this in, tongue pausing in its shy exploration of the bacon grease on her lips. I lay my fork down and lean back. "But that's a 'blow this motherfucker up' sort of job, and I don't think either of us is ready for that. Murdering a King is like throwing a rock into the water. It makes ripples. The closer you are, the more you feel them." Moving my finger up and down in the air, I explain, "You're way too close to that rock, Little Bird."

To my surprise, she says, "You're right." Not breaking my stare, she brings the bacon to her mouth, ripping off a bite. "It wouldn't help me, anyway." I wait for her to elaborate, but she doesn't.

"So give me something else." I think the growing electricity in my chest might be anticipation. Lavinia wants something and it's big. Big enough to have her locked up for all this time. Important enough that other Kings are involved. I know the seedling of a war when I see one, and it might not be my fight, but I'm down with getting a few blows in.

She tilts her head as she inspects me. That's exactly what it feels like. An inspection. She's measuring me up, eyes descending to my bare chest, cataloging the bits of ink Remy's given to me over the years, but the hardness in her gaze never dissipates. It's almost a disappointment when she asks, "How many people have you killed?"

"How many people have *you* killed?" My face doesn't even twitch. There's a rumor. Unconfirmed, but everyone in Forsyth has heard it.

She reacts, but only by cramming the last of the bacon into her mouth and rests her hands in her lap. "Fine."

I raise an eyebrow. "Fine?"

"There's something I need," she explains, throat bobbing with a swallow. "If you can get it."

I shrug, not missing that her eyes flick to my chest again. "Depends on what it is."

She nods, surely having expected this much. "It's a box. It's at my—" I wait, watching her grit her teeth. "I mean, at my father's house. It's under my old bed."

I grin, tapping my knuckle against the table. There it is. *Intrigue.* "What's in it?"

Her eyes fly back to mine, jaw sharp. "None of your fucking business."

I hold up my hands, palms out. "Chill, Little Bird. Can't I be curious?"

Sharply, she answers, "No."

I wave this off, not in a mood to push it. "Okay. I'll break into your father's heavily fortified mansion, under threat of certain death, to bring you a box of mysterious value. And in return?"

"Let's not get ahead of ourselves," she says, scoffing.

I give her a threatening grin. "Oh, let's absolutely get ahead of ourselves. A guy needs some incentive, doesn't he?" When all she does is glare at me, I shake my head. "Plus, all the hot water you're in? I doubt this will be a one-and-done job. This is going to be a *service.* That means long-term."

She gives me a threatening grin right back. "This isn't anything I can't do myself."

"You and I both know that's not true." I lean back, kicking my feet up on the table, "One of us has been Lionel's prisoner for the past two years, and it hasn't been me." I throw her a sarcastic grimace. "You have that really embarrassing habit of getting caught. Face it, Lavinia, dealing with the Kings requires a certain finesse that you just don't have."

"Fuck you." She rolls her eyes, looking away. But below the

table, I can hear her heel tapping against the cheap vinyl flooring. "Cut the shit already. What would you want?"

I'd think that should be obvious. "Say you'll be our Duchess. Without argument or backtalk, or the need for—" I glance toward the elevator. "—discipline."

She swings the full force of her glower on me. "Say I'll suck your dick and cook your meals like a good little cutslut? Go fuck yourself."

"Who said anything about being a cutslut," I snap, flinging a hand in the direction of the door. "Cutsluts stay downstairs in the party room. They're easy pussy. Christ, you're a lot of things, but easy will never be one of them." I run my fingers through my hair, tugging on the roots. "The Duchess can be whatever we want her to be. If you want to lay out terms, then let's hear them." Before she can start, I warn, "And I'll lay out mine."

Her eyes narrow in response, but I can see her mouth purse as she considers. "I get to leave whenever I want."

I give her an exasperated look. "'Murder my dad, let me do anything I want'. You really aim for the fucking moon, don't you?" I dust the bacon grease from my fingers, countering, "You get to leave when one of us is with you." Her mouth falls open in outrage, but I add, "But no restraints."

She falters. "None?"

"If you play nice," I clarify. "And by nice, I mean no biting or kicking or stabbing. No burning. No punching, slapping, shivving, kneeing, head butting, cutting, flaying, slamming—"

"Christ, I get the gist!" She gives me an exasperated look, but I see the spark of hope in her eyes. She must really hate that elevator. "No bodily harm."

"And," I add, "you have to sleep in our beds."

"No." She brings her bound wrists down onto the table with a decisive *clunk*. "In fact, I get my own room."

I peek through the arch that leads into the main room, gesturing with a hand. "Three bedrooms, four people. Do the math."

She twists her neck to look. "No one's sleeping up there."

I realize she's looking up at the loft in front of the clock face and it's an effort to keep my face straight. The old Dukes used to make their black lab sleep up there. "You want to make the loft your own space? Fine by me." No door, no locks, no walls—just bars. She can't keep us out of it. It's a cage with the flimsiest illusion of freedom. It's perfect. "But you still have to sleep with us."

"No."

I stare at her, thinking none of this is worth it. I could just force her and forget about compromising. But I think back to the sound of her slamming her body against the insides of the elevator. Her screams—not cries of anger, but *howls*. Desperate, keening, full of panic.

Can't fucking do it.

I offer, "On weekdays. You can have weekends off."

She scoffs. "Fuck that. One night a week, *if* I want to."

"Christ, you're shit at compromising." I rub the bridge of my nose, my thoughts going to those beers in the fridge. Bitch is about to drive me to drinking. "Here's my best offer. A day of the week for each of us, and you have to do what we want." At her horrified look, I reason, "That's less than half the week, Lav. It's not going to get any better than that."

"I'm not being your sex slave for a day!"

The corner of my mouth quirks up. "Who said anything about sex? Maybe we just want you to scrub our floors?"

Her nostrils flare angrily. "Your brother acts like he wants to throw me down that flight of stairs, Remy wants to wear my skin, and *you*..." She shakes her head, barking a harsh laugh. "God even knows what you want, but I'll never be into it." She levels me with a stony look. "*Ever*. If you fuck me, it'll be assault. Assault is off the table."

I let my eyes drop to her body, hidden beneath Remy's hoodie. "That's a bit over-the-top for someone I've seen get wet for me." When she just stares at me, unblinking, I yank my feet off the table to lean forward, voice hard. "Maybe this whole negotiation thing is confusing you, so let's get something straight, Little Bird. Your pussy is mine, Duchess or not." She pushes away from the table, like she's going to storm off. I reach out to fist the hoodie, slamming her back to her seat. "If I want to fuck you, then that's what I'm going to do. If my brothers want to fuck you, then it's only because I'm allowing them to. So instead of being a brat about your precious fucking virtue, you might want to start thinking about how I can make it good for you."

She raises her chin, muscles so tense that I can see the strain in her neck. "How can you possibly make it good for me?"

"Easy." I give the sweater one last crush in my fist before letting it go. "If you're a good girl, then maybe I'll take your position on the matter into consideration."

She blinks, voice a perfect deadpan. "Wow. The possible consideration of my consent. Don't break your back *not* being a piece of shit, Nick."

"I won't." I try to stuff another slice of bacon into her mouth, but she turns away, jaw clenched. Laughing, I muse, "God, you really are a Lucia, aren't you? Every woman in this place knows her pussy is her best bargaining chip, but you think yours is diamond-studded." Leaning back, I decide to tell her something that may come as a surprise. "You ever think that's the reason I want it so bad?"

Her gaze meets mine slowly, filling with a suspicious glint. "Bullshit."

I used to think it was just Daniel and all his rules. Lavinia the jail bird. The one thing I couldn't touch, and goddamn, my fingers would positively itch for it. I used to lay in that shitty South Side bed at night and imagine taking her. Throwing her into my car, driving somewhere secluded, no cameras or foot soldiers to see me ripping her clothes off and stealing it, touching every inch of her skin, forcing my way inside.

Ruining her.

I reach down to adjust my cock, already full mast just imagining it, but the truth is, it wasn't just the Kings' rules that made me want her so bad. She's just such a haughty little bitch, thinking her pussy is above me. Makes a guy want to own it.

And now I do. "No bullshit," I tell her, willing my dick to stand down. "But understand one thing, Little Bird. I'm not Daniel Payne. I don't collect nice things and lock them away to rot. You've had no control over anything for the past two years, so maybe this will make sense to you." I grab her bound wrists, pulling her against the table. "I'm *going* to fuck you, Lavinia. That's a given. It's not something you have control over. But," keeping my eyes locked on hers, I pull a knife from my pocket, flicking it open, "it's up to you how it happens. You can make me work for it—I don't mind that—or you can make me have to hold you down and fuck that nasty attitude right out of you." With one clean yank of the blade, I cut her zip ties. "For the record, I don't mind that, either."

She jerks her hands into her chest, the chair's back legs clattering as her weight slams into the seat. "So that's it, huh? You're going to fuck me and there's nothing I can do about it?!"

"I'm giving you something worth taking advantage of." Feeling slightly annoyed, I mention, "And stop acting like you have it so bad. I read the Lords' contract with their Lady earlier, and you wouldn't believe some of the shit they put on paper. They micromanaged that bitch down to the soap she washed her cunt with."

"And how exactly," she growls, "do you expect me to make you work for it?"

I close my knife, shrugging. "That's up to you. I don't mind waiting." Lowering my chin, I stress, "For a while."

Her eyes tighten. "And in the meantime?"

Stuffing the knife back into my pocket, I give a cold laugh. "We could do nine months of that." I point to the elevator and her eyes follow. "But I doubt either of us wants to, so we need to come to some kind of understanding. What's it going to take to get you to settle the fuck down?"

She looks down at her hands, wringing her knuckles. "I want clothes," she says, and I refrain from smirking victoriously. She's actually going to barter here. "*Real* clothes, not those rags your cutsluts donated to me."

I don't bother hiding my grimace. "I mean, I wouldn't mind. But outside of the tower, there are expectations for a Royal woman. Slut-wear is just part of the dress code. You know this." Nevertheless, I compromise. "I'll get you some things to wear around here."

"And shoes," she stresses, rubbing her wrists. "I'm not walking down those million flights of stairs in heels. If the three of you want to kill me, there are less annoying ways of going about it."

I give a slow nod, thinking. "I guess that's practical. You could always use the elev—"

She slams her palms on the table. "No more elevators!" When I tear my gaze from the red marks across her wrists, I see that there's a deadly sort of alarm in her eyes. "I'll negotiate with you, Nick. I'll try to find some meager fucking illusion of comfort with this, but I'm telling you now, if you put me into that elevator again? We're done. I'll make you have to guard me every second of your goddamn day." Her eyes turn flinty. "That's as non-negotiable as the fact my pussy is apparently yours now. Do you understand me?"

The chances of me never having to lock her up again are appallingly slim. But this can at least buy me a few days of peace, so I agree, "Fine. But if you try to run again, we really *are* done, and that means I won't think twice about tossing your ass in there. Do you understand *me*?"

"And if you do make me fuck you again..." she says, eyes tight.

"*When.*"

She scowls, but continues. "You have to wear a condom."

I laugh. "Not a chance. And just so we're crystal fucking clear, withdrawal is off the table, too. The only thing in this tower that pulls out is that sofa over there."

She crosses her arms, pushing her tits together. "Then no joy. I'd rather jump from one of these windows than get knocked up with one of your demon spawns."

I pause, half chew into a piece of bacon, turning that thought over in my mind. Somehow, it hadn't occurred to me until just now.

Lavinia Lucia, belly all swollen with the things I plan to do to her. Suddenly, it's all I can see.

Even so, I know better than to push. At least for now.

"You'll get on birth control, don't worry." It's a statement. No further negotiation. "I'll set it up. You need a new tracker, too."

Her back straightens. "No."

"Yes."

Louder, "*No.*"

"You're fucking terrible at this," I sigh, head lolling back. "You have to offer me something, Lavinia."

She tosses her hands up. "Fine, I'll clean or something!"

"Not good enough." I rub my chin, thinking. Of course, I want her body. Her mouth. Her pussy. But all of that's going to be mine, regardless. "I have some rules. Nothing major. Agree to them, and I'll consider letting the tracker go."

Her eyes narrow suspiciously. "Like what?"

"Kissing."

"You want me to kiss you?" She looks distinctly unimpressed.

My eyes zero in on her mouth. This was always an issue with making her Duchess. Sharing her with the others. It's why it had to be Remy and Sy. They're the only people I could see her with and not want to shoot. That doesn't mean it'll be easy, though. "I want you to *only* kiss me."

She takes a dramatic glance around the tower. "I don't see anyone else lining up, so consider that a done deal. What else?"

"When I'm here or downstairs, enjoying some downtime, I want you in my lap."

"Should I expect a little collar with a bell on it?" Lavinia's cheeks get really, intensely red when she's mad.

It's fucking adorable. "Don't tempt me. I do deserve a little something extra from you to sweeten the pot, considering you can't even be a proper Duchess."

"*You* deserve something from *me*?!" Her cheeks get redder and redder. "How the fuck do you figure?"

"You're not pre-med," I point out, swiping a piece of bacon for myself. "The Duchess is supposed to be our cutwoman. Our medic. Now we're going to have to trust some outsider. It puts us in a bad way." This is something Sy has reminded me of, frequently and *with feeling*, for the last two damn days.

"You think I can't handle your poor little boo-boos?" She gives me a sneering smile. "Please. I was stitching up Royal bitch-boys before you even graduated high school. Find me a pre-med who knows how to handle a dislocated shoulder."

This is news to me, and I sit up, brows knitting together. "No shit?"

She sits straighter too, eyes flashing. "I'll do the lap thing. I won't kiss anyone. I'll stay in your stupid fucking tower and not kill you all. And in exchange?"

I dust off my hands. "I'll break into your daddy's house and get whatever you want. You can also have the loft, new shoes, clothes for home, and my sparkling fucking benevolence." I slide the fork and omelet to her. "In return, you'll be in my bed once a week, minimum. The others get a day for themselves. You'll keep the violence in check, and you'll act like the fucking Duchess, in this house and outside of it."

I offer her my hand, and even though I still see the flicker of defiance in her eye, she shakes it, sealing the deal. "And know this." I tighten my grip and pull her toward me, the two of us meeting over the table. As I speak, low and deadly, I watch a lock of her blue hair sway with my breath. "If you spit in my face again, I'm going to slap the piss out of you."

Her eyes flick to mine, catching the threat in my tone just as much as my words. "Spit in your face? Is that figuratively or literally?"

I reach up to sweep the lock of hair away, tucking it gently behind her ear. "Fuck around and find out, Little Bird.

9

Lavinia

Thirteen days.

It's almost midnight, and the clock above me is still as a stone. I spend a long time staring at it from my makeshift nest on the floor. The pile of blankets smells awful, like a dog rolled around on it, but I'm too stubborn to go to the couch downstairs. Instead, I pull my shirt to my nose, block out the smell, and track the slow creep of the moon through the cloudy glass. Strange to think those heavy iron hands used to move, ticking away above the streets, and now they're just another part of this gigantic, looming, decrepit statue. But that's Forsyth for you. Every bright thing gets snuffed out here. It's Forsyth's blessing and its curse.

Everything here goes still eventually.

I turn my back to it, shifting my gaze to the main room. It's as dead as that clock, but I can still hear sounds from Remy's room. An hour ago, they were startling, putting me on edge, dreading the thought of that door opening. Somehow, tucked up into my nest, I've lost my nervousness. It's easier up here.

Easier than the elevator, certainly. I keep finding my eyes

wandering to the shape of its door, as if the mere thought of it existing has carved an ominous hole in the world. My bones are tired from its walls. My muscles are sore from each surge against them. My lungs ache with the memory of being inside, desperate for a breath that wasn't saturated with my own exhale.

Right now, I could run. Sure, Nick took all the keys and weapons away before herding me up into the dark loft, but I could still escape. Having nowhere else to go is better than the dark holes they keep putting me in. But then there's potentially nine months of that elevator if I get caught, and the throb of my bruises makes me consider that perhaps Nick had a point. I'm not very good at escaping. I'm good at enduring. The question is, how far will that endurance get me?

I remember Nick in the ring on Friday night, taking Perez down so smoothly. All that raw strength and understated power. Deadly. That's what he is. It's not the polished, clean sort of violence the Counts favor, either. Nick's not afraid to get dirty, to cut through flesh with a dull knife, to saw through bone. He's more than just a murderer. He's a murderer who understands the game.

And he thinks he loves me.

It'd be stupid to think I can harness it by taking him up on his offer, but I find myself wondering. What would it be like to have a soldier of my own? Someone to stand between me and the world. Someone who fights dirty. Someone who wants things I can never give him, because he's also someone who'd put me in a box when he realizes it.

I should absolutely run.

I fall asleep, imagining the hands reaching toward the top of the clock, as if it were taking a long overdue stretch. A bear coming out of hibernation. A bird raising its wings.

Twelve days.

IT's the first thought that fills my head when I wake up. *Twelve.*

The second is that Nick is an annoyingly early riser.

I blink open my eyes to watch him puttering around the main room, pulling on his shoes, scrolling on his phone, lazily combing his fingers through his hair. Unlike yesterday, when he was shirtless and unoccupied enough to stare unabashedly at me from dusk until dawn, today he moves with an economical purpose.

"Are you going to my father's house now?" I ask, blearily watching him shrug on his leather jacket. There's a blanket tangled around my ankle when I go to stand and I shake it off. It's a little chilly up here, but in truth, it's not so shabby. Wide open spaces, no door to lock me inside, this big clock face standing between me and the world. Somehow, I managed to catch entire hours of sleep last night. "I want to come," I rush out, trying to get down the spiral staircase without breaking my neck.

But Nick distractedly answers, "No." I hate how he has this way of saying things, firm enough that it's clear he's made up his mind, but also indifferent, like he can't be bothered to revisit it.

Stumbling to the bottom of the staircase, I insist, "I can help. I know the way in and out. It'll be faster if you take me." I spent yesterday going over all the particulars, even going so far as to sit at the table with him and draw him a map. But there's no possible way the idiot heard me. He kept staring at my mouth and reaching over to toy with strands of my hair, smirking every time I jerked away.

He's not taking this seriously.

"It'll be a *liability* if I take you." He checks his pocket for his wallet and car keys. "And that's not where I'm going, anyway."

"It's not?" I try to keep the urgency out of my voice. It's obvious they don't know shit about the arrangement my father made with Daniel. I need to keep it that way, but I also need that box. Immediately.

Twelve days.

He hoists a black leather backpack over his shoulder, finally turning to me. "Don't be surprised or anything, but it turns out the first requirement of being a Duke is a willing subjugation to academic excellence." When I do nothing but stare blankly at him, he dryly explains, "I've got class."

My eyes flick to the tattoo beside his eye. "They don't have an issue with the fact you look more like a felon than a frat boy?"

He shrugs, throwing his arms out wide. "Whatever it takes to get another Bruin in the belfry, this fine establishment is ready to entertain just about anything." On someone else, that might sound pompous and entitled, but Nick says it with this wry, bitter twist of his mouth.

Maybe I'm not the only one making compromises.

"So I just stay here all day?" I ask, tugging at the hem of Nick's hoodie. He'd taken Remy's from me last night and all but demanded I wear his instead. It doesn't matter whose hoodie I wear, though. My bare legs are cold in this drafty place. "And what am I supposed to do while you're off playing Dutiful Duke? Clean? Cook you dinner?" I hope the sarcasm in my voice is more audible than the worry, but my eyes flick nervously toward the elevator anyway.

I can't spend a day in there.

I'll die.

"You can hold off on the rat poison for another day, Little Bird." He jerks his chin over my shoulder. "You're spending the day with him."

In a moment of utterly perfect timing, a door opens behind us.

Heat and apprehension swirl in my stomach. I'm not ready to spend any more time with Remy alone, not after what happened Saturday night. But, to my absolute non-relief, Remy isn't standing behind me.

It's Simon. Lurker.

Fuck.

Stone-faced, hateful, huge-dicked Sy.

Fucking fuck.

Having sex with these guys is something I know for a fact will happen. I didn't need Nick's lecture over breakfast yesterday to make that known. Being prissy little fuck-puppets is what Royal women *do*, and I'm a Duchess.

But having that thing inside of me wouldn't just be sex. It'd be literal torture.

I turn to Nick, mouthing a panicked, "No way."

Nick just steps forward, his solid wall of body dwarfing my own. "I can't stay with you all the time, and you can't be trusted on your own. This is how its gotta be. Unless...?" He follows my gaze to the elevator, eyebrow rising.

Fuck.

"No." I try to make my voice firm and decisive, but the thread of fear still comes out, drawing his eyes to mine.

He reaches up to touch my chin. It's gentle in a way I'm not expecting, because that's how he is—a mystery grab-bag of hurt and tenderness that I'm never adequately prepared for. When he leans down to clear the distance between our mouths, I lean back. *Way* back. I lean back so far that Nick strains to catch me, eventually snapping upright to glare down his strong nose at me. "One day," he says, tucking his thumb under the strap of his bag and crushing it in his fist, "you're going to regret being such a bitch to me."

In a mere moment, he's already gone down the stairs, feet echoing off the steps.

I curl my hands nervously, turning to Simon. "Look—" I start, but he cuts me off.

"Put some fucking pants on and get ready. I have somewhere to be." He must be an early riser like Nick, because he's impeccably dressed, a large gym bag already clutched in one of his large hands.

I wrap my arms around my middle. "I don't have any normal pants. Just the shit those cutsluts gave me."

He shrugs. "You know what they say. If the slutty shoe fits."

The comment grates, but fuck this guy. I've done enough compromising these last few days. I stride across the living space to the small corner where my loaned clothes are stacked on a chair, and get to shuffling through them.

"Seriously?" I mutter when I can't find a single pair of normal jeans. The closest I can find is a pair of faux-leather, skintight leggings. I bend to slide my foot into the leg, and since I've got nothing but this hoodie and those ridiculous lace panties, I instantly feel the cool air against my exposed ass.

Behind me, Sy grows suddenly silent.

There isn't a single shift of fabric, a whisper of a breath, or disturbance to the air. Tensely, I chance a glance behind me and find him standing there. Staring.

Not just staring. Sy is basically sodomizing me with his eerie blue eyes. The muscle in the back of his jaw ticks and he shifts his weight to one foot, gaze plastered to my ass. Fist clenching and unclenching. I think of making a comment, but instead, I yank the leggings up my calves, as if ignoring it will make it go away.

Until he mutters out a low, "Goddamn it," and the next time I glance back, it's to the sight of the bathroom door slamming shut.

I spend a moment blinking at it, slack-faced in confusion. But these walls, I've come to realize, are glorified cardboard. I'd be surprised to find an inch of insulation between the sheetrock. This is why, when I hear the muffled rhythm of grunts mingling with subtle fleshy sounds, it hits me.

My jaw drops in outrage.

I didn't have brothers growing up, just my sister, but we were surrounded by my father's foot soldiers. I'm never surprised when a guy is disgusting; they're pigs. At the same time, hearing one jerk off in the other room, a guy who has made it clear he thinks I'm trash? I do the only thing I can: be happy he's using his hand and not shoving that baton up my twat.

I finish pulling on the leggings, shimmying them onto my hips. I sniff my hair. Does it smell like a dog? There's no way I'm going into the bathroom to check it out, so I wrangle it into something presentable. When Sy emerges from the bathroom, red-faced and drying his most likely cum-stained hands, I'm ready.

"You done?"

His eyebrows drop to a dark glower and he tosses the hand

towel aside, snatching up his gym bag. "Well?" He gestures belligerently toward the door. "I don't have all day."

More of that outrage bubbles to the surface—he was the one jerking off like an animal—but I keep it to myself, pulling on the uncomfortable strappy shoes that were donated to me. "Let's go then."

His broad shoulders are all I see as we take the long trek down the stairs of the tower. Sy doesn't talk. He doesn't even glance back at me when I audibly struggle to keep up, palm pressed to the stone wall for support. He's too fucking fast for a guy his size, but maybe that's just a result of the hot, furious energy radiating off him. It's a relief for more than one reason when we finally reach the bottom, my feet aching.

He pauses at the door leading outside, hand on the big brass knob. "Nick says you won't run."

"I won't." It hurts to say it, but it's true. Before I can do anything, I need that box, and as much as I loathe Nick, he's more likely to get it than I would be. If he fails, he fails. My father might even kill him. Too bad, so sad. Either way, I have to at least let it play out.

Sy gives me a long, dark look. "If you try, I won't play nice like him when I catch you."

I stare at him. He thinks the way Nick treats me is 'nice'?

"We made an agreement. I won't run." I draw a dramatic X over my heart with my finger. "Cross my heart."

His eyes narrow and it's enough to let me know he's not privy to the full negotiations Nick and I made. These are the little details I keep and file away. The Dukes are just like Remy's unfinished gallery of star paintings. Parts of a whole that don't quite fit.

Outside, he unlocks the SUV and I get in the passenger seat, dourly remembering being behind the wheel a couple of nights ago. Inside, I instinctively lean to the side, pressing against the door. Sy locks the doors, starts the engine, and exhales an irritated sigh. "Oh, knock it the fuck off. I'm not going to fuck you."

"What?" I blurt. Then, before I can stop myself, "Why?

He answers nonchalantly, "I don't fuck whores."

"I'm not a who—"

"Do you have a pussy between your legs?" He doesn't wait for an answer. Good thing. It's lodged in my throat. "Then you're a whore. *All* of you are."

All of *who*? The girls from the Velvet Hideaway? Royal offspring? Counts? Or is he talking in the most basic sense? Girls. All *women* are whores.

Jesus Christ.

I know very little about the Bruin family dynamics other than how they all started. Simon and Nick share the same mom, and once upon a time, she was a Duchess. They have different dads, but both men were her Dukes. Nick's father should have been King, but before they started popping out their little Duke freak-spawns, they exited the Royalty stage left and let Saul take the kingdom for himself. I know the story well enough. My father used to love to laugh about it over inter-kingdom meetings.

It does make me wonder exactly what Daddy Bruin thinks of Nick claiming his legacy.

The car jerks to a stop and we're back in front of the gym. It looks different in the daylight. More gray. Less festive. Kind of sad and tired, like it's still recovering from the weekend. That makes two of us.

Sy doesn't speak to me on the way in, just grunts for me to follow. Inside, the gym is bustling with men working out. I glance over at him. "For the record, I'm not into exercise. Or dressed for it."

His eyes rake over me. "I'm shocked." He lifts his chin toward an office in the back. It has a wide window that overlooks the gym. "I'm here to train. You're going to wait in there until I finish."

"I'm just going to wait? By myself?"

"No, not by yourself." He looks at me like I'm stupid. "You may have promised Nick not to run, but I don't buy it. Lucky for me, the gym comes with a built-in babysitter."

Before we get to the office, the door swings open and a woman steps out. Long dark tresses teased with enough hairspray to probably choke someone frame a heavy-looking set of cleavage. She's in a black leather jacket and skin-tight pants, not that different from my own. High-heeled boots that could double for shit-kickers come up above her ankles and there's a heavy flash of gold on both her fingers and earlobes. A pair of winged reading glasses hangs around her neck from a chain. She's dressed like a cutslut who aged out of the institution and couldn't accept it, and the crow's feet around her eyes make her look older than the rest of her skin suggests.

She crosses her arms as we walk toward her, propping her side up against the doorjamb. "Ten minutes late," she notes, jaw working a piece of gum between her molars.

Sy gestures limply to me. "We're still adjusting."

It's truly hard not to mention that his jerk-off sesh in the bathroom is what held us up.

"I guess this is my babysitter?" I ask, eyeing the woman.

"This," Sy says, with the only measure of respect I've heard come out of his voice so far, "is Mama B. I'd tell you to watch yourself, but to be honest, I'd love to see you try."

I look her up and down, understanding. Mama B is more than a garden variety cutslut. The shrewd arch of her eyebrow at my scrutiny is a sort of warning, but she pushes her chest out, straightening her shoulders.

She doesn't mind being measured up. "You done eyefucking me?" she asks, raising a hand to the open door. "Then come on in."

MAMA B IS leader of the cutsluts.

I know not only because she's been notorious in this capacity since as far back as Leticia or I could remember, but also because I'd heard the girls talking about her during the party on Saturday. It's well known that she keeps the rowdy DKS fangirls in line, but I'm surprised by what I see when I follow her inside.

If her having the only actual office in the building is any indication, she must actually run this joint. From the neatly labeled folders, baskets, and bins, I assume she governs the matches, maybe even pays the bills and coaches. Mama B is more than a glorified cutslut. She's management.

She's also, I gather from the state of her office, incredibly organized. Everything is perfectly in place. Her desk is spotless, other than tidy paperwork and a flat calendar jotted with neat handwriting. File cabinets with little labels line the back wall. Framed photographs of different girls all huddled around Mama with bright smiles and scant clothing. One girl shows up more than once, and the resemblance is striking. A daughter? I also spot a few guys, sometimes mid-fight, sweat glistening off their bodies. It's another piece of the Duke's puzzle, one I wasn't aware of. Counts would never put a woman in a position of power. Leticia was as close as it gets. The only thing that doesn't fit—or maybe disturbingly does—are the obnoxious inspirational quotes dotting the walls in loopy, glittery script.

You can't climb the ladder of success with your hands in your pocket!
Believe you can, and you're halfway there!
Victory is always possible for the person who refuses to stop fighting!

"You want something to drink?" she asks, slipping on her glasses.

"No, thank you," I say, not prepared to ingest anything these people give me.

Her lips form a thin line, giving me the impression I've caused offense. She shrugs and sits behind the desk, picking up a pen. She clicks the end with her thumb and starts sorting through an organized stack of papers.

I spy a magazine on the end table. *Muscle Monthly*. A hulking, tanned, veiny couple clings to one another on the front, overly white teeth bared like fangs. I creep my fingers over and snag it. I've settled on an article about the benefits of protein shakes when she says, "You look a lot like her."

I look up warily, searching her worn face, and try to remember if I've heard anything about beef. I learned long ago that Forsyth is a field of landmines, but keeping all the rivalries and hostilities tabulated in my mind is enough to give me a migraine.

Clearing my throat, I reply, "People say that. That I favor my mom over my dad." I guess it's not a surprise she knew my mother. She was the Countess, of course, and this woman, Mama B, probably attended Forsyth at around the same time.

My mom died when she was thirty. Leticia and I were still toddlers, so we never really knew her. All anyone ever talks about is her death. A handful of pain pills and a bottle of gin, and that's all she wrote. I think there must have been a time when I resented her for leaving me alone with my father and all his cruelty. But that's long gone. I don't even know what kind of person my mother was. Maybe she was a Leticia, cold and ruthless, and would have made my life even worse. Maybe she was a good person who found herself trapped in a shitty situation, in which case, I can't say I blame her for taking the express route out. Either way, there are too many terrible people currently living to waste my resentment on the dead.

I pretend I'm not unnerved by this woman knowing more about me than I do about her. "Guess I've got that going for me."

"I don't mean your mother." Her head tilts, jaw working that piece of gum. "Although I see that, too. I'm talking about your sister."

My blood freezes. "My sister?"

"Yeah." She narrows her eyes. "Same nose. Shape of the mouth. Chin, hair, complexion. Not your eyes, though. Those are like your father's."

No shit. I hastily redirect the conversation. "When did you see my sister? I didn't know she ever came down to the West End."

Twelve days, my mind echoes.

"Oh, it was a while ago." She scribbles something on the paper. "Two years, maybe more. I don't know if she was even at Forsyth yet. It was only once. She came in looking for someone and then left."

"Looking for who? One of these guys? Simon? Remy?" I don't even dare say Nick.

Humming, she spins the chair around and pulls out a drawer from the file cabinet, long, pointed nails flipping through the tabs. "Can't remember."

Mama B doesn't seem like the kind of woman who'd forget a pretty girl intruding on cutslut turf, but I've gone this far without letting on my interest in Tisha's whereabouts to these people. I'm not letting it slip now. That doesn't stop my mind from spinning and a thousand other questions forming. Why was she down here? Was she alone? Who the fuck was she looking for that would send her to Duke's territory?

Just another missing piece in the Leticia Lucia puzzle.

"I admit, it was surprising to see the Count's daughter waltzing through our doors." She lowers her chin, looking over her winged glasses at me. "But not as unexpected as Killian Payne trotting you out the other night." Looking back to the ancient computer monitor, she adds. "I definitely didn't see the Duchess thing coming."

There's judgment in her tone that sets me on edge. The lie comes easily. "That makes two of us."

"Just doesn't seem like you've got that certain Duke-branded flair." Her narrow shoulders lift. "No offense."

I give her a tight grin. "Yeah, because being a cum dumpster takes a lot of raw talent." Her eyes flash at me, and I coolly add, "No offense."

She clearly has something cutting to respond with, but a quiet tap on the door interrupts us. A doe-eyed redhead sweeps in, looking like something out of a skincare commercial. The strappy top she's wearing screams 'cutslut', but the jeans, sensible shoes, and overall soft demeanor makes me think otherwise. I recognize her as the girl from the photos around the office.

Mama's face lights up. "Hey, baby, you headed to class?"

"Yeah, organic chem starts in an hour. Trying to get a jumpstart on a lab assignment." She hands her a slip of paper. "Just wanted to drop off this receipt before I left."

"Thank you." Mama's eyes flick to me, the brightness in them dimming. "Verity, this is the new Duchess. Lavinia, my daughter, Verity."

Verity turns to look at me, but the spark of shock in her expression is short-lived. She quickly drops her gaze, shoulders curling inward. "Uh—hello." She reaches up to tuck her red hair behind an ear, looking awkward. "I, um, sent you some shoes and lotion, actually."

"Oh, thanks," I reply, voice caustically sunny. "It's been a lot of fun climbing sixteen flights of stairs in these bad boys." My heels make an energetic tap against the floor. "A lot of people want to kill me, but you..." I bring my hands together in a slow clap. "You're inspirational. Seriously, mad respect."

Mama B's face contorts with her scowl, but Verity visibly cringes. "Yeah, sorry about that. I just had them lying around, so I thought—"

I cut in, "You thought the bitch who stole Duchess right out from under you would be miserable in them." Nodding, I concede, "Well-played."

She cringes even harder at the realization I know. I perfectly remember the discussion between the Dukes the night they won me.

What happened to Verity? She was the obvious pick.

I can see what Remy meant before, about her being too breakable. She obviously hadn't put much thought about coming face-to-face with me. Her face blooms a bright scarlet and her hands start wringing. Single child, I'm guessing, and I bet she hasn't gotten away with a lie a day in her life. This is like punching a hamster. Not even enjoyable. Rolling my eyes, I put her out of her misery. "Look, don't sweat it. I would have done worse."

She exhales tightly. "I might have some old flip-flops in my trunk?"

I wave this away, fanning the magazine open once again. "Oh, Verity, don't give up now. Don't you want to see how long I last?"

She answers with a grimaced smile, giving her mom a little

finger wave before leaving the office, a dejected curve to her shoulders.

Mama B isn't amused. "My Verity is a good girl."

"I know." The grunting sounds of intense working-out float in through the door she'd left open. "Too good for them, probably. I did her a favor." I stand and look out the window that overlooks the ring. Sy is in the middle of it, shirtless and in a pair of shorts. He's not boxing—not in the traditional sense. His style is more MMA, but less dirty than Nick's. Arcing kicks and violent knee jabs with perfect posture. His back is rippled with hard muscle, skin coated in a thin layer of sweat. His opponent seems more of a partner than a foe, giving him pointers along the way. Something about him is familiar, but I can't quite place it. In any case, it becomes obvious very quickly that Sy is a powerful fighter.

"He's good," I say as much to myself as anyone.

"Nick might have the Bruin blood, but Sy is the real fighter in the family." The perfume and the clink of jewelry signals Mama's no longer in her seat but standing next to me, also watching. "It's not a game to him. It's a mission. The boy fights like the axis of the earth hinges on him winning."

"You'd think with all that exercise, he'd be a little less of a..." She raises her eyebrow and I finish, "...asshole."

She lets out a puff of laughter. "I'll tell you the same thing I told my daughter when she was being groomed for those shoes you're wearing." She looks at me, gum smacking. "Every powerful man has demons. The things they do to gain it leave a mark on their soul."

"They leave marks in other places, too." I touch the tattoo on my shoulder, face darkening. "Some visible. Some not."

Mama whips around, grabbing the hand on my shoulder blade. Her sharp nails dig into the soft skin on my wrist. "That mark may have been painful, Duchess, but it's also a gift. You're protected. Coveted. *Claimed*." She says it like it's a good thing, and when I look in her eye, I see that she means it. It's like what Nick keeps saying; I should be grateful. She lets me go, nodding. "Around here, girls your and Verity's age are one of two things: Spoken for, or spoken of. You didn't do my little girl any favors."

The truth is that until Leticia went missing, no one cared about what I was doing, who I belonged to, or what I wanted.

Now, I'm just like she said. Spoken of. Vulnerable. Suddenly, monsters are coming at me left and right, chomping for their pound of flesh.

A grunt from out on the floor draws my attention. Chest heaving, Sy wipes his brow with the back of his hand and spits blood on the floor. But he goes back in for another round, exactly how Mama B had described it. Like a man on a mission.

But that's the thing about powerful men and their demons.

They can be slayed.

I have twelve days to figure out how.

10

Simon

Swing, jab, kick.
Bruce dodges and darts around every attempt.
Slam!
"Goddamn it!" I shout, reeling from the hit. "Are you fucking serious?"

"You still asleep, Sy?" he taunts. If it were anyone else, I'd jump him and pummel that smug face for talking to me like that. Bruce is my regular sparring partner and a DKS, though. We've spent the last three years in a non-stop competition from our pledging and hazing days, to comparing our wins at Friday Night Fury. He even tried and *failed* to earn a Duke position, which has only increased our rivalry. Ever since, he's made it his life's mission to belittle and piss me off.

Mission accomplished.

"Heard you guys had a party the other night," he says, bouncing tiredly. It won't be hard to wear him out. I've got more stamina. "Maybe you need some coffee?"

Mostly, I know what I don't need: a distraction like Lavinia Lucia, all up in my space, being flaunted around by my brother, disappearing with my best friend, taking off her goddamn pants in my living room. I shake it off and get back on my toes, calculating my strategy.

You'd think rubbing one off right before I left the tower would've helped me focus. At least cut a little of the tension that's buzzing like a livewire under my skin. But nope. Still wound tighter than a priest's neck band.

The worst part of all this Duchess bullshit is that I'd shed the constant, ball-nagging lust for girls like that ages ago. It wasn't easy. Every guy would love nothing more than busting a fat load. But I'm not every guy. I watched as Remy, Nick, and even Tate got regular tail, chasing skirts like salivating dogs, not even caring that they were slaves to it.

But not me. Just like the lust for the fight, every time I feel that inkling of red-hot *want* creeping up my spine, I visualize the calm water of my inner ocean and throw myself into something productive, worthwhile. School work. Weightlifting. Training. Paperwork for my dad, data logging for my pops, yard work for my mom. It's not like girls never want some, because they do. They flirt and dress as whoreishly as possible, dancing around me like little painted slut-dolls, and I rebuff them all. Too mean, Tate used to tell me, eyes disapproving. But the meaner and colder I was, the less they'd try, because here's my truth:

I don't need pussy.

This is all I need.

My fist meeting Bruce's jaw with an audible click, sending him stumbling back. I bear down on him, slamming him back hard enough to hear the breath escape his lungs in a painful-sounding wheeze.

The commotion is enough to catch the attention of the other guys around the gym, and as I'm wiping the blood off my lip, they crowd around the edge of the ring. They're all DKS. The gym is members-only, other than a few trainers and younger, aspiring fighters. Potential DKS. Oh, and the cutsluts. They're always around, like I said. Little painted slut-dolls. I recognize faces from the party this weekend. It's one thing to let that bitch get in my head, but it's another to embarrass myself in front of these guys.

I—*punch*—fucking—*jab*—hate—*kick*—her—*slam!*

Bruce flails backwards, arms hooking in the elastic ropes around the ring to keep from falling completely. "Jesus." The guys behind him push him back to his feet, shouting out to the both of us. He grins. "That's more like it."

The energy escalates between us, the normal friendly competition sliding into an undercurrent of hostility. I don't like it. It's too close to how I used to be—unstable, like a live-wire. The biggest part of my training these last few years has been cutting off emotion from the fight. I never do it out of anger or frustration or resentment. Not anymore.

Only these last couple weeks, I've been feeling the fury slithering up my spine with every hit.

Bruce would have made a good Duke. He's got the leadership qualities and the drive. He did well enough, defacing the Barons' altar over the summer, but once we came back with the video of Lavinia—what we did to her, a King's daughter—it was over. Swinging at the Counts and the Lords in one fell swoop? No one could top that.

We also had an ace up our sleeve. Nick and his precious fucking blood legacy claimed the third spot right out from under him. I already said I was sorry, but it wasn't exactly sincere. Even after everything, even after Nick turning his back on us and becoming South Side trash, I'd still rather have him on my six than anyone else. I think Bruce could probably tell. The next time I saw him, he was full on overcompensating with his flashy new muscle car and sleek luxury watch, brushing it off like he couldn't care less. It's all a bit pathetic, the shows people put on.

His fist shoots out, but I dodge, narrowly missing the hit. I use the momentum to spin around and swipe his leg out from under him, sending him crashing to the mat. Whoops and cheers come from the guys around the ring, catcalling and taunting as I wipe the sweat from my forehead and prepare to take Bruce down a notch.

It's for his own fucking good. We've been equals for three years, but that's over. I outrank, overrule, and out-dominate him. He needs to know his place.

I pounce on him while he's still on the ground, legs pinning him to the mat. I hold up my fist, prepared to claim the win, but a shrill whistle cuts me off. It's a familiar and universal signal—Mama wants our attention.

"You got off easy," I tell him, making it clear I could've kicked his ass.

His chest rises and falls from exertion. "Whatever, bro."

I hop up, and despite the restless agitation whirling in my chest, offer him my hand, tugging him off the mat when he begrudgingly grabs it. One of the girls tosses me a towel and hands me a bottle of water. "Good job, Sy," she says, leaning over the rope. I ignore her tits, unscrew the cap, and peer over the ropes. Mama's standing a few feet away, my twitchy-looking Duchess at her side.

Mama B taps her wrist. "Sorry, Simon, but the clock's up. I've got a few errands to run." From the quick, sidelong glance she casts at Lavinia, it's clear this is a nice way of saying she's done babysitting for me.

Nodding, I let my head hang, catching my breath. "Bruce was about to get his ass handed to him, anyway. Probably a good time to stop."

"Fuck you, Perilini," he shouts, wiping his face. "I was plotting my comeback. If anyone here is lucky, it's your slow ass." His eyes dart over to Lavinia and a rankled heat runs up my spine.

Hooking the towel over my neck, I climb through the ropes and jump down to the floor. I give Mama a polite kiss on the cheek when I reach her. "Thanks for helping out."

Her mouth purses in an annoyed fashion, but I can see the affection in her eyes. "It's fine, but don't make it a habit. I've got a lot to do around here."

"I won't." It's a slight admonishment, but I'm aware of what she's really unhappy about. Lavinia was never supposed to be Duchess. Her daughter, Verity, was at the top of our list—unofficially, but Mama B had to know. I wasn't opposed to it. *Easy*. That's what Verity would have been. She understands the role of a Duchess, so there would have been no need to train her. She's certainly compliant. Her mother raised her to understand her place in the hierarchy of the system. She's like a little sister—not the kind of girl that gets my dick hard. Plus, it would have made Mama happy.

Instead, we're stuck with Lucia's bitch offspring.

I jerk my chin at Lavinia. "Come with me."

She follows, shivering a little. They keep the gym cold because working out is a sweaty business. The guys love the chill in here. It makes the cutsluts' nipples hard all the time. Lavinia is no different, futilely trying to cover her tits with her arms. It just pushes them together, forcing me to fight the urge to look. It's bad enough that I've been waking up in the mornings with soiled boxers like some goddamn middle schooler. Does she really have to traipse around like a cutslut in those strappy little shirts and shorts? *Fuck*.

Teeth grinding, I push the door to the locker room open a little too hard, causing it to slam back into the wall. I catch it on the swing back and hold it open, waiting. When all Lavinia does is shuffle to the side, I raise a hostile eyebrow. "What the fuck are you waiting for? Let's go."

She freezes, looking between me and the open door. "You want me to go into the men's locker room with you?"

The sound of running water and male voices echo off the tiles. "I need to shower and change," I tell her, like I'm talking to a very dumb child, "and you can't be trusted on your own."

"I'm not going anywhere," she insists, balking. "Nick and I worked out a deal."

"Yeah, well, you and I didn't."

We stare at one another for a long moment, and she drops her arms, likely thinking I'll cave at the sign of her hard nipples. I don't. Ultimately, she lets out a beleaguered huff and walks in. When she passes, I get both a waft of her shampoo and a high-definition view of her ass cheeks shifting beneath shiny, tight fabric. Like a dog to a pork chop, my dick immediately perks to attention, making my fists clench.

This, I remind myself, is Nick's fucking fault.

Silently seething, I direct her to the row of lockers, halfway considering if grabbing her and tossing her into them would make my situation better or worse. Figures I'd have a freak libido to go with my freak of a dick.

Ignorant to my inner turmoil, she leans against the metal doors, her tight little body a deceptively casual curve. It takes just as much discipline to tear my eyes away from the jut of her hips as it did to let Bruce up before. Fighting and fucking. My brain keeps trying to get me to crack, but I won't. I imagine my ocean, tucking it all beneath the surface of the waves.

I'm better than this.

I open my locker and begin pulling out my stuff, desperately trying to think of anything else. Bruce's boisterous laugh bounces off the walls, which is a useful distraction. He's definitely still pumped from the fight. Turning away from Lavinia, I drop my shorts and hastily wrap a towel around my waist. I don't need any more commentary on what's swinging between my legs.

Sure enough, when I spin back to her, she's wide-eyed and pointedly looking at anything but me. "That guy you were fighting. He was with Rath when I—when they brought me here." She touches her neck, casting a cagey glance toward his voice.

"Yes," I confirm, just feeling more pissed about Nick going behind our back, ordering DKS to do his dick's bidding. "Unlike other people, Bruce does what he's told."

She scowls at the floor. "And what am I supposed to be doing?"

"Sit," I tell her, pointing to the bench. "And don't fucking move or I'll make one of the fighters supervise." She scowls, dropping heavily on the bench, head turned so far away from my crotch that I can see the tendon in her neck straining.

I stalk around the bank of lockers to the showers and duck myself under the hot water, making it quick. I scrub off the sweat and blood, struggling to clear my mind of her hips and ass and tits, but it's frustratingly difficult to disconnect. Usually, I'm pretty good at distracting myself from the disgusting swell of need that crops up every now and then. Problem being, ever since that night we broke into the brothel, 'every now and then' has turned into a daily war against my dick. I might not want to fuck, but my cock?

It twitches halfway to life under the spray of the shower like an excited puppy.

My dick is like a fucking dowsing rod for pussy all of a sudden.

Two shower heads away, Bruce turns off the water and says, "The new Duchess is pretty hot." He dries off with a white towel. "Lucia or not, I'd fuck her."

I turn the handles, bringing the water to a halt. "You'd fuck a warm mattress."

"Who says it needs to be warm?" Bruce laughs, but I can hear the thread of interest in his voice when he glances back toward the lockers. "Seriously, though. I got a nice feel of her when I put that tracker in, and I saw the video. Your brother broke her in nice and hard, but what about you? You feed her that monster yet? Torn her up?"

"She's a cutslut, minus any of the charm. I'm not putting my dick into Count trash." I scrub my hair with a towel. "You and my idiot brother might be indiscriminate, but I actually have standards."

Bruce snorts, because he's heard my song and dance before. It's true, though. All these guys give it up for free, but dick is a gift. They think it's because I'm so unnaturally hung, but they're wrong. Truth is, bitches around here talk a mean game about wanting a monster dick, but when push comes to shove, they can't handle it.

And when they can't handle it, it's never *their* fault, is it?

Before I can get started, Bruce walks out of the shower stall, passing the row where Lavinia is waiting. Her expression is passive, but her shoulders are tense, eyes on alert. I cut down the row back to my locker and notice her gaze darting over my shoulder, flashing in alarm. I look back and see Bruce leaning against the door to his locker, buck-naked, dick semi-erect between his legs as he eyefucks her.

"Come on, man." He reaches down to fist himself. "If you're not going to fuck her, how about giving me a shot? I'll stretch her out, get it ready for you."

Snorting, I shove my toiletry bag into the locker. "First of all, Nick's bigger than you."

Bruce scoffs, "Not fucking likely," but I talk over him.

"Secondly, the Duchess' pussy is for Dukes only. You didn't make the cut." It's a low blow, but I'm not feeling generous today. My skin feels hot, my balls tight enough to ache. The fight, this *bitch*. The whole damn thing has me on edge like an exposed nerve, and no matter how much I jack off, I can't seem to purge it.

"How about we fight for it," Bruce suggests, visibly changing tack. "Winner takes all."

"How about you use that shining personality of yours and get your own pussy," I reply, knowing good and well Bruce has worked his way through the cutsluts a dozen times over. That information pisses me off even more. The girls want his cock. Crave it. They don't act interested only to look at him like he's a freak when the time comes to pony up.

Two other guys have wandered over by this point: Dave, in a pair of skin-tight black boxer briefs, and Kent, who isn't even bothering to cover his nakedness with the towel he's got hanging around his neck. DKS snaps to the promise of a winner-takes-all like moths to a flame, but I'm not in the mood to compete—certainly not for this piece of trash. They're all waiting around for me to answer and there's something about the fact Bruce has to ask—that he needs my permission before he lays a hand on Lavinia—that makes me pause, considering.

"Give me that watch you keep flashing around," I decide, nodding at his locker, "and I'll let you have a go. Assuming you can handle her."

"What?" Lavinia gasps, the first words she's spoken since we came in here. "You can't be fucking serious!"

I ignore her. "Just stay away from her ass. Remy's already called dibs on it, so it's off-limits."

"Don't worry, babe," Bruce says, reaching into his locker for the watch and tossing it to me. "I can handle you just fine."

I catch the watch with a skilled snatch from the air, doing my best to hide my surprise. It's a really nice watch. The kind of watch douchebags like Bruce won't even call a watch. They call it a 'time-piece'. I weigh it in my hand. There's no way she's worth it. But the bloodless, contorted, horrified thing her face is doing? That sure as hell is.

She's off the bench in a heartbeat, but Bruce has got killer instincts. He leaps over the bench, dick swinging, and easily pins her against the metal door. Lavinia gets a knee up, but he blocks it. Her teeth come next.

"Oh, by the way," I say casually, "she's a fighter."

I reach for my boxers, listening to the sound of their bodies slamming against the metal doors. "Jesus," he grunts. "Grab her arms, will ya?"

I know he's not talking to me, and that's confirmed when Dave and Kent both get their hands on her—one on each side. I yank up my shorts while she continues fighting, heavily outnumbered. Still, she's wild enough that they have to wrangle her to the hard floor. Bruce straddles her hips and pushes up her shirt, exposing her black sheer bra. Yanking the cups down, he fans his hands over her tits, squeezing them tightly.

"I think you like it rough, don't you?" Bruce says, rocking his hips against the leather pants.

She thrashes, some unholy marriage of a growl and a shriek clawing its way from her strained throat, and for a moment, I'm struck with a strange sense of disappointment. *She should be better.* She's our Duchess, for fuck's sake. She's supposed to be strong and unyielding. A flash of memory—that night at the Hideaway—grips me like a vice. She'd been held down by two men then, too. Lavinia's full of piss and vinegar, but in the end, she's just like any other girl. Small. Weak. Easily dominated. I remember the shape of her beneath my hands all too well. The way she looked while taking my brother's cock. How she laid so still for Remy and me as we jerked our dicks over her used cunt.

My cock fills inside my boxers, hard and thick, and there's no stopping it. Not while I'm watching Bruce pant like a dog, dragging down the waistband of her tight pants. Not while I watch the other two, eyes sparking in anticipation and mirth as they wrestle her into submission. Not while I watch her snap and grunt and detonate with panicked fury.

Not while I imagine—*crave*—being in Bruce's place.

"Get out." The words are a low rasp, barely audible. Dave laughs as Bruce pries her knees apart. I slam my fist into the metal locker, barking, "Get the fuck out!"

Dave and Kent drop her arms immediately, obediently following my directive. Bruce is too caught up in the fun, so I lunge at him, hoisting him off her body and tossing him across the room. "Are you fucking deaf?!" Unthinkingly, I toss him his watch, not caring when he jumps to his feet, muscles coiled tight. "Get out."

"What the fuck, Perilini?"

I march toward him, flinging a towel into his chest. "Don't make me say it a third time."

He drags in a long, hard breath, nostrils flaring wide. "She won't be any good after you've had her, anyway."

A moment later, it's just me and her. The locker room thrust into a charged silence. I press my palms against the door and lean my weight on them, panting as I try to shove the impulses down. *Why is this so goddamn difficult?* Years, and I've been fine. Now, I can feel that primal, animalistic need clawing its way up, and it's almost as if it doesn't care what it gets—fighting or fucking—but it's going to get something. I turn to face her, my cock blistering hot, skin pulled taut. I'm almost afraid to touch it out of fear that I'll come.

I'm better than this.

I am.

But she isn't.

Lavinia scrambles to her feet, tugging her shirt down with one hand while the other pulls her pants up. "You son of a bitch!" she starts, face a vivid, scarlet red, but I don't let her continue.

"You did this," I hiss, pointing to the obscene tent in my boxers as I stalk toward her. She backs away from me, but suddenly bumps up against a locker, nowhere to run. "You've been doing it for days! Making me feel this... this fucking..." But I can't find a word for it.

Apparently, she can. "You're blaming me for being a horny freak?!"

Freak.

I grab a fistful of her hair, chest swelling in fury. "You bitches always go for that word, don't you? You want to know why? It's because you're all the same."

Her neck tightens as she strains away, eyes looking just as enraged as I feel. "It's because it's true, and you know it," she sneers, flashing her teeth. "I bet people think you're the normal one out of the three of you, but they're wrong. You're the most fucked-up."

My other fist rears back, ready to feel her bone beneath my knuckles, but when I snap it forward, I stop a bare inch from making contact. Fighting and fucking, fucking and fighting.

Her body might go rigid, but she doesn't move.

Doesn't flinch.

I'm not going to wail on a girl a quarter of my size.

"You have two options." Chest jerking up and down with angry breaths, I shove the top of her head down, forcing her to her knees. "Either you get rid of this," I say, pushing her cheek into my hard-on. "Or I'll bring them back in here and let them have free rein."

She tries to pull away, straining against my hold on her scalp. "If you're asking me who'd I rather fuck, then you might as well call them back in. I'm not impaling myself on your horse dick!"

"Then use your mouth!" I bark, shoving the elastic waistband down. "You made it happen. You take it away!"

She breathes hard, eyes fixed to some vague point behind me, refusing to even make eye-contact with my dick. "I'll choke." My dick reacts to that possibility with an excited twitch that sends pre-cum dribbling from the tip. Her eyes jump to the motion, face contorting in outrage. "Oh my god, you'd get off on that, you fucking—"

I buck my hips, the tip of my dick rubbing a wet trail over her cheek. "I guarantee you it'd be better than taking all three of them."

"Been there, done that," she snarls, recoiling venomously from the head of my dick. She eyes it with skepticism, like she's unsure if she can take it.

"Not at the same time," I threaten. When she doesn't argue back, I grab the back of her neck and pull her forward, ordering, "*Open.*"

I tighten my grip on her neck, a nonverbal way of letting her know that I *will* retaliate if she does something stupid. Still, it takes a long moment for her face to shift. It's a subtle change—the crumple of her brow, the gleam of agony in her eyes—and she hides it fast enough, shuttering her expression. But I still catch it.

She's accepting her loss.

The festering heat inside my chest swells at the knowledge.

Yes.

Know your place.

Slowly, her pink lips part just enough for me to detect the wet flash of her tongue behind her teeth. Too high on the buzz to wait, I thrust against her mouth, the head of my dick slotting into the gap. Her cheeks scrunch into a grimace, but I barely notice it, too busy testing by pushing in further, finally understanding what it means to feel a hot, slippery tongue against my leaking cock head. I grab either side of her head and hold her there, soaking it in. The sight of her mouth wrapped around it—even just the tip—is almost enough to send me over the edge.

I've gotten handjobs before. Back in high school, when I was still under the delusion that sex meant something, the girls used to talk a big game, but would always end up chickening out. They'd wrap their fists around my shaft and give me half-cringing jerks, like they were just praying to god I'd blow my load and do them the mercy of not expecting anything more.

But none of them would ever dream about sucking me.

It'd be a joke to think this was any better than those hand jobs, because Lavinia barely does anything. She closes her lips around me, but keeps her tongue still, hands coming out to brace against my hips when I thrust against it, coming with a tight, shaken sound.

I don't mean to. It's just the sight of her lips wrapped around me. The knowledge that she's holding me back, but I could easily force my way into the back of her throat.

In the end, I realize I've squandered it.

As she flings herself away, spitting a thick wad of my cum onto the floor, sputtering messily, that's the first thought that hits me.

I should have pushed her further, made it last longer, forced every drop of my spunk down her throat. It's like when I saw her pussy that night bathed in our cum. It's all I've been able to think about, and now, *this* is all I'm going to be able to think about: her mouth, those lips, and the way she looked on her knees.

One thing it doesn't change is how much I fucking hate her for it.

11

Lavinia

The drive back to the tower is spent in a tense, bleak silence. Sweat beads up on my forehead. I can feel it settling into my lower back. Sy never so much as glanced at me, sitting stiffly behind the wheel. He drives like a robot, barely moving, eerily efficient. For no tangible reason, I get the sense he's avoiding the urge to look over at me. Maybe it's the subtle twitch below his eye or the way his fingers keep tightening around the steering wheel, knuckles going white.

The small, desperate sound he made when he came is still thumping around in my head.

"Roll down the window." It's a desperate demand that shatters the silence like a grenade. I frantically flip the up-down button, but nothing happens—locked. I force myself to face him. "Roll down the goddamn window before I puke your cum all over the dash."

Whirrrrr

The blast of air is humid but still welcome. I breathe in and out, trying to keep the nausea at bay. As much as I'd like to hurl spunk all over Sy's spotless SUV, I don't really want to taste it all over again.

It's not like I've never sucked a cock before. It's not even like I've never been forced to taste another guy's jizz, because before that night at the Hideaway, Nick had cornered me. Once—last Christmas. Daniel had given me to him as a 'bonus'. No touching—those were the rules—but Nick didn't have to touch me to leave his mark. He made me watch as he jacked off over my face, covering my mouth in his cum. It was the only time, but it was enough that Daniel made a new rule; Nick could never be alone with me again. Nick just enjoyed it too much, I guess. He took it and turned it into something that didn't exist by deciding I was his.

Must run in the family.

I can still sense Sy in the hinge of my jaw, the strained invasion of a too-big, uninvited obtrusion. At least Nick hadn't forced his cock inside. At least he hadn't made me feel the shape of him on my tongue, swollen and perverse. Nick might be hung, but Sy's is grotesque.

"Oh god." Another wave of nausea rolls over me, and I stick my head out the window like a dog.

"Give me a break," he mutters. "You sucked dick for three whole seconds and you barely swallowed anything. Fucking drama queen. I should've just let Bruce have you."

"Yeah, maybe you should have," I bite back. "At least he's not a mutant."

The car screeches to a stop, flinging my head into the window's gutter. Before I can recover, a hand grips around my throat and drags me back in.

"One day, bitches like you are going to realize that a dick like mine is too good for your rancid, used-up cunts." Lip curling, he adds, "*Not* the other way around." He gives me a shove, face set into a tight scowl. "And here I thought living at a whorehouse for a year would teach you a thing or two about handling a real man. Guess I'm wrong."

"A real man?!" I bark out a wheeze of a laugh. "You're a freak and a goddamn rapist."

His fingers tighten around my throat, nostrils flaring. "I gave you a choice. Don't whine to me because you can't handle the consequences of your own decisions."

I swear to god, these men have been living in their own alternate universe. I knew the Royals were bad. I knew their ideas were antiquated and fucked up, but the bitter rage rolling off this one is more than I can handle.

We stare at one another for a beat, his fingers squeezing against my throat, and I get the distinct impression that he'd love nothing better than to crush my windpipe and be done with me for good. I fight to swallow, to breathe, and I think he may just kill me here and now. If I was a suicidal bitch, I would spit in his face.

But the time for that is done.

I grab his hand, wedging my fingers between our skin, and grind out, "You'll have to answer to your brother if you kill me."

His jaw clenches, and then he abruptly releases me. Again, I grapple for air, slowly taking it in as he shifts the car into gear. "You have no idea," his fingers constrict around the steering wheel, "no *fucking* idea how much of a rapist I'm *not*." He flicks two belligerent, icy eyes at me. "Lords like to conquer their pussy. Barons like it all solemn and sacrificial, because it makes them feel like it's worth something. Princes? To them, pussy is a tool that gives their sorry asses some purpose. And Counts... well, you know what Counts think of theirs." He slides me a menacing look. "But Dukes are better. We don't take our pussy, we win it. To the victor go the spoils." There's a tense beat of silence before he goes on, "I could have ripped my way into so much pussy these last three years. Pussy that's attached to someone who wouldn't sit in my passenger seat whining about it afterward. But I haven't. Not once. And do you want to know why?"

Unthinkingly, I lob back, "You love yourself too much to cheat on your own right hand?"

Head shaking, he coldly answers, "Because none of you are

worth fighting for. You're all fake. Every piece of ass in this town is just looking for an angle to get something—you most of all."

Bristling, I ask, "What the hell is that supposed to mean? I never asked to be—"

"You think I don't see what you're doing to my brother?" He glances at me, even though it's clear he doesn't want my answer. "This little agreement you have? Look at everything you are. Lucia's daughter, the Kings' asset, murder suspect, Countess in the making. Nick might be too busy chasing your skirt to see it, but I'm not." His smile is bitter and grim. "You're just a Daniel with tits."

I blink, staring unseeingly through the windshield as we zip past a slow station wagon.

A Daniel with tits.

Doesn't sound too bad, really. "You talk a lot of shit about being above the game for someone who just forced his donkey dick into my mouth."

"That," he bites out, "was a mistake."

I give a disbelieving laugh. "A mistake? Did you trip and bust your nut down my throat? Because that's not how I remember it." Staring out my window, I watch the world whip by. "You're just a Nick without any of the finesse."

He doesn't answer for a long time. We pass the turnoff for the Avenue and start heading toward campus, passing a fender bender, cutting through the warehouses of the West End. "It won't happen again," he eventually says, voice low and hard. The funny thing is, he actually sounds like he believes it.

I don't have that luxury.

～

. . .

WHEN WE GET BACK, loud bass thrums from behind Remy's closed door. Sy goes straight to the kitchen and fills up a glass of water. Then he walks to Remy's door and pounds on it. I watch from the kitchen archway, taking off my shoes as he waits, impatient, shifting from foot to foot until he beats his fist on the door again. A moment later, the music decreases slightly, and the door opens a small crack. The shock of platinum hair appears first, then Remy's sharp cheekbones.

"I'm busy."

"Not too busy for this." Sy gives him the glass of water and then holds out a palm. I can't see what he's holding, but Remy frowns down at it. Firmly, Sy adds, "You promised."

"Fine." Remy takes whatever it is—something small—and pops it in his mouth. *Oh. Medicine. Right.* Remy takes the glass of water next, throwing it back. His throat bobs with three hard swallows before handing the glass back to Sy. "I need to get back to work." He shuts the door, leaving Sy standing there with a hung expression.

Instantly, the music is back to the same thrum as before, reverberating obnoxiously through the thin walls. Continuing to ignore me completely, Sy drops the glass off at the kitchen before disappearing into his own bedroom.

I stand there, waiting to be told what to do, where to go, but Nick... isn't here. He still hasn't returned from class or whatever he's up to, and for the first time in months, I'm semi-alone, unrestrained, in a room bigger than a shoebox. Naturally, my first instinct is to bolt. See how far I can get. There's a reason Nick calls me his 'Little Bird.' That urge to fly away is imprinted in me, as imbued into my flesh as the unfinished serpent on my leg.

But Nick was right.

It may be time for me to adjust my plan. To use the Dukes. To be his new Daniel. To embrace what being a Lucia is. I've lived through my father's wrath, Daniel's imprisonment, that awful night at the brothel, and now Sy.

They won't break me.

Twelve days.

The first thing I do is grab a handful of clean clothes from the cutslut pile and lock myself in the bathroom. I strip, catching a glimpse of myself in the bathroom mirror. I'm too skinny and the bruises from those two nights in the elevator haven't faded yet. I washed off Remy's marker ink last night, but even though I barely had his design on me for more than fifteen hours, it somehow feels strange to look down and see the original, shitty art that had made him so outraged. I don't... miss it, necessarily. His artwork is good, but Dahmer levels of disturbing. The dragon was detailed and elaborate—undeniably beautiful—but the pointed tail stabbing at my cunt?

It just makes me remember the orgasm he gave me in his room.

I'm starting to get it now.

To Royal men, sex is a weapon just as much as an indulgence, and these three are no different. Sy might think the Dukes are better or above it, but he's kidding himself. In the end, it's all about power and ownership. It'll only feel good when they want it to. The problem is, they know how to wield it.

I mean, other than Sy, who probably couldn't find a clit with a compass and a map.

Nick and Remy, though? I have to remember that they touch to hurt, even when it feels good.

I step under the sputtering spray of the shower and start scrubbing the afternoon from my flesh. The semen and sweat, the dirt and deceit. Facing the nozzle, I let the hot water blast on my face, burning away the strained sense memory of Sy forcing his way inside. I don't move until it runs cold, then step out, freezing at the sight of the sink.

There are four toothbrushes.

I tilt my head, staring at the little cup holding them all. It's an odd, jarring display of unification, as if someone has stripped the Dukes and me down to the bare essentials and shoved us together on the back of this sink.

If only Leticia could see me now. We fought over everything.

From as early as I can remember, she was glaring at me, trying to put me in my place. In some fundamental, inexplicable way, there just wasn't space for both of us. My whole childhood was spent in a struggle to extend my arms—to spread myself out—but my sister was always there to shove them back to my sides. She'd get really into it, too. Every time I thought I'd found a footing, she'd find some creative way to push me back down. Lying to our father about something I'd done, planting evidence in my bedroom, even going so far as to strike her own cheek just to blame me. That's the thing about Leticia. She didn't mind getting hurt if it meant bringing me down a peg. I suppose we've always had that in common.

When I'm dressed in my hand-me-down panties, a black tank, and a pair of cut-off shorts, I head back into the main room and go up to the loft. In the light of day, not only does it smell like a dog lives up there, it looks like it, too. The dirty blanket I slept on is twisted on the floor, and a gnawed shell of a tennis ball is abandoned in the corner. It's dusty, drafty, and mostly bare, but strangely, I find it doesn't matter. It has an open, lofty feel. Wide open, with no tight walls or locks, and a clear, vast view of the living area, including the front door. The glass in the clock is not transparent—clouded with dirt and weather residue—but it provides a nice amount of light. It'd be perfect for reading. I rest my elbows on the railing and take a deep breath, surveying the area.

If it didn't mean being a slave to three rapey pieces of shit, this might actually be my dream home.

I head back down the spiral staircase, and just as I hit the bottom, Remy's door flies open. The same loud, bass-thumping music spills into the common area as he steps out, freezing at the sight of me. His wild eyes are underscored with dark bruises beneath them, cheeks pale and gaunt. He looks more like a strung-out Avenue junkie than a Royal. Face blank, his gaze drops to my leg, fixing there for a long stretch of cold silence.

I clear my throat. "Do you know if there's a broom?"

He jerks at the sound of my voice, eyes flying up to mine. "A broom?"

Right. I doubt he's ever swept a floor in his whole life. "Cleaning supplies," I elaborate, nodding upward. "So I can straighten up around here."

The corner of his mouth curls. "What are you, Cinderella?"

I shrug. "If you think I'm bad, you should see my fairy godmother." Especially after what happened with Sy, Mrs. Crane's words from Friday are still fresh in my mind.

"You may have to spread your legs for them, suck their dicks, cook their food, and wash their clothes. So what?"

Remy gives me a couple of slow blinks before turning toward the kitchen. I follow wordlessly, watching the broad line of his shoulders shifting beneath the fabric of a faded and worn band t-shirt as he stops in front of a door, gesturing limply to its antique knob.

I wait until he's turned toward the fridge, reaching in to grab a sports drink, before opening the closet—well, a pantry, I discover. Small. Cramped. Enclosed. Swallowing hard, I ease my head inside, fingers clutching the jamb as I inspect the contents. There are canned goods, bags, containers of rice, and sure enough, tucked to the side is a collection of supplies. I spy a bottle of disinfectant, a pair of rubber gloves, and sponges.

"Nick and Sy's mom brought those over." I whirl around, surprised to find Remy so close, and instantly fling myself away from the space. Remy doesn't miss how tense I've become, eyes taking in my posture. "Can't wait to see what she says about you."

I open my mouth to respond, but he's already halfway to his room, guzzling down the red drink, slamming his door behind him.

My breath gusts out in a loud, relieved exhale.

I turn back to the pantry, fidgety at the thought of walking inside, but distracted by the little collection of supplies. So Nick and Simon have a mother who cares enough to bring them these things. Does she care about them holding a woman captive for their own sexual pleasure and abuse? Probably not. She was Duchess back in her day. She's likely one more woman I'll have to suffer a lecture about being lucky from.

I gather everything I can hold in my arms, carrying it all up to the loft. I spend the rest of the afternoon and evening scrubbing it down from top to bottom, getting into every nook and crevice. I toss the dog blanket and the old toys into the trash. I know they want to treat me like an animal, but there's a line I won't cross.

It takes me a while, but slowly it comes together. I find a few extra blankets and pillows in a different closet and arrange them in a pallet on the floor. I carry the cutslut clothes up to the loft and arrange them neatly. A dresser would be nice, or even a mattress or a chair. Any of those would also imply that I'm staying.

Twelve days.

It's late when I finish. Neither Simon nor Remy have left their rooms. Nick hasn't returned, and that does make me apprehensive. Class was obviously over hours ago, which means maybe he went to collect the box from my father. It also means that maybe he got caught.

I'm not sure which one makes me more excited. Getting the box or him getting caught. Both have their positives. I settle in my bed —ignoring the hard, worn wood a few layers below, and take a deep breath. Soon enough, we'll know which turns out to be true. Whichever it is, my father is always the one holding all the cards.

12

Nick

The Kings have beef that goes back to the dark ages, but for some reason, they all live in the same place, buying and inheriting their homes in the glitzy suburbs north of Forsyth. If anyone asks, the Kings will be the first to insist that it's not *true* North Side, because it's well outside of territory. Naturally. They'd never want to raise their families in the muck they've created. What they don't realize is that it's all the same to the rest of us—the foot soldiers, the worker bees, the ones who put our asses on the line for it all. To us, north is north.

Point being, Lionel Lucia has the unique privilege of playing both sides. When it benefits him, he'll say he doesn't live in North Side. He's just a guy looking to give his family a nice life, and that's where all the best opportunities lie. But when he wants to jack off his henchmen and Royals, he'll say he lives a Northern life, through and through. The worst part is that neither is entirely disingenu-ous. Count money is coated in drugs, blood, and sex, traded in dark alleys and on shitty street corners. It's natural he'd raise his family in an ostentatious McMansion smack in the middle of the suburbs. On the other hand, Counts are responsible for the North Side's prosperity. While Kings like Daniel and Saul are content to take the money from their own respective territories, the Counts and Princes take their money from other places, leaving the North Side and the East End to thrive off it. Kind of shitty, considering.

I park the car three blocks over and travel to the gated community by foot. The streets here are too quiet—too serene—for my shitty car to go unnoticed. It's not the first time I've been here for sketchy business, but it's the first time I've done it in service of pussy.

When I get through the main perimeter fence, I pause for a second to really appreciate this fact.

Is she worth it?

The negotiating, the compromising, the constant fucking sting of rejection when she turns away from me? But I already know the answer: It doesn't matter.

She's mine.

Her body is mine, her attention is mine, and like it or not, her problems are mine. Royals are historically shit at keeping their women, but not me. If keeping her was as easy as dicking her down raw and rough, then what would be the point? No, keeping Lavinia Lucia is going to mean getting my hands bloody. And, I realize as I jump over the wrought-iron fence surrounding the Lucia compound, I've possibly missed it. Daniel kept me in rough work for a long time, and I've spent the whole summer restless and itching for something to do. It's obvious Saul doesn't quite trust us —or me, specifically—enough to dole out the Dukes' dirty work yet. I guess it's up to me to make my own trouble. Well, with a little help from my Duchess.

"There's a foot soldier that walks around the property. Fifteen-minute intervals," she explained, showing me a hand-drawn map. *"On Tuesdays and Fridays at six sharp, he holds a meeting for Count business. No one else knows, but he turns all surveillance off for it. That's your window."*

I wait four minutes before the guard shows. He's a big guy, broad shouldered, and I instinctively touch the gun holstered to my side, poised to pull it if I need to. Luckily, he lumbers by, completely unaware, and I start the timer on my watch. Once he's out of sight, I dart from tree to tree, keeping to the shadows. There's a pool out back, and I can make out the outline of a miniature-sized replica of the house. I tilt my head as I inspect it. A playhouse? A massive swing set sits abandoned in the corner. Looking at this, you'd almost think Lionel gave more than half a shit about his two daughters, except one's vanished and the other's been sold.

I stop at the back door and look at the numbers I inked on my wrist hidden below the edge of my glove. The code Lavinia gave me to the backdoor servant's entrance. *"They'll be in his study,"* she told me. *"There's a back stairway off the kitchen..."* She gave me directions to her room from there. *"In and out. He'll never know you're there."*

I press in the series of numbers, pausing before I push the last one. I'm not so hypnotized by her pussy that I haven't considered the possibility of this being a set-up. Lucia's men could be waiting to ambush me. It'd be a smart move; one I would orchestrate myself if needed. Maybe all of this is an elaborate ruse to take out the Dukes. I think back to the conversation with Lavinia—the very specific item she asked for—and decide there's something going on here. Something bigger than a rivalry between Dukes and Counts.

Guess I'm about to find out.

I stab the final number on the pad with my gloved finger.

Other than the sound of the bolt unlocking, nothing happens.

I wait for a tense beat before turning the knob.

I step in carefully, quietly, casting my eyes around the kitchen. It's immaculately clean, every surface sparkling in the low light. The first step I take is cautious, mind racing with the knowledge that Counts are here, somewhere in the house.

Her directions are easy enough to follow, so I turn toward the staircase to the right of the backdoor. I take the steps two at a time, avoiding the fifth step, which—according to her—is squeaky as hell. On the landing, I stick close to the right side. The left is open, a balcony that overlooks the study below. Warm light casts up to the vaulted ceilings. I don't risk looking down, but I do freeze when I hear them. Voices.

"Are you suggesting I stop looking?" Lionel. His voice is low and lethal, and it's Perez's familiar voice that answers.

"I'm saying we should be prepared."

I don't need to be down there to feel the tension between them. It's a good enough distraction, allowing me to continue on, up the stairs and to the second floor landing.

"There are three doors on the left side. Two on the right. My room is the second door on the right."

The door opens with no problem, and I duck inside, carefully closing and locking it behind me. I take out my phone, flipping on the flashlight. It's not until I'm in here, surrounded by her things, her scent, that I realize I'm in a treasure trove of Lavinia-related things. It's ravenous, this hunger uncoiling inside of me, desperate to clutch at anything of her. I inhale deeply, catching the scent of a girl I never knew.

"Gotcha, Little Bird," I whisper, flashing the light over her dresser. It's spotless, recently dusted. I run my fingertip over the smooth, dark mahogany of a jewelry box. When I lift it open, a figurine of a ballerina whirrs to life, spinning. Hastily, I close it. A bottle of perfume sits beside it and I can't help but pick it up, lifting it to my nose for a furtive sniff. Lavender. Interesting. There's a single tube of lipstick on the middle of the dresser, conspicuous in its solitude. I pick it up and pull off the top, revealing a bright crimson color. I place it back on the surface, lifting my attention to the mirror. Tucked into the edge are various mementos. Among them are ticket stubs to concerts that took place two-to-five years ago. Pop, punk, rap. Lavinia didn't seem to be too picky, but I bet it was all the same. Fast, energetic, alive.

And then there are the photos.

One is of a group of high school-aged kids. It takes me a long moment to find her, crouching in front of the group with her mouth opened wide, her crimson lips framing a pink, pierced tongue. I lick my own lips reflexively, imagining that stud against my cock. Shame she didn't keep the piercing.

Another photo is of two girls, a little older. They're both dressed in private school uniforms, plaid skirts and white shirts hidden beneath bright red sweater vests. They look similar, one smiling, one not. That's how I know which is Lavinia. That sharp fuck-you frown. I've seen it enough. Her features are less defined here, the subtle hint of fading baby fat still curving her cheeks, but she was still fucking hot.

I return the photo and open the top dresser drawer. Bingo. An underwear drawer can tell you everything you need to know about a girl. It's mostly black and white panties, plus a few bras with lace edging. I lift a pair of the panties to my nose, smelling the clean, soft fabric. She may not have been a virgin when I took her, but this drawer tells me she's not experienced. There's nothing special or overtly sexy—although, add in the school-girl attire and a pair of white cotton panties and my spank bank is full.

I grab a few pairs and shove them in my backpack. She'd bargained for clothes to wear around the tower, and I magnanimously oblige, adding in shirts and pants.

I turn and shift my focus to the bed. It's as outlandish as everything else in this house. Massive dark wood with spindles on each of the corners sits beneath an ornate canopy. The shithole Crane motel and Velvet Hideaway were definitely a downgrade for our Duchess. No wonder she's so bitter. She might not have been her daddy's favorite, but she still grew up like a spoiled little Countess.

At the foot of the bed is an intricately carved cedar chest. She hadn't asked for a blanket, but, hey. Am I not benevolent? I open it up, intending to find some bedding, linens, maybe even pillows, but instead I find the most Lavinia thing of all.

Jack-shit.

I shine the light in there before closing it, idly noting that it looks pretty beat up compared to the opulent polish of the outside. That's a Count for you.

I approach the bedside table next, sliding open the drawer.

Inside are three books, one a novel, a page marked with a candy wrapper. Every time I went to see her at the Hideaway, she had some god-fucking-awful book nearby. The novel is *Dead Souls*, so... you know. Light reading. There's also a thinner, well-worn book that looks like it was written for a middle schooler. There's a yawning kitten on the front and the title '*A Practical Approach to Kittens*'. The last book is...

I squint at the title.

A lawn mower maintenance manual?

Shrugging, I grab all three and shove them in the backpack. I flash my light around the drawer, still feeling that gaping hunger inside of me—still starved for all her secrets—and spot something wrapped in a baby-blue hand towel. Pulling it out, it jumps to life, humming in my hand.

Jackpot.

I stare at the little orb, mouth spreading into a smirk. I look over at the bed, cock growing hard as I imagine her on it, legs spread wide as she got off—*right there*. It happened between those sheets, her pussy dripping as she thought of getting fucked. I push out an even breath, forcing myself to hold that thought for later. A vibrator. Maybe our girl has a few more urges than she lets on. That, too, goes in the bag.

She didn't ask for this stuff, but now that I've worn her down and got her to negotiate, it's not going to hurt to have a few more pieces of leverage up my sleeve.

Satisfied, I focus on the main event.

I drop to the floor, pulling back the edge of the rug and shucking off a glove. Underneath, I spread my hand over the floorboards, looking for the right one. "*The edge is slightly uneven; your nails will catch on it. Pull on it and it'll lift up.*"

Over and over, I do like she said, searching for the catch, but I can't find it. I'm about to say fuck it all—I've got everything I need—when the tip of my pinky snags an uneven edge. Using my stubby fingernails, I finally gain purchase, lifting the corner up and removing one board and then the other.

Inside is a wooden box—a cigar box. The scent of stale tobacco wafts out of the hole, bringing back a sudden sense of memory of my Pops' office. Shaking myself out of it, I realize it's wrapped in an intricate web of colorful elastic bands. Someone else might assume they're placed randomly, but I know better. This is a jacked-up DIY security system. I bet she knows each color and orientation, every band's exact placement, just as solid as a password. I shake it, hearing the contents rattle inside, but I don't have the time to snap a picture and recreate the pattern of the bands after I've opened it.

Annoyed, I shove the whole thing in my backpack and zip it up.

I check the time. Eleven minutes. If I get down there fast enough, I can make the first fifteen minute security sweep. Double checking to make sure everything is back in place, I head to the door, pausing in front of the mirror.

I can't say what makes me do it. Maybe it's the way Lavinia looked when she woke up that morning, all rumpled and lost. She probably thinks she hides it well enough, wrapping herself up in that bitchy dignity that's as bulletproof as Kevlar, but I see it. It's the look of someone who's used to not belonging. I look around this bedroom, collecting little pieces of the puzzle, and doubt most of this stuff is really hers. The bed and the trunk, the canopy, the satin sheets, the lush pink rug...

It all screams *I'm a princess.*

I'd sooner expect her walls to be painted black, slashed with red, covered in posters and sheer tapestries, ripped jeans cast aside on the floor, boots haphazardly tipped over by the door.

But there are certain things I can tell are just... her.

I lift the bottle of perfume and the lipstick, sliding it in my bag. On a whim, I snag the photo of Lavinia and her sister, too, tucking it into my back pocket.

Halfway there.

I head back the way I came, creeping down the hallway with my back to the wall. This time, the voices are louder, no longer softened by the quiet cruelty Counts are so known for. I cross over, keeping to the shadows, and can't help myself. I peer down into the study where Lionel Lucia sits in a leather armchair. At his feet is a massive black and brown dog, its head as big as a bowling ball.

A Rottweiler.

I narrow my eyes.

That would have been some relevant fucking intel, wouldn't it?

Lionel has more than one attack dog, though. Perez is occupying the winged sofa across from him, the other two Counts flanking him. A yellowish bruise mottles the side of his eye, evidence of the beating I gave him.

Lionel's holding a crystal tumbler in his hand, half filled with amber liquid. "Nothing you've done lately inspires confidence that you're up to the task at hand. First, the disappointing results with the Lords when you kidnapped their Lady," the ice clinks against the glass, "and then the utter humiliation of losing the fight over Lavinia."

"Sir—"

"Not to mention your complete inability to secure Leticia when she was handed to you on a silver platter." Lionel shakes his head, glaring into his drink. "I gave this kingdom two daughters, and what do you do with it? Squander them."

Perez's jaw tightens. "I've done my best—the Lords... no one anticipated their attachment to their Lady. And Nick Bruin? Don't tell me you saw that one coming."

"Excuses," the older man says. "You and I had an arrangement and we both know failure is *not* an option, for either of us." Lionel spins the serpent ring on his finger. "You're running out of time. Less than eight weeks now."

My watch buzzes, giving me a one-minute warning. I cover the sound, but the dog's ears perk up, nose rising from the ground. I dart back across the hall to the shadows and carefully make my way back down the stairs. I open the door, not latching it entirely— afraid it'll make too much noise—and crouch behind a thick shrub. The instant the guard passes and goes around the corner, I make a break for it across the yard. I'm at the first tree when I hear quick paced footsteps racing through the grass. I keep running, not looking back, but it's not the guard. The deep, bone-vibrating bark announces the dog.

Shit, shit, shit!

I get to the fence, throwing my backpack over first and pulling myself over in one swift leap. The dog rushes to the fence, barking and claws scratching at the metal. Jesus Christ.

I need a minute to catch my breath, but I don't take it, grabbing the pack and running like hell through the neighborhood. I don't stop until I'm in my car. I don't fucking breathe until I'm on the road.

Whatever's in the box better have been worth it.

13

Lavinia

I can't even remember the last time I had a good, real, *deep* sleep. Not at the Hideaway, regardless of the nice bed. Not in the old Crane roach motel. Certainly not those three days and nights my father had a hold of me after Leticia disappeared. If I'm being honest, not even before that, back when the tension was building between us, three grown vipers trapped in a dark hole, always coiled to strike. In those tired, hectic high school days, it was almost like gravity was watching, laughing at the way we slithered around one another in anticipation of our own fangs. The apple doesn't fall far from the tree. That's always been our curse.

Tonight, I'm curled up on the hard floor, the clean blanket pulled up to my chin. When I hear footsteps on the metal spiral staircase, I don't flinch. I heard him come through the door, could smell the scent of the city clinging to him, ozone and car exhaust caressing the back of my throat.

Even though he was my lifeline for the past two years, this may be the first time I'm truly relieved to see Nick. If he's here, then it means one of two things: He succeeded, or he failed. Either of those will mean a new path lies ahead. It's progress—an 'after.'

Eleven days.

It's just after midnight. His footsteps reach the loft, a dark silhouette against the cloudy clock face and the glow of the city beyond it. He remains still for a long moment, head tilted. I can't see his eyes, but I can feel them on me like a weight. "You didn't tell me about the dog."

The deep timbre of his voice pierces the silence, vibrating through my bones. "Ah, Amos." It's not that I forgot about Amos. Father loves that dog more than he's ever loved me. I give an innocent, "Oops," and sit up. If he thinks I'm making anything easy on him... well, he's dumber than he is pretty. "Did you get it?"

There's a backpack hanging loose in his fingertips. I've seen it before. He carries it everywhere. I've learned there can be anything inside. Guns, knives, tampons, candy. What I need now is for it to have the box from my bedroom.

When he doesn't answer, I impatiently grab for it, but he jerks it back, out of my reach. "You cleaned up the loft."

"Yeah," I say, looking around the tidy space. It'd taken the better part of the afternoon and evening to scrub and disinfect the floors, but the worst part was the blanket. I'd washed it under the bathtub spigot and left it to dry over the clock cables overhead, so it's still a touch damp. Better than asking Sy or Remy to show me to a washing machine, and it definitely needed one. I peer up at him, mouth slanted wryly. "You failed to mention a dog to me, too."

I can hear the smirk in his voice more than I can see it. "Fair point." He finally lifts the backpack, casually tugging the zipper open. "I almost didn't find it," he says, pulling out the box. Even in the low light, I can tell it's the one. I'm half expecting him to yank it away before my fingers touch the wood, but he lets me take it.

I inspect it carefully. The elastic band system is still in place. "You didn't open it."

If he hears my soft, surprised tone, then he ignores it, reaching into the backpack again. This time, he pulls out a small bundle of clothes and a book, setting them on the floor beside my nest. I recognize the novel as the one I was reading the night Leticia disappeared. *Dead souls*. Apt title.

He straightens, slinging the strap of the bag over a shoulder. "You sleeping here tonight?" At my nod, he exhales, sharp, edged with the same impatience I'd felt before. "That makes two days." He looks at the bundle of blankets. "Can't be comfortable."

"Yeah, well..." I look around the nest I've made. It's hard and uncomfortable and cold, but it's as close to being mine as anything will ever get around here. I see that now. "I had a long, shitty day. This is better than the alternative."

His eyes narrow. "What happened?"

I clutch the box and book to my chest. "Your brother happened. Ask him about it."

There's a stretch of tense silence before I hear the shift-shuffle of him crouching down. "He fuck you?"

The words are spoken in this low, flippant tone that makes my stomach drop, but the second I look at him, I see it. The clenched jaw, the possessive territorial heat in his eyes. That expression's never been comforting before, but if it keeps Simon from pulling a stunt like he did today...

Well, maybe there's some use to Nick's obsessive streak.

"No," I answer, watching some of the lethal fire fade from his eyes. I make sure it doesn't go too far. "He was going to share me, actually. Some of his fellow gym rats wanted to give your new Duchess a spin. He traded my pussy for a wristwatch."

It's not fire that sparks in his eyes, though. It's a complete, unfathomable, bottomless pit of darkness. "He traded you," he repeats in a blank voice.

"For a watch," I remind him. His eyes slide from mine to Sy's bedroom door below, and it doesn't matter that he's crouched down, looking for all the world like we're having a calm, civil conversation. For a moment, I get the sense he plans to do something excessively violent. *Interesting*. Sighing, I put him out of his misery. "But he reneged. Threw them all out of the locker room and decided to use my mouth instead."

His eyes instantly fall to my lips, brows crouching low. "You sucked his dick?"

I balk at the anger in his voice. "It was either that or get ripped apart by his three pals. Which would you have preferred I choose?"

His mouth presses into a tight line when he rises to his feet again, staring down at me. "This counts as one of your nights."

"I know."

His eyes dart to the book. "I want something for that."

"For what?" I look down at it, confused. "A half-read book? Seriously?"

"I didn't have to bring it," he snaps, adjusting the strap on his shoulder. "But I did, so now you owe me."

I see then how it's going to be. One negotiation after the other. It's exhausting, but it means he's willing to play, and that's something I can use.

Plus, I really want the book...

Shoulders falling, I wonder, "What do you want?"

His gaze drops to my mouth again. I'm so sure he's going to order me to suck him off that it takes me a second to process his answer.

"Kiss me."

I blink up at him, everything thrown off-kilter. "*Kiss* you?"

"A real kiss," he clarifies, a hardness settling over his features. "No fighting, no bitching, no turning away."

It's such a small thing in comparison to what Nick's done to me. What Remy has done to me. What Sy's done to me. A kiss. Simple. I should be grateful it's not worse. But a feeling of dread builds in my stomach. A week ago, my answer would have come easily—-probably in the form of my knee jabbing into his balls. Now, I'm sitting here thinking that it's not so bad. That it's not eight hours in the elevator. That I should be relieved this is all he wants.

I should be *grateful*?

What the fuck?

It's not the thought of a kiss that makes my blood run cold; it's the new certainty of what I'm willing to do to avoid the next worse thing. What Nick wants is something I can't give to him. He's a monster. A killer. A man who can lock me in a box and walk away. I don't care if he's suddenly decided to play college boy, he's dangerous. Lethal.

I can't forget that.

Wordlessly, I rise to my feet in front of him, lifting my chin just as much in defiance as agreement. His forehead creases skeptically as he searches my eyes. I'm sure he expected a fight, but I'm too damn tired to give him one. I won't be grateful. I won't be supplicant. But I'll do what I need to, if it means getting what I need.

He steps forward, shoulders tensing as he lifts his hand to my face. His fingertips are gentle as they press into my jaw, tilting my face up. If I thought the worst part of this would be having my mouth violated for a second time today, then I'm wrong.

So fucking wrong.

The worst part is easily the way he looks at me. I've spent my life being second, third, fourth best. Never special to anyone, never worth a second glance. Leticia was prettier and smarter. It was easy being invisible next to her.

But the way Nick looks at me pierces right through whatever sad armor I've wrapped around myself since the first night I met him in that parking lot. He looks at me like he *wants* me, and maybe it's in all the twisted, perverse ways that a girl should never feel good about, but goddamn it.

It's really hard to remember why.

It doesn't get any easier when he tips down, touching his lips to mine. His eyes are a blurry pair of hooded darkness, and I'm not expecting it. The way he pecks at my bottom lip, coaxing it open. The subtle gust of his sigh when his tongue peeks out, warm and wet, slipping into the crease. I don't expect the way his fingers nestle into the curve of my waist, folding me into his body as he kisses me.

I don't expect it to be so... tender.

His jaw is strong, but for once, not forceful. He licks inside like he's savoring it, slick and unhurried as he tilts his head, deepening the kiss. His tongue feels rough and soft, all at once, and it's the sound he makes more than anything that sends my mind spinning —his long, self-indulgent groan shooting straight to the most vulnerable part of me. My breath hitches shamefully, but I'm too caught up in the solid breadth of his body against mine—stubble rubbing against my chin—to think much of it.

And then he wraps around me, forearm pressing into the small of my back, and hauls me up against him.

He's rock-fucking-hard.

Suddenly, I'm flooded with the memory of that night in Hideaway. That sloppy, rough kiss he'd given me through his ski mask. The burn of him forcing his way inside. The harshness of his breaths into my ear as he fucked me, hard and unforgiving.

I get my hands against his chest and shove with all my strength, jerking away the second the connection is broken. My back crashes into the loft's metal railing, and I lift the bottom of my shirt, wiping my tingling lips with trembling hands.

He doesn't get to do that. To be sweet. Sexy. *He's a monster*, I repeat to myself. A monster.

He's breathing hard, head still tipped down as he looks at me through his lashes. My stomach plummets as I realize this will mean a punishment. My father used to do it by the hour. Back talk was an hour—two if I cursed. Hitting my sister? Two hours in the chest. Breaking curfew—three hours. Spilling something on the carpet, breaking the swing, scratching the slide—four hours. Anything over five hours was the result of something more serious. A call from my principal, a bad report card, the neighbor ratting on me for sneaking out. Those were dependent on his mood at the time, but the longest times were always reserved for an injury to the Lucia reputation.

When Leticia went missing, it was days.

Now I have a new warden, and my heart lodges itself into my throat as I tell myself this is good. It'll give me an idea of the scale.

What is a rejected kiss worth? Three hours? That's a metric to go by. It'll give me a standard, something to measure up my future infractions to.

But instead of dragging me down the spiral staircase, Nick just stares at me, a slow smirk quirking his lips. "Enjoy the book, Little Bird." Lifting the backpack over his shoulder, he starts for the stairs. I wait, heart thumping wildly against my ribcage, until I hear his bedroom door close. It's only then that I move, collapsing in a breathless, relieved heap.

Still trembling, I bring my things to the pile of blankets on the floor.

I remove the elastic bands, slowly taking them off, one by one, and set the box in my lap. I flip the little gold latch and lift the lid. The scent of Cuban cigars wafts toward my nose. The smell is both calming and repulsive. It immediately conjures up my father— every moment of our lives together. Leather and wood. The salt of tears. Scotch and barbed words. I fight back the anger and nausea it brings, because of course, this is the box she would choose to hold her secrets.

The box isn't mine.

It's Leticia's.

After she went missing, I searched every inch of her room. It was only when I got down on my hands and knees that I remembered the floorboard hiding place. We'd discovered them when we were little. I hadn't used mine in ages, but when I lifted the board, I discovered the box—elastic bands in place. Inside were objects and pictures. I didn't understand their relevance to my sister, but that wasn't a surprise. We hadn't been close in ages—if we ever were.

One of the items is a photo. In the foreground of the picture are two striped, sock-covered feet, toes leaning toward one another. Beyond the feet—one ankle showing half of a blurry tattoo—is a view of water. Maybe a lake. Maybe even the river. The water is crystal clear, and the trees on the opposing bank are shades of yellow, orange, and red. It was taken in the fall from a high vantage point, perhaps an overlook. Aside from that, there's a white ribbon stained brown with blood, a crinkled pharmacy receipt with the numbers '4009' scribbled on the back, a random single bullet, a dried wildflower, and a smooth granite rock.

Those objects are all still in the box—including the one I added myself. I remove the envelope. It's crinkled from the few times I've read it. The word '*Daddy*' is written in Leticia's immaculate cursive across the center.

I remove the paper from inside. It's a sheet of off-white stationery with the name '*Lucia*' embossed at the top. The handwriting is unmistakably my sister's.

Daddy,

This isn't the way I wanted to do this; however, you've given me no choice. But when have you ever given me a choice in what I do with my life? I've found the one thing you can't control and I'm finally ready to do it.

I'm not the person you want me to be. I can't marry Perez. I can't marry any of the Royal soldiers. I know you see this as a betrayal, an assault on your title, but it's not. For once in your life, I wish you could understand there are some things that aren't about you. This is one of them.

This is the last you'll hear from me. Consider me dead. You'll never find me or my body. You taught me how to do that. If only you could have accepted me for who I am, and not just as an extension of yourself.

Leticia

Each time I read the letter, even now, I search for clues or something I've missed. Leticia left the letter the day she vanished. I'm the one who found it on Father's desk, the envelope crisp and clean. It was a week before her twenty-first birthday. I hadn't seen Leticia in a full day, but that wasn't unusual. If we went days without speaking to one another, I counted it as a blessing. Everything had become impossible. The pressure from Father. The impending wedding. I knew she was sneaking in and out of the house, but I didn't know why.

When I found the letter, I took it. Sliding it into my back pocket. I should have given it to my father when she came up missing, but he was so angry and suspicious. Maybe there was a part of me that enjoyed it—just a little bit—the way my father instantly turned on me, assuming I'd done something to her. It was, in his own way, almost flattering. He thought I was conniving and vindictive enough to harm my own flesh and blood. There's really no higher compliment from Lionel Lucia.

But having the letter made me look even more suspicious. It also was the only clue. She'd vanished without a trace. No one could find her. Not the Counts, not the police... no one. No witnesses, no sightings, no body. She'd simply disappeared.

Just like she said she would.

My father didn't need to know that. He needed to think she was out there somewhere. Alive. Waiting to be found. Available to be married to Perez. Because if she isn't, there's only one person who can take her place.

Me.

~

Eleven days.

"Son of a..." I wince, my side aching from a night on the hard floor. I roll on my back and grunt again, shifting only to remove the hardback book wedged between my shoulders. I lie like that for a long moment, staring up at the broken clock, trying to work out the kinks.

It's the smell of bacon that finally gets me vertical.

"Morning sunshine," Nick says as I stumble down the spiral stairs, still rubbing the sleep out of my eyes. This time, Sy is working the stove and his brother sits at the table, plate in front of him. Nick raises an eyebrow. "You look like shit."

"You would too if you'd slept on the floor all night."

"Your choice, Little Bird." He looks me in the eye as he sinks his teeth into a ripe berry. There's a gun sitting next to his elbow, and when I zero in on it, he picks it up with inked fingers, lifting the back of his shirt to tuck it away. "There are three available beds just waiting for you to grace one of them with your sexy body."

I ignore him and rub my face. "Is there any coffee? Or do I have to eat someone's ass for the pleasure of caffeine?"

"Not my kink," Nick answers, looking nonplussed.

Sy grunts, barely managing to jerk his head in the direction of the coffeepot. The motion is small, but it is enough for me to see something that wasn't there the day before.

A bruise on his jaw.

Was that from the gym? I try to remember as I pour myself a cup. I know he and Bruce were sparring kind of intensely, but I don't remember any swelling when he forced himself on me in the locker room.

Nick lifts his fork, which is when I notice his fresh, red, raw knuckles. I look between them as I take my seat, trying to read whether or not it was done on my account, but Nick stops me. "What are you doing?" he asks, fingers clamped around my wrist.

I blink at my coffee, then at him. "What does it look like I'm doing?"

"It looks a lot like you aren't holding up your end of the bargain," he answers, giving his lap a pointed glance.

My jaw goes slack. "Here? *Now*?"

There's a hardness in his stare that makes my belly swoop nervously. "I'm here, aren't I? Enjoying some downtime. Sit." He gives his thigh a pat, but though his words are polite, the flint in his eyes is anything but.

Limply, I set my coffee on the table and turn to him, lowering myself to perch on his knee in stilted, reluctant increments. His arm hooks around my waist, yanking me into the hard warmth of his body.

"Sy, how about a plate for our Duchess?"

I expect Sy to throw the plate at me after he fills the dish with eggs, bacon, and fruit—partly because of the sharp glare he sends me, but also just because he clearly just hates me. I won't say there's no aggression when he drops it on the table in front of me—right beside Nick's—but he keeps it in check. *Brothers.* I don't understand how they work, but I do happen to know a thing or two about sibling rivalry. Shit gets complicated.

"I'd ask you how you slept, but that's been discussed," Nick says, resting his chin on my shoulder. "Anything you want to share about the package I delivered to you last night?"

"No." I shove a forkful of eggs in my mouth, forcing down a happy groan. *Damn,* they're good. The Master Bater is an excellent cook.

"I see." He takes a sip of coffee, and slowly, his other hand creeping up my sweater, rough calluses skating over my ribs. "Aren't you hot in this?"

A shiver threatens to roll up my spine, but I clench down against it, going stiff. "Aren't you supposed to be getting me actual clothes?"

He hums just as his fingertips reach the underside of my breast, tickling the skin there. "I keep my word. Although... I do like seeing you in my sweater. What do you think, Sy?" Even though he's talking to his brother, he says the words right against my ear.

Sy answers, "I think if you want to feel up your whore, you should find somewhere else to do it."

Nick's chest bobs with a silent laugh, and my eyes fall closed in dread, because if there's one thing I know about sibling rivalry—

Yep.

There it is.

Nick cups my breast in his wide palm, squeezing, making sure Sy notices. To me, he adds, "Well, everyone has things to do today. You can stay here, Little Bird."

My eyes whip toward him, widening. "Locked up?"

"Obviously." He keeps his gaze fixed on mine, which is why he sees me looking toward the elevator. He gives a subtle shake of his head, thumbing my nipple. "Just up here."

"Oh." I stare diligently at my plate, trying to ignore the way he's fondling me. "What am I supposed to do all day?"

"Meditate? Masturbate?" He gives his now empty plate the same pointed glance he'd given his lap. "Clean?"

I narrow my eyes at the sink full of dishes. "At least Auggy gave me books to read."

Nick shoves his other hand up my sweater, and I wince as it latches onto my other tit. "You mean that trash you always had sitting beside your bed? Your horny books?"

"Romance novels," I correct, ignoring the nasty look Sy shoots at me. When Nick squeezes my breasts together, I'm quick to add, "And I'll read anything. It doesn't matter. That just happened to be what she brought me. I wasn't—I mean, I'm not..."

"Horny?" he whispers into my ear, making me squirm. Nick nods up toward the loft. "I just gave you a book last night."

"I finished it."

He scoffs, skating his knuckles along the sides of my breasts. "You didn't read half of *Dead Souls* in one night."

A derisive snort comes from Sy's direction, making my mouth purse. "You're right. I didn't read half of *Dead Souls* in one night. I read it *all*."

Nick pauses, finally pulling his hands free from my sweater. "Yeah, right."

"I'm a fast reader," I explain, pinching a piece of bacon in my fingers. "So if you plan to keep me from going completely insane with boredom, you're going to have to do better than a single Gogol novel."

I feel his shrug against my back. "What do I look like? A fucking library?"

"I can't just sit here all day. That can't be the job of a..." I clench my jaw, forcing out, "Duchess."

A quick glance reveals the corner of his lip curving upward at the word. "You're right. Most Duchesses would be escorting us to class, sucking us off in the parking lot, and taking a fat load as her lunch. But most Duchesses are also students *and* trustworthy. You're neither." He grabs me by the hips, hitching me up against his obscene erection before pushing me off his lap. "I have class."

Relieved, I scurry to the empty seat next to him, tucking into my food before another ridiculous demand comes out of his mouth. Between bites, I notice Sy exiting the kitchen, only to cross over to Remy's door. He bangs on it with three demanding raps. A moment later, Remy emerges, looking no better than the day before. If anything, he looks even more strung out, his hair limp and hanging about a gaunt, colorless face.

"What?" he snaps. Or, at least, it seems like he tries to snap. The word ends up falling flat, landing between them like a deflated balloon.

"Come eat breakfast." Sy puts his hand on Remy's shoulder, a gesture that might seem friendly and casual to most, but I can see Sy's bicep flex as he pulls him forward, away from the bedroom.

Maybe Remy could fight him if he didn't look like a walking corpse—and probably feel like one, too. Instead, he walks out, shirtless, wearing the same jeans he had on the last time I saw him. Ink stains his fingertips and there's a long, dark smear of charcoal slashing across his defined pecs. Sy leads him back to the kitchen and puts a full plate of food at the spot Nick just vacated —next to me. He adds a glass of juice and drops three pills next to it.

"Come on, you know the drill." Sy shoots Remy an expectant look until he finally perches on the stool.

There's something about the way he's moving, limp but mechanical, that makes the hair on the back of my neck prickle. It's like being in the presence of something artificial. Too precise and economical. That, plus the tattoos, sallow features, and pale green eyes, sends a shadow of a shiver down my spine. Lifting his hand, Remy's long, stained fingers slide the pills around the tabletop, shifting the little shapes in a circular motion.

Sy gives him a hard look, leaning down to speak close to his ear —probably hoping that Nick and I won't hear. We do. "Don't think I don't realize what's going on here. You've been in that room for days, barely eating, barely sleeping. We both know where this road leads, Remy. Take your meds, or I'll have to call your dad."

Nick looks between them, frozen.

Remy's green eyes shift to Sy, and then to the pills. Wordlessly, he scoops them up and crams them into his mouth, swallowing hard. "Satisfied?"

"No," Sy answers firmly. "Show me."

Sighing, Remy lifts his chin and then opens his mouth, sticking out his tongue. "Christ, it's like being back in Saint Mary's," he mutters, shoulders curling inward, hunched over his plate.

"Thank you," Sy replies, turning his back to us. "You're on filing duty this morning, and then your first class is at eleven. I need you ready in twenty."

I glance over at Remy just in time to see him discreetly spit the pills onto this plate, hiding them beneath a pile of scrambled eggs. I get this crazy urge, like I'm twelve all of a sudden and Leticia is beside me, breaking the rules, and I could turn to my father and tattle, watch her get punished.

Only the punishment never came.

Not for her.

Never for her.

I swallow the urge down with a sip of coffee. What do I care if this guy doesn't give a shit about his health? And betraying Simon? Well, that's just a cherry on top of this fucked-up sundae. No, I keep my mouth shut. I learned that lesson a long time ago. Plus, I have to figure a day of filing papers is punishment enough for someone with Remy's energy,

I watch from my periphery as Nick gathers his things. Wallet, keys, book bag. I notice he doesn't take his gun out, meaning he either drives to campus with it, or stashes it downstairs. The second he stops beside me, tattooed fingers tapping an even rhythm against the chipped wood, I know what he's going to ask. It still makes the tips of my ears explode in a flash of heat when he says, "Suppose it's too much to hope for a kiss goodbye?"

God, that fucking kiss.

Even five hours spent with my nose buried in *Dead Souls* wasn't enough of an escape from it.

I answer by cramming a forkful of eggs into my mouth, chewing aggressively.

He hums, reaching out to run his fingers through my hair. "I could bring you back more books. Something...*thicker*. Hornier?"

I squirm away from him, making my hip bump Remy's. "Forget it. Even a *good* book wouldn't be worth having your mouth on me again."

Nick goes still beside me, hand still caught in my hair. The next thing I know, my head is being yanked back and my gaze is locking with sharp, blue eyes. "Do you really think this attitude is helping you any?" he asks in an acidic tone, knuckling hard against my scalp. "Don't push me, Lavinia. I have other ways of keeping you put for the day." He never mentions the elevator—doesn't even look at it—but I hear him loud and clear.

Every time I reject him, I'm playing with fire.

My neck protests the angle until he releases me. That dark shadow in his eyes doesn't dissipate at the low, pained sound I make. "Clean the fucking kitchen," he mutters, turning on his heel and marching out.

A second later, the door to the stairwell slams shut behind him.

After a few minutes of him pretending to do more than pushing his food around the pills, Remy slides off his stool and dumps his food and meds down the disposal, saying, "I'm going to get ready." When he turns, he gives me this hooded, warning look, like he knows I've just seen everything. "Imagine a snake without its forked tongue," is what he says, muscles shifting beneath his bare shoulders as he walks away and shuts his bedroom door behind him.

Captive and alone, again.

Eleven days.

Suddenly, my breakfast doesn't seem so appealing anymore. Ignoring the guys' stacked plates. I rinse mine off and put it in the dishwasher, removing any trace that I've been here. Being their cleaning lady isn't part of our negotiation. If Nick wants me to scrub their filth, he's going to have to pony up something a lot more compelling than a hair pull. I grew up with a sister, for fuck's sake.

I shut the dishwasher door and face the main room, taking a few deep breaths. All of this is better than closed, cramped spaces, I try to remind myself, but occasionally it still feels the same. Locked doors, limited air, high walls.

This whole tower is one big elevator shaft, isn't it?

But on the positive side, it's the first time I've been truly left alone in the tower. No one here to threaten me, glare at me, or grope me. It's a different kind of freedom, and for the first time since waking up, I allow myself to really breathe, exhaling the tension.

And then I do what any rational person would in my situation. I snoop.

It's obvious the guys haven't been here long enough to make much of a mess, but the tower isn't bare. The furniture is nice but well worn; I assume provided by the fraternity. I know there are budgets, legal fees, property management. They're as much a business asset as anything. One wall is comprised entirely of composite photos, rows and rows of each pledge class dating back to the very beginning. I skim over the faces of hundreds of men; the scourge of the West End, the fists of Forsyth. At the top of each class is a trio of leadership—the Dukes for that year—and I idly find myself wondering what they did to earn their spots in this tower. I know the Royals rotate out their leadership, with positions won during a series of contests and games that are meant to seem like fun, garden-variety delinquency on the surface, but often end up with someone shedding blood. No one knows that better than me, still remembering the blood swirling down the drain as I washed all traces of them from my cunt that night, weeks ago.

That's when I see it. There are small oval photos right underneath each year's trio. It's not another man, but a young woman.

Their Duchess.

I go from composite to composite, looking at the smiling girl in each photo. I search their eyes, looking for any sign that they filled this tower with their own misery, the dark shadows that reflect back at me when I look in the mirror. I try to find her, the one who didn't want it, the one who fought, the one who felt hopeless.

If she's in any of those photos, then she hid it better than I ever could.

Maybe Nick's right. Maybe these women did find it to be an honor to be the Duchess and serve the Dukes. Maybe they spent their summers hoping, praying, to one day be in this very tower, hopping from bed to bed, escorting them to classes. Maybe each and every one of them wanted nothing more than to be a good little bitch for the fists of Forsyth.

Too bad I'm not other women.

I turn away and focus on the adjacent wall. There's a long stretch of shelves and cabinets that I haven't had the chance to explore. The shelves are mostly frat memorabilia—stuff that's too nice or sentimental to keep downstairs in the ruckus room. None of it looks like it has much financial value; it's just a collection of trophies, bear statues, and Forsyth swag.

I crouch and swing open a set of double doors. Inside is a filing cabinet, and without thinking twice, I pull it open to reveal rows and rows of files. A little rush runs through me at the sight of just... so much *information*. A lot have 'Class of...', and a quick flip through those reveals lists of every pledge class. I spend a few minutes looking at the names, wondering when these three pledged. Freshman year for Simon Perilini. I don't know Remy's last name... or his first. The closest I can find is a Remington Maddox, sophomore year, but that can't be right. The Maddoxes are their own kind of royalty, filthy rich and powerful enough that I can't see one of them slumming it in the West End as a fist of Forsyth.

Nicholas Bruin isn't in here anywhere.

Gotta love that nepotism.

I thumb past the rosters and on to files dedicated to the tower itself. I see one that's messily labeled 'Clock' and pause, glancing over at the enormous, motionless clock face. I bet it was amazing, back in its day, ticking away. Was it loud? Did the cables above my loft rattle? When did it stop? The curiosity doesn't surprise me—Father always did say it was my worst quality—but the intensity of it does.

Pulling it out, I open the cover and fold my legs beneath me, settling in to read it. It's an entire chronological history of the clock: maintenance, repairs, receipts for parts, historical register paperwork. Apparently, about a decade back, there was an attempt to apply for a restoration grant, but there's no indication it was ever approved. Looking back farther—the paper getting thinner, more wrinkled, ink fading—there were attempts ten years before that, and ten years before that. Whatever this tower meant to Forsyth, the local government obviously seems content to let it rot. Of course, with Barons mostly holding the keys to anything political in this town, they're probably the hands that need greasing. Knowing the rivalries around here, I'm betting Dukes would sooner let the building crumble.

The most recent repair receipts involving the clock itself are almost fifty years old, the work orders tattered and barely-readable. Buried under everything else is a manual. *Introduction to Horology: The Art of Making Clocks and Watches.*

My belly swoops in excitement.

I take a paranoid glance over my shoulder before removing the manual, shoving the file back in its spot, and closing the cabinet.

This should definitely keep me busy for a while.

14

Remy

I disappear up the stairs while she's in the bathroom, doing whatever it is girls do in there.

Or whatever my mind seems to think girls do in there.

I don't turn on the light to the tiny stairwell as I climb to the room below the belfry. I already know where every step is, can feel the handle to the door at the top, without having to see it. It's not because I've been here so long, either. This is only the third time I've ever been up here.

I'll say this, it sure smells real. Like old metal, dust, and damp. I've always been good at that, though. The details. It's why people want my ink on them. They want the small things, the shit no one else would notice or care about, but I'm happy to spend hours agonizing over. The precise way a shadow falls below an eye. The hatched lines that fill it. The texture, the shade, the perfect curves of a circle.

The density of stars.

Black glass. Blonde hair. Red lights. Blood on the trees.

I think I do pretty well.

It's the problem with not having made anything I'm happy with in so long. Sometimes my brain just decides to pour all of its effort into something elaborate.

Like, for instance, filing duty.

It's pointless to do work here. I know it, feel it, acknowledge it, and yet I still sit down on the stool and flip the switch, bringing the drill press to life. I used to know this guy at Saint Mary's who kept swearing we were all machines. Maybe not in the most literal sense, but there is some truth to doing things automatically, a muscle that flexes itself without being told to, like a heartbeat. There's work to be done, so my hands start moving. We're all mechanical up to a point. I believe that shit down to my marrow. Bag of flesh made up of cogs, cables, and rods, not too unlike that dead clock downstairs.

Filing duty isn't new to me. I did it all summer for Saul, so I picked up the little nuances. The way the drill falls when I lower it into the metal. The sound of the shavings being kicked up. The noise of the mechanics, the texture of the steel. If only Sy could appreciate how exact it all is, maybe this version of him wouldn't keep looking at me the way he does.

Like I'm broken.

I know I'm working perfectly when I finish the first one. The five fine holes I've drilled into the surface of the metal are smooth, but not too smooth. Rough, but not too rough. Fucking nailed it.

And when my phone rings, I feel my mouth quirk in a triumphant, bitter smirk, because it's my dad's name flashing across the screen. Of course, he'd call me when I was feeling the smallest bit of pride. My mind is fucking amazing.

Because three days ago, I fell into a dream.

And I never woke up.

"Yeah?" is how I answer, eyes narrowing suspiciously. Sy *had* threatened to call him before. Am I turning on myself already? That happens sometimes. Can't help it.

"You aren't in class." The tone of disappointment is so real—so goddamn perfect—that I nearly laugh. I've definitely got that one down. "I was going to leave a voicemail."

Looking around the room, I decide to let this play out. I have places to *be*. "I've got work this morning. Class at eleven."

"Oh." He sounds just south of surprised, as expected. "So I take it you haven't ruined your future quite yet. Otherwise, are you well?"

I tap my fingers against the table, wondering which value of 'well' he's asking about. I guess that's up to me. "I haven't read a single syllabus." Tapping my fingers faster, I add, "I've been late twice, I'm in the middle of securing some studio time, and I fucked my Duchess' brains out with a marker over the weekend."

There's a stretch of silence on the other end of the line, and then my father's exasperated, "I think you're supposed to use your cock for that."

"Oh, that's what it's for?" Kicking a foot up on the table, I shrug. "Wouldn't know. Some complete jackass put me into a middle school with abstinence-only education. Shittiest parenting imaginable."

"This is your senior year." His voice takes on that serious, authoritative tone that always makes my teeth ache. "You wanted an art degree, and despite knowing the best thing it can get you is something to wipe your ass with, I've paid hand over fist to make sure you get it. How's that for shitty parenting?"

"Gets a little shittier each time you throw it in my face." I rub my chin. "Ever wonder why you can't call me without throwing a few jabs in?"

"Probably the same reason you add another tattoo to yourself every time you're throwing a fit." He sighs, all long-suffering. Hard work, being my dad. "I meant, are you *well*? Any side effects? Are you sleeping? You haven't answered a single one of my texts, and Doctor Weatherby says you haven't scheduled a session in weeks. You know the arrangement. I need to be kept informed about—"

"I'm doing fine," I insist, cutting him off. Doctor Weatherby is the last person I want to see. For years, I've had it drilled in my head.

Don't think about the stars, Remy.

Turn away from the stars, Remy.

Stay in the light, Remy.

I'm not allowed to look, but that night of the party, I did it. I glanced down—it wasn't like I meant to—and the stars were there, and now I'm caught in a web of them, waiting for the red lights and the blood and the black glass, and *goddamn it*. I *need* to see them. I'm tired of being told I can't. They said my name and made me look, and now, if I could just get back to them, I could find out why.

It's the snake.

Vinny.

She makes the stars burble up like a bad chemistry experiment.

Smoothly, I lie, "I've been sleeping like a baby. The kind who has loving parents, even. Modern medicine is amazing, really."

There's no sigh this time. For all that, he's a gigantic shithead. My dad has always been lazy enough to believe me when I say everything is all good. Less work for him. "Well, since you're so fucking splendid, then I guess I can inform you that it's time to be realistic and plan for grad school."

"Ah, it's been a few months since we've had this talk, hasn't it?" Fuck, I am *so good*. "So where you wanna do this?"

Sounding confused, he asks, "Do 'this'?"

Nodding, I elaborate, "Yeah, you know. Where do you want to lecture me about the 'sorry course my life is taking'? Because I know you like to keep it hush-hush that I'm the family fuck-up, and since I can't see you coming to campus, we have a few options." Before he can answer, I offer, "I've always liked the country club. It's not my scene, obviously. But they let us sit in that room—the one with the Rubens painting? It's the one with all the thick asses. Anyway, I think I'm pretty close to determining that it's fake as hell, so if we could go there, that'd be cool."

I can practically hear him rubbing the bridge of his nose. It's one of the reasons I'm so drawn to Sy. He does this thing where he rubs his thumb with his forefinger. A fidget. It reminds me of my dad, just without all of the festering resentment. "Do you really think that attitude is going to get you anywhere in life?"

I get this sudden flash of Nick this morning, yanking Lavinia's head back. Stars. That's what I see when I look at her now. Blonde tendrils of hair. The sound of her scream. The flashing panic in her gray eyes. Red lights. And anger—so much fucking anger—burning hot enough that it could flatten this whole goddamn city to rubble and ash...

"Do you really think this attitude is helping you any?"

The words are almost identical. That can't be a good sign.

I run my fingers through my hair, pushing it back, blinking as I try to reorient myself. "Can we do this later? I'm not really feeling great."

My dad's voice drops an angry octave. "Don't brush me off. Either you're doing alright, or you're not. You don't get to play both sides whenever it's convenient for you. You know our agreement. Make an appointment with Weatherby, or else—"

I rub my temple. "Set up a time with the club and I'll be there."

"Remington!"

I hang up, letting my phone fall to the workbench as I clutch my head. Stars—so many goddamn stars. Blonde hair. Red lights. Panic. Anger. Wind. The memory is beginning to hurt again, a sharp, hot throb behind my eyes. It's all smudged, like a charcoal sketch that's been handled too many times, the edges indistinct.

I've tried to get back to it. I don't know how or why, but I know it's what I need to do. It just feels so far away. Even when Lavinia is right in front of me, it's not quite right. Not yellow enough. Not red enough. I thought if I just stayed here, it'd come back to me. I thought if I played along, let my brain work out the kinks in this whole thing, that I'd get to go back to where it all started.

It's not working.

I power down the drill press, going through the motions of closing up shop as my temples throb painfully. The longer I wait, the worse it gets here. My dad will come. Sy will turn away. Nick will leave. Lavinia will fade, just like the stars.

If they aren't going to come to me, then I'll just have to go to them.

15

Lavinia

The staircase to the belfry is behind an undersized doorway in the loft. I'd noticed it earlier but wrote it off as little more than a hiding spot for spiders, so I left it shut. I seriously consider following my gut when I finally heave the heavy metal from the frame, flipping the light switch just inside.

Cramped.

That's what the staircase is. Narrow, enclosed with high stone walls. The main tower staircase is roomy compared to this. Practically cavernous. Just the thought of walking up those steps, knowing the walls are so close to my shoulders, makes sweat prick up on the back of my neck, stomach lurching with panic. I gulp as I stare into the dimly lit space, peering up the stairs to the door at the top. Five seconds if I sprint. Ten if I don't. And I don't even know what I'll find once I reach it. Maybe it's a closet, and I'm just trapping myself into the worst space imaginable.

Fingers flexing into fists, I square my shoulders.

And then I sprint.

Two steps at a time, swatting webs out of my way as I go, I dart up the staircase to the tall, industrial-looking door ahead, as if it's the only thing that exists.

When I finally reach it, wrenching it open with constricted lungs and a hammering pulse, I'm not expecting what I find.

It's... bright.

Brightly lit.

I stumble through, closing the door behind me as I gasp for air, letting the panic bleed out of me in waves. It's not a closet, but instead, a large, busy space full of the clock's inner workings. I peer openly into the musty space, instantly seeing that all the brass rods and cogs are dusty from disuse, probably jammed in a million different ways. I'd skimmed the manual, but seeing the sheer enormity of the guts up close is a whole different perspective.

I take the book from where I've had it tucked beneath my arm, intending to flip through the pages in an attempt to figure out what parts do what. Or what part stopped working? But I pause before my finger can dip between the pages.

Something is off.

The floor isn't clean, which is why I can see the well-worn path leading toward the center of the room. I follow it without thinking, my mind full of the fact that this doesn't feel like an abandoned chamber of an ancient clock tower. I can't explain why, but it simply has this... energy. An odd buzz in the air, like someone's been here more recently than fifty years ago. Maybe even more recently than last month.

It isn't until I cross to the other side of the tower, ducking around cables and clock stuff, that I see the crates, open and visible to anyone who can manage to gain access to the highest room in Forsyth.

Guns.

Entire cases of them.

I stand there stunned for a long moment, even though I shouldn't be surprised. Everyone knows the Dukes run the gun trade in this town. I just wasn't expecting them to be...here. So close to campus. So fucking *obvious*. The Counts would *never*.

I crouch down to inspect a pistol, shiny and new-looking, and feel a zing of jubilation. I could take them all down with one of these babies. I test the weight in my hand, running my finger over the barrel, and feel an odd, raised spot to the metal, like it's swollen and rough.

Looking up, I catch sight of a drill press in the corner. Some other complicated machinery sits beside it—the source of the buzzing I've been feeling—and suddenly, I'm reminded of Sy's words earlier.

"You're on filing duty this morning…"

Not filing papers, I suddenly realize.

Remy's filing the fucking serial numbers off.

Gooseflesh springs up over my skin as I whip around, looking for signs of his platinum hair and gaunt cheeks. I don't see anything, though. And that's another problem. There must be a hundred guns here—maybe more—but not a single box of ammunition.

Irritated, I put the pistol back in its place.

Thump.

My eyes spring to the ceiling, muscles tense. Everyone knows there's one last level to the tower. The belfry. A quick scan around the space doesn't reveal a door or staircase, but there is a ladder. It's in the southeast corner, illuminated by a weak bulb.

I climb it, fully appreciating how stupid it is to do so. The main living area of the tower is restricted for anyone but Dukes, but the belfry is basically considered Fort Knox. From the way people talk, the Dukes basically treat it as sacred. I don't think I've even known anyone that's been up here, unless you count Saul—and who does? At best, I'm admitting to poking my nose into places I don't belong. It'd just be showing them that I've seen the guns, that I know too much now to be let free.

This could get me *days* in the elevator.

I spend about five minutes gnawing a thumbnail before deciding I have to see it.

At the top, I push up a heavy hatch, arms straining under the weight. I'm met with a gust of wind, blustery and warm as I rise out into the late morning air. The enormous iron bell that hangs overhead casts me in shadow, and I crawl on my hands and knees to get out from under it. I don't realize how tight my chest is until I'm up here, inhaling air like a man dying of thirst would swallow water. I circle around the big bell and rush to one of the arched openings to suck it in. The air, the view, the openness of it all. As my muscles unwind, I take in the landscape below. It's spectacular, looking out over the city, each of the four corners of Forsyth visible from such an extreme vantage.

I went to bible school when I was smaller—for, like, a dozen heartbeats. My father thought it'd be a good luck for us—Leticia and me. It wasn't long before both of us were thrown out for having a 'problem with authority.' I got punished. Leticia didn't. In any case, I spent enough time there to realize I'm not religious.

But if there is a heaven, it'd be just like this; no walls, open space as far as the eye can see.

I'm soaking it in, staring out over Forsyth with jubilant awe, when I hear, "I knew you'd come." Jumping, I spin, startled at the voice behind me.

It's Remy, just as I expected. He's strolling up from the other side of the bell, leaning to casually rest against the support to the west-facing archway. He's wearing a baseball cap, but it's backward, haphazard locks of his hair twitching in the wind. Even if he doesn't look as imposing as he had before, there's still that empty wildness swirling in his eyes. His skin is paler in the sunlight, and although he's looking right at me, the dark orbs of his pupils make it seem like he's a million miles away.

This isn't Remy at all.

It's Maniac.

"You have class in twenty minutes," I say, fidgeting nervously. It's a passable ruse, the pretense that I've come up here to remind him, but if the lack of reaction on his face says anything, he isn't buying it. "Nick never said I couldn't come up here." I press my back to the stone wall. "I just wanted some air."

His eyes fall to my fingers, which are twining around the draw-string of Nick's hooded sweatshirt. "You're not supposed to be wearing that."

I glance down at it—dark gray, bearing the tongue-in-cheek 'FU' insignia that always sells well around here—and shrug. "He basically forced it over my head yesterday. It's not like I stole it or—"

"No." Something crosses over his face, tight and frustrated. "I mean, this isn't how it went. Not exactly. You're not..." His head tilts, eyes narrowing. "Why aren't you blonde?"

I pause, face screwing up. "Because I dyed my hair?"

The frustration smoothes out, leaving him with a bland expression. "It doesn't matter. I think I found out how to go back."

"Go back?" Now I'm the one who looks frustrated. "You're not making any sense. Use your words!"

He lifts his arm and I finally see the flash of crimson. It's running down his forearm to his wrist, over his palm, dripping from his lithe fingers. He watches the sluggish stream of blood, looking disinterested. "This obviously didn't work—not completely."

"*Shit...*" I start forward, though I don't know why at first. I just know that Remy is standing in front of me with a huge gash on his arm, and for some reason, I need to fix it.

Nick is going to think I did this.

That's what's going through my mind as I lurch forward, snatching his wrist from the air. "Lift your arm, you fucking moron!" I raise it over his chest, hoping to stem the bleeding, but it's heavy and limp and he's looking at me with those fucking *eyes*.

"I'm just re-tracing the steps." His fingers are suddenly grazing my jaw. "I saw you falling into the stars. I don't remember what they said, but I heard you scream. You had... all this blood..."

It's then that I realize he's smearing it across my cheek. I drop his wrist and lurch back, frantically wiping it away. "What is wrong with you?!" But then a flash of light draws my attention to his other hand. A gleam of silver. A knife. I come to a slow, gradual realization, edging further away from him. "You did that to yourself."

His eyes move from my cheek to the knife, and he lifts it, inspecting the blade. "It was supposed to wake me up." Shrugging, he raises the blade and calmly slashes another cut into his skin. "It's not like I'm an expert on my own psyche. I usually pay people to take care of it. It's just..." The frustration comes back, carving a divot between two angry brows. "It's really confusing in here sometimes."

I take a deep breath, teeth clenched. "Remy, you're off your meds. I saw you spit them out. That's why you take them, right? It's why Sy gives them to you? Because you're cr—" His eyes spark in a way that makes my mouth slam shut. Gently, so as to not provoke the armed lunatic, I finish, "Because you're *sick*. You're just not yourself. You don't know what you're doing."

"Oh, I know exactly what I'm doing." He lifts a bloody finger, tapping his temple. "Got it all figured out. I've just been stuck in here too long. It's adapting, tricking me into thinking it's real. But it's not."

I throw my hands up, exasperated. "Stuck in where?!"

"The dream!" he snaps, face transforming into a furious pinch. "*You* did this. Drawing on you, sleeping with you...it made me dream. This is all *your* fault. You fell into the stars and left me up here! Where the fuck did you expect me to go?!"

I pull my hair back from my cheeks and breathe. Because this? This is actual insanity. I'm standing in front of a madman. "Remy," I try, keeping my voice even and calm, "you're not yourself."

"Then why," he demands, shooting forward, "why do I keep remembering the stars and the blood?"

I jump back, startled. "I don't know what you're talking about!" Only, I realize, maybe I do. Blonde hair, blood, the night sky? Grasping at straws, I ask, "Are you talking about what happened the night you broke into the brothel?"

His pale lips mash into a tight purse. "This is the problem. No one ever listens to me. They'll look, but they won't hear. Everyone wants to see my brain. Everyone wants to look at the paintings and the drawings and the fucking tattoos! But no one wants to hear it." Looking away, he starts pacing a small circuit in front of the bell, muttering in an agitated voice, "How do I even know?! How do I know the brothel actually exists? Maybe I created you just for this, because I'm telling myself to wake up." He freezes, whipping his wild green eyes to me. "Fuck, of course. It explains everything. That shitty tattoo on your leg? I couldn't finish it because I ran out of ideas. They're not stars. They're not, like, infinite, you know?"

Feeling at a loss, my attempt to be firm falls as limp as his arm had before. "Remy, this isn't a dream. You're awake, you're—you're *right here.*"

He lets out a laugh that sounds relieved, tipping his face up toward the sun. "That's why you're here, isn't it? Maybe I've been dreaming about this for months. Fuck, maybe I've been dreaming it for years. You showed me the stars because you know I need to wake up, and maybe when I do..." His head jerks back, like he's just been physically hit, eyes unblinking as they fix to mine. His face goes dark with such a terrible sincerity that it makes my stomach plummet. "Maybe when I wake up, Tate will be alive."

My blood turns to ice. "Who...who's Tate?"

His jaw works around a soundless reply as he stares at me, hard and wide-eyed, like I've just horrified and awed him all at the same time. "Maybe I never left. Maybe that's why it hurts." Fingers pressing into his temple, he let out a slow exhale. "But we can make it stop. Can't we? You should know what the stars said." When all I do is shake my head, completely lost, he leans over the edge and gestures for me to look. "See? Down there. Don't you see?" I slowly move next to him and peer over. There's nothing down below but a terrifying drop and hard pavement, which is made all the more obvious when a gust of wind catches the brim of his hat, sending it over. Watching its fluttering descent, I draw back, stiffening when his hand lands on my back, pressing down. "You know how this ends, don't you?"

My heart pounds, feet scuffing the stone as I struggle backward. "Remy, let's go back downstair—"

"I have to wake up now." He moves abruptly, arms and legs fluidly pulling him up onto the ledge. He rests a hand on the arch, looking so casual about it. So calm. "If I wake up, then maybe we can be together again." He looks at me, green eyes piercing, and the thing is, he's crazy. He really fucking is. But he looks at me and all I see in his face is a bottomless despair. "The four of us. Like it should be."

"The four of us?" I ask, waving a finger in a round gesture that's meant to encompass the Dukes and me. It's only then that I notice I'm trembling. "I think we can probably do that downstairs, away from the—you know—horrifying drop to our gruesome deaths?"

His laugh is a jagged, broken sound. "You? No, not *you*. You'll be gone, back to your snake hole in my brain. But Tate will be here."

He sways, legs and arms loose. *Too* loose. Without thinking, I lunge forward to grab his hand. "Remy, look at me. This isn't a dream. You're having some kind of episode. You don't know what you're—"

"I know. I have to wake up now." His green eyes drop to the ground below the tower, pale lashes brushing the tired hollows beneath his eyes. I can hear it from all the way up here. Traffic. Distant sirens. The static of voices and wind and life.

And I know that he means to jump.

People think I'm a murderer. They're wrong, but it's not something I can shake off with a few impassioned refusals. It's going to take time, proof, preferably a whole-ass body of evidence. If Remy takes some batshit swan dive from this tower, I'm through here. I have his blood on my face, my hands. No one will believe I'm innocent. And I might not understand it, but Remy is beloved. To DKS. To Nick. *Jesus*, to Sy.

This isn't just a few days in the elevator.

This is my dead body being shoved in there for transport.

Eleven days.

"Remy, look at me," I order, keeping my voice firm. This is some fucking nonsense, which means there's only one way to deal with it. *Better nonsense.* I wait until his distracted eyes pass over mine to say, "You're right. The stars talked to me. I know everything."

His attention snaps to me, as sharp as the blade in his hand. "They did?"

Nodding, I carefully take the knife from his loose grip, tucking it into my hoodie pocket. "They said you'd come up here. They told me to tell you the truth. Don't you want to hear it first?"

His eyes move from me to the street below, a seed of skepticism on the wrinkle of his brow. "I already know the truth."

I shake my head. "Fine, I'll keep it to myself." It's a risky bluff, but I turn to walk away, pulse hammering in my head as I brace for the sound of his jump. I've seen someone die before. Once. But I was too young to remember it. In the recess of my mind, I wonder if it felt like this. Was I scared? Did I try to stop it?

Did I fail?

Instantly, I hear the soles of his designer shoes meeting the stone. "Wait! The stars." Turning, I raise an eyebrow at his impatient expression. "Where are they? Why can't I see them?"

Because it's daytime, you fucking lunatic?

I keep my sarcasm to myself for once, knowing what I need to do. "You need to go lie down. Have another dream. You liked that before, didn't you?" At least that's how it seemed the other day when Nick was congratulating him about it, as if such a feat were impressive and new.

There's another strong gust of wind that blows his hair into his eyes, platinum locks brushing his cheekbones. He turns to toss a glance over his shoulder at the ledge, fingers twitching. "Go to sleep so I'll wake up?" He actually has the nerve to sound incredulous, like *this* is the craziest thing he's heard all day.

"Not exactly. Come on." I reach out for his bloody hand, watching his eyes flick to the movement. I keep my movements slow, placating, coaxing him away from the edge. "I'll show you the stars. I'll tell you everything." All I want to do is get him away from this belfry—away from the ledge and air and deadly drop. I want it so badly that I don't even think twice about offering, "You can draw on me again. You can fix my snake, make me how you want."

His first step is reluctant, but the second is solid and sure, allowing me to pull him toward the bell. He follows without protest or question, ducking down to the hatch when we reach it, and I try to ignore the twist in my gut when he pauses there, glancing up at me like I hold all the answers to the universe.

"I think I did a pretty good job with you," he says, face cast in the shadow of the bell. Then he's down the ladder, giving me a moment of reprieve to brace my palms against my knees, chest shuddering in relief.

"Yeah," I say, unsure if he can hear me, "you did a really good job."

16

Lavinia

The Dukes have some hardcore first aid supplies.

I guess it makes sense. Everyone knows the true role of a Duchess is to piece her men back together after their fights, and not all of their battles are as structured and self-contained as Friday Night Fury. I pilfer through the cabinet, which I'd spied earlier in my snooping, and begin pulling out what I'll need, glancing behind me every few seconds to make sure Remy's still in his room.

My hands still have a subtle tremor.

Because of this, I detour to the kitchen, swiping a bottle of bourbon from the counter before looping back around to the main living area and crossing to his door.

If I'd been curious about what he was doing, holed up in here for three days, then being inside doesn't give me any answers. He's obviously destroyed every drawing—and a couple canvases—he'd been occupied with. The floor is covered with torn bits of paper bearing black smudges and smears. The bed is unmade. Art supplies are strewn about like a bomb's been detonated. I have to step around a mangled canvas to get to him.

Luckily, he's still on his tattoo bench—the most sterile place in the tower—one leg stretched out on the foot of it as he waits. The bold mania in Remy's eyes has dulled to an aloof sheen as I dump the supplies onto his drafting table. The difficult thing about Remy —I mean, aside from the fact he's completely guano—is that he looks so disaffected. It's easy to believe he's too preoccupied to pay any mind to other people, plus, he's hot. Like, attractive in the sort of way girls like me write off as too complicated to fuss with, because there are probably *other* girls, and anyone who *can* be picky usually is, and *Jesus*, that's just way too much work.

He's got his uninjured arm thrown back, tucked beneath his head as he watches me, eyes following the bottle of bourbon to my mouth. He waits until I've taken a swig to inform me, "That was a gift from Saul. Vintage, I think."

I look at the bottle. "Really?" At his nod, I take a longer drink, feeling the heat descend from my throat, to my chest, settling heavy in my gut. "Good. Fuck that guy." I bury a cough into my wrist as I pass the bottle to him, nodding. "Might want to hit some of that. I haven't stitched someone up in years."

He doesn't react beyond a brief twitch of his brows, tipping the bottle to his mouth. "You said I could draw on you again," he says.

"Yep." I grab his wrist, pulling his hand into my lap to finally get a good look at the gashes he'd made. I'm relieved to see the cuts are clean, if deep.

"You'll take off your clothes."

"No."

His eyes narrow. "You'll be a good girl. Tell me about the stars."

My lips press into a tight line. As a rule, I don't mind lying. Actually, I sort of count on it as a way of life. And despite the fact I'm being gentle and even considering getting naked for the man who might have shoved me off a tower an hour ago, I don't actually give a shit about this guy. Let him lose his mind for all I care. This is survival.

But one glance at his dark, intense eyes tells me that this is playing with napalm. If I'm trying to make Nick my weapon, then Remy is an unguided ballistic missile. Powerful, but too unstable to harness. Playing into his delusions is all risk and zero benefit.

I spot a box of black, disposable, sterile gloves, and help myself to it, tugging them over my fingers. "The stars would want you to know how to find them," I begin, cradling his fist in my hand. "You see them in your dreams, right? So I'm going to teach you."

Ignoring the dark, too-aware tingle of his eyes watching me, I grab a pile of gauze and antiseptic wipes and get to cleaning the blood away. The fine lines of his tattoos appear more clearly with each pass and I let myself appreciate them in a detached sort of way, how they cover his veins and shift with the tendons. For a second, his whole speech about considering curves and flesh begins making sense, as if the mere flex of his fist is suddenly bringing a sparrow on his forearm to living, breathing sentience.

"I used to get these... I don't know, nightmares, I guess," I begin, applying pressure with the gauze as I rip open the wipes one-handed. "They were so real, sometimes I'd wake up in the middle of running away, or beating on the inside of the—" The words slam into the back of my throat and then scurry back inside me, but I can still hear them throbbing in my ears.

I'd wake up beating the inside of the chest.

The issue was that sometimes it wasn't real, but *sometimes it was*.

I clear my throat. "It got to a point where I just couldn't know what was real or dream." Possibly the only good thing to come out of being handed over to the Lords is that I haven't had one of those nightmares in ages.

Not until Nick threw me into that elevator.

"But dreams are never as exact as we think. Like reading, for instance." He doesn't flinch when I run the antiseptic over the wound, even though it has to sting like a bitch. "If I can read, then I know I'm awake. When I'm dreaming, it's all just a big, confusing jumble of gibberish. But there are all kinds of tests.

Counting your fingers, stopping your breathing, checking a mirror…"

Ironically, Leticia taught me that. "*So you'll stop screaming in your sleep*," she'd said, eyes narrowed into an irritated glare. Reading has always come easy to me and has more uses than one. 'Gifted', my teachers used to call me, as if I'd go on to be some amazing academic prodigy. Instead, I've found more practical uses for it. I only need to read something once, and then I can remember it, and re-read it in my head later.

When I'm locked up, I think, trying to shake out of it.

"What I mean is that there are a lot of ways to make sure you're awake," I say, twisting to retrieve the suture kit.

"I'm not crazy." The words emerge quiet but decisive enough that I freeze, glancing up. His cheeks have found a little more color with the bourbon, and his eyes bore into mine with an intensity that borders on uncomfortable. "With all the people fucking around inside my head, everyone should be grateful I'm not rocking in a goddamn corner. Have you ever been told you're not allowed to think of something?" There's a beat of silence where I shake my head. Firmly, he repeats, "I'm not crazy."

I give a skeptical hum, tearing open the sterile needle and thread. "I'm going to assume you're not skittish about needles. Just stay still."

Stitching up wounds is sort of gross, but fairly straightforward. I watched a doctor do it once. Some guy my father used to pay to work on his soldiers when they got in a pinch. Someone discreet enough that he had no problem bringing him to my room, showing him my injuries from a particularly rough night inside the chest. When I got old enough to make myself 'useful' by saving my father the expense, I ended up being the one brought to bloody people at two in the morning.

My stitches aren't as intricate or sophisticated as his, but they get the job done. We're both quiet as I work, pulling the skin taut with each knot, but from the way his other hand starts tapping on the vinyl of the chair, I can tell he's still agitated, growing restless.

This becomes even more evident when his fingers wander over to my thigh, pushing up the hem of the hoodie I'm wearing.

"Wait." I shoot him a stern look.

He rolls his eyes, sinking back into the seat. "You said I could draw on you again," he repeats as I finish up.

I squint as I cut the thread free, surveying my work. Not too shabby. "Under one condition."

His lips tip up into a cold smirk. "You don't get to make conditions. You're mine. I can do anything I want with you."

Nodding, I reply, "True. You could tie me down and have your way. But you won't. Want to know why?"

He arches an eyebrow. "Why?"

I start bracing myself for the task ahead. "Because I'm going to prove that you're awake and I'm real."

I WATCH the top of his head as he fills in the snake on my calf.

It was the only way he'd agree to following my orders, so I lie here, just like last time, and let him have his way. The 'way' apparently involves a lot of black and red markers, and I allow myself to watch the design itself come to life. Last time, he'd turned it into a three-headed dragon, but this time, it's an intricate vine of flowers. The head of my snake appears from a bed of thorns, and for a moment, I'm incredibly fucking annoyed. I spent hours agonizing over this half-baked snake tattoo and twice now he's just shouldered in and created effortless masterpieces out of it.

Fucker.

Unlike last time, I'm still fully clothed—or as 'fully' as I can be in the tiny little cutslut shorts I've been given. It's still enough skin for him to rise to my knees, my thighs, his fingers grazing over flesh in a way that still evokes a sense of heat and restlessness.

"Don't tell Sy what happened up there," he says without stopping. "He'd get the wrong idea."

The wrong idea? What the hell does that mean?

I don't speak the words aloud, but Remy answers anyway. "He just overreacts sometimes."

"Tell me about it," I say, twisting to get a better look. "But sure, I can keep my mouth shut."

Although I do add this little piece of information to the list of secrets and lies these 'brothers' keep from one another...

"You should be naked," he mutters as I fight down a shiver. His eyes rise to my center, marker pausing. "I can't see the stars when you're in all these clothes."

"Tough shit," is my response.

His fingers tighten around the marker, but he goes back to drawing, jaw tensing every time he bumps into the hem of my shorts. I think I do a pretty good job of suffering through it, but when he begins pulling my knees apart to get higher on my leg, I jerk it away, eliciting a grunt of frustration from him.

"Time's up."

I'm fully expecting him to ignore me at best, hold me down at worst, but to my astonishment, he just frowns, stepping back. "It's shit. I told you, I can't visualize!" He gets the same look in his eye that I'm betting preceded all the sketches being ripped to shreds like confetti on his floor.

I'm in no hurry to see how such an impulse translates to human flesh, but it's the only thing I think can work with him. "I want you to ink me—for real." I tug my hoodie up and point to a spot on my hip. "Right here."

When he shifts his frustrated gaze from my leg to the patch of skin I've designated for him, his jaw loses some of its sharpness. "I don't ink bitches."

I parrot his words from before. "But you already marked *me*. I still have the Brass Bruin, remember?" His lips press tight, brows furrowing, and I get the sense that he's having an argument with himself. I add, "I drew it. It's not your art. It's nothing, just a few lines." At the curl of his lip, I offer, "Or just give me the needle and I'll do it myself."

"Nobody touches my gun." Wordlessly, he walks to the drafting table, glaring at the design I've drawn in a half-destroyed sketch-book while he worked on the snake. He taps at the simple outline of a seven-pointed star with his marker. It's not good, but it doesn't have to be. "*This* is supposed to prove you're real." It comes out a shade sarcastic, but he's also pulling on a pair of gloves, mouth slanted wryly as he inspects the drawing. "How the fuck is a shitty star going to do that?"

"Because we're here. This moment between us is real. The tattoo proves it. It won't wash away or disappear." I'm worried the instant I say it out loud that it sounds trivial and add, "Whenever you're confused, you can check."

He frowns, clearly displeased with my display of logic. "And you want it here." He hooks his forefinger into the waist of my shorts and wrenches it down.

"Not that low!" I snap, tugging them back up.

He pulls it down again, easily overpowering me. "If you'd take off your clothes, then I could see the fucking—"

I growl, "Draw the goddamn star, Remy!"

His head snaps back, eyes filling with fire. I had him pegged from the first moment I stepped in here. I can absolutely believe he *is* Remington Maddox, because Remy is clearly a spoiled little rich fuck. I bet no one's ever yelled at him before, told him to shut his mouth and get down to business.

"Look," he says, tone clearer than I've ever heard it, "If I'm going to break my code of not tattooing bitches, then I need you to cooperate a little. I'm not half-assing it. My art is a gift and I decide where it goes and how the process is going to happen." Ironically, he's looking at me in much the same way I'm looking at him. Like *I'm* the spoiled little Lucia bitch who's never been told what to do. "Pull down your shorts and let me find the right spot."

I shimmy the tight shorts lower, revealing my hip and most of my pubic area. His fingers brush over the skin, like he's reading the fine lines on a map. He stops on a smooth swath of flesh an inch from my hip, closer to my bikini line, and presses down. "Here."

"It's a little lower than I'd like—" He glares at me. "But it's fine. Fine!"

He turns away and opens a tall cabinet, revealing a complete set of tattooing instruments, including the autoclave for sterilization. Methodically, he pulls out everything he needs.

The intensity of his focus returns when he starts sketching the star on my skin, quick and sure, even though he glances over to the sketchbook every now and then for reference. The artwork is a million times better than my own, thank god. I already have one shitty tattoo to regret.

The sound of the gun buzzing to life is enough to transport me back to that night, pressed face-down into the Hideaway's mattress as he pricked their insignia into my shoulder. My hands curl, muscles going taut as the needle makes its first touch.

There's a perverse pleasure in this pain, the needle stabbing in and out like the barb of a stinger. I hate it at first, but the sensation spreads across my flesh. I almost regret that it's fast work, the design small and simple, because I feel the desire to sink into the vibration. Maybe I've spent too much time around this psycho, because the second he pops up, forehead creased into a sharp frown, I can tell he's itching to make it better.

Instead, the gun goes silent.

There's a long moment where he cleans the excess ink away, soothing the sore skin with something both astringent and good smelling, and I get the sense this is a bit ritualistic for him. As I watch the crease in his forehead slowly ease, I wonder how many times he does this. How many times does he tilt his head in contemplation of someone else's skin?

"Count them," I order, watching the way his platinum hair falls into his eyes. "Count the points."

Limply, he says, "Seven," and I shake my head.

"Use your fingers. *Count.*"

His green eyes ping to mine, flashing in annoyance through the strands of hair, "I'm not a Count, I'm a Duke." Despite this, he aggressively obeys, jabbing his glove-covered fingertip into each point. "One, two, three, four, five, six, seven. How the *fuck* is this supposed to prove anything?"

I scowl back at him. "It doesn't, asshole. You have to do the second part."

"What second part?"

Rising from the bench, I ignore the way his eyes instantly drop to my thighs, darkening. "Now, we sleep," I say, gesturing to the bed. "And when you dream—if you see me—you won't be able to count the points. So when you wake up, you'll know."

"Assuming I'm not already, what makes you think I'll even have a dream?"

I have no way of knowing he will. If nothing else, it'll go a long way to easing the shadows beneath his eyes, and maybe some rest will help him see reason. I give a helpless shrug. "You did last time, didn't you?"

Tilting his head, he notes, "Last time you were naked."

"Jesus fucking Christ," I mutter, hands slapping angrily against my thighs. "You know what? Fine. I'll get naked... *if* you take your pills."

His eyebrows rise hopefully and then crash into a scowl. "You think a lot of yourself. What makes you think your tits are worth me dosing myself into oblivion and making shit eleven times more confusing?" His words lose a little of the effect, seeing as how half of them are yelled from the bathroom next door. He walks back into his room with three bottles, not even sparing me a glance as he pops them open, one by one, and sets them on the table in a neat little row. He picks up the bottle of bourbon and finally looks at me, leaning back against the drafting table to pin me with his eyes. "Well?"

I point at the pills. "You first."

"*You* first."

Rolling my eyes, I shimmy my shorts down my legs and fling them with a kick of my ankle, arching a brow.

Eyes locked on my bare thighs, Remy picks up one of the pills and puts it into his mouth, swallowing it down with a swig of bourbon. "More."

I reach beneath the hoodie to slip off my panties, my awareness prickling at the way his eyes track their descent.

He takes the second pill. "More."

Sighing, I grab the hem of the hoodie and lift it over my head, wishing I'd thought to wear a bra today. The moment it clears my head, sending my hair into a wild cascade, Remy is already pitching forward, licking his lips. "Take it," I say of the third pill, my arms still in the sweater sleeves.

He obeys absentmindedly, and I'd had this whole plan to make him open his mouth and lift his tongue, but I know he's swallowed it when he takes a couple more sips from the bottle, throat bobbing as his dark eyes take me in.

I gesture to the bed. "After you."

I'm an idiot for not expecting what comes next.

Remy begins undressing, just like last time. "I told you before, Vinny," he says, smirking when I turn away. "I can only sleep naked."

"Great," I mumble, crossing my arms over my tits as I shuffle to the other side of the room.

The bed is messy, but I've been sleeping up in the loft, on the cold, hard floor, for so long that it's annoyingly inviting. Remy doesn't stop to clean it off, just falls into the bed, grabbing me on the way down.

I dive quickly beneath the twisted blankets, covering myself, but he's already doing the same, slotting right up against me. Remy's a touchy fucker, so I'm already tense in anticipation when his palm covers one of my breasts, thumb sweeping over my nipple.

"You know," his erect cock brushes the outside of my thigh, "last time I made you come."

"*Forced* me."

I'm looking pointedly away from him, but I can still see him in my periphery, propping his temple on his fist as his other hand squeezes my tit. "I could make it quick."

"I could make you a eunuch."

"I could make you scream."

I turn to him, finally meeting his hooded gaze. "Remy. Aren't you tired?"

"No." It's a lie, and from the way he drops his gaze, he realizes how obvious it is. He heaves out this long, beleaguered sigh and finally lets me go, collapsing to his back. I watch as he pushes his hair away, staring up at the ceiling for a long, silent moment. "Vinny?"

"What?"

"I don't think I'm awake." His voice is a rumble that's almost as grim as the lines around his mouth.

I turn on my side, drawn to his profile in some inexplicable way. A single slant of noon sunlight is cutting through his blinds, casting an eerie glow over the curve of his cheek, and I'm swept with the notion that he's asking me for something. Something only I can give him. Not an order, but more of a plea.

Maybe that's why I ask, "Why not?"

"I can't be," is his sleepy-slurred answer. "Because if I'm awake, then it means... this is just how it is. It means it doesn't get better." His eyelids dip low on a slow blink, cloaking something lost and hurt. "I'm probably asleep." His hand becomes limp, a sign he's finally drifted off.

Tucking my hand beneath my cheek, I trace the lines on his face with my eyes. He's callous and cruel and volatile, and right now, I'm not sure if I've ever resented anything more than the creases etched into his sleeping face, because it stirs something inside of me. This is the face of a person who's been hurting for so long, his face has forgotten the concept of slackness.

Turning away, the lie comes easily. And why shouldn't it?

I tell it to myself every day.

"It'll be better when you wake up."

～

Banging pounds in my head, loud and disruptive. My eyes fly open, and I jolt up at the same time the door swings open. Nick consumes the space, jaw tense, fists balled, gaze roaming over my body.

"What the f—" I start, voice scratchy from sleep.

"Jesus Christ! Don't fucking move!" Remy shouts and I freeze. I dart a look across the room where I see him perched on a stool in the corner. He's buck naked, holding a marker in his hand, with a thick pad of paper propped on his knees. "The door was closed, motherfucker," he barks at Nick. "We made a deal. I don't lock it if you don't barge in!"

"It's been eighteen-hours," Nick replies through clenched teeth. "I had to make sure the two of you were alive! What the fuck are you even doing in here?" He marches over to the bed and I see it. That dark, defiant flash of possessiveness that's always made me want to strike out. "And for god's sake, at least give her a blanket," Nick adds, lifting one up off the floor and tossing it over my body.

I still haven't moved, not exactly sure what's going on here. The last thing I remember is watching the noon sunlight peeking in through the blinds as Remy breathed deep and even beside me, his skin warm and electric against mine.

"Son of a motherfucking—" Remy's muscles ripple, cock swinging heavily between his legs as he dives for the blanket. He catches the corner and yanks it off. "I'm in the middle of something and you're ruining it! Why do you always have to ruin everything?!"

It's a loaded statement—the whole exchange is full of them, from the locked door to Nick's shuttered expression at Remy's words. There's so much history between these two—these *three*— that it's getting harder and harder to position myself outside of the line of fire. These are old wounds, but they're also fresh. Re-opened. Chafed raw. Normally, pouring some salt into them would be a good time, but I spent hours yesterday calming Remy into the dark-eyed, naked mess of fixation that stands before me right now. I don't need Nick coming in here and riling him up again.

"Nick," I say, trying to move as little as possible. "Remy obviously needs a little more time. Whatever you came in here for can wait until he's finished, can't it?"

His eyes meet mine and there's a tension there, like he wants to fight me. "I got something for you," he says, reaching into this pocket. He pulls out a rectangular plastic card and holds it aloft. "It's for the University library. You can go with one of us while we're on campus."

A rush of emotion hits me. It's too tangled up to put a name to; part surprise, part trepidation, and a spike of longing so intense that my reply emerges softly and choked. "What do I have to do?"

I know it's too big before Nick's mouth can even form the slow, malicious smirk. "I haven't decided yet." Ignoring us, Remy bends to roughly arrange me back into whatever position he had me in before. Nick's gaze moves to him, flickers of jealousy sparking underneath his stone mask. "What the fuck is *that*?"

Remy pauses, following Nick's gaze to the tattoo, and he flinches at the sight of the star. "She made me do it," he answers, and when he begins pressing his fingertip to each point, lips moving soundlessly with his counting, I find an odd sort of relief. "Seven is good. It's four, but also three. The tower has four sides but three faces. This is... it's empirical." His eyes meet mine, wide with a strange, energetic sort of awe. "I get it now." Remy's warm hands grip my thighs. I blame Nick and that library card for not expecting what comes next. Remy's finger dipping between my legs and parting my lips. My body stiffens at the first brush of his fingertip against my clit.

I try to slam my knees shut, squeaking, "Wait—!"

But he easily forces them apart. "You're real, Vinny. That means you're nothing. It means you're ours. Do *you* get it yet? Have you learned what it means to belong to us?"

I fight the shudder that threatens to roll across my skin. These fucking Dukes. Give them an inch and they'll take a mile.

"What are you doing?" Nick asks, jaw tight.

Remy's eyes are fixed on my center, swirling with fascination.

"Just enjoying the sights, Nicky." Glancing at him over his shoulder, he adds, "You know how she looks when she comes."

Nick's eyes flare angrily, because he doesn't. Remy's the only person in the world who knows what I look like when I come. But even though there's something black and furious in his stare, there's also an eagerness to the way he watches Remy touch me. "How does she feel?" Nick asks.

"Warm. She's already wet for us, Nicky." Remy pushes his fingers inside, wrapping his other hand around my thigh to spread me wider. He glances at me and there's a vicious mirth to his smile that wasn't there yesterday. "You ever wonder what ouroboros tastes like?" Holding my gaze, he pulls his finger from my pussy, only to slip it between his lips.

My fists clench against the sheets as I attempt to remain still. "I helped you," I remind him, as if that'll spare me.

Remy hums, pulling his finger free from his mouth. "Tastes like honey and static."

Nick's blue eyes glaze over as he watches Remy poke and prod my cunt. "Lick her pussy," he says, lids heavy, "make her come."

"*No.*" It emerges from my throat in a low, decisive growl that makes Nick's eyes narrow.

He lifts the library card. "If you want this, you'll spread your legs and take it."

But Remy's already dropping between my thighs, tongue sweeping a wide, hot path up my center. Without really meaning to, my fingers grab for his hair, belly tight with the tension of wanting and hating them for it.

I wonder when they'll realize I've won.

Maybe when I throw my head back against the pillow, toes curling as Remy's tongue flicks my clit, Nick will realize this isn't exactly the punishment he means it to be. Maybe when Remy dips low to plunge his tongue into my cunt, drawing a soft keen from my throat, it'll occur to them who's on their knees for whom. Maybe when my hips buck, back arching with a hitched breath, Nick will understand that he's just a spectator to a fight he's already lost.

My fingers clench against Remy's scalp, and I don't even try to push back the searing waves of pleasure that crash into me with every flick of his skilled tongue. My chest heaves with shuddering gasps and I guide his head, forcing him to my clit. I'm rewarded with a low rumble that vibrates through my core like an earthquake. Remy's good at taking direction here. His hands curled around my thighs as he makes a mess of me and all my slickness. I know I'm close when I wonder how terrible it would be if he were to rear up and shove his cock into me. I sink my teeth into my lip, muscles coiled tight, just in case.

Just in case I'm lost enough to ask for it.

Ten days.

I make sure I look at him just before the band of tension in my belly breaks free. *Nick.* He's watching with this slack, idiotic expression. Mouth barely parted. Blue eyes glazed. Hand shoved into jeans that have been hastily unbuttoned. There's a divot in his forehead that so closely resembles pain that it makes my fists clench in Remy's hair. Suddenly, I think I understand Auggy.

Because there's power here.

It's in the way Nick freezes when I moan. It's in the clench of my thighs around Remy's head, trapping him. It's in the way Nick's body seizes with mine, thick cum dripping over his fist, both of us diving off that jagged precipice with nothing but our own pleasure in mind. I cry out without really meaning to, back arching as Remy holds me down, growling ravenous sounds into my cunt.

My body falls heavy and slack, and for a long moment, I gulp in air, trying desperately to sate my lungs. The sweet aftershocks of my orgasm make my thighs tremble as Remy continues, uncaring of how sensitive I am. I try to pry him away, but it's a weak, halfhearted gesture that he easily shakes off.

It isn't until I hear the grunt ripping from his chest that I realize he's been fisting his cock. I feel his release more than I see it, rocking through my center in a sharp burst of vibration. Sticky, wet semen coats my thighs.

For a long moment, there's nothing but the sound of the three of us catching our breath.

Nick is the first to compose himself, jaw going sharp as he shoves himself back into his pants. "Get your shit done and send her out. Sy is taking her to campus today. I've got to meet Saul." He tosses the library card at me and it lands on my chest, right between my tits.

It's probably meant to be demoralizing. Payment for my 'service'. The whorehouse has churned out another worker bee. A commodity to be used. I suppose the shame is there, deep down, buried under the layer of armor I pulled over myself long ago. But I wasn't on my knees. I didn't have to take either of them into myself. If his goal was to make me feel like a whore, then he lost.

I pick up the library card, wetting my chapped lips.

To the victor go the spoils.

17

Simon

Whore.

I hear her shut up in that room with Remy and Nick, but even if I didn't, I'd still know. It's in the air, charged with sex and disgusting, private things. I spend too long frozen in front of the door, straining to hear their grunts. Her gasps. The moans and breath. The soft creak of a mattress' springs.

And I'm hard.

So goddamn hard, all the time now.

I gather it up and shove it down with the anger, my fists curling into tight, shaking fists as I tuck the feelings away. An ocean. That's what I use. It churns inside of me, white-caps of rage frothing it up, but I'm good at keeping it below the surface, always hidden under the depths. It's the only useful thing my mom ever taught me. Visualizing, meditating, learning to make myself tidy and even. Even though it sounds like wishy-washy nonsense, there's science behind this. Research. Verifiable evidence that it's effective.

So why is my ocean suddenly so goddamn difficult to still?

Nick is the first to come out. I wait from the entryway into the kitchen, leaning against the arch as my eyes track his path to his bedroom. He's flushed and heavy-limbed, fucked-out probably. I wonder how he took her. Did he bend her over Remy's drafting table? Did she spread herself wide for him on Remy's bed? Did she take them both, one after another? Or at the same time? Did Nick take her pussy while Remy fucked into her asshole? Did they fill her up, their cum leaking from her holes, dripping down her thighs like—

"*Oof!*" Slamming into me, Lavinia staggers back, a sheet fluttering to the floor around her. "Jesus Christ!" She scurries to cover herself with the sheet, but it's trapped beneath her. "Wear a bell, *Lurker.*"

She says it derisively, with a curl to her lip, but I'm too distracted with the sight of her naked body to pay her insolence the attention it deserves. Her shoulders are bare, two stark clavicles framing a delicate-looking sternum. Her tits are round and heavy-looking, two perfect handfuls crowned with two pert nipples.

The next thing I know, I've got her shoved up against the wall, my fingers digging into her warm flesh. She smells like sweat and honey and pussy, and god*damn*, I'm going to fuck her. I'm going to rip my way inside and slam into her little body until I can't anymore. I'm going to put my ocean into it, pumping her cunt so full of my cum that she'll be weeping it from her goddamn eyes. I'm going to—

"—off me, you fucking psycho!" Lavinia's fists beat against my chest, which is the only thing that sends me careening back to myself. My erection is pressing into her belly, pinning her against the wall just as much as my own two hands. Hands. One is gripping her shoulder while the other palms her full tit. I blink at it for a suspended moment, wondering when I started losing grip on my own internal tides.

But I already know the answer to that, don't I?

When all she does is gape at me, I snap, "Cover yourself up! I know you just got double-teamed, but believe it or not, this isn't the Velvet Hideaway!"

Lifting her chin, she grits out, "I did *not* just get double-teamed!"

My anger flares anew, almost satisfied by her flinch when I surge against her, gripping her breast. "Don't lie to me. I heard you in there, taking their cocks. Probably at the same time. Which one got your ass?" Her jaw drops and I scoff. "Remy, of course. Nick's too full of himself. He always comes in through the front."

Her teeth visibly clench. "I didn't take anyone's cock. You watch entirely too much porn."

"You're lying!"

"Am not!"

It's the heat of her eyes just as much as her skin that drives me to spin her, my hand landing between two smooth scapulas, pressing against the delicate bumps of her spine and crushing her into the wall. My other hand dips down and I force my fingers to her soft, warm center, blood boiling at the slickness I find there.

"You're a fucking liar," I growl into her ear, sliding my fingers into her wet cunt. "You're a goddamn—"

But she's tight.

Too tight, too tense for someone who's just had my brother inside of her. Nick isn't as big as me, but he's still big. She'd be fucked open if he'd had her—and chafed, swollen and raw if Remy had.

Jaw clenching, I pull my fingers from her cunt just to slide them up an inch, finding her asshole puckered and taut.

Huh.

She's smooth down here. Hairless. Wanting. So much heat is radiating between her plush cunt lips. My mouth parts against her ear as my fingers run up and down her slit, learning the topography of her sex. If this is how she feels around my fingers, then I can only imagine how it'd feel around my cock. Constricting. Slick. The sound of her muffled cries as I pushed her face into a pillow and *took*, sinking into the depths of her, my fist tangled in her hair.

I'm three fingers deep into her pussy when I slam back to reality, a sharp, pained squeak coming from her throat. Fuming, I fling myself away. "That's what you get for bouncing around here like a whore!"

She whirls on me with lava in her eyes, hastily gathering the sheet up. She wraps it around herself like armor, and the thing is, it's convincing. For a split second, that flash of fire in her eyes makes her look less like she just got violated and more like she's about to do the violating. "You're just as cracked as your friend. I hope someone's put you on medication, too, because I'm done stitching psychopaths' knife wounds! The next time one of you is carving yourselves up like a Christmas ham, I'm just going to stand back and let you go to town!"

I pry my eyes from the patch of skin above the sheet to ask, "What are you talking about?"

"Remy?" She gives me that haughty, condescending look that always makes me want to slap her. "Six-four, super rapey, likes to draw on everything and slice his arms up? Ring any bells?"

This time, when I slam her against the wall, it isn't to get my hands on any part of her body. It's forcing her gaze to mine. "Tell me what happened," I demand, fingers digging into her chin.

And that's how I learn about what went down yesterday. Through her fiery glare and tense jaw, Lavinia tells me about Remy cutting his arm.

"He looked me right in the eye, and just..." She makes a slicing motion, her eyes conveying the gravity of the situation with a flinty sort of anger. "He might as well have been using a marker. That's how casual he was about it."

It rests in my gut like a boulder that gets heavier with each revelation. My grip slackens, my shoulders fall, and my feet shift as if they're tiring of lumbering my body around.

I leave her there against the wall, falling into a chair at the kitchen table. "Fuck." I drop my head into my hands and exhale. He's supposed to be better. Meds and rest and a solid routine. It was supposed to make shit like this a thing of the past.

"I stitched him up," she says, shuffling her feet in an awkward, impatient gesture. And then, "Who's Tate?"

The question, just as much as the person asking it, makes my spine go rigid. I turn to look at her over my shoulder, noting her bedraggled, powder-blue hair, and the curious tilt to her head. "Don't," I say, voice full of warning. "You did Remy a solid earlier, and I won't forget that. But don't you ever say her fucking name." Without waiting for a reply, I pick up the plastic bag I'd walked in with an hour earlier, thrusting it into her arms.

Brow furrowed, she fumbles with it, her sheet almost slipping. "What's this?"

"A necessity." Folding my arms, I chew the words through gritted teeth. "According to my brother, we're supposed to take you on campus with us. I don't drive there—I run. It's part of my workout. So, on the days you go with me, you need to be dressed like someone who isn't prepared to get penetrated by the fists of Forsyth."

Shooting me a glare, she peers into the bag, seeing the pair of sneakers and athletic attire I'd bought for her. Out of my own goddamn money, too. A wild laugh rips from her chest. "You want me to *run* with you?"

"I don't want you to do anything but get the hell out of my life, but since that's not happening..." I pause to wait for her eyes to finish rolling, reaching out to jolt her chin up. "I've decided that I'm not adjusting to you. You can adjust to me. I'm leaving in five minutes. Get changed."

Jesus fucking Christ.

This was a terrible idea.

And there's no one to blame but myself.

When Nick first told me it was time to take Lavinia on campus, I knew why. He's kept her locked up in the tower, and he's salivating at the chance to show Forsyth who she belongs to now. I didn't need him to remind me that it's part of the game. Flaunting females is a Royal flex—one I've earned and one that's respected. I agreed for those reasons alone, but I had my own caveat. We're running there. Not just because of my workout process, but because I need to expend as much energy as possible when I'm around this bitch. Exercise helps more than anything.

Or it would, if we were actually running.

I bark, "For fuck's sake, Lucia! We're in Prince territory here! You want to run out of it before we get shanked, or what?" I'm a block ahead, finally outpacing the scent of her hair like it's the boogeyman or something. Every glance over my shoulder reveals her tits bouncing in the strappy contraption I'd bought for her. *Athletic wear*. Skin tight. Curve hugging.

Fuck the absolute entirety of my life.

"I told you I don't exercise," she gasps back, red-faced. Even when she slows to a lumbering gait, hands on her hips, chest heaving with big, strangled gulps of air, her tits pulse at me like two firm beacons, and now I'm remembering. I had one of those things in the palm of my hand. *Fuck*. "What'd you think? That I was doing Cross Fit in my various cells over the last two years? Fuck the Princes; I'm already fighting for my life here."

Irritated, I stop, waiting for her to catch up. The townhouses on either side of the road stand over us like a threat, making my neck prickle. It's too visible, but I've been running this loop since freshman year, and I'm not about to chart a new one just because I've become a Duke. The closest townhouse is PNZ—Psi Nu Zeta, the Princes' frat—and it's just what I'd expect. A cash-money facade that reeks of stale beer and generational disappointment. There's something pungent dripping from the balcony two floors up, and I stop just short of walking into it.

"I thought you looked like you were in pretty good shape." I try not to look at her body as I say it, but it's impossible. I know she's fast. She got a swipe in at Remy that night at the Hideaway, but that may have just been adrenaline. In the light of day, her arms are thin and feminine, although there's some slight curve to her bicep. Her stomach is flat, but on closer inspection, I don't see a lot of muscle underneath. You'd think that a female primed for a life of selling her pussy would have better stamina than this.

"I guess looks can be deceiving," she says, finally catching up. She leans against the concrete wall of the townhouse, pressing a fist into her side. "Like you." She squints up at me, a lock of her blue hair fluttering with a gasping exhale. "You look like a normal guy and not a circus freak with a dragon dick tucked in his sweats."

It'd be easier if it were just the rending claws of anger. I could shove it below the surface of my ocean and let the rhythm of the waves take it. It'd even be easier if it were just the lizard-brain spike of lust that I had to wrestle beneath the ripples, starving it of attention.

The problem with Lavinia Lucia is that I want to kill her almost as much as I want to fuck her.

That's what propels me forward, and the fear that flickers in her eyes is enough to bring both raging to the surface. "I'm about to look like the guy who strangled your ass in the East End and let the Princes take the fall for it. You think you're special because you sucked a couple of cocks a few hours ago? You're not."

Her head jerks back in outrage. "I didn't suck their cocks!"

Scoffing, I counter, "Please. I know my boys and their afterglow. If they didn't fuck your cunt or your ass, they definitely fucked your face." I've discovered the more I accuse her of being a whore, the more she reveals.

She proves me right, pulling her shoulders back to glare at me. "For your information, the only person getting head this morning was me!" At my dumbfounded expression, she smirks. "That's right, while you were picking out sports bras for this little cardio sesh, your buddy's face was planted firmly between my thighs. And while I was riding his tongue like a goddamn stallion, your brother was jerking off to it."

I blink at her for an extended moment because I'm building it in my head. The ocean gets swiped away like sand on marble, making room for the vision of Remy licking her pussy as Nick watched. I don't need to wonder what she tastes like. That bit of investigation was solved the moment we parted in the kitchen doorway, my tongue curiously sucking her from my finger.

But why?

Neither of them fucked her afterward.

What was the point?

Before I can think of a retort, we're startled by the sound of a door opening above us, making my hackles rise. There's a split moment of rowdy music, the static of distant life, and then the door slamming shut, casting the alley in silence once again.

Or *near* silence.

There's a small, soft cry overhead.

Lavinia's eyes dart up. "Do you hear that?"

Mostly I hear my molars grating. "Hear what?"

She holds still for a moment, head tipped back, palm raised. She points overhead. "*That.*"

Looking up, I see what's unmistakably a tiny white paw batting between the bars of the balcony. "It's a fucking cat."

She pushes off the wall and walks out toward the other side of the street to see better. "It's a kitten, not a cat. They just—they just threw it out there!" Her face hardens as she peers up at the thing. "Psi Nu cocksuckers. Shouldn't be in charge of a Princess, let alone a kitten." The ball of fuzz spots Lavinia and starts meowing in earnest. It's small, about the size of my fist, but it cries like it's a grown thing, long and pitiful. Lavinia's face falls, her eyes dropping to mine. There's a moment of tension that I don't quite understand until she pleads, "Come on, can't we get it or something?"

"Excuse me?" I look between her and the balcony. "That's not our cat, and more importantly, *no.*"

Rolling her eyes, I watch as she calculates the height of the balcony, gives her feet a testing bounce, and then takes a loose run at the townhouse. I see the attempted jump coming from a mile away. Before her feet leave the ground, I catch her, arms wound around her waist, and jerk her back toward the street.

She slaps ineffectually at my forearm. "Hey, you fucker!"

"I'm going to be late," I growl, tugging her away. "And if you want to have any time in the library, then you need to get your ass in gear!"

The kitten lets out an even sharper cry and Lavinia jolts away, glaring at me. "That kitten is too little to be out on that balcony! It could rain or get cold or—"

"Not my problem."

"But—"

I force her to keep walking. "It's not either of our problems. That kitten has a home, unlike *other* annoying pets." I slide her a significant look. "Someone put it out there for a reason." The little cries get louder the farther we walk away. "Probably because it's annoying as fuck."

"Wow." She glares at me through the awe. "You're just an asshole all-around, aren't you?"

Snorting, I say, "Tell me something I don't know, Lucia," and start jogging toward campus.

The library isn't a typical spot for Royals to congregate. They tend to hang around the student center or the fountain in the middle of campus. Wherever they can flex and be seen. Nick would be into that—Remy too, when he's feeling more like himself. Remy loves to be in the middle of shit—feeds off the energy of a crowd, the attention. It's why he loves the fight so much. But not me. Sometimes the worst part of a fight is the din of the crowd, the heat of their bodies, and the thrum of their energy. I'm beyond letting it distract me in the ring, but before and after? I could do without it.

It's the winning that does it for me. The thought that I've come out on top. The feeling of having conquered. It's just like I told my Pops about becoming a Duke. I never would have been happy as a mere Forsyth alum, and I never would have been happy as a regular DKS. If there's a step in front of me, I'm going to climb it—conquer it.

My major is no different.

"Is there a reason, other than torture, that you can't work on one of the two floors we just passed?"

In my mind, I thought I'd bluff my way through tucking her under my arm and publicly claiming Lavinia. I've seen the other Royals do it with their females. The Lords basically piss on their Lady, marking their territory like a pack of wild dogs. The Counts may as well lead their bitch around on a collar and leash. The Barons crowd around theirs like they don't want anyone to see her, but we all know it's bullshit. The Princes are the worst. They could carry their Princess through campus on a palanquin, and it wouldn't even surprise me.

Point being, I'd planned on making a show, but the second our arms brushed coming in through the doors, my cock grew harder than a lead pipe, which sent my ocean into a tempestuous froth. Twice today I've lost my grip. If it happens again, it could go one of two ways. I punch someone in the face, or I blow my wad in my shorts. Neither is acceptable.

I look back and see her half a flight of stairs behind me, flushed and breathless. I'd made her put on the sweatshirt she'd had tied around her waist before we walked in. It's cold in here and the last thing I need is her nipples staring at me all afternoon.

"It's more quiet," I reply, although I owe her no explanations. "And the books I need are up here."

She drags herself up the last few steps, eyes skating over the sign hanging over the entrance to the floor: *Behavioral Sciences.* "Huh," is all she says—whether it's meant to be judgmental or just due to the fact she's still struggling for breath. I cross the room to the bank of computers in the back corner and grab a seat, pointing to the one next to me. She drops into it with a loud sigh, sprawling out like she's been on her feet for days instead of two hours. I turn away from the sight of her spread thighs and open the screen.

"Behavioral Sciences..." She peers over at the screen. "Which one?"

I slide her a look that's full of warning. "You know, the amazing thing about being at the library is there's no reason for small talk. It's in the rules."

"Uh, huh. And you seem like such a rule-follower by nature." She reaches behind her head and yanks out the elastic holding her hair back, shaking it free. "Fine. If you won't tell me, I'll guess." Her eyes narrow in assessment, and I avoid them at all costs. "Economics? Seems boring, but then you're not exactly a paragon of adventure, are you? Or maybe Poli-Sci?" She hums to herself, looking way too comfortable here. "I guess that could come in handy, dealing with the Royals. Especially if you were going to be King. Which you aren't. Your brother is lined up for that spot."

Her voice is increasingly like nails on a chalkboard. Fucking stuck-up, know-it-all, big-tittied pain in my balls. We could have had a sweet girl like Verity, but *no*.

She bends over, flipping her hair forward to gather it up into her hands. While she can't see me, I take her in—the pale blue hair that doesn't go to the roots, her long slender neck, the gentle jut of her shoulder bones, and I'm hit with one immutable, striking fact.

She's mine.

I could have her anytime I wanted.

With a sharp whip of movement, she rears back up, smoothing her hair into a neat ponytail. The scent almost overwhelms me.

"Pre-law? The Dukes could use a good lawyer, but that's also a shit job with a terrible life expectancy, so I'm crossing that out." I glance over and see her tilt her head dramatically while tapping her finger on her chin. "That leaves sociology or psychology."

Not liking how good she is at this, I snap, "Didn't you want to come to the library to look for a book or something?"

She pushes a scoff through her plump lips. "And what, you're going to just let me wander around on my own?"

I fling a hand toward the stacks. "Go for it! Anything to shut you up so I can get some work done." She perks a little too much to be comfortable, but I don't really want her around to see what I'm looking up anyway. "Just stay on this floor and don't cause any trouble."

Before I can even finish my sentence, she's off, nearly sprinting toward the stacks. I watch as she takes a minute to orient herself and then disappears down the closest row. I have to trust that whatever deal she made with my brother is solid enough to ensure she really doesn't run. If she does? I'm not sure that's the worst thing either. At least not for me.

Once she's gone, I open the PsyGui portal and type in a few search terms; parasomnia, hypomania, mixed affective states, emotional dysregulation. All things that describe Remy's recent behavior.

At first, I thought it was just the transition. Moving into the Dukes' tower was always going to be a big adjustment for him. Remy has a thing about structures—homes, buildings, rooms. It's not just that he grows attachments, but also that he's so weirdly selective. Nick could probably sleep on a sidewalk if it's quiet enough, but Remy needs his wall scrawlings and what he'd once described to me as 'purple energy.' Whatever the fuck that means.

Pausing, I think of him eating Lavinia out this morning, and add hypersexuality to the list. That's the only thing that can explain *that*. It's not a surprise he's obsessed with her. It was one of my concerns about bringing a Duchess into the house, and it didn't help that we'd already had the dust-up with her in the Hideaway. But it's been a long time since Remy refused to take his meds. Since he legitimately tried to hurt himself. Since he actually succeeded. This is some freshman year shit, and if I don't find out why—and how to stop it—then I really am going to have to call his dad.

It's the deal I made when Remy got out of the hospital. We convinced his dad to let him enroll, to let him pledge DKS so I could monitor his moods and symptoms. Truth be told, I was naive enough to believe that, like me, the structure of training would help him level out. It's not that simple for him, though. Remy and structure go together like eight-balls and good decision-making.

It's why I chose psychology as my major. I figured I'd go into athletic training and really focus on developing the talent at the gym. But when shit hit the fan three years ago and Remy really started struggling, it clicked. My mother, predictably, was both ecstatic and worried. Happy I'd decided to follow in her footsteps. Worried about my motivation.

She's wrong about both. I'm not following in her footsteps. She's a goddamn *psychologist*. I'm a double major—psychology and biology. I'm going to be a *psychiatrist*. A *real* doctor. Remy doesn't need to talk out his feelings to get better. He needs to fix his chemistry. And most importantly, he needs someone who'll give a fuck. Not his dad, who'd be happy to lock him away in a padded room.

"Oh, wow, who's the hottie? I wouldn't mind him guiding me through freshman orientation."

"Ew. No. That's the one we were talking about," the hissed female voice floats over the computers, too loud to be unintentional.

"Which one?" the first girl replies.

"You know! The one with the giant donkey dick." My eyes flick up, and I see the Count's bitch, Sutton, standing next to another girl, openly watching me.

"Oh god, you mean the one who—"

"Blew his wad before he even got it in Richelle's pussy? Yep. That's the one."

Richelle. The name brings sour bile to the back of my throat. It all went down at the Fourth of July party on the river, sophomore year. It's one of the few events where we're forced to co-mingle with the other frats. The University requires it as an attempt to keep us in the spirit of brotherhood and community service, just like the dumb charity carnival. The royal women take the brunt of it by having to work together for planning, while we mostly get drunk, fucked, and have a good time. This particular Fourth party was no different—until this blonde with big tits and a barely-there bikini started following me around. She wasn't local, and had no idea who I was, which was admittedly a selling point. She started rubbing up against me in the boat dock, smelling like coconut and spiced rum, and I couldn't even think of a good excuse.

It was a weak moment. A bad day. I was coming off a dirty fight —the kind of fight you feel like Superman for winning—and I had enough shots and Jell-O shooters to fuel a fucking jet engine. I let her grind her ass against me to the music, and then I let her drag me to her car. Ten minutes, one kiss, and some unskilled fumbling later, I was shooting off into the soft skin of her thigh.

On the upside, she never had the chance to get weird about the size of my dick.

Sutton's eyes meet mine. She flips her hair over her shoulder as she crosses the distance between us, approaching me with an unearned swagger. "Perilini. How's the Royal life treating you?"

I keep my eyes on the research, scrolling the mouse. "Better than the case of clap, you're probably nursing."

Sutton's not new to the game, and she shows it by smoothly sliding her ass onto the desk, her bare, smooth legs crossing. "I was just curious. Things must be pretty chilly, considering."

"Considering what?"

She gives a delicate hum. "A Bruin in the belfry again. He's got the keys to the kingdom, and you're just riding bitch. Figuratively speaking, of course." I hear her smirk more than I see it. "Plus, he brought that sneering bimbo with him. You realize Lavinia Lucia is a murderer, right? To tell you the truth, we thought the Dukes were better than royal dumpster diving, but it's really nice of you to clean up our trash. Recycling is *so* important."

I click the mouse, already bored. "Since you're their bitch again, you'd know all about Count trash being recycled."

There's a long moment where the only sound is my typing, and then, "I'm being serious." When I finally feel irritated enough to look up, Sutton's eyes are hard and grim. "Duke or not, you're pre-med, like me, so I'm going to give you some advice. Get rid of her, Perilini. Take her to some abandoned West End warehouse, put a bag over her head, pull the trigger, and give the Barons a nice stack to get rid of the body." Her face is inscrutable, except for the flicker of displeasure when she looks away. "Lavinia is trouble, but her blood runs North, which means she's ours. She's *theirs*. The longer you have her, the worse the Counts are going to get."

The chuckle comes involuntarily. "You royal bitches never stop, do you? You're the pettiest, most insecure cunts in all four corners. I'm going to let you in on a little secret." Pitching forward, I keep my voice low and even. "The Counts being this wound up about it—so much that they make their pet whore risk life and limb to scare me away? It's the only good thing about Lavinia being my Duchess. And that's exactly what she is now. *Ours*."

She arches an eyebrow. "You really want to kick a nest of vipers?"

"I really want to whip out my donkey dick and *piss* on a nest of vipers, but taking Lucia as my bitch is a close second."

"They're only going to get worse," she insists, fingers tightening around the edge of the desk. "And they're already bad enough. Trust me."

"Is there a reason you're whining to me about your problems?" I ask, trying to figure out why the Cuntess is even talking to me.

"I thought you were smart, Perilini." A long beat pulses between us, and she leans in just like I had before, voice soft and secret. "I wasn't sent here to scare you. I was sent here to distract you."

"Shit." I jolt to my feet. "Where is she?"

"Aw, did you lose your Duchess already?" With a cluck of her tongue, she drops from the desk, turning away. "Don't whine to me about *your* problems."

I push past her, trying to remember which row of books Lavinia went down. I take a calculated guess and rush down the narrow aisle, craning my neck to search. It's empty and so is the next. I'm midway down a collection of medical journals when I hear two voices on the next row.

Fucking Perez.

"You and I both know this can't last," he's saying, the words uttered in a harsh whisper. "If you think kneeling for those meatheads is enough to save you, then you're about to be disappointed."

There's a sharp cut of laughter. "Poor Bruno. You look like a goddamn mess. Daddy must really be putting the heat on you. I imagine he's pretty disappointed in you for losing that fight." There's a pause, and then her voice emerges with a reedy tone. "Not to mention your trigger finger."

No one calls Perez 'Bruno', yet here's this little girl, calling him out.

"You cockteasing bitch," he mutters, followed by the sound of books dropping. "The only reason I lost that fight is because you can't keep your mouth shut! When are you going to stop fighting and accept—"

"I'm *never* going to stop fighting." The hatred in her voice is so full of venom and steel that it even brings me up short. "I'm never going back to him, and most importantly, I'm never going to be yours."

There's a quiet, pained sound, and then Perez hisses, "You think I want you? You think the Dukes want you? No one does. News flash, you Smurf-haired slut; you're the consolation prize. You're the bronze fucking medal of the Lucias. People take you because it's that or nothing. Leticia was better than you in every conceivable way, and when I finally have my collar around your neck? You're going to pay both your debts."

I stalk down the row, turning at the end, and feel the ocean inside me rage when they come into view.

Lavinia is pressed against the shelf, a pile of books at her feet. Perez has his forearm shoved against her throat, lips pulled back into a sneer. Spitting right into her face, he says, "The clock is ticking, sweetheart. Even you can't manipulate your way around a King's order."

My fists tighten, vision going red in that very particular way. It's been years since I got into a scuffle outside of the ring, which is the only reason I unhinge my jaw enough to speak.

"Ten seconds." Perez doesn't flinch at the flat, threatening sound of my voice. In fact, when he turns just enough to glimpse me over his shoulder, he barely looks surprised. "That's how long I'm going to give you to take your hands off my property. I'd say five, but honestly, I don't like her very much. Not that it's going to make a difference for you." I stride toward him casually, as if I'm taking a stroll through the titles, but the truth is I can't even feel the surface of the ocean anymore, dragged under by the thrum of my veins. "She belongs to the Dukes, to *me*, which means I'm about to make whatever my meathead brother did to you look like schoolyard roughhousing."

Lavinia's eyes ping from me to Perez, and the closer I get, the more I realize they're welling with tears. It brings me up short, because a few hours ago, I had her in the same position. I can say what I want about Lavinia, but this bitch is anything but soft. Her ability to take a little abuse is the only redeeming quality she possesses. It'd take a lot more than a little manhandling to break her.

This means, "You've upset her." Lavinia's forehead creases at the fury in my tone, but it's wiped away the second I snatch Perez by the neck. "Only I get to do that."

The ocean is a whirling, brackish froth now, and it's made all the more turbulent by the fist Perez swings out at me, still bandaged from his amputated finger. It's easy to dodge, to catch his wrist in my hand, to look at the forearm he'd had pressed into *my Duchess' fucking throat*, and let the ocean loose, releasing the dam.

Just a trickle.

Just enough to clutch his elbow and bring my knee up, jabbing hard into his ulna.

The bone snaps audibly, a crunchy, fleshy sort of human sound that echoes through the aisle, just as brittle as the pages around us.

Perez's face goes slack, but only for the smallest moment. The yell comes next, strained through his gritted teeth as he flings himself back, cradling his broken arm. Redundantly, he screams, "You broke my arm!"

This is always the hardest part, tucking the ocean away. Stilling the waves. Calming the currents. In a perfect world, I could bury the fist I'm flexing into his jaw a few good times. Maybe a couple kicks to the kidney while he's down. Fuck, it'd be glorious.

But I wouldn't stop.

This isn't the gym. This isn't a fight. There's no rules, no boundaries, no structure. I'd keep hitting and jabbing and crushing, until Bruno Perez was nothing but a lifeless lump of tenderized meat. He'd deserve it, but I wouldn't. He's not worth doing hard time.

So I breathe hard, fighting to pull the rage back into myself. I think of my parents and the look on their faces if they got the call. I think of Nick stepping into my shoes and taking over. I think of Remy, because if I were sent away, all it'd take is one bad day, and he'd be locked up in a different kind of cell.

The reality of the consequences cycle in my head, over and over. But they're not what finally snaps me back to rationality.

It's Lavinia, lurching forward and slamming her fist right into Perez's grimacing face. "I don't kneel to anyone, you piece of shit!" She pulls her fist back again and I see it in her eyes. This is a girl with no ocean.

She's not going to stop, either.

It takes more of my strength than I'd expect to haul her back, arm hooked around her waist as I drag her out of the aisle. Even two rows down, she's still struggling, mouth pulled into a snarl.

"Calm your goddamn tits," I growl, pulling her toward the emergency exit behind the records department.

By the time we reach the door, the fight's mostly drained out of her. "Let me go!" With one solid wrench of her body, she frees herself, shooting me a glare. "I could have gotten a few more shots in."

I glare back. "You always get your knuckles wet on someone else's kill?"

She flings her arms out. "If the opportunity arises, then why not?"

"That was pathetic," I tell her. "If he'd had a weapon or wanted to, he could have fought back."

She rolls her eyes, turning a tight circle. "I'm fine, Simon. Thank you for asking."

"And that punch was just..." Shaking my head, I don't bother disguising the awe in my voice. "Did you really tuck your thumb? Has no one ever taught you how to hit someone before? That shit is embarrassing, Lucia." Strangely, I find my lips twitching. "You hit like a girl."

Her eyes flash angrily and damn. She might not have the form or skill to back it up, but the pure determination in her glower could probably get her by, to a point. "I kick like a man, if you want a demonstration."

I turn to walk toward the social sciences section, knowing instinctively she'll follow. "I think you've demoralized yourself enough for one day."

As expected, the sound of her sneakers scurrying behind me makes my ears prickle. "You broke his arm."

Unapologetically, I confirm. "Ulna. Clean break. He'll be out of the game for a bit."

There are a few moments where I hear nothing but the sound of her shoes, and then her quiet voice, full of malice. "Good job." It's the tone that gets me. All patronizing and smug.

"Let's make one thing clear." Whirling around, I catch her shoulder, stopping her in her tracks. "I'm not your goddamn attack bear, Lucia. Perez got his due because you belong to the Dukes. You're not untouchable because you're special." Reaching out, I brush my fingertips over the red, angry skin on her neck. "You're untouchable because *we're* special. Don't forget that."

She follows me to the second floor without needing to be told, but her footfalls sound weirdly resentful, like she's dragging them along. Probably glaring at my back.

"So long as I'm untouchable."

～

The knock on my door is soft but determined, and there's no

doubt who's behind it. I consider not opening it at all. It's almost eleven, and I've had a long, bullshit day filled with bullshit hurdles and far too much Lavinia Lucia.

I just want to get some fucking sleep.

Tap, tap, tap.

"Jesus Christ," I mutter, resting my book on the bed. Sure enough, Lavinia, dressed in an oversized DKS hoodie and leggings, stands a few feet back, shifting her weight from foot to foot. I'd spent an hour in the shower scrubbing the scent of her off me, while pretty much rubbing my dick raw, and here she is again, assaulting me with her... goddamn fucking *everything.*

My eyes flick over her head to where my brother leans against his own doorjamb, arms crossed over his bare chest. A hard expression is plastered across his features. Jealousy, if I know Nick as well as I think I do. This is exactly the kind of shit I didn't want to get into.

"It's late," I snap. Her eyes pin to my chest before roaming down to the band of boxers. I fight the urge to cover my crotch with my hands. This bitch is on my turf. I'm not hiding my cock from her. "What do you want?"

Her gaze travels back up my body. "I know this isn't ideal for either of us, but..." She seems to find some spine, straightening to her full height. "I'm sleeping here tonight."

Again, I look over at Nick. He's watching us with a quiet intensity, but the knot in the back of his jaw tells me everything I need to know. I raise a hand toward him. "You realize my brother would throw a goddamn parade if you slept in his bed?"

Her jaw works from side to side, weight shifting, and I've only spent a handful of hours with this bitch, but somehow I can read the dull, wary cast to her eyes.

The problem isn't that Nick doesn't want it.

It's that he does.

Heaving a labored sigh, I step back into the room. "Why can't you just sleep in the loft like a good dog?"

She quickly follows me in, shutting the door behind her—probably more to keep Nick's glare off her back than anything else. "I made a deal. This is part of it. Three nights a week. Last night was Remy and the two before that were my nights off."

I know that's only part of the answer, but it doesn't matter. I know why she's here and not across the tower. Nick has attachment disorder the strength of an h-bomb. My brother never wants something at a reasonable level. We're alike in that way. 'Coming on too strong' is probably an understatement. Nick hasn't formed a healthy attachment in his whole goddamn life. I still don't see why that means I have to share my bed with this skank. Verity would have never made me do this shit.

Irritated, I point to the chair in the corner. "You can sleep there."

She rubs her temples. "It has to be the bed, or it doesn't count."

I glare at her. "Are you fucking kidding me? You negotiate worse than you punch!" Seething, I burst, "Fine. Take the left side of the bed."

The bed is king-size, but I'm not a small man. I move my textbook from the middle of the mattress and replace it with two pillows to act as a barrier, giving myself the majority of the space.

Lavinia stares at it for a long moment before shaking her head. "God, you're weird."

"Stop acting like this isn't the reason you'd rather sleep here." I reach for the pull on the lamp on the bedside table. "You'd better sleep like a goddamn rock, because the second you wake me up, I'm going to take it out of your ass." I pull the quilt up to my stomach. "And don't steal the blanket. If you piss me off, I'm taking you back to him. He can fuck you into corpsehood for all I care."

I yank the pull, shrouding us in darkness. It's not enough to block her out entirely. I can still sense her, but I drag the pillow over my head and roll away, pushing my back toward her.

I don't exactly know what my brother is trying to do with all this. Make me as crazy as Remy? Whatever it is, I've worked too hard on my self-control, my discipline, to let a pathetic little girl like Lavinia Lucia destroy all of that just by moving into my house.

18

Lavinia

The little nest I'd made in the loft is just what I wanted. I spent all afternoon and evening tucked away up there, reading the books Sy had impatiently allowed me to snatch from the shelves under his watchful gaze. I got a pretty good spread. A couple more Russian novels, a textbook on pharmacology, a medical triage manual, and—the result of a quick trip through the library's antiquarian section that had Sy nearly apoplectic—a book on 19th century classical engineering.

The loft is great for reading, not just on account of the natural light from the clock face, but also because I can watch the guys come and go and know they're focused on something that isn't me.

The problem with my nest is that it's uncomfortable as fuck.

This must be why it's so easy to fall asleep next to these men.

I knew it before, when I dozed off next to Remy's bare, warm body for an entire day and night, but Sy's bed is just as comfortable to fall asleep in.

Waking up, however, isn't so easy.

It's not the dark that makes me struggle for breath—although it doesn't help. It's the stillness. The sensation of being closed in, unable to escape, the feeling of being *surrounded*, and that's exactly what I'm feeling now. It's been a long time since I've woken up like this. Stiff with panic, convinced I'm still in the chest, sweaty and shaken and helpless. Ever since those two nights in the elevator, I've felt it lingering on the edge of my awareness, prepared to sweep me up in its grip, but I've managed to remain vigilantly on the other side of it.

Until right now.

The dreams—the night terrors—used to be the worst. Leticia taught me how to know what's real, but nothing ever touched *this*: waking to the feeling of being restrained, trapped on all sides, unable to move.

I'm lying on my side, that much I'm sure of. My chest twitches with a quivering inhale, and I can lift my eyelids far enough to make out a dim slice of night, but I *can't move*. My legs are trapped. There's a solid wall against my back, and weight bearing down on my ribcage. The pressure of a hard rod crushed between my ass cheeks pulses. There's something else, though. Something distinctive. A sort of... heaving flutter against my back. An undulation.

My brain erupts in a confused flurry.

I was bad.

How long have I been inside the chest? Is he going to let me out soon? If I scream, he'll make me stay longer. Father doesn't suffer disturbance. But sometimes I can't help it, and I can feel it building now. The scream. It's wedged in my diaphragm like a bomb, and the fuse is sparking to life.

But then the wall shifts behind me, dragging me against it.

The undulation is the rod, pushing into my ass in these small, rolling waves. The heaving flutter is warm against the top of my head, seeping through my hair. My breath begins coming in tight shudders that wheeze through my nerveless jaw like a whistle, because this isn't the chest. This is something new.

The elevator?

The image of my father's face in my mind morphs into Nick's. I glimpse the tattoo on his temple, but the numbers are indecipherable, blurry shapes. What were they, again? Two, seven....something. His blue eyes burn into mine with so much anger. I'm being punished, aren't I? Wouldn't go to bed with Nick. Chose his brother instead. Tossed into the elevator and shut in until morning. Too hot. I can't breathe in here. Why won't he let me go? Doesn't he know I'll die here? Doesn't he care?

The undulating suddenly stops.

So does the fluttering warmth.

There's a moment of such utter stillness that I almost wonder if I've fallen asleep again, but then the weight on my ribcage gets snatched away, the wall behind me disappearing. There's the shuffle of fabric and then my body rocks a little. I'm surrounded by a scent that's almost recognizable: wood and coldness, an undertone of mint, and something aggressively masculine.

A voice cuts through the darkness. "Calm down." It's a strained, yet somehow sluggish rumble that resonates through my bones. The whistle between my teeth quickens. There's a sigh, and then something touches my shoulder. "You've got sleep paralysis. Wake up."

Everything begins clicking together. I know this smell, spicy and cold. I know this voice, plowing through the night with all the bluntness of a hammer. Nick hasn't thrown me into the elevator.

It's Sy.

I went to sleep in his bed, and that must be where I am. I can see the back of his door and the faint light bleeding through the crack beneath it. But I can't fucking *move*.

There's another touch on my shoulder and then Sy is rolling me to my back. Everything is blurry and dark, too hard to find the edges of. I can feel them, though. Sy's hand shaking me. The jut of what I'm now realizing is his cock pushing into my thigh. His hand moving to my neck, my throat, fingertips pushing into the tendon.

He's checking my pulse.

My vision swims, and for a moment, I get a clear visual of him hovering beside me. His face is little more than a blot of shadow, but a slice of light from the moon casts his jaw line into sharp relief.

The pressure on my jugular eases. "Still can't move?" he mumbles, voice thick with sleep.

Can't move. Can't speak. Not even when those fingers begin sleepily wandering to my collarbone, trailing a line of fire toward my sternum. They pause there for a brief moment, and in the fog of my vision, I see Sy's head tip down, a lock of curls flopping over his eyes.

The first brush of his palm against my tit is nothing like it was earlier. That one had been harsh and painful, full of contempt. This one is testing, his thumb grazing curiously over my nipple, which I can feel pebbling beneath the oversized shirt I'd stolen from Remy that morning. I hear more than see Sy wetting his lips, shoulder shifting as his palm gives my breast a squeeze. It's soft at first, almost...considering.

And then it's harder.

At some point, my breathing began to calm. But he has done the opposite, the gusty sound of his breaths loud in the space between us. It gets louder and deeper with every press of his cock into my thigh, a vestige of the undulating from before, hips rolling against me.

My vision begins sharpening when he rolls on top of me. That's how I know he's only half awake himself, eyelids heavy as he parts my thighs and begins rucking up my shirt. There's some distant part of my mind, too trapped by the pull of sleep to fully surface, that's thrashing and snapping and still afraid. This might not be the chest, but it's not safety, either.

It's Simon Perilini, fist of Forsyth, surging into the cradle of my thighs.

My eyes track the ridges of his pecs and abs as he braces himself above me, quietly thrusting his massive cock against my crotch. The quiet of it—no barbed words, just quick, hushed panting—is so incongruous to the Sy I've come to know that I can almost deceive myself into believing I'm still asleep. There's no hatred here. No glares or slurs. Just the tight curve of his jaw as he braces on his forearms and... uses me.

That's what he's doing.

I'm a warm body for him to position how he likes, one of his big palms wrapping around my thigh and hitching it over his hip. I'm an opponent without a weapon. Here in the dark, it could even be a secret. Something that happens in the thin void between oblivion and wakefulness.

"You're sleeping." His voice is barely a whisper, and his eyes are drooping heavily. I don't know whether he's speaking to me or himself. The crush of his brows as he thrusts against me, muscles tense and coiled, is too deep and desperate to be anything but unconscious.

His eyes close, lips parting, and every rolling press of his pelvis against mine makes the tip of his nose drag against my temple. Instinctively, I know he'd never show this distressed urgency if he were completely awake. There's no dignity or power here. Just pure, lizard-brained lust.

He's hunched over me, his warm, spearmint-scented breath washing over my face, when I begin to feel the stirrings. His cock dragging over my clit sends a cascade of electrical pulses deep in my belly. I chase them, these fiery sparks of life leading me through the dark and into the light. Somehow, I know they're the way back.

My first free movement is a small twitch of my hips.

Sy freezes, chest jumping with his short breaths, and god, I can *feel* him. His erection throbs against me like a living thing.

The next movement he makes is a hard jab of his hips that jolts my whole body. His cock stutters against me. It's how I know he's still wearing his boxers, and I'm still wearing my leggings. It doesn't feel nearly as messy as it should, because my next moment of awareness is that my panties are soaked.

At some point, my jaw has eased, meaning my breaths are less of a whistle and more a series of increasingly eager gasps. My toes curl, and then I gain movement in my knees, my thighs, and I could probably find a way to wedge a foot between us and kick him off, but instead I'm wrapping them around his hips, pulling him close.

Sy makes a sound into my cheek that's ragged and torn and *damn near inhuman*, and the instant I regain movement in my hands, reaching blindly for his shoulders, he's shoving them back down, pinning my wrists to the mattress. I know I'm awake when the pain hits me. It's not the sharp shock of hurt I'm used to. This one is bone and flesh, his pelvis grinding so tightly into mine that it's painful. It's the pressure of his weight pinioning my arms to the bed. It's the drag of his chest against my sensitive nipples, the flash of his body heat that fills my veins with fire.

Through it all, I can see him, dark curls swaying against a creased forehead as he slams his body into mine. In that barely cognizant way of being too swept up in the pleasure to think of a good reason why I shouldn't, I lift my neck to watch. It's dark in the room and even darker between us, but I can still see the edges of a body that's carved from stone. The flex of muscles beneath Sy's warm, brown skin.

Briefly, I'm fascinated by the art of it—and that's exactly what it is. Sculpture made flesh. All those muscles, all this power, all the raw, unrestrained hunger in his lurching movements, fixed on me like a burning thing. If Remy could see this, he'd probably have something horrifically poetic to say about it, and I'm taken by an urge to know what it'd be.

Even when his breath begins punching from his chest in these strained, agonized grunts, it's still so strangely quiet, as if the dark has made the two of us evanescent and hidden. The rhythm of the friction doesn't make me any better, my gasps coming faster, sharper, fed by the electric pulse that's building in the apex of my thighs. I tighten my legs around his hips, my heels digging into the tight, muscular curve of his ass, and I can't look away.

The tip of his massive dick has escaped the elastic of his boxers.

It's horrifying to look at in the light of day—to think of it ripping into me—but here, in our odd sleepy trance, it's just like his body. A monument of masculinity. I'm too far gone to flinch away from the fleeting thought of my wet, aching cunt falling prey to that monster.

My orgasm rips through me in a flash of white-hot sparks that are swallowed by the darkness. My soft cry folds itself into the cadence of sound around us. The creaking mattress. Sy's frenzied panting. But I know he feels it in my body, my feet slamming to the bed as I dig up against him, savoring the pressure of his thick cock rutting against my clit.

He takes in a ragged gulp of air and seizes, pelvis crashing painfully into mine. "Oh, god," he groans. "Oh, *fuck.*"

I feel his cock erupt.

Warm, sticky cum surges between us, coating my belly with wet heat. The tips of my fingers prickle with numbness because he's still holding my wrists, cutting off the circulation. It's the only thing that keeps me grounded as I soar, throwing my head back to take in more air, more air, more air.

It feels like we float our way to a slack collapse, like a pair of autumn leaves fluttering to the ground. My shirt, I realize, is tucked up over my breasts, wedged beneath my armpits. The weight of his chest against mine is almost too much—too heavy, too warm, too slick with sweat and cum to be comfortable—but without it, I might just float away.

There's a long moment where we just breathe into each other, my chest caving with his exhale, his chest dipping with my inhale, and I get a lungful of his scent. It's delivered to me by the softness of his curls as he turns his head.

His mouth brushes against my jaw.

It's as if he's falling back into slumber in the cradle of my body. It's a slow, uncoordinated gesture that probably isn't a gesture at all. It's barely even damp, hardly fit to be accused of tenderness.

But it's almost...

It's almost like it could have been a kiss.

I wrench myself away from him. I don't know how, with his body being so heavy and limp, but I jolt from under it as if I'd just been electrocuted.

"What the fuck are you doing?!" I smack my palm against the light switch by his door.

Sy is up in an instant, but he's off-balance, hastily tugging his boxers up. I watch it in perfect detail, the shift from his half-asleep trance to the towering mess of hatred I've come to know. It's a miracle that all that tension and contempt snapping back into his posture doesn't knock his sorry ass right over. It bears down on me through the force of his glower. "You planned this," he snarls. "You fucking—I was asleep and you—you *made* me!"

Frantically, I tug my shirt down, torn between outrage at the accusation and disgust at the feel of his cum cooling on my skin. "You're the one who—!"

But he barrels right over me, teeth clenched as tightly as his fists. "You think you can come in here and pussy whip us, don't you?" His wild blue eyes jump to the bed, and I don't know how to process the flash of panic I see within them. "You laid here and waited for me to fall asleep, and then you fucking baited me!"

"I couldn't even move. You saw me, I was—" What's the term he used? "Paralyzed! You knew I couldn't move! If anyone got violated here, it's me."

But he's tugging at his hair, looking about two seconds from losing it. "That was all your fault! I knew you liked that night at the Hideaway!"

I gape at him, utterly at a loss. "I bet people think you're the stable one, don't they? Normal, respectable Sy, the only Duke who has it together." I give a low, bitter laugh. "I thought Remy was the insane one here, but he's the only one out of the three of you who doesn't bullshit himself."

Sy doesn't stop me when I wrench the door open, fleeing back to my cold nest in the loft.

Nine days.

～

THE NEXT AFTERNOON, I'm standing awkwardly outside of Remy's door. The never-ending, pulsing music vibrates from the room, and I'm hesitant to interrupt him on account of it being impossible to know which version of the guy is going to open the door. The rich, entitled Duke? The rapey, artistic prodigy? Or the brain scrambled maniac that rambles on about stars and colors and forces me to be his canvas.

Inhaling deeply, I lift my fist and rap on the wood, hoping it's loud enough for him to hear over the thudding bass. The music lowers a beat before the door flies open, making me take an instinctive step back. He stands there in a dark gray button-down shirt, although the actual buttons are conspicuously missing, revealing a swath of his tattooed torso. My eyes drop to a pair of black leather pants molded to fit his lithe, long body like a glove.

A gust of weed hits me in the face like a physical force.

He looks me up and down with heavy, bloodshot eyes. "Did you come to yell at me for not catching you?" The question is asked with a sour tilt of his mouth, as if such a motive were plausible but inconvenient.

I blink at him for a second. It's ten in the morning and after what happened between me and Sy twelve hours ago, I'm too exhausted to bother untangling Remy's enigmatic comments. I cut to the chase. "Do you have a paintbrush I can borrow?"

His head snaps upright, some of that weed-fog draining from his expression. "Type?"

Blankly, I repeat, "Type?"

"Round? Flat? Fan? Mop? Filbert?" he asks, eyebrows rising with each word. "There are a dozen different styles. Glaze? Angle?"

I shuffle my feet uncertainly. "Uh, something that I can use for dusting in tight spaces? I won't be painting with it."

Even though he doesn't look away from me, his eyes go unfocused again. I think it might be whatever passes for pensive when it comes to Remy. Without answering, he abruptly turns on his heel and crosses to his worktable, picking through cups of brushes. He plucks one out and stares at it pensively, running his thumb over the bristles.

He returns with a slow gait. "This work?"

"Yeah, it should." I reach for it, but he holds it up, out of my reach, nodding to my hip.

"Let me see it."

Pausing for only a moment at the unexpected request, I hook my thumb in the waistband of my leggings and tug it down on one side, revealing the star. It's still red, irritated at what happened last night with Sy, and coated in a thick sheen of ointment. But the lines are stark and clean.

Frowning, he reaches out to graze his thumb over the northern-most point, counting them in a clockwise motion. His touch is gentle, sending an unwanted shock down to my core. My goal had been to give him a literal touch point—something to help him navigate the lines of reality—but now I'm wondering if that was such a good idea. Shit's getting really confusing here.

He trails his touch away from the star, glancing quickly across my pubic area before pulling away. "Here it is." Bracing a palm against the doorjamb, he hands it to me, eyes tracking my fingers as they take it. His chin falls in a nod. "Good brush, nice and thick. Fucked a redhead up the ass with it last year."

My hand freezes, suspended in the air between us. "Fucking *seriously*?"

"No." His impish grin is the thing of wet dreams, I'm sure of it. He's probably pulled that out and leveled a whole room full of girls with nothing but that evil twinkle in his eyes.

I really need to get a fucking grip. "I'll return it when I'm finished."

"Keep it." He shrugs. "I can buy more."

As if having conceded that I've been tortured enough, he vanishes back inside; the door closing with a click. The music begins thumping to its original, migraine-inducing volume.

I turn around and find Nick sitting on the couch, those blue eyes fixed on me like a laser over the distance of the large, open space. If Remy's stare is mischief personified, then Nick's is the embodiment of intensity. He's in a black T-shirt that pulls taut across his chest, arms spread indolently along the back of the couch. I didn't even know he was home, but I've come to realize that's how he is.

Invisible when he wants to be.

Inescapable when he doesn't.

I start toward the kitchen, and he makes a sharp sound.

"Where are we, Lavinia? What am I doing?"

I stop short, scowling, with my back turned to him. "I just need to look for something in the kitchen real quick." When I get no reply, I glance over my shoulder, catching the way he's looking at me—dark and full of warning.

Mother of all fuckers.

Deflating, I turn and cross the distance between us, insides flaring angrily at the way his face transforms into a stony smugness. This asshole is like a needy hellhound.

When I drop into his lap, he hooks his arms around me, arranging me how he likes. I guess the two brothers have that in common. Nick's not happy until I'm turned to the side a bit, his growing erection beneath my upper thigh. Like this, I can't avoid his stare. "What was that about?"

"What was what about?" I ask, locking my eyes onto his face tattoo. Two-three-seven. It makes me remember seeing him in that dream, the numbers an indistinct blur.

"You're not the right type of pretty to pull off that level of dumb." He tugs down my waistband, revealing the star. The muscle in the back of his jaw twitches when he lowers his gaze to it. "Remy said you made him do this. Why?"

I squirm. "I just liked the design."

"You're lying, but I'll let it slide. For now..." Nick is exactly pretty enough to pull off 'dumb'. I wonder if I should take it as a compliment that he never tries it on me. "Why were you at his door just now?"

"I needed something."

"Of course you did." He raises an eyebrow at the paintbrush and then clamps his hand around my wrist—which is still sore from last night. I do a pretty good job of hiding my wince, tightening my grip around the thick wood of the brush's handle. "What were you going to look for in the kitchen?"

I give a resigned sigh, leaning into his body. "I need a wrench and a screwdriver."

I can feel his patience fading. "What for?"

"The clock," I relent, voice sharp enough that his eyes narrow. "I wanted to knock around up there, see if I could find out what's wrong with it. That is," I add bitterly, "if it's alright with you."

His eyes flick up to the cables overhead, forehead furrowing at the lifeless clock face. "Jesus, girl. That piece of junk hasn't worked in decades. I don't know if there's anyone living who's ever seen the hands turn."

"So you're saying there's no wrench or screwdriver?" I roll my eyes, tugging against him. "Is it so fucking hard to answer a basic question?"

He wrenches me back. "Apparently. You've been skating around all of mine." His arms are like steel around my waist, crushing me close. "You let Remy touch that ink on your hip for a paintbrush. What will you give me for the tools?"

"How about a working clock?"

A sardonic punch of air escapes his lips. "I don't give a shit about the clock. I want something else. Something worthwhile." His eyes travel down my body, like he's pondering the possibilities. But I know the moment he smirks at me, meeting my gaze through his lashes, that this is something he's had in mind for longer than the span of this discussion. "I want a blow job."

"I bet you do." I snort, but it's easy to slip back into the push pull of negotiation. Lifting my chin, I offer, "You can touch my tits."

A wave of defiance crashes into his features, which is all the warning I get before he plunges a hand up my shirt, grabbing my tit. "I know I can," he says, voice hard. I shrink back at the menace in his stare, but he follows me, his palm unrelenting. "I can touch your tits anytime I want. Morning, afternoon, night. These?" He gives my breast a squeeze that's aggressive enough to make me wince. "These are *mine*. If I need to offer you something so I can stick my dick in your mouth without the risk of you biting me, I'll do it. But it doesn't make you in charge of this." Pointedly, he pinches my nipple. "A man has needs and you've been sorely neglectful of your duties as Duchess. Maybe having that library card—reading all those goddamn books—is a distraction from what you're meant to do here."

It makes me recall waking up last night, convinced he'd thrown me in the elevator for spurning him. With all of his 'gifts' and barters, it could be easy to forget what Nick is, but he's never slow to remind me. There's a small part of me that flinches against a sense of hurt and I look away, refusing to let him see it. The library card had been such a big gesture, it almost made me believe he wanted to give me something big. Something important. Something thoughtful.

He's just building something he can tear down later.

God, he really is like my dad.

One mention of that elevator and he could make me give him a blow job—hell, a dozen of them, every day. But instead, he's doing this. Making me cave to it, bit by bit, step by step, in ways that only I'm to blame for. With every boundary I barter away, I begin to wonder which is worse. The blunt certainty of powerlessness, or the gradual, escalating supplication to it.

Tonight, I'll have to sleep in his bed. Maybe it's better to set up the expectations first. "I'll... give you a hand job."

A satisfied smirk tugs at his lips. "That's more like it."

"But I don't need another paintbrush. I need everything on this list." I reach into the narrow pocket down the side of the sleek athletic leggings Sy got for me and pull out a scrap of paper. "Not just the screwdriver and wrench. *Everything.*"

If we're going to barter, then I'm going to get something worthwhile.

He takes my list and skims over it, muttering the supplies out loud. "Oil, large s-hooks, cable, wire..." His eyebrow shoots up. "This is going to fix the clock?"

"I don't know. Maybe, with an understanding of the mechanics. I've been doing a lot of reading." Not appreciating the dull cast of skepticism in his gaze, I burst, "I need to do something! I'm stuck here every day with fuck-all in the way of stimulation, and it's going to drive me up the wall. The last thing this tower needs is another mental health crisis!"

If he's taken aback by my outburst, then he hides it well enough. "Fine." He tucks the paper in his back pocket, hips bucking into my ass as he lifts. He gestures at his crotch, the bulge already pronounced. "I'm ready when you are."

I give him a sullen look. "Now? Seriously?"

He grins, dark and sadistic. "It's called a 'job' for a reason, Little Bird. Show some work ethic."

We stare at one another for a long moment, and it becomes obvious that he expects me to do the work of unbuckling his jeans and getting this started. I refuse to let him see my nerves, although I don't keep the revulsion off my face. Rolling my eyes heavenward, I grab his belt, gingerly unbuckling it. The skin of his lower belly, and the rough trail of hair beneath it, is warm against my knuckles. I lower the zipper and pause, waiting for his hips to lift before reluctantly inching down his pants and boxers. His lower abdomen dips as I make contact, and he reacts by spreading his arms across the back of the couch again, getting nice and comfortable.

The light thatch of hair nestled above his cock greets me first, but just below I can see he's already erect, the hard length of his cock straining against the crotch of his jeans. If it weren't for the fact I've seen his brother—I can still feel the tender bruise on my pubic area from Sy's sleepy, late night railing—I could say Nick's the most hung cock I've ever seen.

After a couple aborted approaches, I finally woman the fuck up and tuck my fingers into his pants, touching his hard, hot flesh and pulling it out.

"You really are turning this place into your whorehouse."

I turn and see Sy standing in the middle of the living room, jaw clenched so hard that it looks painful. Nick's cock twitches against my palm and I recoil, snatching my hand away.

"Hey, hey, Little Bird. No need to stop." Nick grabs for my hand but I shift away, cheeks flaming. The last time I saw Sy, he was looking a lot like he did now—pissed off and a few seconds from hitting something—only this time, his abs aren't covered in his cum. Nick looks between us, probably noting the simmering tension. "My brother's a raging prude, but he can handle it. He'd probably jerk off to it later."

Sy's fists curl. "This has nothing to do with being able to handle something or not. It's time for dinner and Mama will kick our asses if we're late." He stalks over to Remy's door and pounds on it. As soon as the music inside halts, Sy barks, "Time for dinner! We're leaving in five minutes!"

"Dinner?" I ask, looking between the two of them. Nick winces as he stuffs his boner back into his jeans, spitting a low curse. "No one told me about a dinner."

"Family dinner," Sy hostilely informs me, "is every Thursday night at the gym. It's so we can carb-load for Friday Night Fury." He gives Nick a pointed look. "Everyone knows that."

Remy's door flings open. He's still in the leather pants, but he's put on a clean shirt, and this one even has buttons—although they don't start until halfway down his sternum, revealing his toned, inked chest. He shrugs a jacket over his shoulders; the bottom flaring at his hips. He seems more alert than he has in days. His eyes instantly dart to me and Nick on the couch. "Something going on?"

"Nothing that can't be postponed," Nick says, dragging his fingers under my hair, against my neck. "A deal's a deal."

I don't bother leaning away from him, because it'll just make his grip on my neck tighten punishingly. "I keep my word, asshole." I still need the tools, and I know better than to think he'd just give them to me.

"Tonight." He dips forward lightning quick, pressing an open-mouthed kiss to the pulse point on my neck. My body clenches with the struggle of hiding the shocked shudder that ripples down my spine, but he lingers long enough to feel it, his words fluttering a hairsbreadth from my ear. "For the best, really, since you're sleeping in my bed. That way you can take your time, do it up right." Suddenly, my whole life narrows down to the closeness of the moment, his breath and scent, and I get this vivid image in my mind of Sy on top of me, face contorted with desperation.

My eyes flick to his.

Sy stares back.

Whatever spell I'm under is rudely broken when Nick rises from the couch, holding my head long enough to thrust the bulge in his pants against my cheek. It's a crude, half-joking gesture that makes my stomach swoop in humiliation. It doesn't get any better when he chuckles, giving my head a patronizing pat. "Go change into something acceptable for a Duchess. Tonight is your first real appearance in front of the club. You need to make a good impression."

"Show off those pretty tits," Remy says, spinning a marker between his fingers. "Something with cleavage."

Scowling, I jog up the stairs to my loft, depressingly grateful for the scant distance to collect myself. There are times when I feel a little bit of control and it seems like I can do this—I can handle them—but then there are other moments when I realize I'm just an object for them to put on display, to use for their pleasure, to *possess*.

It'd be no different with the Counts.

Sometimes I wonder why I'm fighting it at all.

19

Lavinia

The gym has a different vibe than I'm used to when we step through the doors. It still has the overwhelming scent of sweat and testosterone, but it's mingled with the thick, garlicky aroma of Italian food. I've never seen the DKS frat gathered all at once, and certainly not like this—clean, well dressed, and good-natured. Even the cutsluts seem to have tamed it down a bit for the event.

Which royally fucking sucks for me because I look like a hooker sent to fulfill a thirteen-year-old's dreams.

"Why did you tell me to dress so slutty?!" I hiss, punching my fist into Nick's side. His arm is looped around my shoulders, wrist loose, hand grazing my breast with every step we take.

"I like it when you dress slutty," he says, looking down at me—or rather at my tits. The top I'm wearing had gotten Remy's approval, low cut and pushed high. The wire from the bra stabs into my ribcage like a skewer.

I scan the room, face falling. "Everyone else is dressed all...nice."

'Nice' isn't exactly the right word. I was raised in the North Side where any gathering ranking higher than a random grocery store run-in necessitates a show of the nicest finery and frippery one can dig from their four-hundred square-foot closet. These people aren't dressed 'nicely' for Count standards.

But they certainly are for the Dukes'.

The cutsluts are all wearing cute little dresses—the kind girls their ages would wear to Sunday school in the East End. Besides the top, I'm wearing a tight pair of burgundy pleather pants with diamonds cut down the side—hip to ankle—showing off plenty of skin. The cutsluts are also hard at work carrying huge pans of food and placing them on tables arranged on the back wall. The area typically used for floor seats has been transformed into a dining hall with long tables and chairs filling the space. Frat boys are gathered in clusters around them, all obviously eager to eat. Every eye in the room swings toward us as we enter, and I know they're not just looking at me.

The four of us are a spectacle.

Remy alone looks like some kind of glam-rock god, not even raising the sunglasses that are hiding his weed-glazed eyes.

Nick is... well, *pretty* is an understatement. But it's the effortless, fundamental kind of pretty that means he doesn't even have to show an effort.

And Sy? He's obviously dressed for the event, looking casually superior in a dark gray V-neck sweater with a white-collared shirt underneath. I've gleaned enough of their history to understand that these are *his* people. He called it a family dinner and now I see why.

But I'm not family.

Duchess or not, I'm an interloper at best, and an enemy at worst.

"You look perfect," Remy says, resting his hand on my ass, his thumb tucked under the waistband on the side of the star. I stiffen, never sure if he's going to push things or not, but he just gives my ass a firm squeeze. "Our sexy little snake."

I spare a glance at Sy, who kept quiet the entire car ride over. I suspect he has a few choice comments about my outfit, but his attention is pointedly focused across the room as he waves to Mama B.

"Boys," she says, waving them over. She gives them each a quick hug and a kiss, bracelets clinking with every move. She very intentionally ignores me. "Nice of you to finally show up. We've got a lot of hungry young men here, and they can't eat until you do."

"Sorry, Mama," Sy says, pulling back. Her lipstick imprint remains on his cheek. "Took us a few minutes to get out of the tower."

"Better late than never." She licks her thumb and wipes off the lipstick mark, fussing over him like the mama bear she is. "First family dinner as head of the house. How's that feel?" Mama brushes Nick's hair off his forehead, beaming at him.

"Like a long time coming," Nick says, surveying the room. A wistfulness falls over his features, a flicker of something uncharacteristically hesitant. "I guess this is what it's all about."

Remy is next to greet her, darting around me to swoop her into an aggressive hug. "Mama Bad Bitch! Those cubs running you ragged?"

She gives a boisterous laugh. "If they didn't, I'd get worried. Can't remember a time I didn't have all you cretins underfoot, driving me to drinking."

There's a strange affection here, much too physical for my tastes. In North Side, the Counts show deference by bringing in revenue, and they show respect by not getting wasted until business has concluded. Here, there are hugs and back pats, kisses and playful tackling.

It makes me tuck my limbs in close.

Mama gives Remy's stomach a lighthearted jab. "Where's your muscle mass gone, boy?" Her eyes flick over to me and then back up to him. "You eating enough? You look like you've spent the last two days in a South Side alley. You aren't getting into that viper junk, are you?"

Inwardly, I balk at the look she cuts me.

"Nah, not me," he says, finally lifting his sunglasses. They push his hair away from his face as he tucks them up on his head. "Just had a few rough days. Went off my meds for a minute." This makes her lips purse tight, and there's a current of tension so palpable that I can practically see it running between the five of us. Remy easily casts it off. "Please tell me you made your world-famous garlic bread. My dick's been hard for a loaf since I woke up."

She works her mouth into a bright smile, giving his cheek a fond pat. "I saved two loaves in the back just for you. Verity will get you all settled."

"Sweet." He kisses her on the cheek and walks off toward a group of guys, bumping fists and slapping hands along the way. The celebrity of Royalty has never been lost on me, but it's still odd to see it bestowed on the same guy who babbles nonsensically and slices his arms up.

Mama turns to Sy, eyes dark. "Should I be worried? Is he stable?"

Sy shifts his feet, dropping his gaze. "Maybe? I don't know. It's hard to tell with him sometimes." I know Sy's more worried than he's letting on. I saw the books he checked out of the University Library. I might not have told him about Remy almost jumping from the belfry, but I get the impression Sy can sense that things are worse than they seem. "But I'm thinking it was just the transition, you know? All the changes."

She nods. "You're probably right." The boys start toward the long tables, Nick pulling me along. But before we can pass Mama, I feel the sharp prick of her nails digging into the back of my arm. "Hold it." I stop and Nick looks over, catching Mama's sweet grin. "I need a word with your Duchess, if that's okay?"

Nick gives her a long, measuring look, and I think for a moment he may refuse. He'd be well within his rights. Inside the tower I might have bargaining power, but out here? There are appearances to keep.

He reluctantly slides his arm from my shoulder, relenting. "I'll save you a seat, Little Bird."

Mama and I watch as he departs, the confidence in his saunter to the group. A cutslut immediately intercepts him for a hug, stretching up to throw her arms around his neck. The sight of his hands landing on her hips has my mouth pursing in annoyance.

I deliberately turn away, facing Mama. "Look, I'm sorry about the outfit. The guys wanted me to get dressed, and they... well..." I cup my boobs, "asked me to show a little tit. I didn't realize dinner had a special dress code."

Mama's eyes flick over me, narrowing as she crosses her arms. "I don't give a shit what you wear. Come to dinner in a potato sack for all I care. The problem is that you were supposed to be here two hours ago. You're the fucking hostess of this thing."

"Me?" I stare at her in astonishment, head snapping back. "I'm not the hostess. *You're* the hostess! They called it family dinner and you're the Mama."

Her face tightens to stone. "I know you spent your life as a spoiled little North Side brat, but you're not in your Daddy's kingdom anymore. Don't stroll in here like a goddamn queen. You haven't earned that title—not yet." She snorts. "You've barely earned the title of Duchess. And I doubt you ever will if Lionel has anything to say about it." I blink and she nods. "Yeah, I know all about your daddy and your sister and how totally fucked you are." She arranges the bracelets on her wrist, revealing an old, faded bear's paw. "My roots run deep with the Royals, Duchess, so here's a bit of advice. If you want a shot at staying in that belfry, you better step up your game."

I give a low, incredulous laugh. "First of all, I don't want to be in the belfry. And second, it would help if someone gave me a fucking heads up that I'm supposed to do something other than suck cock, clean dishes, and talk maniacs off of ledges." I jerk my head over at the Dukes, who are currently hovering over one of the tables, surrounded by their brothers and cutsluts. "You think those three can take a break from their libidos and power trips long enough to give their trophy bitch a primer on house duties?"

"Oh, please." She rolls her eyes. "Don't play that game with me. You're a smart girl, Lavinia. I think you can figure out how to manage this life." She turns her gaze to the cutsluts, jaw hardening. "Dozens of these girls have spent years in training to serve DKS, and a few for the Dukes specifically. If you're so lost that you require direction, then maybe you should consider lowering yourself to ask one of them."

I open my mouth to say something snide back, but her fingers clamp around my chin. She gives it a tight, threatening squeeze. "Verity's in the kitchen. She can tell you everything you need to do. And while you're taking advantage of that, you might want to reflect on *why* she can tell you everything you need to, and show some goddamn grace." She drops her hand, which is good, because I'm one second from removing it myself. "If that's something you're capable of, that is."

This ancient bitch thinks she knows me—my history—but she's wrong. Only one person knows what it was like to grow up under my father's thumb, and she's gone. It's not like Dukes are ruled so harshly. As if being under Saul Cartwright's thumb ever accomplished anything worth crying about.

I walk away before I do or say something I'll regret and head toward the kitchen door at the back of the gym. I feel the eyes of everyone on me as I cross the room. The only ones not particularly interested in me are the Dukes. The three of them fit in easily here. Nick is engaged in telling some kind of animated story, and Remy has his arm slung over the back of a chair, a trio of girls surrounding him. Even Simon looks relaxed, beer in hand as he tutors a pledge on his fighting stance. I guess they have me where they want me.

Serving them.

I wouldn't put it past any of them to have planned it this way, setting me up to be scolded by Mama like an unruly child. The thought bristles inside of me like a storm, and when I step into the kitchen, I'm fuming hotter than the heat of the room.

What kind of gym has a goddamn kitchen, anyway?!

The girl I met the other day, Verity, is removing a pan from the oven, while another cutslut picks up a large salad bowl and moves toward the door I'm blocking.

"'Scuse me," she mutters, giving me such a wide berth that I have to wonder if she thinks stigma is contagious.

"Yeah, sure," I mutter back, not bothering to step out of her way. The crouch of her brow as she inches around me is the closest thing I'll probably get to satisfaction today. To Verity, I say, "Your mom sent me in. Is there something I can do to help?"

Although it's a million degrees in here and she's juggling a dozen tasks, other than a quick assessment of my outfit, Verity is unfazed. "Yeah, the bread needs to go out, along with this bowl of sauce. The salad dressing is in the refrigerator—oh, and the parmesan cheese."

I open the refrigerator and grab the items she listed, cradling them in my arms and hands. Carrying them out, my eyes are drawn to the table where the guys are sitting. It's fucking ridiculous that someone like Mama can accuse me of arrogance when the Dukes are sitting at the head of the most prominent table, clearly distinguished from the rest of them.

Except, of course, for the cutslut sitting in front of Remy, like an appetizer.

She's on the table with her legs spread, making room for him to lean in and press his marker to her throat. Her head is tilted to the side, and even though she's grinning at another girl a few seats away, her teeth are digging notches into her bottom lip.

He's drawing a design down her throat, dipping low to her sternum.

I stop mid-step and stare at them without really knowing why at first. Something indefinable twists in my gut. The feeling is too hot to be called disappointment, but too unhappy to be called irritation. I just know that he's pitching forward, those green eyes fixed on this bitch's skin, and it makes me think '*no*'.

Verity passes in front of my line of vision, nodding at the crowd. "We need to get this on the table or there's going to be a riot soon."

I blink, snapping out of it, and follow her over to where the food is already stacking up. It looks to be buffet style; the spread arranged in a calculated order. I intuit it quickly, placing the dressing by the salad at the beginning of the intended circuit, and the cheese over by the meatballs.

Verity pulls the aluminum foil off a dish of pasta and looks over at the table. "You don't have to worry about Haley. She's not poaching your man."

My back straightens and I busy myself with taking off the dressing caps. "I'm not worried about some random cutslut."

"Haley's not just a cutslut," Verity says, a bit of sharpness in her voice. "She's a ring girl."

I raise an eyebrow. "What's a ring girl?"

"A ring girl is a fighter's biggest cheerleader." She carries serving utensils to all of the dishes. "She helps him warm up before a match, wraps his wrists if he needs it, fetches water, snacks—whatever they need, really. She'll promote him on social media and have his back on campus. She's a total hypewoman."

"Haley does this for all of DKS?" There are at least forty guys in the frat, all fighters of one level or the other.

"Haley, specifically?" She shakes her head. "No, she just works with Sy and Remy. I mean, those two are joined at the hip, so it makes sense that they'd share a ring girl. She knows what they need."

Why?

Why does that sentence make me rankle?

"She knows what they need."

Part of it is ingrained within me—this aversion to failure. I'm the Duchess. *I* should know what they need. But another part of it is an odd sense of indignation, as if being on the receiving end of everything that's miserable about being Duchess should make me privy to the praise of it.

If I'm theirs, then why the fuck aren't they *mine*?

"What about Nick?" I sprinkle some cheese on a dish of lasagna—something to keep my hands busy. "Doesn't he have a girl?"

She gives me a strange look. "He wasn't here last year, or the year before that. You didn't know?"

I hold back a scoff. "Trust me, no one was more aware of that than me." Nick wasn't here because he was busy being down in South Side, keeping me captive.

Nodding, her confused expression doesn't leave. "Well, Nick doesn't have a ring girl. He doesn't need a ring girl." There's a beat of silence, as if she's waiting for something to dawn on me. "He has a Duchess."

Oh.

So *Nick* is mine.

Fucking figures.

I glance over at the table. Haley has her head tipped back now, feet swinging leisurely as Remy draws something intricate enough that his brows are furrowed in concentration. Feeling that same hot, inner twist, I shake the container of cheese and the shredded pieces fly all over the place. "Shit."

"It's fine." Verity collects it all in a napkin and wipes it into her hand, glancing at the frown I'm too slow to hide. "Are you okay?"

"I just..." I don't know how to word this or why I even care. "It seems like the Duchess would do that stuff for all of them. Why do Sy and Remy even have a ring girl?"

She laughs and tosses the napkin and cheese into the trash. "Ah, you don't know a lot about DKS, do you? I mean, you know about the Royal stuff, obviously, but not about our frat or the West End." It isn't said in a snotty sort of way, but it still makes my teeth gnash. "The West End doesn't have a lot of resources," she patiently explains. "The gym is great, don't get me wrong. We have a lot of trainers around here, and sometimes Saul can spare someone from the Athletic Department, but for the most part?" She tilts her head toward the frat. "The fighters are responsible for their own team. That's why the Duchess is always pre-med. It gives the Dukes a better medic than we're used to."

I give her a wry look. "So, what, they're using Haley because I'm not training to become a podiatrist or whatever?"

Verity averts her gaze, an awkwardness settling across her features. "It isn't actually my business, but if I had to guess? They probably just don't think it's something you'd want to do. Or maybe it's a trust thing. They've had Haley for a long time, and you're..."

"The enemy," I mutter, straightening the salt and dressings. Everything seems ready. "Look, is there a manual for all this somewhere? Because I'm going to need one to know when I'm supposed to be somewhere early, or when I'm supposed to just sit still and look like a whore." Jaw tightening, I add, "Or when I'm *not* supposed to look like a whore. Is there like a dress code chart or something? Showing up looking like a hooker at a church picnic isn't my jam."

She grins. "You look fine."

"*Not* according to your mother."

She sighs, throwing a look in Mama's direction. "Hey, I'm sure the Dukes think you look spectacular." *Well, at least two of them.* Beaming, she adds, "And they're the only ones who matter."

"Yikes." I grimace. "You girls don't just drink the Kool-Aid, you chug it."

Rolling her eyes, she starts back to the kitchen. That's the cool thing about Verity compared to these other people. She seems able to take a few lighthearted barbs. That must be why something niggles at the back of my brain. Straightening my spine, I follow her in, finding her standing in front of an open drawer, sorting through a huge container of flatware.

I lean against the counter, watching. "Can I ask you something?"

"Sure."

She hands me a bundle of forks that I need both hands to grasp.

"You've known the guys for a while, right? Longer than just them being in DKS?"

She nods. "Yeah, my Mama knows their parents from back in the day."

"Right." A few forks slip and I squeeze my hands tighter. "Do you know who Tate is?"

She freezes. It's almost indiscernible, but I catch it. "Tate who? The guy's Tate?"

"Yeah, I guess so." I readjust the bundle, watching Verity carefully. "She just... Remy mentioned her. It seemed like they're close."

"Boy, it's been a while since I've heard that name." She grabs her own handful of utensils, but again hesitates, this time looking up at me. "I know you want to understand how to be the best Duchess. Sometimes that means not picking at old wounds."

"I'm not trying to pick at any wounds here, I'm just..." Huffing, I glance at the door, thinking of him out there, using another canvas, and wondering why that's rubbing my insides so numb. "Remy had this really scary episode the other day. It just seems like the more I know about him, the better I can navigate his issues. This Tate girl seems important to him." Important enough that he's risking every- thing to change history. "Just tell me, Verity."

She holds my gaze for a suspended moment, searching my eyes. Whatever she sees there makes her sigh. "Tate Cross used to run with them when they were kids. They were all crazy inseparable, like... best friends. Everyone figured if they pledged, she'd end up being their Duchess, but the truth is, Tate wasn't Duchess materi- al." She tosses me a significant look, grinning. "Tate wasn't *guy* material, if you catch my drift."

I process what she says, realizing. "So she wasn't like...a girlfriend."

"No more than Remy is." Verity laughs, but her smile is short- lived. "She died a few years back. Suicide." Her eyes move to the door, a sadness etched into her features. "It really messed them up. I think... I think maybe they blame themselves. Or maybe they blame each other. Either way, after Tate died, Remy was never the same. Nick ran off to South Side and joined up with the Lords. Sy dedicated himself to the fight." She meets my gaze, voice lowering. "Don't tell my mom, but a small part of me might be a bit relieved I didn't get picked for Duchess. They're amazing, but I doubt they'd ever let another girl in. In a way..." Her head tilts as she assesses me. "In a way, I guess it had to be someone like you. Someone who isn't a friend." She pulls back a little, eyes widening, "I mean... I *don't* mean... that's not to say they hate you, or—"

"Chill out," I say, halting her. "I get it. Or, at least, it doesn't bother me. My shitlist is as long as my forearm, and they might not be at the top, but they're pretty fucking close."

She nods, smoothly accepting this. "Plus," she adds, throwing me a wink. "Now that I don't have to be pre-med, I can drop my organic chem class. Silver linings. That's my thing."

20

Nick

"Vinny," Remy says, pushing his nose right into her cheek. "Be a good girl and get me a drink."

We're at a table of twenty DKS, most too absorbed with their food to notice this little exchange, but Sy and I make eye contact across the table. This is probably as close as Remy gets to asking nicely for anything, and Sy seems as curious as I do to see how she'll respond.

She pauses, fork hovering an inch from her mouth, and slowly lowers it back to her plate. She's been quiet and solemn the whole dinner—probably pissed about us not telling her all the criteria for her Duchess position. If I had to wager a guess, I'd say she's under the impression we did it on purpose in an attempt to humiliate her. That's probably easier to swallow than the truth, which is that none of us actually care about her public-facing role as Duchess. She's here for *me*, not DKS. That's why I want her looking like this, all hard and soft and sexy. Let everyone see her skin and know whose fingers get to touch it. All I want to do is peel those pants off and play with what's underneath, but unfortunately, *we* have obliga-tions. Sitting through this dinner is one of them.

Remy's arm is curled around her hip, thumb tucked under the waist of the leather pants. From the placement and shift of the shiny leather, he's rubbing small circles over the tattoo he'd put on her. It still chafes to know he did it. I can count the number of chicks he's inked on one hand, and Lavinia somehow takes two of the spots. The brass Bruin was unavoidable, but the star?

What the fuck is that all about?

"Sure." She swallows back her hesitation and untangles herself, taking care not to place her hand on me for balance as she squeezes through the chairs. "Lemonade or tea?"

He turns to give her that lopsided grin that girls around here always go crazy for. "Mix a little of both together?" When all she does is turn to the drinks table, he calls out, "Thanks, Vin!"

I watch her retreat, eyes tracing every counter of her ass in those pants. "What did you do to her, Remy?"

He stabs a few leaves of lettuce on his fork. "What do you mean, what did I do? She's here to serve us, right?"

"I think what Nick is asking," Sy says, leaning on his elbows, "is how did you get her to do that without scratching your eyes out first?"

I watch as she begins filling the cup. "To be fair, there's still time for her to slip some arsenic into your drink. Or at the very least, spit in it."

"We all know it wouldn't stop me." When Sy and I just stare at him, waiting, Remy shrugs. "You saw her talking to Mama before. I think this attitude adjustment is more about being on the receiving end of a lecture than anything else." His lips curl and I have the fleeting thought that he looks better today than I've seen him in weeks—maybe even years. "Or it could be that I just ate her pussy *that* well." His tongue flicks out, wagging obnoxiously.

"Jesus Christ," Sy mutters, pushing his almost clear plate away. "I'm trying to eat."

Remy reaches out to emphatically tap the table. "One day,

brother, you're going to learn that licking a woman's pussy is the best meal a man can get."

Sy responds by sliding his chair back and heading for the dessert table.

As I watch him go, I see someone enter the front door. "Shit," I mutter, back straightening.

"What?" Remy asks.

I tilt my head toward the door. "Saul just walked in."

His gaze follows mine, watching as Saul strides across the gym, his expensive shoes gleaming in the overhead lights. It's been a few days since we've spoken. He's giving us time to bask in our victory, to adjust to living in the belfry, but the Kings never rest for long. A new semester means new business. It's always busy on the Royal front, and the crime trade around here doesn't slow for regime changes.

It's not unusual for a King to show up at a frat wide event, nor is it a surprise that he walks straight to us. I stand and drag Remy to his feet, appreciating the protocol. I don't have any more respect for him than any other King, but Saul is our boss. I've never been a Duke before, but playing deference to a King?

I know that shit like the back of my hand.

"Pretty Nick Bruin," he says, flashing me a grin. His hand thrusts out, and I catch the glint of his ring before shaking it. The worst thing about using my name to gain entry into the royalty is the fact I have to share a ring with him. "How's the belfry treating you?"

"Good," I say, matching my grip to his. Saul's history is linked a little too closely to my own—my family's relationship intertwined with his. "It's an adjustment, but nothing I can't handle." Over his shoulder I see Lavinia turn away from the table, a cup in each hand. She pauses when she spots Saul, instantly turning back to the drink spread. "I like a good challenge."

"Yes, you do," he replies, gaze moving to my right. Saul never quite looks like he knows how to approach Remy, but he keeps trying, and it's no wonder why. Remy is heir to the Maddox fortune, and that makes him more valuable than any other DKS, no matter how unbalanced and strange he might seem. "And, er, how about you, Remington?"

Remy's not quite as into following protocol as I am, so only half his attention is on Saul. The other half is on the piece of garlic bread he just crammed into his mouth. "Fine," he says, chewing with a thoughtful expression. "The tower's soul hasn't wasted me yet, so that's a plus. A lot of people look up there and see decay, but it's just a skin, and that," he jabs the bread toward Saul, "is something I can work with."

"That sounds... positive." I don't really like the way Saul smiles at him, the tilt of his mouth a touch too patronizing. Remy's not a goddamn child. He doesn't even sound crazy once you understand his language. He's just saying the tower is better than people give it credit for. He's saying he respects its history, which means he respects the institution. It's a fucking compliment.

And Saul has the nerve to look all indulgent. "You've always been quite the character, kid. You just tell your daddy that the tower could use some work. The West End needs business from people like him." I'm careful to keep the scowl off my face when Saul puts his back to him, speaking directly to me. "So, look, I need to take care of some business with Miss B, but you three come find me when you finish dessert. We need to talk."

"Yes, sir," I reply, locking gazes with Remy as Saul claps me on my back. The two of us watch as he heads over to where Mama's standing, arms crossed, leaning against the office door. Everyone knows they go way back, but the way she looks at his approach is a mixture of exasperation and endurance, so who even knows what that history looks like. Saul runs his hand down her arm, leaning in to say something to her. When they step into the office, closing the door behind them, I finally let my glare free.

"You shouldn't let people like him treat you like that," I tell Remy. "He talked down to you, and then he basically shut you out. Fuck that shit."

But Remy just gives me a blank look, shrugging. "People like him only know two ways to treat me." Instinctively, I know which people he's talking about. The Kings. His dad. Old, powerful shitheads who see Remy and wonder why he isn't locked in a padded room. He looks at his slice of garlic bread a little too intensely, jaw going sharp. "Trust me, this is the better of the two."

We're interrupted by Sy, who lets out a loud whistle, getting everyone's attention. He's standing at the head of the room, watching as all eyes turn on him. "Tomorrow is the second Fury of the semester!"

There's a sudden burst of cheers, so loud that Lavinia's shoulders rise toward her ears as she shuffles over from the drink table. As soon as she hands the drink off to Remy, I grab her arm, hauling her into my side.

Remy nudges me with his elbow. "Isn't that supposed to be you up there?" Dukes only have one leader—the King—but I'm a Bruin. I'm the blood legacy. Everyone's expecting me to be the face of the belfry, but I'd rather be its fist.

I shrug.

It just feels right that it's Sy up there, commanding the crowd with nothing but his quiet power and simmering intensity. If DKS is expecting flash, then they're not going to get it. Not in the way they're expecting.

Looking sour, he continues, "I know you're all used to the Dukes hyping the suspense of which house we're going up against on Fridays. Throwing out clues, making you guess, running bets. But we're not those Dukes." His eyes pass over the members, skittering over the cutsluts. "No frills, no fuss, no bullshit. Tomorrow night, we fight against the Beta Nu."

I watch as the news rolls over the room, fists rising in the air as the guys cry out in approval. Jaiden Spann yells out, "Hell yeah! Fuck the Barons!" and everyone echoes, "Fuck the Barons!"

Sy doesn't savor it, his voice slicing easily through the celebration. "It's not about who we're fighting. It never has been. It's about showing Forsyth that the West End is still in the game. It's about *winning.*" His dark eyes land on Remy's. "I don't know about you, but I'm sick of everyone else coming out on top. The Princes, the Barons," his eyes land on me, "the Lords," and then Lavinia, "the Counts. Every year, they steal our glory. This is the only hype talk you're going to get, so listen the fuck up."

He raises his chin, and for a second, it's just like we're kids again—Sy bossing all of us around, but being so competent at it that we never thought to push back very hard. "This year, we're going to win the game. It might get ugly. It might get bloody. Some of you may go to jail or get permanently injured." He shrugs. "But that's a sacrifice we're willing to make."

There's a swell of playful 'boos' that makes Sy's lips twitch.

"It's a new year with new leadership, and it's time to prove you're worthy of being part of the Bruin Family." He holds up his fist and shouts, "To the victor go the spoils!"

"Wow," Lavinia says, from next to me, "Your brother really gets into this, doesn't he?"

Instinctively, I pull her close. "It's in my blood, but he's the one born for it," I admit. "He wants this—needs it—more than me, anyway. Ambition is what keeps Sy's robot parts chugging along. It's one reason I came back."

"How so?"

"He could've been a Duke without me, but there would have been a challenge over leadership. With me here, there's no question. I'm the true legacy, but Sy can take the reins. Being King isn't my goal. But Sy?" I send her a look.

Her forehead furrows and I'm sure she's trying to figure out why a guy like me would walk away from power. I like power as much as the next guy, but I don't like being locked into a system. I smooth her forehead out with my fingers and say, "We've got to meet with Saul before we head out. You can help the girls clean up, and we'll meet you back out here in twenty."

"Whatever you say, your highness." She bows dramatically, voice dripping with sarcasm, but my cock twitches between my legs and I drag her back.

Dipping my mouth to her ear, I whisper, "Don't forget I'm

collecting on our negotiation—tonight." I lick a hot, swift stripe along her neck, smirking when she hurls herself away from me, burning me with a scowl. In response, I pass her, giving her ass a sharp smack. "Stay frosty, Little Bird."

Sy gives me a hard look as I walk up to him and Remy. "If looks could kill. You'd be a smoldering corpse right now."

"Don't worry. I plan to lock up all the weapons in my bedroom. Well..." I grab my cock. "Except for this one."

I grasp the knob to the office door and turn, pushing it open. I hear the knocking first—the *bang-bang-bang* of the pencil holder on the desk—but then I get an eyeful of Saul's pasty ass, pounding into Mama. Her skirt is pushed past her hips, knees bent around his waist.

"Oh, shit! My bad." I back out quickly, pushing Sy out of the way so I can slam the door.

Remy frowns. "What's up?"

"You know how there's that rumor about Saul and Mama having a history?" I don't bother hiding my grimace. "Well, it's not a rumor anymore. He's fucking railing her in there." Short, breathy cries come from the office, confirming my statement. Sy shares my look of disgust, but Remy lets out a barking laugh.

A few moments later, the door opens.

Mama gives me a hard, admonishing look. "Next time, knock, Nicholas." She smoothes down her skirt, and shit, what a total G. She isn't even blushing.

"Miss B," Saul calls, tucking in his shirt. "You're always good to me, darlin'."

"Yeah, well, I wish I could say the same about you." She pats me on the cheek and walks back into the gym, waving over her shoulder. "Don't take too long, boys. Tomorrow's going to be a long day."

"Yes, ma'am," Sy says, nose wrinkling as we enter the office. Saul is now completely put back together, no sign of what just took place other than the toppled pencil cup on the desk. He moves behind it and settles into Mama's chair, looking disgustingly relaxed.

Goddamn, I know it's a sad day when an old fucker like Saul Cartwright is getting more action than me.

"It's time to get the gears turning on business this year, boys," he says, leaning back. "I've got a job for you."

"What kind of job?" Sy asks.

"You get the filing done?"

"Drilled and welded, just like I was taught," Remy replies, leaning indolently against the door. "It's all packed up, ready to ride."

Saul nods. "Good, then it's time to drive it. It's just a standard pickup and delivery. Simple, but important."

"Sure," I reply. "No problem."

"I know it isn't," Saul responds, giving me a long look. "You did some deliveries for Daniel, didn't you?"

Killian would get his panties in a twist if I were going around yapping about the Lords' business, even if it wasn't his, so I keep my answer vague. "Here and there." The truth is that Daniel was big on the ladder system. Delivery work is a grunt's job. Everyone had to do it at some point, even his own son. The thought of starting a new climb from the bottom rung lingers bitter in the back of my throat.

He nods and picks up a paperclip. "How's the Lucia girl doing?"

The three of us share a quick look and there are too many undercurrents there to itemize. "She's a pain in the ass." Because his undercurrent is mostly hostility, Sy begins aggressively listing off, "Disruptive, defiant, depraved."

Saul smirks. "Gets your dick hard, huh?"

Sy crosses his massive forearms over his chest. "No."

"She's not so bad." Remy says this with a knitted brow, like this is something that's just now dawning on him. "And really, when you think about it, stars are just big balls of fire. That's what Vinny is. A pinpoint of light from far away, but get her close enough, and boom. Bitch goes supernova." A slow smile creeps onto his face. "Never a dull moment in the belfry."

I push my hands into my pockets, knowing I have to choose my words carefully. Saul taking interest in my woman would be a problem. "She's adjusting. She's out there right now cleaning up with the cutsluts."

Saul laughs darkly. "You could have had any one of those girls. Mama B says she has a nice crop this year, all trained up right. Instead, you want the enemy. You're as bad as the Lords, picking the only bitch they couldn't have." He shakes his head, and I just barely restrain myself from correcting him. The Lords *have* their Lady. But Saul gives me an exasperated look. "I knew nothing would come easy with you. The blood of a Bruin and the nature of a Payne? God fucking help us if the Count bitch has any influence on you." He points to Sy. "Now your brother? He's got the discipline of a Duke. That's what I need."

Unconcerned, I shrug. "I may not be easy, but I get the job done."

The Bruin thing is getting to him. It's as obvious as the cum stain beside his zipper. Saul's had three years to mold my brother into the seasoned, dutiful fighter he is today. I guess I get it. Back then, Sy was the biggest threat to his crown. Now it's me.

And he has no control.

He taps the paperclip on the desk. "I'm worried about you, Nick. You're a good soldier, but you run hot." At my unblinking stare, he explains, "I got a call from Lionel Lucia the other day. Seems like someone broke into his mansion. Well, 'break-in' may be a generous term for someone who waltzed right through the door with his own security code."

There's a lightness to his tone, one I know not to mistake for approval. I lift my chin, not bothering to lie. Saul needs to learn just how hot I run. "The Duchess wanted something from the house, and I got it for her."

From my periphery, I can see Sy's head slowly turn to stare at me. I haven't told him I broke into the mansion. I knew he'd tell me not to do it, or worse, we'd fight about it, and those fights never help either of us.

Saul's expression is stone. "Did it ever cross your mind it was a setup? An opportunity for the Lucias to take down a wet-behind-the-ears, cocky-as-fuck Royal?"

"Yeah," I say. "Of course it did. But if that was the plan, they failed."

He stares at me for a long moment. "Do you want to tell me what was so important to the girl that you risked getting captured, mauled, or worse?"

"I don't know," I answer, sounding purposefully bored with the discussion. "I didn't look."

"Jesus Christ," Sy hisses, shoving my shoulder. "What the fuck, Nick? It could have been a weapon!"

"For fuck's sake!" I shout, tired of them assuming I'm an idiot. "It wasn't a weapon. It was an opportunity." I look at Saul. "You let me in because I'm a Bruin, but everyone in this room knows my name means jack shit. I'm an asset because I'm quick on my feet and I can take care of myself. I know more about running between Kingdoms than anyone here, so don't call me cocky for being good at what I do."

Saul went rigid about halfway through that rant, and now he's just sitting there, silent, eyes narrowed. He lets the tension in the room grow before speaking. "You have Royal blood, and you did a lot of dirty work for Daniel, but you didn't grow up in this world, son. Your father abdicated his position. *To me.* I want you to take a few days to think about what that means." He flattens his palms against the desk, standing, voice rising with each word. "This is a fragile ecosystem. There are rules and procedures, and in *no goddamn way* do you fuck with a King without approval!" He holds my eye, veins bulging. "Especially not Lucia! Do you understand?"

This argument has nowhere to go but nuclear. It's why I concede, "Yes," and I even shrug as I say it, like it's no skin off my back.

"Good." He gestures to the door. "I'll text you the drop-off location tomorrow night, and then you can prove to me how well you actually follow orders."

"Yes, sir," Sy says, and the three of us leave the room.

We stand in the hallway for a suspended moment, stiff with the tension of the argument. I know Sy's going to speak before he even turns to me, voice low and cutting. "You son of a bitch."

I smirk. "I don't think mom deserves that."

"Seriously," Remy says. He's been quiet this whole time, but now he looks at me, and I don't like what I see in his expression. It's wary, distrustful. "What the hell was that? You broke into Lucia's place?"

I push my hair back, grinding my fingertips into my scalp. "Give me a break. She wanted something. I needed leverage. You know how we work." Ignoring Sy's judgmental stare, I insist, "I was careful! It was barely a job—in and out. If I'd done something like that back in high school, you would have laughed your asses off and begged me for details."

"That was before we ever had to question your loyalty," Sy snaps.

It lands just as sharply as he means it to, making my expression shutter. "You're questioning *my* loyalty?" I thumb the corner of my bitter smile, looking between them. "Where was your loyalty when you believed the police report about Tate?"

There's a short pause, both of them staring at me, before Sy answers in a flat voice. "What the hell are you talking about?"

"I'm talking about the two of you, actually buying that Tate killed herself!"

Sy looks at me like I've just suggested the moon is made of cheese. "She *did* kill herself. You saw the evidence, Nick. We all did!"

Despite the resentment settling heavy in my chest, I keep my voice even. "She was murdered."

There's a moment where Sy looks at me with such utter confusion that I almost think he's close to getting it. But then it falls away, his shoulders easing, and what's left behind is even worse.

"Nicky," he begins in this infuriatingly patient tone. "Grief is complicated. I know you need someone to blame—something to fight. But Tate wasn't—"

I surge forward. "Did you know she put down a deposit on an East End apartment two days before she died? She never moved a single thing in. She never got the chance." When all they do is stare at me, I insist, "Who puts a deposit down on a new place if they aren't intending to live?!"

Sy shakes his head, and I almost wish he'd get in my face again, because this quiet, solemn thing he's doing? It's void of anger. Empty of fight. "Nick, that's not how it works. Suicide can be an act of impulse. It isn't always planned. Tate had a sickness, and she didn't want us to see it, but that doesn't mean—"

I stab a finger into his chest. "She never would have used one of our guns." To Remy, I stress, "*Never.*"

Tate abhorred the gun trade in the West End. While being a fist of Forsyth was fun to her, being its bullet was never her destiny. There were days we talked about it—becoming Dukes, running the firepower. Tate wasn't interested, but she also wasn't surprised. Part of me likes to believe she had faith that we'd find a way to do it better, bring some change to the system. But she hated it. Sometimes she refused to even get into a car if she knew we were packing. By contrast, the three of us never cared much. Hell, back in high school, I used to flaunt it. My very first gun, given to me by my Pops, was a prized possession.

And they think she used it to put a bullet in her head.

Tate never would have put that guilt on me.

Not intentionally.

It doesn't matter that we had fundamental differences about it. Tate respected us—loved us like her own flesh and blood—and it didn't matter that she had tits. She was our brother. In a lot of ways, she was the only thing that held us together, and it strained her. I fucking *know* it strained her. But she wouldn't have checked out like that. She would have fought until her last breath.

I look at Remy, whose face has turned to ash, and I almost feel bad for putting this on him. Another lecture Sy is sure to give me—a reminder that Remy's too fragile for something like this.

I'm just so fucking sick of the suspicion and snide remarks.

With a dead-eyed stare, Remy wonders, "Who would want to kill Tate?" and I know what he's thinking. To us, she was so full of life.

"I don't know." It might be the worst part of this confession, admitting that I don't have the answers. "But if I wanted to find out? If I wanted to be *loyal*?" I turn toward the gym, bumping Sy's shoulder as I pass. "I'd probably start by infiltrating South Side."

I LOST my virginity when I was fourteen to a girl from Preston Prep in the backseat of her brand-new BMW. It was after a football game. Preston had some all-star quarterback, Emory something or the other, and we were getting slaughtered, so I went out to the parking lot to smoke a joint. This beautiful girl in a short red and black plaid skirt came up to me and took a hit. We got high, and I pretended to be cool, kissing her like I had a fucking clue. I'd never had a boner so hard before. When she asked me to the back of her car, I thought I'd come before she got my pants down, but she was good—experienced—and her cunt was deliciously warm. Or at least that's my memory of it. It's definitely the way I told the story to Sy and Remy when I got home.

But really, what I took away from that night was the smell of the car's rich, buttery leather. That's why, to this day, when I smell expensive leather, I think of pussy and get a little hard.

Lavinia isn't wearing real leather. It's some kind of pleather synthetic, but that doesn't stop my dick from expanding as I watch her peel them off.

The first time I saw her, years ago, she wasn't much to look at, panting down at the asphalt, all small and pitiful looking. I remember being disappointed, because this girl was supposed to be dangerous. She was the epitome of North Side. Spoiled, raised by its King, Royal down to her golden hair—supposedly a murderer. But there she was, this little slip of a thing, eyes wide and ringed with exhaustion, posture screaming defeat.

But I was wrong.

Minutes later, the sole of her combat boot slammed into my jaw. I wrestled her down into the leather of Daniel's backseat, touched my tongue to a loose molar, and that was that. I was in love.

I've been hard for her every day since.

A part of me misses the motel days. Those nights, I'd unlock the door to her shitty room and step inside. Sure, she'd give me this pissy, snobby look like I was to blame for everything wrong in her life, but that second between the door swinging wide and my foot stepping over the threshold, I'd see it.

Her whole face would brighten.

Just a flash—blink and miss it. It'd be a stretch to say she was happy to see me instead of whatever food or other necessity I was lugging in for her, but it didn't make a difference to me. Sometimes the sight of it would be the only thing that got me through. That's something Sy and Remy wouldn't understand—how fucking empty it could get in South Side. No one trusted me. No one liked me. Damn sure, no one was ever excited to see me.

No one but my Little Bird.

"That smile makes you look so fucking deranged," she mutters, pushing the pants to her ankles. Getting out of those tight mother-fuckers takes work and I'm happy to supervise.

Eyes locked on her creamy thighs, my grin widens. "I'd believe that if my name was Deranged Nick, but it's not, so I know I'm as handsome as ever." She rolls her eyes and sighs—oh yes, this is a burden—before pulling her shirt over her head.

God, her tits are spec-fucking-tacular. The kind of tits that are begging to be cupped in a palm, caressed by a tongue, and I take my own shirt off at the sight of them, thinking of how they'd feel against my bare chest. Unfortunately, she won't hear about coming to bed naked—although I don't fucking know why. She does it with Remy. Lets him feel all her flesh against his. Lets him bury his mouth between her thighs and get a taste of her cunt. But me? I have to keep coming up with shit to bribe her with.

Shit's getting old.

I didn't give her a chance to go back to her loft when we got home from family dinner. I just announced, "It's bedtime," and pointed to the door. I was prepared for a fight—looking forward to it, actually—but she just kicked her shoes off by the door and walked right in here.

Sy and Remy disappeared up to the belfry and I haven't heard a word out of them since.

I guess it's meant to be like this. Them on one side, my Little Bird and I on the other. Just like old times.

I watch as she works her arms into the shirt I left out for her—my compromise. It's an old Friday Night Fury t-shirt my dad gave me in middle school. It's soft and worn almost through. Her nipples press at the thin fabric and the hem grazes the bottom of her ass. My cock jumps eagerly. It's been this way since she shoved her hand down my pants earlier, when my stupid brother cockblocked me.

When all she does is stand in the middle of my room, arms crossed, I nod to the empty side of the bed. "What are you waiting for? My brother isn't going to interrupt this time. No one's going to save you."

She scowls, walking over to the side of the bed. "I don't need saving." She doesn't get in, though. She pauses and looks around. "Why don't you have anything of your own in here? Sy has books and frat stuff. And Remy... well, his room almost has too much of himself."

I look at my bare walls. Other than the bed, the room came with a dresser and a desk, a ladder leading up to the catwalk toward the duct. My backpack and laptop are on the desk. My clothes are in the dresser and closet. "I don't like extra shit. I have everything I need," I say, giving the empty swath of bed a pointed look. "Or I'm about to."

She finally relents, perching on the edge of the mattress. "It's just kind of weird," she says, fingers toying with the blanket. "I have more personal stuff in the loft than you have down here. I mean, I'm actually the one being held against my will, but you live like you're in a prison cell. What's that about?"

A flicker of annoyance runs through me. "Why are you asking all these questions?"

She shrugs. "I guess I'm curious."

"Curious about me, or about why you can't find something to manipulate me with?" I lunge for her waist and drag her the rest of the way on the bed.

"Paranoid." She reclines stiffly next to me, hands folded against her stomach, refusing to be arranged.

I explain, "You're not getting more about me than I want you to have."

She turns her head, staring at me. "What are you talking about?"

I touch the soft curve of her jaw, mapping out the patches of skin I'd like to greet with my mouth. *This one*, right below her ear. That's where I'd put my teeth. "Come on. You know this dance we're doing, Little Bird. This tit-for-tat arrangement where we hold leverage over one another? It's a Royal game. A *King's* game." My fingertips trail down her throat, skating over her chest. "I'm sure you learned plenty from your father, but I learned it from Daniel Payne, and I guarantee you he was better at it." Her hand is soft when I reach it, knitting my fingers between her delicate knuckles. "You're not going to see anything about me that I'm not ready to show you."

She let me move her hand to my crotch, pushing her palm against my cock. She even has the good grace to not look like she wants to stab my eyes out. Her gaze follows her touch as she warily squeezes me through my jeans. I wonder what happened at family dinner to make her like this—quiet and thoughtful and testing— but mostly I just feel *hot*. Like fucking sweat springing up, skin burning, wanting nothing more than to rip that shirt off her body and press mine against all of that cool softness.

Breath deepening, I reach out to touch her chin, turning it toward me. "Kiss me."

Her mouth thins into a tense line. "That's not part of the deal."

It takes every ounce of self-control I have not to fist my hand into her hair and take it for myself. I could—we both know it. But it wouldn't be as good as it was last time, when she tipped her face up to me, inviting me inside.

So I clamp down on the instinct, and for my troubles, her fingers begin inching toward the buckle on my jeans.

I link my hands behind my head and wait.

Her movements are methodical, measured. The clink of the buckle as it slips away, the tines of the zipper spreading apart—all of these things are done with an exacting precision that electrifies my every nerve. The barest touch of her knuckle against my skin is enough to make my belly cave and my balls clench.

Lifting onto an elbow, she rolls onto her side, hooking her fingers into my waistband and shoving it down my hips. I savor the sight of it, the little aborted movement she makes when my cock gets trapped inside my pants, the way her mouth scrunches up when she has to push harder to free it.

My cock springs out of my pants—*finally*—lobbing with weight, and impatiently, I kick the legs of the pants off to get them out of my way. I fight the urge to grab her by the back of the neck and force those lips down on my cock, to flip her over and pound into her pussy. Because if I did, I'd miss the way her teeth trap her bottom lip as she looks at me, gaze fixed on my cock like a tangible heat. It's not the first time they've been face to face—briefly. I wonder if she's thinking about last Christmas—but it's the first time she's looked at it with something other than disgust.

She tilts her head like she's assessing a particularly baffling task.

It makes my dick jerk, clear pre-cum seeping down the hood, and she flinches at the sight of it. But she also kicks into gear, reaching out to glide her thumb over the tip. A deep, bone rattling shudder runs through me, and my hips rise.

"Yeah, Little Bird. Touch me."

She frowns but skims her fingers down my shaft, sending tremors across my nerves. Again, my hips fight to buck, but I breathe deep, happy to take the scenic route.

"Cocks are weird," she blurts.

Her voice is muted by the blood pumping in my ears. "Huh?"

"Dicks, cocks, penises. They're fucking weird." She looks at me from under her eyelashes. "Your brother's is a beast."

I snort. "A demon that rides on his shoulder more than swings between his legs." Her lips curve at that—the barest hint of a smile—and it's almost as exhilarating as her fingers wrapping around my shaft. It's why I ask again, voice low with strain. "Kiss me."

The smile vanishes. "No."

Rejection burns in my chest, but I push past it. "I bet you can't find anything weird about my cock. I've never had any complaints."

She studies it for a moment, actually running her palm down the shaft. A hum builds in my throat and my balls threaten to burst. "It's got a slight curve." She dips her head and raises an eyebrow. "And your balls are fucking huge."

"That curve is what makes it feel so good inside," I tell her, placing my hand over hers. I force her fingers to spread, to clamp around the shaft, then guide it up and back. "And my balls are legendary around these parts. It's why no one fucking messes with me."

The sight of her fingers wrapped around me is almost enough to finish this. One of the best things about Lavinia is how un-fussy she is. Her nails are tidy, not painted and sharp. Her hair always smells clean, not weighed down by noxious products. There's no artifice to her. No mask. No bullshit. She's beautiful without ever intending to be. I spent two years in South Side and Lavinia Lucia was the only real thing about it.

I force her hand up and down, building a rhythm as I watch her, that studious gaze locked on my dick. Her eyelashes fan against her cheeks with every slow blink, teeth raking over her lip as she takes over, moving her fist. I release her hand and touch her chin. "Kiss me, Little Bird."

"We didn't agree to that."

"Every—" Her hand pushes at the tip and I grunt. "Everything is negotiable. You know that."

Her movements take on a life of their own, wrist twisting on every upstroke, brushing my balls on every downstroke. She's toying with me, eyes flicking to mine with an experimental squeeze. When I bite out a soft curse, her tongue peeks out to soothe the notches her teeth have made in her lip.

"It's too much," she says, seemingly unaware of what she's doing to me. Is that possible? That she's unaware? Doubtful. She's the smartest Royal woman I've met. "There's nothing you can give me that'd be worth it."

"There has to be something." I push up, running the tip of my nose along the line of her jaw. "Anything. More books? One of those digital readers? More shit from your house?" Her nails graze my balls and I hiss. Fuck, this is good—better than I expected. She's hot, her tits pressing against my shirt, her hand moving in quick, firm motions. I should be happy with it, but I'm smelling her hair and panting into her neck, and I want more.

I want *everything*.

I want to dig my way into her cunt. I want to hold her down so tightly that she can't even breathe. I want to *hurt* her, just to be the one who makes her feel something worth screaming for.

"Tell me what you want, Little Bird." My mouth drags over her cheek, damp and stuttering. "Tell me and it's yours. Just give me your mouth..."

She keeps her eyes down, staring at my dick. "Well, there's one thing I want. Maybe..."

"Anything," I shoot up, wincing at the ache in my balls. I grab her face with both of my hands while she keeps jerking me, my mouth hovering so close to hers that I can taste her breath. "Anything you want, I'll do anything."

She finally glances up, eyes heavy and bright. "I need you to steal something for me again."

I nudge my lips against hers, eyes falling closed. "Deal. Whatever it is, I'll get it for you."

"You promise?" She whispers it against my waiting mouth, making me shudder.

I barely even recognize the sound of my own voice, tightened with strain and desperation. "Fuck, baby, whatever you want, just—"

Her mouth opens against mine.

My hands clamp against her head as my tongue plunges between her lips. She's waiting for me, her tongue greeting mine with a slick, warm curl. The sound I make into her mouth is breathless and feral, and she doesn't fight when I tilt my head, crushing her closer.

I always knew this would be the hard part with Lavinia. Pulling myself back once I got a taste. Not devouring her. *Not ruining her.* I struggle with it now, assaulting her mouth with frantic, bruising kisses. She follows me perfectly, mirroring my sucking retreat, only to let me back inside, her tongue meeting mine.

Eagerly.

Lavinia kisses just like I always hoped she would; impatient and a little bit mean. Her teeth nip into my lip, and then her tongue appears to push a bead of blood into my mouth. It pulls a ragged sound from my chest and she feeds it back to me, her hand jerking me relentlessly. My fingers knit into her hair and I know I'm probably pulling it too hard, but the whole universe narrows down to the tip of her tongue and the warmth of her palm, and when I yank her head to the side, sucking wild, frantic kisses into her neck, I begin babbling.

"So fucking good for me," I'm saying, teeth scraping against her neck as the tickle builds behind my balls. "Can't wait to fuck you again. It's all I ever think about, Little Bird. Being inside you, watching you come for me." Her rhythm escalates and I can feel my orgasm speeding toward me like a freight train. "Fuck," I growl, pulling her mouth back to mine. I speak my next words on the crest of a gasp, slick against her tongue. "I love you."

That's how I come, kissing the refusal from her lips. I know she doesn't want to hear it—doesn't want to believe it—but I know deep in the pit of my wandering soul, this woman is mine.

Even if she never loves me back, I'm never letting her go.

21

Lavinia

Sleeping with Remy is like trying to find rest in a hurricane. He's not very touchy once he falls asleep, but his presence— the thrumming energy of him—keeps my subconscious just alert enough to avoid sinking too deep. He's a restless sleeper. Always moving, it seems. It probably helps that I'm always naked when I'm in his bed. Either way, I'm always being pulled back from the edge with him. It's not a bad sleep. If anything, it might be some of the best rest I've ever gotten.

Sleeping with Sy was like falling—if falling was more about the landing than the flight. It's no wonder he and Remy are such good friends. Sy is some kind of black hole. I didn't understand it at first, but now that I'm lying here in the dark, my brain running like a hamster on a wheel, it's all I can think about. Sy is a goddamn sponge. It's like his mere presence has a way of drawing out energy.

Which sucks for me, because I was somehow able to reach a depth of sleep that was... problematic. To say the least.

Sleeping with Nick is something else.

After the hand job, he pulled me half on top of him, hitched my leg over his hips, and instantly nodded off. But Nick doesn't sleep like Remy or Sy do. Where Remy is chaos and Sy is a vacuum, Nick is inertly wary. He never loses the tension he carries throughout the day, and even though his breathing is even, chest rising and falling in a measured rhythm, the hand he has clamped around my thigh never loses its grip.

Nick sleeps like a man who's trying to hold the world together.

In any case, he's warm and still, and even though he's clutching me like a toy he's reluctant to let go of, he's not holding me down.

My lips are still sore and bruised from his kisses.

It's my first time seeing Nick in repose, and I can't help but map the lines of his face, forehead creased even in sleep. His love might not be real, but he thinks it is, and I know enough about our world to understand that's probably the best a woman around here could hope for. He's handsome and strong—and *fuck*, let's face it—hot as hell. If I were a little better about lying to myself, I could even see myself giving in. Path of least resistance. It probably wouldn't even be bad—not all the time. The sex would be explosive. I know that much from the way he kisses me, touches me, surges into me like a wave hitting a shoreline. He'd make it feel so fucking good. He'd protect me like a prized possession. Maybe the more I gave in—the more I relented, stopped fighting—the nicer he'd be.

But I'd never have a choice.

Not really.

Because Nick was right. This thing we're doing *is* a Royal game. A King's game. Owning, dominating, consuming—it's all a Royal man knows. The bartering thing we do... it's just a thin veneer of control for me. He does it because it makes it better for *him*, not for me. I can't forget that. Being possessed, being dominated, being consumed—it's all a Royal woman knows.

And I'm sick—*so goddamn sick*—of being locked in a cage.

If there's one thing life has taught me, it's that there's always a box. It might be a chest at the end of my bed. It might be a metal elevator. It could be a closet. It could be a trunk. It's a big world out there, full of little nooks for girls who haven't learned their place yet, and for men like Nick?

They're tools.

With my brain running as it is, I self-indulgently imagine being free. It'd be much like being up in the belfry. Clear skies. A wide landscape. Nothing but air and empty space between me and the rest of the world. With the loss of my awareness before nodding off, hand loose against his tattooed chest, I imagine Nick is there in front of me, standing between me and the world. Is he keeping me away from the world, or is he keeping the world away from me?

I choose to believe the latter.

If I can't feel free, then at least I can feel safe.

Eight days.

THE BANG STARTLES ME.

My head snaps up. I look down at the living area from my loft and realize Nick's returned. It's only nine in the morning, but I've been up since dawn, having realized his side of the bed was vacant and cold.

It threw me for a loop, because I'd been fretting about how waking up beside him might go. Another demand for a blow job? An offer for full-on sex? Or maybe, like his brother, he wouldn't have bothered with the pretense. Maybe he would have just woken up hard and pinned me down, made me take it.

Instead, he left me there in bed, alone.

Remy and Sy came out of their bedrooms not long after I climbed the spiral staircase, pulling out the books and clock diagrams that have held my attention these last few days. Remy's on the couch with a sketchpad on his knee. Sy has been making him come out of his room a little more since I told him about the arm slashing incident. I don't know if it's that Sy wants to keep an eye on him, or that being alone in his head isn't exactly the best place for

Remy to be. Either way, he seems a little more grounded, pausing his sketch to look at Nick.

Nick, who's shucking off his leather jacket and dropping onto the couch beside his brother. He nods toward the big metal box he'd just dropped onto the coffee table. "Special delivery," he says, watching as I descend the stairs. I'm still wearing the shirt he'd given me to wear the night before, and his eyes drop to the way it hangs on me, pupils dilating.

Walking to the table, I ask, "Is this...?"

He unlatches it and swings it open, presenting it like a gift. "Sufficient?"

I answer by dropping immediately into his lap, not even having to be ordered. A spark of shocked satisfaction fills his eyes, but I'm too busy inspecting a hammer to care much. "This is perfect," I say, peering at the contents of the metal box. There are wrenches, screwdrivers, pliers, all kinds of bits and cutters.

"I know how you can show some gratitude," he says, eyes flicking to my mouth.

"So do I." I give him a sharp, sarcastic grin. "I did it last night. The only one with a debt here is you." In my periphery, I see Sy's head rise, feeling the weight of his gaze on me.

I can see Nick remembering that he'd promised to steal something for me last night, eyes narrowing. "I don't think edging a guy from his nut just to get a promise out of him would stand up in the court of human decency. But that's alright, Little Bird." he reaches out, fingering a lock of my hair. "I keep my word. As you can plainly see."

I look from him to the toolbox, considering that it really is a nice set. We're still playing the game. The Royal game. He wasn't wrong before about his bedroom. If he had something personal in there, I might be able to figure out its importance. I might gain something to hold over him. Luckily for him, there's not a single morsel of insight to be gained from his room.

Nothing, except for his own words.

Without thinking too hard about it, I twist, pressing a quick kiss to his cheek. The instant I pull back, I consider that this is a rocky path to go down, because there's a stunned, delighted gleam in his eyes and a slackness to his mouth, and *fuck*, Nick Bruin is easy. But he's easy for a reason and that can turn on a dime. Today, I'm good, but what happens when I piss him off?

Sy suddenly stands up, drawing our attention. "I'm going to get ready," he says in this curt tone, as if I've somehow managed to annoy him.

Clearing my throat, I pick up a wrench, giving it a couple taps against my palm. "I don't know what's wrong with the clock, but I assume it hasn't had any maintenance in years." I look between Nick and Remy. "Since it isn't a weapon and doesn't have a pussy between its legs, I can see how it got neglected."

Nick, having rearranged his expression into something carefully blank, gives my waist a squeeze. "I'm sure you can kick it into submission."

"So," I say, picking up a coil of wire and inspecting it. "I'm thinking Simon and I can do our morning jog, but instead of going to the library, I come back here and get to work." It'll be a shame to miss out on all those books, but spending a large block of alone time with Sy isn't worth the reading material. He's barely said two words to me since I stormed out of his bedroom the other night, and god knows I'm not saying anything to him.

But Nick says, "What morning jog?" and when Sy emerges from his room, he's not in his running clothes.

He's wearing a fucking suit.

I'm so caught off guard that I gape openly, because *Sy is fucking hot*. The notion slams into me like a linebacker, throwing me off-kilter. Of course, I knew he was attractive. He has those pretty genetics, and the ripped physique, plus the warm, brown skin. His handsomeness just always has the open hostility wrapped around it. But now, he's standing there raking his fingers through his curls and glaring at my shirt, and I just think... *wow*. Who knew Sy could be such a stunner? The jacket is draped over his arm, and he's wearing a tie and everything. I look a little too hard at the way his white shirt strains around his bicep and chest, sputtering, "I thought..."

Nick touches my chin, slowly turning my face away from the sight of his brother. "It's Friday Night Fury, Little Bird. None of us have class on Friday. We have to prep."

"But..." I know I haven't quite regained my footing yet when I blurt, "I wanted to see the kitten."

Remy's distracted voice chimes out, "Kitten?"

"Yeah, uh—" My eyes dart to Sy's, unnerved by the way he's looking at me. "On our last jog through the East End. Some asshole threw their kitten out on the balcony. I just wanted to see if it's still there. Maybe I can go check on it alone. Remember last night? You said—"

"You've got a full day ahead, too," Nick says, cutting me off. "All of us need to prep for the fight."

Remy leans forward, agreeing, "It's your first official Fury as Duchess. You probably have just as much to do as Sy."

I start to argue, but there's a knock on the door. Simon opens it and Verity stands on the other side, all smiling and chipper. "Good morning!"

"Hey, Ver," Simon says, features softening when he sees her. "Just in time."

"Just in time for what?" I look at Nick.

Nick's fingers dig into my ribs when he stands, lifting me from his lap. "You'll be riding to the gym with her. She's helping you get ready for tonight. Mama B sent her over."

Sy buttons his sleeve cuff. "So you don't embarrass yourself, *or us*, like you did yesterday," he says, only sparing me a brief, narrow-eyed glance.

Verity gives me a sympathetic look, but I see the awkwardness underneath it. "I'm sure you'll do fine."

I roll my eyes, but I shouldn't be surprised. I showed my ignorance about my role as Duchess and this is Mama's way of putting me in my place. Verity never would have made such an error if she'd been chosen. "Okay, but I was really hoping to check on that kitten…"

Sy finally looks at me—really looks at me, for the first time in two days—and hotly explodes, "For fuck's sake! Get me tools, bring me books, break into my house, get me some clothes, take me to the East End, eat my cunt." He says the last part right into my face, flinging off the hand Nick presses to his chest. "Christ, I bet that piece of junk clock is less maintenance than you!"

I press a hand to my chest, mocking, "Aw, I'm sorry! Are all the tasks associated with keeping a slave inconvenient for you?"

"Oh, that'd make you feel better, wouldn't it?" he says, eyes bugging out. "Poor little Lucia. Such a victim. Look around you, sweetheart!" He flings a hand toward the toolbox. "You give my brother your pussy in exchange for goods and services. You're not a slave. You're his whore!"

I don't even really think about it—it's an automatic impulse that drives my arm back.

My palm meets his cheek with a sharp, resounding crack.

Sy's head twitches to the side, but other than that, the slap barely seems to touch him. Except for that way, he's eerily still, frozen in place as the smack echoes. The whole room goes silent enough that I can practically hear everyone's intake of breath.

And then everything happens very fast.

Sy lunges at me, but Nick darts between us, bodily shoving him back. "Leave it!" he barks.

Remy springs off the couch and catches me around the waist, saying, "You don't want to go there, Vinny. Trust me. *Trust me!*"

But I'm seeing red and glaring right into Sy's furious eyes as I thrash against his hold. "So I'm a whore? Is that right? Then where's my fucking payment for two nights ago, *Simon*? Or for the locker room? I don't remember you paying me anything for what happened at the Hideaway!"

He snarls, "I should knock that goddamn look off your face!" I watch as Sy's fists flex, body coiled so tightly that even Nick struggles to hold him back.

I spread my arms out, bursting, "What a fucking shocker! You want to hit me? You want to fuck me? You want to punish me for not being the perfect little robot girl?" I feel a bitter, dark laugh bubble in my throat. "All that shit you were spouting at the library about you being special? It's a lie. There are fourteen other Royal douchebags out there, just like you. They're just as mean, just as selfish, just as fucking full of themselves." Scoffing, I throw in one last barb. "The only thing that's special about you is between your legs."

I'm fully expecting him to throw it back at me. Something really snappy, like, "I guess that makes two of us." It wouldn't even be a lie. I grew up in this system. I know what women are in this town.

Instead, he just stares at me with this tense, numb expression.

His muscles uncoil so gradually that I don't even notice it. Not until Remy has let me go, bending down to pick up his discarded marker. I watch idly as he tucks it behind his ear and struts over to a frozen Verity. He leans down and her eyes widen, like she's not sure what he's doing, but he just whispers something in her ear. When he tips back to meet her gaze, he asks, "Can you do that for me?"

"Y-yeah. Sure."

He looks up and raises his chin, the heat of his scowl piercing through my anger. "Verity's going to drive by the kitten on the way to the gym. Nick, you and I are going to take Sy." He looks between us—Nick, Sy, and me—and pins us with his green eyes. "And if anyone else feels like throwing hands, then they're going to catch some of mine. We should be saving this shit for the Barons, not each other." His gaze stops on me. "Is that clear?"

Nick, Simon and I all stare at him for a moment. Sometimes it's hard to remember he's clued into anything happening in the room, but the look he's giving me right now says it all.

If I'm drawing a line, then he's going to choose Sy.

"Crystal," I say, feeling strangely wrung out by the outburst, as if I'd had a flame inside me and now I've doused the room with it, leaving a cold, empty space.

Nick gives Sy a long look before saying, "Good, it's settled."

The trip down the stairs moments later feels longer than usual. Nick's at my back, but I can't tell if he's herding me or protecting me. On one turn of the staircase, I glance over my shoulder and catch a peek of Sy, who's looking straight ahead, brows crouched low and troubled-looking.

When we get to the street, Sy and Remy go one way, and Verity and I go the other.

Nick follows me, leading me to a shiny blue Mustang sitting at the curb. It's Verity's, I realize, when she walks around the driver's side. I reach for the passenger door, but Nick darts in front of me, opening it himself. If he's trying to make a chivalrous gesture, then it's dampened by the way he's blocking me from entering.

"Look," he starts, so close that I can smell him, spicy and warm. "This is a big fight for Sy tonight. A rematch with this Baron fucker is going to earn us points in the all-frat competition. Whatever your beef is, this isn't just about him. It's about all of us —and that includes you now. That means your job is to look sexy and supportive." When I don't respond, he ducks his head, forcing me to meet his gaze. "You don't ever want to square up with Sy, Little Bird. I can't always be here to protect you. He'd fucking cream you, and then I'd have to kill him, and then my parents would kill *me*, assuming Remy didn't get there first." He reaches out, thumb brushing my lower lip, and I fight back a shiver at the darkness in his eyes. "You should leave the fighting to me."

Suddenly, I'm hit with the memory of falling asleep last night. The notion of having the whole world in front of me, and Nick standing between me and it. The reminder that he's not always keeping me away from the world. Sometimes, he's just keeping it away from me.

I know I'm getting soft when the idea strikes me as sort of...

Sweet.

Before I do something impulsive, like give him another kiss on the cheek, I get in the car, avoiding his eyes as he slams the door. He leans down for a second to nod at Verity before patting the hood, sending us off.

"Jesus," Verity says, cranking the engine with a powerful roar, "it's just not fair that he's that good-looking."

As she speeds off, I don't tell her that Nick's pretty looks aren't what draws me in. It's everything else—all the bad stuff, the ugliness lurking under the surface, the all-consuming need to survive in the darkest of places.

It's the parts of him that remind me of myself.

22

Lavinia

The cutsluts have their own locker room—or I guess, more accurately, a lounge. It's certainly nicer than what the guys get and smells more like lotion and perfume than mildew and sweaty ballsack. The floors are made of hardwood, and the front room has soft velvet couches, like the powder room at the country club. The next section has a long row of lockers on one side of the room and then brightly lit mirrors and dressing tables on the other.

"Sit," she says, pointing to one of the chairs. My shoulders tense at her commanding me like a dog, but I have a feeling that challenging this girl would get me into a world of hurt not just from Mama, but from the guys too. I don't need the headache, and honestly, in her own twisted way, she's trying to help.

"Please don't tell me you're going to do some kind of makeover."

"Okay," she says, swiveling the chair to face the mirror. There are personal items on the dresser, photos of Verity and her mom, a jewelry box, various trinkets. "I won't tell you that, but tonight is pretty important, and after the Family Dinner, it's clear you're in over your head."

"I know how to dress," I reply, shooting her an annoyed look. "My style is just... less gym-rat-hooker and more—" I pause, frowning in thought. "Well, I don't even know what it is anymore. I haven't exactly had a say in the matter these past few years. But if I had a choice, it would be a shade less prostitute." I give her a tight smile. "No offense."

"None taken." She picks up a brush and holds it to the crown of my hair. "The cutsluts have a unique style. We're not ashamed of it. The Dukes like it and that's all that matters." She yanks down the brush, not being gentle with the knots and tangles. "The Duchess needs to have her own brand, but it needs to be *on*-brand, if you know what I mean."

What she means is that, for the next two hours, I'm subjected to an extended version of what Auggy put me through my last night at the Hideaway.

I sit still as she trims and teases my hair, even when the other cutsluts begin filtering in. They stop and hug her from behind, or squeeze her ass, or give her head a little pat. When she moves to my fingernails, painting them a deep, almost black-red, the cutsluts fall into action, assisting Verity when she needs it, finding tweezers and exfoliators and clippers. Never has it been more clear to me that Verity was groomed to be in my position. The other girls defer to her without any snide comments or glares. They work together as a unit, talking nonstop, continuous chatter about any and all things. TV shows, celebrities, food, and sex.

They act like I'm not even here.

I suppose it's an upgrade from the party and the dinner, where I'd be subjected to suspicious glances, tinged with contempt. It doesn't occur to me that Verity's had some hand in it until a short, black-haired girl walks in with three outfits.

Verity arranges the sets of hangers, asking, "So, which do you think?"

I'm in the chair, my hair in rollers, fingers fanned out over each knee, and I can't think. I can barely move. It's some bastardized version of what happened that night in Sy's bed. *Paralysis.* That's the word.

I look between the three sets. One is a tight, sparkly red dress. One is a fitted, corset-like top with a pair of tight, slashed up jeans. The last is a loose crop top, a worn leather jacket, and a dark mini skirt.

This paralysis drags out as my gaze moves between them, and I swear I can feel sweat springing up. I don't choose. I take what I'm given. It's been like that for years. The books at the library were one thing. I was being rushed and pressured, and there wasn't much choice. There were things I needed to know, so those were the books I got.

But this?

Shifting uncomfortably, I say, "What do *you* think?"

Verity blinks at me, pinging her gaze to a couple of the other girls. "Er... well, you have a really nice figure. I'm sure you'd look great in whatever. Right?" She asks *them.* The cutsluts.

One of them gives a hesitant nod. "Uh, sure. You have a good body."

It isn't until Verity mentions, "The dress is very... North Side?" that my brain cells begin kicking into gear.

"You're right." I reach out and toss it on the floor. "Give me the one with the leather jacket, but the jeans from the other one."

"Sexy punk. Good choice." Verity gives me a pleased nod, hanging the winning outfit beside the mirror. "I'm going to run out for a second so all your stuff can set. You'll be good back here." She doesn't phrase it as a question—to neither me nor the other girls— she just leaves. That's how I end up sitting quietly, awkwardly observing such elaborate pre-game rituals as bra swaps and topless selfies.

By the time Haley, Sy and Remy's ring girl, walks in, I'm high from the fumes of everyone else's hairspray and nail polish. I watch her in the mirror's reflection, stripping off her dress and going through her locker, just as topless as the others. She's wearing a pink lace thong and looking pretty blasé about it. None of the girls seem to have a shred of modesty.

Haley decides on a rainbow-striped, stretchy, sequined tube top and pulls it over her head. "Cheyenne," she calls to the girl in the next locker, "can I borrow your red lipstick?"

"Sure, babe," the other girl says, sorting through a makeup bag. "Try this shimmer gloss on top. It'll spark off your sequins."

"You're a lifesaver," she leans toward the mirror next to me and applies the lipstick. "Is Bruce ready for his fight?"

"He's pissed he's not the main event, but I know he'll get his chance. Sy's the draw." Cheyenne gives Haley a little pout. "Which means you are, too."

When she says Sy's name, Haley's eyes meet mine in the mirror. I could look away, but I don't. She may have on the sequins, but I'm the Duchess. She glances back at Cheyenne and says, "You meeting Bruce before the fight? Like usual?"

"God, yes, you know how he is. Superstitious and horny as fuck. I blow him before one goddamn fight he just so happens to win, and now I have to get on my knees before every match."

Haley laughs, and tugs on a pair of black Lycra booty shorts. "You know you love it."

"I know it makes him happy, and that's my job." She walks over, kisses Haley on the cheek, and strides out of the room. "See you out there, girl."

Haley pushes her feet into knee-high boots and spends a long time fussing over the laces. When she throws her head back to spritz on some perfume, I get a full view of the faded design Remy drew on her skin during Family Dinner. It's a drawing, I remind myself. Not real ink.

Verity walks back in. "Mama's looking for you, Haley," she says, nodding at my feet. "You should be good now."

Haley strides out of the room, leaving us in a gust of peach-scented body spray.

"Did your mom really want her?" I ask, pulling wads of tissue from between my expanded toes.

"Yeah, they're doing some photos beforehand for promotional stuff." She rolls her eyes. "Social media. It's really big in the West End. Everyone here creams themselves for a good flex."

"Who all's doing photos?"

"Haley and Sy, and the other fighters and their ring girls." She moves behind me and fusses with my hair a bit more.

I wiggle my toes, flexing them out. "And then what? There's a while before the fight. Do they practice?"

She gives me a quick look and hands me the denim jacket. "I mean, you *could* call it practice, but most people call it fucking."

"Bruce and Cheyenne," I state.

"Definitely. They have some routine." Her eyes meet mine. "What? Are you wondering about the guys?"

"I don't care who they screw."

But even as I speak the words, something about the thought of it—Remy bending someone over a table, Nick railing another girl in some dark back room, Sy showing someone that silent intensity I'd seen a couple nights ago...

It makes it feel impossibly crowded. More elements at play. More sweat and lust and hands.

I'd just really fucking rather they wouldn't. "But it'd be good to know where they're sticking their dicks, right?"

The look she gives me makes me feel hot and uncomfortable, and it's not because of the jacket. "The Dukes and their Duchess always have their own arrangement. That's between you and the guys." I stare at her as she speaks. "But I guess I could tell you that Remy and Haley used to be pretty hot."

"They fuck?" I ask. "Regularly?"

There's a cringe in her eyes. "Lately, less so. I don't think they've done anything since you became Duchess. You know, if you're worried about STDs or something. It never struck me as anything beyond physical. Remy's not really the type. Honestly, neither is Haley."

The knowledge twists inside of me like something barbed, and I can't help but picture it. Haley's sexy, I guess. I bet she'd take it without any fuss whatsoever, spreading her thighs for him, uncaring of whatever litany of nonsense is pouring from his mouth as he fucks her.

"What about Simon?" I blurt, not meaning to.

"If he wanted her to, she would, but I think pre-match fucks aren't really his thing. Or they haven't been, as far as I know. I haven't seen any... signs." She arranges the makeup table, forehead creasing. "The other girls actually have experience with sex stuff, though."

"You don't?" I ask, eyebrows shooting upward. "You're a virgin?"

She nods, and wow. Who would have thought, with all that cutslut gear? "I was saving myself."

"For *them*?"

She laughs at my tone. "Not Sy, Nick, and Remy, like... specifically." She lines up the nail polish again. For a third time. "Just whoever the Dukes would be. It was always meant to be my place— to be Royal." She sends me a brief look. "And we all know what Royals like. A virgin in the street and a slut in sheets."

I'm still hung up on the thought of anyone saving themselves for three random jerkoffs. "What if they ended up being...?" *Creepers? Lurkers? Maniacs? Assholes?* It's not like the current batch could get much worse, and she was clearly down for that. "What if you didn't like them?"

"It wouldn't matter," she replies simply. "It's not about the guys —not really. It's about being Royal. Belonging to something bigger than yourself. Helping your community, making your name mean something. I guess liking them would be a bonus." Before I can tell her how insane that is, she goes on, "Sy seems more like he'd punch walls to psyche himself up for the fight or something." She gives me an awkward smile and a long beat settles between us.

Finally, I ask, "Why are you being so nice to me?"

She frowns. "I'm a nice person."

"No, I mean..." I wave a hand between us. "Let's not bullshit each other here. You're obviously better suited to be Duchess than I am, and plus, you actually wanted it. Like... enough that you were willing to save yourself for three potential psychos. Doesn't it piss you off?" Quieter, I ask, "Doesn't it hurt?"

She pulls one shoulder toward her ear, half shrug and half wince. "Not in the way you're thinking. Not because of *you*. You seem nice enough." She cuts me a sly look. "For Count trash, at least."

"Gee." My voice is deadpan. "Thanks."

Her responding smirk is teasing enough to lighten the words. "It definitely messed up a lot of plans, but if I'm being honest... not all of them were mine." The look she gives me runs right to the pit of my chest, because I know it. I saw it in Leticia, and sometimes, I see it in myself. It's the look of someone who has expectations to live up to. "I'm nice to you, because even though I didn't get chosen, I'm still loyal to the Dukes," she says, matter-of-fact. "I'll do anything they ask of me. Won't you?"

We stare at each other.

I know she's remembering my little scuffle with Sy earlier when she bursts into laughter right along with me. Whatever pang had settled into my chest before is purged when I throw my head back, shrieking with deep, belly aching laughter. "Yeah, right," I snort, dabbing wetness from the corner of my eyes. "Fuck, I needed that."

"That's probably why it has to be you." Her grin fades, but doesn't completely disappear. "The Dukes are fighters, and I wouldn't resist anything. I bet they're never bored with you." She opens up the makeup bag, flicking her wrist in a motion so similar to her mother that it startles me. "Don't worry about the other girls. They'll come around once they get it."

"Once they get what?"

"That you aren't here to spy or sabotage our guys." She begins dropping all of her polish and supplies into the bag, adding, "Because that's why they've been—Sy and Remy, at least. Ours, for the last few years. But now?" She stands, pushing out a decisive exhale. "Now, they're yours."

It's impressive how three words can say so much when they're spoken so resolutely—so fiercely. I don't need to see the warning in her eyes, because I hear it.

The Dukes have more than their own six fists.

~

VERITY WALKS me to the ring. I get the feeling she's been told to keep an eye on me until I'm back with the Dukes. In a crowd like this, there would be ample opportunity to make a run for it. But I'm not running. I'm biding my time.

Eight days.

As Verity has made perfectly clear to me tonight, the entire Duke system places value in their Duchess. For now, it's the best I can do.

Friday Night Fury has a different vibe when you're not being dragged in by an intimidating Lord, micro-chipped, and offered up as the prize in a bitter rivalry between gangs.

Not that I'm still not on display.

Nick watches us approach from the other side of the gym. He's standing against the outside of the ring, arms slung lazily over the top rope. He must have been watching the door to the dressing room. It's the only way to explain how his eyes find me from across the crowded space, which was empty hours ago, but is now taking on a rowdy demeanor. His gaze never leaves me. The closer I get, the straighter he stands, his blue eyes taking in every part of my body.

I hadn't really been able to think much of it at the time, but the outfit... it's exactly the kind of thing I would have worn back in high school—when I actually had the chance.

When I begin rounding the ring toward them, Nick nudges Remy, making me subject to his intense gaze, as well. The area is shrouded; the spotlights focused on the center mat, but I can see Nick's fitted black button-down shirt and pants. I'm used to seeing him covered in blood splatter or half-naked. Like this, he doesn't just look pretty, he's gorgeous.

They both square up to meet me, hopping down from the platform, but Nick's the one to reach out, tugging me forward by a belt loop.

"I see we're going to need to reconsider your wardrobe situation." Leaning down, he speaks directly into my ear. "I've never seen you hotter than you are right now." He punctuates this by squeezing my ass, fingers poking through one of the slashed rips right below my ass cheek. It's why I'm not wearing panties, and from the way he freezes, a low, strained sound escaping his throat, he can tell.

I fight back a shiver and try to blame it on the crop top. My entire bottom torso is exposed. I'm pretty sure if I lift my arms, my tits are going to peek out of the bottom.

But at least I get to wear boots.

He reacts by wrapping his other arm around me, hitching me up close to rasp. "One day, you're gonna let me fuck your pretty cunt again. Name your price, Little Bird, I'll pay it." Another squeeze of my ass brings his forefinger in dangerously close proximity to things he hasn't earned a right to. He doesn't make me fight him off, spinning me around to face Remy. "See?" he asks him, winding his arms around my neck, chin propped on my head. "Do you see it now?"

Remy is definitely seeing, but I'm not sure *what* he's seeing. His eyes are roving over me like someone who's deciding whether or not the car he just bought is a lemon. Whatever he's looking for, he doesn't seem to find it.

Not until he hooks a finger into my waistband and shoves it down, revealing the star.

I watch him mouth the numbers, the divot in his forehead easing. He steps back, giving me one last sweeping look, and then nods. "Yeah, I see it." His eyes flick up to mine, and then Nick's. "She's a fucking Duchess, bro."

Nick gives me a shake that feels strangely victorious, as if he's the one who's won a fight. "Damn right she is. Let's do this."

I cringe from their energy, but a part of me unfurls at the same time. It's the first time someone's called me a Duchess without it feeling forced and halfway like a joke. I begin to wonder if I am—if I'd even want to be, even in ideal circumstances. I've known Countesses before, met a couple Ladies, and sold a joint to a Baroness at a local show during my junior year of high school. But this was always Leticia's place. I feel it so keenly that I can almost see a flash of her golden hair in the crowd. I never saw myself as one of them. A Royal woman. Someone people look at when I walk into a room. Someone who becomes the center of attention when Nick grabs my hips, lifting me effortlessly toward Remy's outstretched hand as I'm pulled into the ring. Someone who looks out into a crowd and sees a group of men cheering for something I'm a part of.

For the briefest moment, I think I understand what Verity was talking about before.

Nick circles the mat, fists in the air, flashing his gold ring and amping up the crowd. If this is new to him, you'd never know it. I guess it's just in his blood. The way his tattoos shift against the muscle as he stalks from corner to corner, riling up the masses. The stony look on his face, like he's not even worried about the outcome. I never would have pegged him for a performer, but here he is, commanding his kingdom—no, *their* kingdom—like a master with puppet strings. The crowd is like a drumbeat in my ear—stomping their feet. Some of the frat guys lean toward the ring, slapping their palms against the mat in time to a chant.

DKS! DKS! DKS!

They watch Nick like he's a magnet, and it's clear that they want him—either for his name or his reputation. It doesn't matter. The higher Nick raises his fists, the higher the din of the cheers.

Remy isn't without his fans, though—mostly female. I'm not surprised. He oozes sex as he stalks around the ring, leaning over the ropes to bump fists. He swipes a cutslut's beer and downs it in three big gulps, chucking the cup back into the sea of reaching arms. The same manic energy that's sharp enough to cut is also bright enough to gleam, and he radiates it like a secret, dangerous thing, his messy platinum hair glowing like a crooked halo.

I remain in the back corner, unsure of what my role is here, and I don't feel any less nervous about it when Remy stalks toward me. The weight of his hand lands on my hip, splayed fingers rubbing against the fabric. "You're a star, Vinny," Remy says, mouth close to my ear. "Tell me this doesn't make your pussy wet."

There's an unmistakable energy rolling off of him, and I'm both enthralled and terrified. This is the Remy that may jump off a tower, or shove his hand down my pants in front of a crowded gym. It's a roll of the dice. But one glance reveals that there's no trace of the darkness I've witnessed before. It's all shiny here, the vibration of euphoria building inside of him.

He drags me into the spotlight and lifts my fist into the air. And fuck.

The crowd gets louder.

Part of that may be that my bra is showing.

But a bigger part is just having the position. *Duchess.* The West End is Forsyth's lowest house. The other kingdoms would spit on it, given half the chance. And yet, they fight. Not to be the best. Not to topple someone else. They fight because they don't know any other way—just like me. The epiphany ricochets around my chest like an ache, because I'm one of them. Without ever knowing or intending it, I feel more kindred to this sweaty, heaving mass of bodies than I ever did to North Side.

I look out into the crowd, and I don't see a kingdom that despises me. I see forty—fifty—*sixty* guys that are cheering me on, ready to stand behind the four of us as their ruling house. I see a crowd of men who are built for this. The fists of Forsyth, just as ready to stand *for* something as against it.

I see an army.

Remy lets out a loud, crazed bark of laughter, and then swoops me up, crushing his mouth to mine. I flail for a second, but his arms are like steel around my waist, and I'm not sure if the instinct to kiss him back—open-mouthed and slick—is physical or survival. But I do. I fist a hand into his shirt and taste his tongue, and I can't even hear my own internal reaction, so distracted by the heat of his mouth and the roar of the crowd.

Somewhere off to the side, a random person shouts, "Yeah! Fuck the North Side out of her, Maddox!"

Then I remember who I am.

A Lucia.

That, just as much as the hands prying apart, sends me crashing back to earth. I gasp for air as Nick's stony face glares back at me, and I remember.

The agreement.

"I want you to only kiss me."

"He did that!" I insist, panic swelling in my chest at the prospect of being punished for this. Naturally, Remy just smirks back, raking his teeth over his bottom lip.

"Later," Nick says, wrenching me away from his friend with a bruising grip.

The platform containing the ring is about four feet high off the base of the gym floor, and Nick jumps down first, holding his arms out for me. He catches me effortlessly, lowering me to the ground as Remy hops down beside us.

He doesn't let go, and I know instinctively when he leads us to our seats that I won't be sitting in any of them. The second Nick sits, I curl into his lap, heart pounding with the possibility of where I'll be sleeping tonight. I watch his face carefully as I do, searching for any sign of temper or viciousness.

His expression is inscrutable. Nick is good at that—hiding his reactions, preventing expectations. It's one of the worst things about him, never knowing what comes next. When he finally meets my gaze, there's a darkness within them, and I know better to flinch back when he crushes his mouth to mine.

The kiss is punishing.

There's no other word for the way he forces his tongue between my teeth, licking away the taste of Remy's mouth. It's quick, however, and the moment he pulls away, I feel myself relax. His cock is hard beneath me and he's giving my lips that glazed, satisfied look that suggests he's pleased.

Our seats are nothing special. The same hard bleachers as the rest of the crowd. But we're ringside, and once Nick has settled with his arms around my waist, my eyes take in either side of the room. The cage where they'd kept me last time, and the VIP area for the Kings. The cage is empty, so I guess there's no human prize at stake tonight. In the VIP section, it's not packed like last time, but the Lords are there, including their Lady, and three pretty boys I have to assume are Princes, with their own Princess. It's early in the process, but her belly still looks flat.

On the other side of the ring are two Barons and their Baroness. They're all sitting back, somehow managing to look both tense and bored. This isn't anywhere close to being their scene, which is made all the more obvious by the fact there aren't many Beta Nus in the crowd.

Just one.

He's near the back. The Barons foster the ability to get lost in a crowd. To be the nicely dressed guy who can disappear within the masses. To be masked and hidden and waiting for the time to strike. This one is pretty good at it, but I spot him anyway, leaning against a pillar. He's playing with a device that draws my attention, clicking it into his palm, emitting a green light.

I know instantly what it is.

And I know exactly what I want to do about it.

Remy's hand settles on my thigh, running up and down in long, repetitive strokes. I search the ring and lean toward Nick. "Where's Sy?"

"Bruce is fighting first, then Sy," he says, grinding his erection into my hip. "He'll stay in the back until it's his turn—last minute prep."

I think of the discussion in the lounge. Is he shoving his cock down Haley's throat right now? Overpowering her and making her gag? Or does she take it willingly? It's not important. What's more important is what Nick said before about keeping the peace with Sy. He wasn't wrong. I've always had a hot temper, and I'm not going to pretend slapping him wasn't insanely satisfying. But it's not going to do me any favors. What if Nick wants to put me in the elevator again? What if he wants to hurt me? Nick might be standing between me and the world, but who's going to stand between me and Nick?

I stand abruptly. "I need to talk to him."

Nick pulls me down, scowling. "You definitely fucking don't."

"I need to tell him something."

"So tell *me*," Nick argues. "I'll tell him for you."

I look him in the eye. "Look, I promise I'm not up to anything. I'm not going to start shit. This just..." I glance back at the Beta Nu in the crowd. "It has to be me."

He studies me for a long moment, but gives me a curt nod. "If you try anything, I'll track you down, and all our arrangements—*all of them*—are over. Got that?"

That means the kiss didn't break them.

It means no elevator.

Relieved, I answer, "I do."

The walk to the back is strange. I haven't been in the company of so many people since high school, and it makes me feel prickly and over-sensitive, like being hemmed in and trapped. My muscles feel as tight and strained as my smile when I finally break through the doors.

Haley is in the hallway.

She's smacking on a piece of gum, eyes on the screen of her phone, and she's sitting in front of the door to the locker room like a slutty, sparkling gargoyle. Her eyes flick up at the sound of the door opening, and she raises her chin. She doesn't look like someone who just had their face fucked by a monster cock, but I wouldn't put it past either of them. The cutsluts around here are almost as fanatical as the Counts' dope fiends.

"Where's Sy?" I ask.

She tilts her head toward the door. "Doing his thing. Getting ready." Nodding, I steel myself, taking a deep breath, and then march to the door. Haley blocks me. "Uh, you can't go in there."

I step back, crossing my arms. "He won't care. I've been in there with him before."

"Not before a fight, you haven't." She gives me a patronizing smile, pushing her shoulders back. "Sy has a lot of pre-game rituals. If you mess with one and he loses—"

I roll my eyes, shoving forward. "I'll take that chance."

"Hey!" She tries to grab me before I push through the door, but I'm faster, barreling through.

Sy is sitting on the first bench with two pods sticking out of his ears, but the volume must not be very high, because he whips a white-hot glare at us as Haley stumbles through after me.

"Sorry!" she squeaks, tugging me by the arm. "I tried to tell her—"

"We need to talk," I say, yanking my elbow from her grasp.

Sy is shirtless, putting all of his muscles and russet skin on display. I get this vision of the way he wore that suit earlier, snugly tailored around that broad chest. Something flutters in my belly but turns quickly to stone when he shoots Haley a significant look.

"He can't talk," she tells me in a curt voice. "On fight nights, the second he walks into the gym, he's quiet. It's a ritual, *like I said*."

My face hardens at both her snotty tone and the absurdity of such a thing. "Perfect," I reply, crossing the distance between us. "That means you'll have to keep your mouth shut and actually listen to me. You can leave." I say the last part to Haley, a finger pointed toward the door.

Her jaw drops in outrage. "You can't just—"

I cut in, "I'm the Duchess and I want a minute alone with my Duke." Making sure she hears the possessive undercurrent of authority in that, I add, "Is that going to be a problem?" I can see the hot irritation simmering under her skin, but she spins on her heel and storms out of the room.

When I meet Sy's gaze, he's staring up at me, face composed into a blank mask.

I reach out and take one of the buds from his ear, enduring the flash of hostility in his eyes. "There's a Beta Nu out there with a laser pointer." When all he does is raise an eyebrow, I elaborate, "It's one of those really strong lasers. Like the kind of shit that could probably blind someone. I'm guessing eyesight is kind of important to you, so keep your head down out there."

One of his cheeks scrunches up, eyes flicking to the door.

Impossibly, I know exactly what he wants to say. "I *am* going to tell them. I just—" But I'm not sure how to finish that in a way that isn't horribly transparent. So I go for honesty. "It's an olive branch. You were a shit to me; I was a shit to you. But for better or for *so much fucking worse*, you're my Duke, and that means if you go down, I go down with you." I hand him back his ear bud, not missing the way his eyes lock on my bare stomach for a brief moment. His fingers brush mine as he takes it. "Just because we hate each other doesn't mean we can't both win here." His gaze jumps up to mine, head canting to the side quizzically. "Don't worry about what I'm winning. Just know that taking you down isn't a part of it. In fact, I'd rather see you beat them—*all of them*. Baron, Prince, Count, Lord." I reach out and take the other pod out of his ear, motions slow and gentle enough that he just curiously follows my hand with his eyes. "I need you to hear this—really hear this," I explain with a hard stare. "You can call me a whore. You can push me around. You can hurt me, degrade me, make me feel like trash. And I'll still want to see you take them down. I won't stand in your way, now or ever."

He takes this in with narrowed eyes, flexing his hands. They've been intricately taped, knuckle to knuckle. Idly, I ponder that I'm going to learn how to do that. Maybe there's a book about it. When he gives me a single, chin-dipping nod, I consider it an agreement.

But not until he shakes on it.

He gives my outstretched hand a look that's full of confusion, but he takes it anyway, almost toppling me into his broad chest when he uses it to pull himself to his feet. He towers over me, but he's not scary. I've seen those eyes, heavy lidded and full of need. I've felt this bronze skin sweating against mine. I've heard the sound of his agonized breaths as he rutted himself against me in the dead of night. I've seen him stripped to his most human, basal instincts. And I know what he wants, above all, more than anything.

To win.

Sy is, after all, just another man.

When we exit the locker room, Haley is pouting. She tries to hide it, jerking her chin up at our approach, but I can see the sourness in her eyes. "You're almost up. Bruce is winning." Sy starts to walk toward the double doors leading out to the ring, but pauses when she calls out, "Wait! You're forgetting the tradition, Simon. The Duchess always has to send her Duke to the mat with a kiss." For a second, I get this swell of outrage at the thought of her knowing Nick's rules for me. But when she shoots me a smirk, it's clear that she merely understands just how much neither of us wants to do it. "It's good luck."

Sy turns, revealing a stony sneer, but Haley doesn't realize that I've found a new resolve. The Dukes are my captors. I'll never have power over them. But the rest of DKS?

I walk fluidly to where he stands and strain up on my toes, pushing a quick, firm peck to the pulse point in his neck. In the blink between my lips touching his skin and my retreat, his fingers graze my hip. It's just a quick, involuntary gesture, but when I step back, I see the imprint of my lipstick on his neck and the will in his eyes, and I know he's going to win.

Having three Dukes between me and Forsyth is going to be useful. Being a Duchess is a good role—a strong role. But I'm playing the Royal game now, and only one title will put me on equal footing with my father.

Queen.

23

Remy

This might be the only time the tower's party room has been silent.

The light is low everywhere but here, a large lamp trained right on Sy. There are candles elsewhere, the light flickering around the four corners of the room. From my vantage under the heat of the light, the rest of the tower could be a vast abyss, and that's what it feels like. There are probably three dozen people in this room, but it feels like it's only the four of us. Sy, sitting backwards in a chair, hunched over, arms resting on the back. Nick, watching from my side, his gloved hand reaching out to wipe the excess ink away when my needle lifts. The Duchess and all her starlight as she carefully places a stitch into a cut on Sy's eyebrow.

Someone over by the bar coughs and I watch from my periphery as Nick shoots him a glare. The frat isn't used to this ritual because it isn't theirs. But they're trying. It's a more spiritual feeling than I'm used to, like their energy is pulsing into the stone and mortar, wrapping around us.

These are the most important tattoos I've ever done.

Sy's back piece is a round tribal between his shoulder blades, each ring a part of his native heritage, and the silence is a show of respect. Not for Sy, although he deserves it. It's about respecting the significance—the honor. This is a warrior receiving his badge.

I lift my gun and Nick is there instantly, wiping away the ink. He's the only other person we'd ever allow to be a part of this. The tribal has gotten intricate, bigger over the past three years, each ring a victory, but Nick hasn't been there for most of them. I can see him tracing the rings with his eyes, maybe wondering which fight belongs to each.

With each victory, the rings get bigger, take longer. One day, it's going to be a full piece. I can envision it so clearly in my mind, the rings expanding outward like ripples.

Their dad, Manny, taught me the symbols. The one I'm currently pricking into his skin is his tribe's symbol for change. His dad appreciates the care I take in doing them—so much that, every year, he invites me to their summer ceremony so the tribal elder can bless my ink. We've been doing it since high school, and it's obvious from the first few rings that I was still learning, the ink a little fuzzy. Usually, looking at my own bad work would make my chest thrum with the instinct to fix it, cover it up with something better, but this?

This is sacred history.

Tate was around for some of them.

I look up and see the soft, flickering glow of candlelight illumi-nating Vinny's cheek. She's perched on a chair right in front of Sy, sitting on her knees. Her forehead is pinched in concentration as she pushes the needle through Sy's skin, delicately tying off the thread of a stitch. He'd come off the mat with a river of blood streaming down his eye—the only good shot the Baron really got on him—and Vinny had been the one to toss him a towel. Now she's patching my boy up, her needle on one end of his soul, mine on the other. Something about it is painfully intimate, as if Vinny and I are meeting through the care we're taking for him, weaving together through his flesh and spirit. If either of them asked me why, I don't think I could explain it, but it might be closer than sex.

When I finish the last link on the ring, I let the buzz of my gun cease, and it drops the room into a heavy, expectant hush. Nick reaches over me to give it one last wipe down just as Vinny snips off the last stitch. Sy glances over his shoulder, meeting my eyes, and I nod.

The three of us watch him, waiting. He begins the ritual at sundown, and his silence isn't broken until he either loses, or he's gotten his mark. His back expands with an inhale, and then his gravelly bark emerges. "Fuck the Barons!"

The whole room erupts in a loud, rowdy cheer, and someone's close enough to the lights to flick them on, revealing a room full of excited, half-drunk miscreants.

Fuck, I love this place.

Between one cheer and the next, the music crashes through the speakers like an impatient guest, sending the space into a pulse of deep bass.

I give Sy a pat on the shoulder as he stands, stretching his arms and legs. Verity is there with a beer and a smile, saying, "Congrats!" and he ruffles her hair.

There's a pause before he looks at Vinny, who's gazing up at him with a wary expression. I'm expecting some more fireworks, because these two... I'm not sure they know it yet, but the tension between them is just like his back piece; a ripple of rings, spreading out, glancing off all of us.

I wish they'd fuck already.

Luckily for the vibe of the night, he just reaches out to give her a quick tap on the cheek with the flats of his fingers. It's more of a pat than a slap, and I'm relieved to see her take it as the gesture it's clearly meant to be, giving Sy a small grin as she gathers her medic supplies.

Sy is always a little easier to take after a fight.

From here, it's a proper party. Nick helps me get Sy's back prepped for healing, and I carefully put the blessed ink away, going through the motions of sanitizing the area. My tattoo work isn't over yet. It feels good to have the gun in my hand again, like my art never quite knows if it's real until it's being pricked into flesh as a token of permanence. The pace of it slows me down, the method-ical precision, the humming vibration as the needle buries itself in the flesh. Even when it's easy stuff, like lining the pledges up for their very first paw, it doesn't feel like the end of a ritual. It feels like the middle of one.

I reset the gun and glance over at Vinny, who's currently chat-ting with Verity at the bar. Her cheeks expand with a smile—a real smile—and the sight of it makes me freeze, realizing I've never seen it before. It's as radiant as the sun, and when she laughs at some-thing Verity says, I feel so eager to have it shine on me that I call her over.

"Duchess! Bring me a beer."

Her smile deflates like a sad balloon, and for a second, I regret calling out to her. Stars are always better observed than felt. Some-thing happened to her in the ring. I watched as it stole her away under the glare of the spotlight and returned her to us with wide eyes, mouth set into a new resolve.

Whatever happened, it makes her willing to turn to the senior DKS manning the bar and request a beer. He hands her a bottle from our stash and she carries it over, passing Sy as he pulls on his shirt. I see the way her eyes take him in, the flick of her tongue while he can't see her. She's not the only girl here eyefucking him. Hell yeah, my man could pull a lot of tail if he'd take the stick out of his ass for ten minutes. Cutsluts love nothing more than to be a victor's spoils.

Too bad Sy never takes his cut.

She approaches my makeshift workstation with a beer in one hand and her cup in another. She hands me the bottle, still looking like a fucking firecracker in that get-up Verity put her into. She's lost the jacket, which doesn't surprise me. It always gets too hot in here. Something about the way she's looking tonight just... fits. All those little strappy things Nick keeps putting her in are sexy, but stick to her frame artlessly, as if her very essence finds them disagreeable. Too soft. Vinny needs to be covered in harsh things.

Lucky us.

It makes it harder to shake the feeling that this girl erupted from my brain, fully formed. Sometimes, like this morning's spat with Sy, she seems like this fucking... issue. She throbs around this place like a sore muscle, climbing the staircase to her loft, zipping from room to room, as restless on the outside as I feel on the inside. It's hard to really sink down into my thoughts when I hear her. See her. Feel her.

But other times, a lot like right now, she almost seems too good to be true.

"Thanks, Vinny," I say, swallowing half in one gulp. It dulls the rattling sounds in my head. The questions and second-guessing. I reach for her and drag her forward, pushing down the waist of her pants. The points of the star reveal themselves and I trace them with my finger, silently counting the points.

"So is that post-game tattoo ritual something all of you do, or...?" she asks, glancing over her shoulder at Sy.

"Nah," I say, lingering on the skin covering her hip. "That's just for Sy. It's a native warrior thing—probably not spiritually legit on account of me being white as fuck, but it's what his dad did in his fighting days."

She reaches out, prodding the Virgin Mary on my bicep. "I didn't peg any of you for the religious types."

I let out a grim laugh. "Ah, I was raised Catholic. You know the drill." I shoot up on the bench, raising my voice over the party to sing, "*If you're happy and you know it, that's a sin.*"

Around the room, a handful of DKS respond:

Clap. Clap.

"There's my boys!" I raise my beer to them, smiling wryly at their cheers. To Vinny, I explain, "Some of these fuckers had to sit through mass in school with me. Snorting Ritalin in the sacristy— now that's the ritual of *my* people." I drop back onto the bench, arranging my supplies. "Our Lady of Sorrows," I say of the tattoo.

"I'm lapsed, but some things just stick to you. Seven swords, seven points." There's definitely a little mountain of evidence here that Lavinia isn't real, and I take a moment to count the points on the star again.

It doesn't work in my dreams.

I tried it the last time we slept together, because I saw her. She was blonde—she always is when I'm dreaming. But I finally saw the stars. I saw the red light. I saw the air and heard the screams, but I also saw the tattoo.

And it was just some janky, jumbled blur of lines.

"Wanna help?"

Her eyebrow rises. "Help with what?" There's a wariness in her voice. She's right to have it. I could bend her over my bench and fuck the daylights out of her if I wanted. No one in this room would stop me. That's the kind of power that comes from being a Duke. It rushes through my blood like a stimulant.

I point to the freshman eagerly waiting his turn. "These cubs have earned their marks. You want to assist?"

Her expression clears into surprise. "Me?"

I shrug, grab a fresh vial of ink, and pat the small section of bench between my legs. "Sure."

She hesitates slightly, but swallows the last part of her drink and straddles the bench. I grab her by the hips and yank her back until the swell of her ass pushes against my crotch. Excited warmth spreads through me at the feel of her against my bare skin—my shirt having been lost on the climb up the tower. I fold her body in the curve of my torso like a heartbeat. Maybe Nick's got the right idea with this lap-sitting business. "Okay, tell me which one of these douchebags should go first."

She looks down the row—they've been standing there for an hour—told to do so by Nick. Poor fuckers thought they were coming up all those flights of stairs to get lit. Instead, they're standing in a line for most of the night. That's the life of a pledge. When the party's over, they'll get to clean up our fun.

Vinny searches the line, assessing each kid like she's picking the winner of a beauty pageant. "How about him?" she says, pointing to a punk toward the end of the line.

My eyes narrow. "Why him?" I press my palm against her side, sliding it up beneath the hem of her crop top. "You think he's cute or something?"

Her shoulder lifts in what could either be a squirm or a shrug. "He held the door for me on the way out of the gym. Shouldn't I, like... bestow my Duchessy favor on him or whatever?"

I breathe in the scent of her, rich and sweet, a hint of honey. "If you start doing that, you'll have all these guys scraping at your feet like dogs."

A slow, wicked smirk spreads her lips. "I can think of worse things."

I give her waist a hard squeeze. "Don't forget who you belong to. A guy could get jealous."

"Big words coming from the guy who fucks his ring girl on a regular basis." The scowl she sends Haley's way shocks me enough that my hands freeze on her ribs. "But you could always do your own dog-like scraping, you know."

"You're jealous," I smugly declare. "Fuck me, Lucia. You really keep shit close to the vest, but you actually want our dicks."

She whips around to gape at me. "I'm not jealous!"

"You are," I insist, cock twitching against her ass. "You're like five seconds from clawing her eyes out."

She turns away, spine a touch more rigid than before. "You're delusional."

"You're in denial." Despite this, I press her closer, running my palms under the hem of her shirt. My fingers graze the underside of her bra, her tits heavy and plump, and it doesn't matter that she goes rigid. I raise my thumbs and flick them over her nipples. "Haley's old news, anyway. I haven't fucked her since spring. She's already been told what's off limits. You don't need to have a cat fight on my account. Although..."

This time, she really does squirm. But not before I feel the shiver that rolls down her spine. "Don't flatter yourself."

Laughing quietly, I decide to hold this information for later. "Hey, Ballsack," I call out to the kid she chose. He stumbles forward abruptly, like he forgot where he was for a moment. Probably fell asleep waiting.

"Yes, sir?"

"You're up. Take off your shirt and sit in the chair."

The other guys holler out to him as he leaves the line, slapping his shoulder and giving him high-fives. Vinny looks back at me, her ass twisting and rubbing against my cock in the process. "Is this their initiation?"

"One of them," I say, rocking my hips a little to build friction. "They had to do some shit work for a few weeks to get here, but once they get their cub mark, they'll move through the ranks, gain a few more responsibilities—earn a few more privileges."

"Like a cutslut?"

Ah, the jealousy.

Nick's going to fucking lose it.

"Sometimes." I gesture for Ballsack to take off his shirt and sit sideways on the bench. The mark goes on the upper arm, a bear's paw print to denote their cub status. It's a process every one of us has gone through. I slide my arms between hers and her body and pull her tight against me. "Now, you and I are going to do this together."

Her body tenses. "You want me to tattoo him? I thought you never let anyone else touch your gun."

Ballsack looks over at me, then to her, eyes wide. "*She's* doing it?"

"Turn around and shut up," I tell him. "And never look at my Duchess again." Ballsack isn't a bad kid. None of them are. They've survived a lot to get this far, but it's our job to keep them in line. No one knows better than I do that the fists of Forsyth are chaos goblins, ready to jump at any promise of destruction. They need a firm hand. "Got it?"

His eyes dart forward. "Yes, sir."

"Entitled fuck," I mumble. I push Vinny's hair off her shoulder, letting my fingers graze over the skin on her neck, and settle my chin in the crook where I have a good view of both our subject and the supple swell of her tits below that loose crop top. "And yes, you're going to do it. With my help, of course."

I already have the cub mark prepared on a template, and I instruct her how to apply it, using cold water to leave the purplish temporary dye behind. When it dries, I position the tattoo gun in her hand and wrap my hand around hers. "When you pull the trigger, it's going to buzz," I remind her, "and it'll shake your hand but hold firm. I'm here to keep it steady."

"Okay," she says, tightening her grip. "Like this?"

"Exactly." I wrap my arm around her stomach. "Ready?"

She takes a breath and then turns on the gun. It jolts to life, and she jumps. "You got it, baby," I tell her, rubbing my hand on her flat belly. "All you have to do is trace the template."

I hold her arm still, keeping the vibrations minimal, but wait for her to connect with Ballsack's skin. It takes her a second to get there, but I don't mind. She's so close, and she smells like sex. "He's going to flinch when you make contact," I say quietly in her ear. "Don't move with him. Prepare for it. Keep the needle just under the epidermis. It's more of an etch than a stab." She moves closer and finally the needle touches his skin. Like I said, he flinches, but not much, and I keep my grip solid over her hand to hold her steady. "That's right. Good girl."

She exhales, and I feel her shoulders loosen. Slowly, we trace the outline of the paw print's middle pad together. I pull the gun back when I think she's going too deep, and press it in a bit when she's being too light. It takes half the outline for her to really get a feel for the depth of it, but once she does, my fingers are only covering her knuckles for the novelty of the touch. I don't think I could ever get enough of her skin, all soft and smooth.

These marks are small and won't take long, so I savor it while I can. Last year, when my own pledge group got farther into the process, some of them asked me to cover it up with the actual brass Bruin. Bigger and meaner.

She relaxes into me, and I run my hands up and down her legs. She only needs a little help getting the gun steady, but I let her take control. The pledges seem into it, excited to be marked by the Duchess. She's sexy like this, trapped between my thighs, sharing this moment with me. My cock is rock hard, turned on by the whole scene. She's bright and there's no confusion in my mind—this girl is the Duchess. She belongs to us.

She moves to the outlines of the top five pads without me even having to direct her, and I take a moment to really breathe her in. I've been horny since the day I ate her pussy in front of Nick, but there's just one problem.

Nicky hasn't tapped it yet.

Sy and I talked about it last night, our not knowing what he's waiting for. Nick's never been one to draw out the promise of grati-fication, and he obviously wants her. Worse than that, he obviously *needs* her. Even now, I can see him across the room, bottle tipped back to his lips, staring at her like someone who's been magnetized. She's got her venom in all of us now, but Nick? He's got it bad. I even got a dressing down for kissing her in the ring, as if she isn't mine to do with as I please.

I'd be lying if I said it didn't make me want to do it again.

"Now what?" she asks, pulling the gun back. She tilts her head, considering, and I realize she's done the little claw marks, too.

Shifting forward, I grunt at the pressure against my dick. "I have to change the needle to shade in the middle areas."

I decide to do the rest myself, but when she tries to stand up, I slam her back onto the bench against me, making a low, disap-proving sound. "Tell me, Vinny," I say, beginning to press the bundle of needles into the empty spaces. "Did you like it when I licked your pussy?"

Ballsack's neck twitches, eyes widening, but he obeys orders, not daring to look at the Duchess.

I can't take my eyes off the tattoo long enough to catch her expression, but I swear I can feel her surprised stare against my hand. "It, uh, got the job done."

Scoffing, I move from the center pad to the ones at the top. "Please, your body was shaking like you were having a goddamn seizure." My free hand wanders up her shirt. She should have known I couldn't resist touching her tits when she was wearing that short little top. "I'm good at what I do. No shame in admitting it."

She's still as my palm cups her breast, squeezing. "I'm not ashamed. I got exactly what I wanted."

Ballsack's eyes keep cutting to the side, just shy of actually making contact with her.

"I'm glad to hear you say that." I pull the gun away, revealing Ballsack's finished tattoo. "Just a sec, wardog. Hang tight." I put the gun down and get comfortable with Vinny's chest, sliding my other hand up her shirt.

Her hands clamp around my wrists. "What are you doing?"

"Relax." I tip her back against me, feeling the weight of her tits in my hands. "Ballsack's a good cub. He wouldn't look. But he's made a good impression on you, and that means I need to make a point."

Her chest dips with a long exhale. "What point is that?"

I pinch her nipples, delighting in her hitched breath. "That you belong to us. Your tits. Your pussy. Your ass." Dropping my voice to a whisper against the shell of her ear, I add, "Your mouth..."

Her nipples are peaked now, head resting back on my shoulder. "I think everyone knows that."

"Of course they do." I open my mouth against her neck, giving her tits a hard squeeze as I start sucking. It's been a few days now, and all her bruises are fading. It's a shame. The blue and purple was perfect on her, a little trail of breadcrumbs to every point of her body.

Guess I'll need to make more.

Her skin tastes like copper and sky, the flavor of the moon. Pulling back, I admire the bruise I've made. "But it never hurts to remind them." I reach up to her chin, turning her to meet my gaze. Resting my thumb on her lip, I add, "And it never hurts to remind you."

Her eyelids give me a heavy blink, and I know she's perfect when she immediately figures it out. "You want my mouth."

I answer by dipping down to kiss her, intending to push my tongue between her lips. I've been thinking of them ever since that kiss in the ring earlier. Seeing their imprint on Sy's neck during the entire fight didn't exactly help matters, either. Nick getting his briefs in a tangle over it doesn't make me less inclined.

Vinny obviously doesn't agree, because she whips her head to the side before I can make contact. I follow her gaze right to Nick, who's fisting the neck of his bottle like it's someone's throat. "Don't," she warns, so low that I can barely hear her. "You don't know what he'll do to me."

Of course I know.

People like to think I'm too lost in my own problems to recognize theirs, but it's not true. I see things. I see Sy on the edge of losing it every time she's in the room. I see him sometimes around the tower with his head in his hands, breathing like his lungs are holding all his air hostage. I see Nick, every now and then, sitting on the end of his bed, hunched and silent, eyes so shrouded with darkness that it makes me wonder what he's thinking about. I see him get up every day and try to shake off the layer of South Side that's calcified over his skin, but never quite succeeding. Whenever everyone else sees that tattoo on his temple—two-three-seven— they see an ode to South Side. Mayhem and destruction. A true soldier.

But I see 7:32.

I see them for what they are; fractured, volatile, too internal for their own goods. And I've seen Vinny the morning after Nick chucked her into that elevator—black and blue and red, red, red...

"I want your mouth," I tell her, forcing her to face me. "One way or another."

I can see when it hits her, and Jesus fuck, but that elevator must be really bad, because she doesn't even look conflicted about the choice; her mouth around my cock or being subjected to whatever Nick will have in store for her.

I know the second I pull away that I can't wait. "*Now.*" There's a flash of apprehension in her eyes that doesn't lessen when I stand, putting the obscene bulge in my pants right into her face. Breathing hard, I reach for my fly and say, "Ready?"

Her eyes widen, pinging around the room. "But—"

"Nick won't care. Kissing and fucking are off-limits, but not this." We've already drawn the attention of a few people, and it just makes my dick twitch even harder at the thought. "No one will look. Not unless I tell them to."

She tries, "We can go upstairs," and I shake my head.

"I'm making a point here. Remember?" I nod to the floor. "Here."

A hardness that I haven't seen since this morning returns to her features and she looks around, eyes flitting over Ballsack and the row of cubs pretending they're not hanging on to every word.

"Is this an order?" she asks.

"If that's what it takes to get you on your knees, yeah." I tilt my head. "That or I just make you."

Sighing, she rises from the bench, giving me a steely look as she steps over it and stands in front of me, hands fidgeting. I grab her by the hair and expose her neck, resuming the hickey I'd started on before, dipping down to rub my tongue over the mark. I drag her close, my cock grinding into her lower belly, and then grunt into her neck, reaching down to get two thick handfuls of her ass. It's how I realize she's not wearing any panties. There's a rip just below her ass cheek, and my finger meets skin. If I push it in a little further, it's warm skin. And if I curl into her, sliding my finger between her thighs, it's *slick* skin.

"Fuck," I growl, pulling away from the hickey long enough to get a good look at that plump mouth of hers. And then, in a show of having zero self-control, I duck in to finally steal that kiss. Nick isn't looking. What would it matter?

But she bobs away, straining away from my mouth. "Don't," she repeats, and the flash of panic in her eyes makes me pause.

I wonder if Nick has any idea how effective their agreement is.

It's not real loyalty by any stretch, but even here, cloaked by the party, she wouldn't break it. My knuckles strain against the denim of her jeans as I rub her slickness into the furled tightness of her asshole. There's a loud *rip*, the slash in her jeans giving way.

One of her palms lands on my bare chest, but the other reaches for my zipper, lowering it quickly.

Without warning, she drops to her knees, almost breaking my trapped wrist in the process.

"Hasty," I say, panting as I shove my pants down my thighs. "I like it."

But before she can even get an eyeful of my cock, she's darting an anxious gaze toward the room. There's a slack-jawed sophomore standing at the bar, gaping at the two of us.

"Can't we have... like a buffer or something?"

"A buffer?" I know all the blood in my body is rushing toward my dick, but I don't know what the hell she's talking about.

"Someone to stand between us and... well, everyone else." Her eyes dart to Ballsack still in the chair. To be fair, I haven't told him he can leave.

"That depends." I give my cock a squeeze. "You gonna swallow?"

She bites back, "You gonna let me breathe?"

Ballsack looks like his boner might kill him.

Grinning, I agree, "I'll let you breathe *enough*." She nods. "Then I can arrange that."

"What about her?" she asks, before I can grab the nearest person. She's looking over her shoulder at a group of cutsluts across the room, and I fight back a laugh. *Girls*, man. Catty bitches to the moon and back.

I bark, "Haley! Get your ass over here!"

She doesn't hesitate, skipping up, freezing in place at the sight of my dick in Vinny's face. I tell Ballsack, "Sit here and make sure no one comes over. Keep your back turned." Haley still makes my eyes hurt—diarylide yellow, too brash, too bright—but I still give her an order. "*You* can watch my Duchess take my dick."

Haley rolls her eyes, folding her arms moodily, but I know she doesn't really care. Vinny wouldn't be the first girl she's watched suck me off.

My Duchess, however...

Vinny throws Haley a dark, determined look, and then wraps her fingers around my shaft, making me inhale a hiss of air. Spiteful, stubborn, *and* competitive. "Tell me she isn't the perfect Duchess," I say, chuckling low as I touch her cheek. Vinny meets my gaze and then parts those plush, red lips. Her tongue is the first thing I feel, wet and hot against the head of my cock. I watch, enraptured as my cock surges a bead of pre-cum right onto the rosy tip of her tongue. It disappears in the next instant, her mouth sinking forward, enveloping me in tight heat.

"Fuck, Vinny." I cradle her cheek, coaxing it deeper as Haley looks on with a tight expression. All of the other cutsluts are peering around her, realizing what's going on. Vinny sinks lower, but her tongue isn't doing much. Her eyes keep lifting to mine, like she's trying to figure out whether or not this is doing it for me. That more than anything makes me ask, "You ever sucked cock before, beautiful?" Even as I say it, I know the answer. "Just Sy's, huh?" He wouldn't have given her the space to get comfortable with it—not like I would. I rest my shoulders against the wall, basking in her efforts—pulling back to bathe the tip with her tongue. "Yeah, because you're ours. I bet he choked you, didn't he?"

She gives me a long, significant look.

I tuck my fingers beneath her hair, against her nape. "Don't hold it against him. You're probably the first girl who's ever tried." When she pushes farther, throat jumping with a gag, I grunt, "Don't be a hero. Use your hand, baby." She's aware of the eyes on us, gasps and chuckles drawing more attention than we had initially. I lift her hand from my hip, curling her fingers around the base. I don't need it deep. I just need it like this—wet and slow, the sounds of sloppy suction mingling with the music.

She shifts her knees toward me a bit, twisting her mouth a bit as she pulls back, only to sink back down. I can feel her testing it out, breathing hard through her nose as she reaches beneath my dick to graze a knuckle against my balls.

I shudder, clamping my hand around her neck. "Yeah, yeah, that's good. So good for me, Vinny. Look at your mouth—so fucking pretty. Can't wait to finally fuck you. I bet you'd like it hard, wouldn't you? I bet you'd be mouthy when there isn't a cock stuffed in there."

Haley heaves a sigh, and I shoot her a murderous look.

She shrinks back.

Holding onto Vinny's neck, I urge her faster, thrusting against her tongue. "Come on, baby. Show all these bitches who we belong to now."

That really gets her going, shoulders curling as she takes me in deeper, wetter, her fingers fondling my balls with a little more confidence, rolling them gently in her soft palm. I drop my head back, jaw clenching as I rock against her lips. There's a searing pool of lava settling into my spine, and I know I'm already getting close. I wonder if this is what Sy felt as she clumsily took his beast of a cock, my thighs shaking as she slurps her way up my shaft.

"The fuck...?"

I whip my head around, meeting Nick's eyes.

Or, I would, if he weren't staring at my dick disappearing into Vinny's mouth.

Sy is behind him, watching the same thing.

Most of the party is, too.

"Hey, guys." She tenses at the interruption and I pull her back down, the head of my dick jumping against the flat of her tongue. "Kinda busy. Come back in ten, yeah?"

Haley looks between us, waiting for direction.

Nick is the one to give it to her. "You two can go."

Oh, right. Ballsack is here, too. It's not like either of them have stopped the party from noticing, which was the point. The Duchess is mine—*ours*. She represents DKS but she serves us—exclusively. The way Ballsack walks off with these short, wobbling little steps, confirms he knows it. He's probably packing the most painful boner of his short life.

"Don't stop, Vinny." I rest back, realizing she's also aware of the crowd watching. I massage my fingers into the base of her skull. "You're doing so good, baby. Show them what you've learned."

She takes her hand off my balls and presses it against my abs, fingernails digging divots into my skin as she bobs and licks. Sy's broad shoulders cast us in shadow, but I can still perfectly see the way Vinny darts her eyes toward Nick, nervous at us being caught. She's probably shitting herself, thinking he'll get mad.

He's *really* not.

"Fuck me." Nick's voice is a low, strained octave when he squats down, pulling her hair back to watch. "I always knew you'd make the prettiest cocksucker." He brushes a knuckle over the flushed ridge of her cheekbone, and I can practically see the alarm drain from her face.

Sy's voice rings out, slow and distracted. "We don't have time for—"

"Yeah, we do," Nick disagrees, resting his palm on the back of her head. His pinky rests over my thumb, and when he pushes her down, I can feel the pressure he uses, gentle but assertive. Her movements falter, fingernails digging painfully into my side as he guides her deep, eyes fixed on her stretched lips. She makes a wet, panicked sound and he eases up, running his fingers through her hair as she pops off, gasping for breath. He swoops in, fusing their lips together in a hard kiss. I don't know what to look at—her wet eyelashes or the peek of their tongues meeting between their lips.

A glance at Sy reveals he's rubbing his cock through his jeans with one hand, and taking a swig from a bottle of beer with the other.

"You come yet?" he asks.

Shaking my head, I bide my time, waiting for her to break away from Nick's demanding mouth. The second she does, I'm hauling her back in, feeding her my cock before Nick can have her again. Luckily, he's happy to watch, sweeping her hair away from her neck. He sees the mark I made there earlier, and I know what he's going to do before the irritated knot appears at the back of his jaw.

He leans in and attaches his own mouth to it, sucking his own mark on top.

I can feel the grunt she makes through the shaft of my dick, and my teeth clench. "I'm close." I think I might say it more for Nick and Sy than her, because when they edge closer to watch, I get this odd rush of satisfaction, like I just can't wait for them to see what our girl has agreed to.

It hits me like a sledgehammer in my solar plexus, stealing my breath with a heaving grunt. All three of us look down to watch my dick jolt between her lips. It surges with the first wave of cum, and I'm almost too late to grab the base and yank her back, forcing her jaw open.

"Let us see," I demand, and she quickly complies, opening her mouth just in time for a thick ribbon of cum to shoot onto her tongue. Nick is there to thread his fingers into her hair, holding her steady as I empty my balls into her hot mouth.

My cock twitches with a final, feeble gush, the cum landing more on her chin than her lips. I reach down to gather it up and push it inside with the rest, breathlessly adding, "Remember our deal." Her wet eyes shine up at me, and with a slow, heavy blink, she closes her mouth and gulps with her whole body, forcing my seed down into her belly. "That's our good girl," I say, thumbing the wetness from beneath her eyes.

Nick looks about two seconds from undoing his own fly, but Sy cuts in, voice thin and deep. "Saul just called. It's time to go do the thing. We don't have time." Nick growls, shooting to his feet. Both of their dicks are visibly straining against the confines of their pants. And they're not the only ones. Half the DKS look one second from bending a cutslut over the nearest surface. You're welcome boys. Sy adds, "Lock her upstairs and—"

Vinny rises, eyes full of fire, as she drags a wrist over her mouth. "You're locking me up again?! But I just—!" She points to my cock, as if the prospect of being locked up has made the whole thing obsolete.

"No." The decision comes from Nick, and brooks no argument. "She's the Duchess," he says matter-of-factly. "She goes where we go."

Sy looks to me for help, but I shrug, pulling up my pants. I like having the Duchess around too. She smells good and, well, if I get confused, I look for the star. "Baby bro is right," I tell him. "We take her."

24

Lavinia

Everyone leaves when the Dukes tell them to. Even the pledges who never got their cub mark quickly filter out no argument whatsoever. To West End, the Dukes' word is law. But I've seen them wake up. I've seen them go to bed, leave for class, drive to the gym together, bickering over what music to play. I've seen them clumsily co-exist together.

And these three are a hot mess.

They almost have as many petty differences as me and Leticia. The distrust is ever present in the questions, the suspicious glances, the unspoken words passed between them. It makes me edgy, unsure of which Duke is more or less dangerous to me. Remy certainly hasn't helped, using me to prod whatever wounds are between him and Nick. There's family drama, past traumas, concerns of Remy's mental state, and whatever happened between them that sent Nick running to South Side. It's not that they're fractured. Something fractured would still be mostly solid. These three are broken pieces of a whole.

So the way they move into action is startling.

Everyone seems to understand the assignment. They get dressed in the main room, trading shirts, pulling on boots and shoving knives into them. I keep quiet, my movements fluid and precise. No matter how much I resent it, the truth of the matter is that my pussy is a throbbing mess of ache.

It started with the fondling, and then the neck kissing, and while Remy forcing me to my knees in front of the whole party should have been the equivalent of being doused in ice water, it just helped me make clear to the others that this? The Dukes and the fumbling way they bicker, the barbs they throw, the dark looks, the ledges, the knives, the small spaces, the *large* spaces, the punishment and the praise, the hurt and the gentler touches, being Duchess and all of the status that comes with it?

It's mine.

No one's earned it like me. Haley sure as hell hasn't. Verity would if she had to, but she didn't. I'm the one who's been in this tower, tolerating and enduring. And if I get all the hurt, then that means any shred of good that might come with it is mine to claim, and I intend to.

I change from my ripped jeans and crop top into the athletic pants Sy had bought for me, and one of Remy's expensive, over-sized sweaters, and try not to make it so obvious that I'm rubbing my thighs together, desperate for friction. Was it the thrill of it? Was it the feel of him in my mouth? Was it the eyes—the acknowledge-ment that I'm more than just a ghost that floats behind them?

I don't know.

I just know that I've never been hornier in my entire life.

Eventually, the guns come out, and I watch from the armchair, lacing up the boots Verity let me keep, as each of them smoothly loads their clips. Suddenly they're a single entity, not even having to look at one another to catch a phone tossed over the distance or pass a set of keys.

My father never would have let me be involved in real Count business, but I've been privy to street runs before—have stood next to one of his young soldiers as he weighed out powder for an inter-house junkie who wouldn't take no for an answer. But it was never anything like this, saturated with a tense purpose.

The walk downstairs is filled with a silent focus that I feel nervous to break. I keep my steps even with theirs, not even wanting my footfalls to disrupt the energy of the moment.

I can still taste Remy on the back of my tongue.

When Sy returns with the vehicle, it's not the SUV I'm expecting, but instead a dark van. I stand on the curb, watching with fascination as Nick opens the back doors, reaches beneath the floorboard, and pops some sort of latch. He raises it to reveal a secret compartment. Sy rounds the van to lift the black crate, tucking it snugly in the void above the undercarriage.

"Whose van is this?" I ask, realizing there's a lot I don't know.

"DKS property," Sy says, slamming the back doors. "Officially, it's used to haul the frat's equipment."

"And unofficially, it's used to move gun—" Nick's hand clamps over my mouth, blue eyes blazing into mine with a silent warning.

"Careful, Little Bird." I watch as he twists, looking over his shoulder toward the mouth of the alley. The motion lifts his shirt and I see the black gun tucked into his jeans. "You never know who's around."

I whisper, "The police?"

Remy snorts, his white hair poking out from beneath his dark hood. "The police haven't been a problem in West End since my uncle took over the force. It's the other bastards out there we have to worry about. Someone's always looking to settle a score."

The statement sends a chill down my spine. They're right. A Baron could be out here, pissed about losing the fight. One of my father's soldiers could be out here. *Perez* could be out here. Did I think they'd just stop watching me because I'm with the Dukes? Perez did follow me to the library to deliver that message.

Now I'm the one looking shiftily down the alley.

At least it distracts from the throb in my clit.

"Head check, brother." Sy steps in front of Remy, giving his shoulder a bump with his knuckles. "You good? What's your number?"

Remy jerks his chin in a nod, but there's a crease in his brow when he answers, "I don't know. Hard five?"

Sy's face falls. "Only a five?"

Remy shoves his fingers through his hair, pushing the hood away. Suddenly, he whips his eyes on me, and then he's stalking forward, hooking a finger into my pants. I remain still as he wrenches them down a few inches, looking at the star. A lock of his hair trembles in a passing breeze as he counts, his lips moving silently.

Nodding, he lifts his head, tucking a marker behind his ear like a cigarette. "Nah, we're good. Solid seven."

Sy looks from me to Remy, and then glances down at where the tattoo is. "What's that about?"

It's a question directed more to Remy than me, so I take the out. When Nick glides the side door open, I climb in quickly, sliding across the bench seat. I don't want to be the one to beat my way around the truth. I made a deal with Remy that I wouldn't tell Sy about his almost jumping from the belfry and I've kept it. The cuts on his arm were a different story—too obvious to patch over with bullshit. I keep the truth close, however. Leverage like that could come in handy one day with Remy. In any case, Sy and I have just found something close to peace, and I'm not in the mood to be the subject of his hatred, yet again.

Nick follows me into the van, slinging an arm around my shoulder and pulling me against his side. The charged electricity from the stairwell earlier still clings to him, and the heavy silence of the cabin amplifies it. He touches me like a compulsion, fingertips idly mapping the texture of my inner wrist. I feel the urge humming under his skin, the way Remy's tattoo gun had vibrated in my hand. I didn't expect to like that—the feel of power at my fingertips, watching the needle sink in, the blood oozing from the wound. It was like Remy's energy surged from his body to mine, from his hand to my own.

From the window, I can see Remy's face tilted up toward the streetlight as Sy says something to him, but all I can think about is how I had that man's cock in my mouth twenty minutes ago.

The thing no one ever told me about sucking dick is how powerful it could be. I was on my knees and it rankled. The whole time I was lowering Remy's pants, my words to Perez kept running bitterly through my head.

"I don't kneel to anyone..."

Except I did.

But it didn't feel like submission—not when I had him trembling like a leaf, white-knuckled and punching those little desperate breaths through his teeth. It was like that night with Nick, bringing him off into my fist. I wonder why Leticia, Auggy—hell, even Mrs. Crane—never told me.

Bring a man to the edge of orgasm and he's your bitch.

There's a pressure against my cheek, Nick turning me to face him. The cabin of the van is dark, blotting two shadows into the hollows of his eyes. "What's that little smirk about?"

I'm not sure what makes me shudder more. The quiet, velvety hush of his voice, the memory of his dark eyes watching me take Remy's dick, or the way his finger is tracing my lower lip. "Nothing."

My answer nudges against his fingertip. I don't need light to know he's staring at my mouth. "Open," he says, voice as demanding as the finger he pushes inside.

I obey, more out of nervousness than a sense of requirement, jaw opening to show him my tongue. The pad of his finger rubs against it, like maybe he's hoping I'll suck it. Only the next thing I know, he's diving down and licking against it, his breath hot and foreign as he tastes the remnants of Remy's release. It's more of an obscene invasion than a kiss, his hand trapping my chin as he licks into me, and I get this... sense.

The sense that he's beginning to lose patience.

"Sucking his dick made you horny." His voice is quiet enough that it doesn't cut through the silence. It just ebbs with it, disappearing into my mouth. "I saw you squirming around. I bet you're still soaked, aren't you?"

And then he shoves his hand down my pants.

I turn my face away from his mouth, even though my hips lift to him like an invitation. "Wait—"

"No." He forces his fingers between my thighs. "You broke the rule."

God, that fucking kiss. I knew it would come back and haunt me. "He forced me, it wasn't like I—"

"I know," Nick says, his fingers slipping into my folds. "That's why *this* is your punishment, and not something worse."

My breath hitches. "This?"

"I'll have you finished off before they even get in." His fingers find my hole, and I don't need his responding groan to know what they find. I've been wet since Remy started playing with my nipples at the party, and it didn't get better when I had him in my mouth. "You think Remy's the only man who can make you come your brains out?" he whispers, rubbing my slickness around.

I force my body to open up to him, thighs parting. It's too hard to think when the space around us is warming with our breaths, so quiet and still, but I'm aware enough to understand that this is better than a night in the elevator.

Eight days.

"That's it." Nick speaks against my cheek, whisper-quiet as he runs his fingers through my folds. "This pussy knows who it belongs to, doesn't it?"

It rubs something raw inside of me to wonder if he's right, because I lay my head back on his shoulder and buck into his hand. His fingers find my clit, gliding around it in a tight circle, and I can't help but glance down, watching where his wrist disappears inside my pants. It's the forearm that's been tattooed a solid black. I can almost trick my brain into thinking it's another part of the shadows, just part of the endless void around us.

He huffs short breaths into the side of my face as he works his wrist, fingers pushing hard—almost *too* hard—into my aching clit.

I've been like a livewire since Remy came on my tongue, and now I'm spreading my legs, panting as I mindlessly chase Nick's touch.

He rubs me with a relentless precision, and it's quiet, just like that night with Sy. Like this could be a secret the others would never know about. Through the fog of my body needing the friction, the thought strikes me as vaguely beneficial and I give myself over to it, hoping it's quick enough that they won't see me so powerless.

"Yeah, give it to me," Nick rumbles, rubbing my clit. He's all around me, too close, too warm. The arm he has curled around my shoulders lifts and he palms my forehead, crushing me back into the crook of his neck. "You're mine," he says, harsh as gravel. "Show me how you look when I make you—"

I snap, "Oh my god, would you shut the fuck up and finger me already?!" Grabbing his wrist, I *push* it.

He growls against my jaw, but finally—Jesus Christ, *finally*—dips lower, roughly shoving two of his thick fingers into me. My back arches, and I hate that he's seeing it—the scrunch of my nose, the way I'm biting a painful notch into my lip. But what's worse is my loud, tortured keen as the orgasm rips through me. His palm flies off my forehead to clamp over my mouth, eyes watchful of the others. He surges with my bucking hips, the heel of his hand digging into my clit as his fingers fuck into me, ruthless, determined. He keeps it quiet and hidden, as if he's too greedy to share it with his brothers.

Afterward, everything feels slow and hazy. The drag of his hand against my pussy as he pulls his wrist free of my pants. The tickle of his slick fingertip tracing my lip. The hot-cold of the tip of his tongue, licking the taste of me away. He rests his forehead against mine, inhaling my exhales. "If you ever let one of them kiss you again," he says, knuckles brushing over the curve of my cheek, "I'll cut your fucking tongue out."

By the time Remy and Sy get into the van, Nick looks convincingly casual, but I'm as rigid as steel, his threat resonating ominously in my thoughts. I don't know why I bother staying vigilant with Nick during the good times, because he's always quick to remind me what he is.

His eyes are on alert, scanning the area through the windows. "I think we're good," he says, tapping his brother on the shoulder. "Head out."

The engine rumbles to life, and we start down the road.

Remy gives us a quick glance from the passenger seat, his green eyes flickering on the scant space between our bodies, but he turns quickly forward again. There's a shifting sound, a click, and then the window next to me whirrs to life, lowering a crack.

From my vantage, I can just barely make out the curve of his smirk.

The route seems twisted, and the first time we circle a block only to turn the same way once again, I wonder if Sy is lost. But then it occurs to me that it's intentional, winding through West End in a way that seems aimless, but slowly takes us to South Side, and then East.

Eventually, I realize we're in the area Sy and I traveled when we jogged to the library.

When I finally find the will to speak, it's to ask, "East End?"

"Yeah," Nick says, running his hand down my thigh. "Fifty-Third Street is the boundary. We're in Prince territory now." He pushes my hair off my neck, and it makes me feel whiplashed. How can someone threaten to maim you one second and then touch you so tenderly the next? "Don't worry. We've been invited."

Sy finally parks the van in a dark spot at the edge of an old apartment building. In unison, all three guys check their guns.

"Do I need one of those?" I ask, feeling anxious.

Sy shoots me an incredulous look. "Fuck no."

"Can someone at least tell me what we're getting into?"

He sighs and tucks one gun away, then another. "This apartment belongs to Felix—security for the Princes. They don't do business at their mansion anymore. Not after some lunatic broke in and defiled their creepy ass baby room with blood last year."

I look between them, taking this in. "Barons' work?"

"Probably. They're all deranged," Nick says. "But now we meet off site. It's easier this way, anyhow. This whole area is a shithole no one pays attention to." Nick leans forward and grips Remy's shoulder. "You watch the Duchess. Stick to her like a bitch in heat."

"Wait, what?" I ask, alarmed at the visual.

"Gotcha." Remy turns to me, flashing that creepy Maniac smile. "You're with me, Vinny Lu."

Sy goes around the back of the van to get the goods and Nick follows him, hand touching the gun in his waistband as his eyes scan the street. That's evidently Nick's role—being our cover man as we climb the flight of stairs and enter a narrow hallway. Although the guys seem confident, there's a low level of tension that resonates through my bones. I'm all too familiar with the painful tedium of vigilance. It's how I felt every day of my life with my father. Like a bomb could go off at any moment.

Sy stops at a door and Nick leans past him to knock three times —twice fast, a pause, then a third. I stand back, my side pressed into Remy's as we wait.

When the door finally swings open to reveal a chick, none of them looks particularly surprised about it.

"Felix is in there," she says, jerking her thumb toward the living room. The girl is pretty, maybe young enough to be another student. She's the exact shade of dry, brassy blonde that Leticia used to ruthlessly disparage amongst her friends, and even though she has the posture of a Royal—shoulders back, chin pitched arrogantly in the air—she's lacking the grace of one. There are dark rings around her eyes, like she hasn't slept in days. Or maybe all the effort of keeping her back straight like that has drained her.

Nick pulls out his gun and enters first, keeping it down at his side as he peers into the apartment.

Her eyes flick from the crate up to Sy's face. "You're right on time. The two of them are waiting."

Sy pauses over the threshold. "Two?" There are voices coming from the back, loud but conversational. Sy shoots Remy an edgy look and shoves the crate into his arms, whispering, "If shit goes south—"

"Then come and save our asses," Nick says, fingering his trigger. "I'll never live it down if I die in East End."

Sy's face pinches. "Go."

Remy takes the crate, wraps an arm around my waist, and drags me to an alcove off the entry. Nick gives him a long look, nodding. I don't know what passes between them, but it makes Remy's grip on my waist tighten.

Sy and Nick disappear, following the girl through the foyer and into the main room.

Immediately, the sound of panic erupts; low curses, something falling on the floor, an unfamiliar voice belting out, "Whoa, whoa, whoa! Chill out!"

"Don't you fucking tell me to chill out, Felix," Nick shouts. "Who the hell is this?"

Stupidly, Felix responds, "Bro, chill!"

"You better start fucking talking, Felix!" Sy roars. "What the hell is this? Some kind of ambush?"

"Stop!" the girl screeches, high and alarmed. "Stop!"

Remy has me tucked away behind him and I clutch his stomach, which is hard and coiled. I go to peer around him, but he grabs my sweater, wrenching me back with a glare.

Not before I get a good look at what's happening, though.

The sight of four men in a tense standoff, guns leveled at each other's faces, is burned right into my retinas. There's Nick and Sy, plus a lanky guy I'm assuming is Felix, and then his guest, which... from the looks of it, was unexpected. It's easy to understand why.

"You have two seconds to explain what the fuck is going on," Simon says, voice tight with fading restraint, "or the Princes are about to lose a man."

"Hey, I know that guy," I whisper to Remy, but he's drawing his gun, looking about two seconds from rushing in there. I don't think I've ever seen him so alert before, a hand reaching back to touch my hip.

"If someone fires, you book it, Vinny. Remember, don't be a hero."

But before he can make a move, I duck around him, darting toward Sy and Remy. "Put your guns down, you raging testosterone disasters."

Their guns all swing on me, and then Nick's eyes go tight, his barrel instantly dropping. "Remy!" he snaps, and the man in question is suddenly behind me, yanking me away.

I struggle against Remy's hold. "That's Cash Money! He's just a kid the Counts pay to run their junk. I'll vouch for him, okay?"

Cash lowers his gun next, eyes widening. "Holy shit, *Lavinia*? Is that you?" He barks a laugh, showing a sunny smile that beckons memories of the river from middle school. "Goddamn, girl, I heard you turned coat for the fists, but I didn't believe it. Half suspected your daddy handed you over to the big Bs."

Sy looks between, twitching anxiously. "This fucker's a Count?"

Rolling my eyes, I raise my hand and lower it, gesturing for Sy to drop his gun. "Hardly. He's just a lackey. We go way back."

Cash's head snaps back. "Lackey? Why you gotta hurt me like that, cuz?" He's the first to put his gun away, looking annoyed. "I was just making a routine delivery, supplying the upstanding citizens of East End with the finest, and your boys come rushing in here like a goddamn Fed sting. Lucky this 'lackey' didn't come off with a headshot."

"*We're* lucky?" Nick says, still fingering the trigger. "Talk some more shit, fuck face. See how far you get."

I throw Felix a baffled look. "You scheduled deliveries with two rival houses at the same time? The only one who's lucky here is your stupid ass."

Felix does *not* take this well. "You wanna shut your bitch up and do business, or stand here holding our dicks?"

Nick answers with a quietness that belies his words. "Call our Duchess a bitch again, and the only house we'll be doing business with tonight is the 'big Bs'."

The Barons deal in flesh like the Lords do; only their specialty is getting rid of it. No one knows how, because what the Barons are best at is keeping silent. Their business hinges on a century-long reputation of never having a body found, and never having the customer charged with their murders. Impressive, considering the volume they must see.

The tension falls out of the room like a lead weight, and the girl who's been standing off to the side this whole time, palms covering her mouth, deflates. "I didn't know," she stammers. "When I invited you in, I didn't—"

Felix tucks his gun away, scowling at everyone. "This one was supposed to be here with the drop an hour ago."

Cash shrugs. "No one told me it was do or die, bruh."

"Everyone knows drug dealers' clocks run slower than two snails fucking," I say, stepping away when Remy finally lets me go. "Be happy he got the day right."

"Yo," Cash says, looking between us. "We chill now, or what? I'm not saying I couldn't hold my own, but I smoked a blunt on the way over and I might not perform my best in a shootout."

They aren't chill at all. Nick is still strung tighter than a piano string, and Sy looks like he's struggling to put whatever survival instinct just emerged back into its box. But Remy answers, "Let's get this shit over with," and slams the crate onto the coffee table.

Without being asked, I take the girl's arm and pull her into the kitchen, just off the living room. "We should probably let them do their thing," I explain.

Her face is pale, and she shakily grabs a glass from the dish strainer beside the sink, filling it under the tap. "Jesus Christ."

"You okay?" I ask.

"Yeah, that was just... a lot more near-death than I signed up for."

"Tell me about it." I rest my hip on the counter, keeping one eye on the other room. Sy is taking a gun out of the crate and pointing to the smooth area Remy filed away at some point. "Is this your place?"

She does a half nod, half shrug. "Sort of. I moved in last spring."

"I'm Lavinia," I say, feeling the need to make small talk while the guys do their business.

"Autumn." I nod. The name is vaguely familiar, but I've crossed a lot of paths recently, from the old motel, The Hideaway, and now the West End cutsluts. All these women look the same to me. Snobby and nervous, with that little hint of trauma in their eyes. "Holden moved me in here," she says suddenly, like I should know that name. When all I do is nod blandly, she explains, "He was my Prince. Felix is his cousin."

"You're a Princess?" That explains the haughty posture, but not the haggard appearance. Princesses are notoriously spoiled little poodles.

"*Was*," she corrects, lowering her gaze. "Couldn't get pregnant."

"Ouch." I hold back a grimace, realizing she was ousted. The Princess only gets a few months to conceive, and if she doesn't, she's done—replaced with another pretty Stepford incubation chamber. The awkwardness of the silence is what makes me look away, searching for another topic. Princesses are the most attached to their position. High risk, high reward, and a whole lot of fucking, either way. I doubt any Royal man has it in him to love a woman, and I'm sure most Royal women are the same. Except Princesses. They always seem to fall the hardest. A failed Princess should be put on suicide watch.

That's when I notice the balcony. It's dark out, but I see something moving beyond the glass: a tiny ball of white fur. It faces the window and two yellow eyes reflect in the light. I know when it opens its mouth to cry that this is the apartment I saw on my jog with Simon.

I spin to the woman. "Is that your kitten?"

She follows my gaze, frowning. "Yeah, it's mine."

"Why is it on the balcony?" *All the damn time*, I want to add.

"Felix doesn't like cats."

I look across the kitchen and through the doorway, spotting Felix. He's narrowing his eyes at one of the guns, putting on the flimsy pretense of it possibly not being good enough. Everyone here knows he's going to buy them. I saw the guns myself. They're solid, and the attention to detail with the filing? It's craftsmanship this town has probably never seen before. Felix is tall and skinny, and he's got a dumb look about him—the face of a soldier, not a Royal. *Cousin* to a Royal. *Pathetic.* This girl is far too pretty for him, which just bolsters my assessments of failed Princesses. Suicide watch. Seriously.

"If your boyfriend doesn't like cats, then why do you have one?"

"Holden promised it to me back when we were trying to—" Her jaw works around a word she doesn't look willing to say. She clears her throat. "His Princess just gave birth, so I guess he gave it to me as a consolation prize."

I blink, trying to process her selfish idiocy. "It's not the kitten's fault you got stuck being some douchebag Prince's side-piece."

She gives me a sharp, bitter smirk, swiping a bottle of vodka from the fridge. "Real nice, huh? I can't have his baby, but I can have his kitten. Me, Felix, the kitten. He's just keeping all his pussy in one place." She laughs darkly at her own joke, and it makes my fists clench.

It's so Forsyth. Locking something away just to spite someone else. Putting it into a cage because it's an inconvenience. Not even bothering to care for your own goddamn prisoner, just hoping it keeps quiet until it's useful again.

It's so fucking *Royal.*

Felix sweeps in then, looking like a wannabe gangster in his trucker hat, wifebeater, and shiny jacket. This guy isn't Princely at all, probably pledged to the Psi Zetas because none of the harder houses would take him. He looks between us scornfully, muttering, "...not a goddamn Royal playpen," as he saunters to the fridge. He grabs a single beer—not much of a host, either—and uses the edge of the counter to pop the cap on it. He takes the first sip while staring me down. "So you're that North Side princess?"

I point to Autumn. "She's the Princess. I'm a Duchess."

"But you belong to the Counts," he argues.

"I don't belong to anyone," I insist. "But if I did, it'd be the Dukes, obviously."

"Here's what I want to know." He points the neck of his bottle at me. "Why is it the Dukes get a tight little thing like you, and the Princes get stuck with..." He gestures to Autumn, who curls into herself. "If I'd known there was another piece of Lucia ass floating out there, maybe I would have fought for that instead."

I give him a long, scornful look. "You would have lost. I bet Perez could take you easy." But then something in his words penetrates, bringing me up short. "What do you mean 'another' Lucia? Do you know Leticia?"

But Nick and Sy enter the kitchen, interrupting us. "Is this how the Princes do business?" Sy asks. His stare is just as hard as his brother's, only Nick is directing his at the space between me and Felix. "Disappearing to drink a beer? We don't have all goddamn night. Shit or get off the pot."

Felix looks him in the eye as he takes a long swig from his beer. "Is this how Dukes do business? Charging a ridiculous premium on their pieces?"

Nick unabashedly answers, "Yes."

"All the time," Sy agrees. "Always have, always will. Pay it or stop wasting our fucking time."

Felix hums, his gaze wandering to me. "I don't think they're worth it. But this one..." He tips the neck of his bottle in my direction, sauntering over. He stops in front of me, eyeing me up and down. "Is it true what they say? North Side cunt sparkles, apparently." He grins, tongue sliding over a row of crooked teeth. "Give me an hour to set your bitch straight," he says, reaching out to touch my hair, "and I'll pay full pr—"

I jump back.

Because he's touching my hair.

Because of the sudden '*pop*'.

Because of the warmth that blooms over my face.

Felix's eyes go blank in the millisecond before he tips over, smacking lifelessly against the floor. There's a deafening ringing in my ears that grows shrill and painful, but I don't realize what it is at first, my eyes locked on Felix's limp form. Blood begins pooling around his head, and there's a twitch in his arm, fingers fluttering like a seizure. But then there's nothing, and I don't understand—I don't put it together.

Not until I turn my head.

Nick is standing in the middle of the kitchen, casually emptying the chamber of his gun. His eyes are fixed on the task, lips moving, but I can't hear what he's saying. Everything is so loud. It's only when he glances up, eyes rolling in exasperation toward Autumn, that I realize she's screaming.

Remy and Cash come barreling into the kitchen, guns drawn, but all I can do is look between Nick and the douchebag formerly known as Felix, because he's deader than a fucking doornail.

"You shot him," I say unnecessarily. Even my voice sounds strangely muted, as if my ears are numb to the very core.

Nick gives this little shrug—*que sera, sera*—and reaches behind him to tuck the gun away again. "Can't say I didn't warn him."

Remy rams into Autumn, clamping a hand over her shrieking mouth. Cash is openly gaping at Felix. Sy is berating Nick with this irritated expression, saying, "Now who's going to buy the guns?!" and holding a hand out in Felix's direction, like he's scolding a puppy for making a mess on the carpet. All of these things are happening at once, but all I see is Nick finally meeting my gaze, eyes hard and assured.

"You good?" he asks.

Dumbly, I repeat, "Good?" Something tickles my cheek and I reach up to bat it away. That's when I realize the source of the warmth on my face.

Felix's blood.

Nick steps forward and fluidly snatches a dish towel hanging from the oven's handle. For some reason, I don't flinch when he approaches me, touching my chin to hold me steady as he gently begins wiping the blood away. Strangely, I don't feel anything at all.

Where there should be a sense of horror, there's nothing. No panic. No fear. No disgust or revulsion. There's a quake in my nerves that makes my shoulders tremble, but I don't feel it. Autumn is in the corner losing it, and I'm tipping my face up so Nick can get the space below my jaw. His blue eyes fix to the task with a solemn sort of focus, and while one hand is ridding my earlobe of blood spatter, the other one is brushing through the lock of hair Felix had touched, as if Nick could erase it.

"Uh." From the entryway, Cash raises a hand. "I'll buy your guns."

Sy takes a break from pinching the bridge of his nose to shoot Cash a wary look. "All seven?"

Cash nods. "Cut me a ten-percent discount and swear on your life I was never here. I'll even throw in some of my merchandise."

Sy objects with a sneer. "The West End doesn't want drugs."

From the other side of the kitchen table, Remy's head pops up, eyes wide and hopeful. "Hey, the West End wants *some* drugs."

"You," Sy snaps, thrusting a finger at him, "get *no* drugs. You," he points to Nick, "call in your favor with the Barons and get rid of him. I want this shit so fucking clean, Saul and Ashby will think this motherfucker disappeared into thin air!"

My voice emerges rusty and thin. "What about her?"

Autumn's stopped with the god awful shrieking, but she's sitting beneath their rickety table with her knees drawn up, gawking at the body. "Oh my god, oh my god, oh my god," she's gasping, over and over.

Princesses.

Remy gives her a long look, scratching his head. "Eh, Nicky? Any chance the Barons owe you *two* favors?"

No.

I don't know this girl, but I know that I can't watch her die. Not because some guy wanted to touch me. Not because of Nick, who's so unhinged that he'd shoot a man for it just as soon as carve my own tongue from my mouth. Not because of *me*.

Nick bends to look at her beneath the table, and it's easy. His gun is poking out of his jeans and I just swoop right in, plucking it deftly from the waistband. He rears up, but before he can stop me, I'm reaching under the table and grabbing a thick handful of her hair, pulling her out.

Kneeling down, I jam the barrel beneath her chin, ignoring her plaintive cry. My voice is a lot more even than I feel when I ask, "You know who I am, Autumn? You know what I've done?"

Tears stream down her cheeks, and she's trembling so hard that I can feel the vibration in the gun's grip. "You're the Duchess," she sobs, eyes clenched shut. "You're Lavinia Lucia."

I shove the barrel harder into her jaw. "Then you know what I can do, so I need you to pay attention." I don't know where it's coming from—this strange sense of calm and commanding—but the fact that all of the guys are standing back, watching silently, bolsters my resolve. "You're going to walk out of here tonight and leave the East End. You're going to keep your fucking mouth shut. You're going to tell anyone who asks that Felix here kicked you to the curb days ago."

She's nodding these tiny little jerks against the barrel of the gun, insisting, "I won't—I won't say anything, I swear."

"If you do, I'll find you." I fist her hair harder, hoping she feels the pain. "And you're going to get over Holden! He's never going to love anyone but himself, because that's how these pieces of shit work. You think having his kid is such a goddamn fairytale? Look at what being the child of a King gets you!" I release her, throwing my arms out wide. "A dead mother and two years of confinement! Don't believe the hype, *Princess*." I turn, smoothly handing the gun back to Nick.

Nick's watching me with shrewd eyes, but there's something barely controlled underneath. He hides it by pinning me with a pointed scowl as he tucks his gun away again. "Never touch my fucking gun."

"Kill her and our deal is off," I say. Autumn is pathetic, but she's a Royal woman. A product of her own undoing. She could be Leticia. She could be Verity. She could be me.

"Fine," Nick replies, giving the girl a chin jerking nod. "Get what you need and leave."

I catch a flash of white through the sliding doors. Before Autumn even finds her footing enough to stand, I decisively add, "And I'm taking your fucking kitten!"

～

S*EVEN DAYS*.

Dawn breaks as we finally begin the drive back to the tower.

The van is quiet, illuminated by the dimming street lights and Remy's phone screen. He looks more tired than even I do, his head propped up against the window as he watches some video. In the driver's seat, Sy keeps his eyes straight ahead, his reflection in the rearview wan and impossibly more stoic than usual. Beside me, Nick has his legs sprawled wide, head resting back on the seat, arms crossed, eyes closed. It was a long night.

Evidently, getting rid of a body is a lot of waiting.

I spent all of it hidden away in the van, so I never saw who came. Who took Felix away. *How* they took Felix away. All I know is, one second I'm nodding off to a purr, and the next, they're sliding into their seats.

Naked.

"Clothes are evidence," was all Remy said, looking way too comfortable as he stowed all their weapons and belongings in the center console, cock heavy between his legs.

There's a squirm against my chest and I look down, watching the kitten curl a little tighter. I'd turned my sweater around backward and placed him in the hood, which I figure will be useful on the long trek up the tower stairs. The moment I opened that balcony door, the trembling ball of fur charged at my ankle and climbed me like a scratching post, crying his little heart out. He's so little—barely old enough to be parted from his mother, in my opinion. But he's strong. Resilient. He spent half an hour clumsily cleaning his white fur before finally succumbing to rest.

He's a fighter.

"We'll need supplies," I realize, looking up hopefully. "Food, litter, a box?"

Sy's eyes flick to the mirror, meeting mine with low, angry brows. "No."

"But—"

"Shut the fuck up!" he snaps, knuckles going white around the steering wheel. "I just had to dismember a body because of you! The last goddamn thing I want to hear is another one of your annoying fucking demands!"

Nick sighs. "It's too late for this shit, Sy. Save your tantrum for tomorrow."

"*Please,*" Remy mutters, looking wrung out.

Briefly, I wonder what dismembering a body entails, and whether or not that's something Remy can mentally handle. But even though he looks tired, lounging in the front seat, stark naked, I don't see the Maniac dwelling in his eyes.

Really, he just looks sort of bored.

I give it a long stretch of silence, before reluctantly adding, "The old Dukes had a dog."

"The new Dukes have one, too," Sy grinds out, turning down the alley beside the tower.

My eyes narrow, but I think twice about talking back when I glance down at the kitten. I know then that it's a mistake—that I should set the kitten free somewhere. It'd be foolish to care about anything. It'd be giving these three something to use against me. Something innocent and undeserving. It'd be another way for them to control me. Verity would take him if I asked her to. I'm the Duchess. She could give him a slice of her comfortable freedom.

When the van jerks to a stop, he stirs, stretching out two tiny paws to yawn.

I cradle him close as I step out.

The walk up the tower is quiet and tense, and means staring at Sy's muscular ass and swinging horse dick as he walks ahead of me. Each of them has their guns, phones, and wallets clutched in their hands, and they climb faster than I'm used to, struggling to keep up. I hug my arms around the hood and hope they're too tired to realize I've brought the kitten through the party room, up the stairs, into the main living area.

It's quiet enough that we all hear Simon's phone buzz the moment we step through the door. He glances at the screen and then does a double-take, freezing. "Shit," he mutters, trying to cup a hand over his massive junk. Even soft, that thing is like a firehose. "We have a massive fucking problem."

Remy stretches his arms in the air, letting it all hang out, unapologetic when he catches me staring. "Is it Saul? Word's already reached him?"

Simon shakes his head. "Worse. It's mom."

Nick visibly winces. "What's she want?"

"She's demanding we come over tomorrow for dinner," he says, looking from his brother to me. "And we have to bring *her*."

I freeze as they turn to me. The Dukes look menacing enough when they're wearing jeans and suits and hoodies, but like this? Naked from head to toe, inked and rippling, a study in contrasts? It sends a ripple of panic up my spine. Dealing with one of them is intimidating enough. The sight of their three cocks dangling—each of them twitching to life under my paralyzed scrutiny—is basically like being held at dickpoint.

"We'll deal with that after we've had some sleep," Nick decides.

"I'm sleeping in my room," I announce—just to make it clear that I'm not running. It really is like staring down three bears, complete with the prickle of fear that the moment I turn my back, they'll come chasing after me.

Luckily, none of them do.

I climb the staircase, carrying the kitten up into my loft. The soft light of dawn is creeping through the clock face and I carefully pluck him from my hood, introducing him to my makeshift nest. He spends a moment sniffing around like a spurious powder-puff.

"It's not much," I whisper, running two gentle fingers down his back, "but it's better than being locked on that balcony, huh?"

The kitten spins, rubbing his hip against my wrist, little paws kneading into the blanket. Then he looks at me and cries, big blue eyes squinting with the force of it.

"You're hungry," I note, mouth pressed into a tense line. "I'll see what I can—"

I'm interrupted by heavy footfalls coming up toward the loft, and I stiffen, folding my legs and pushing the kitten behind me. Sy appears in a pair of loose sweatpants and nothing else, halting on the last step of the spiral staircase. The pink light of dusk washes him in muted warmth, highlighting the ridged ladder of his abs. He spends a long moment looking at me, the muscle in the back of his jaw ticking.

"We need to talk." When all I do is stare at him, he... deflates. Head tipped back, he heaves a loud sigh, muttering, "Can't believe I have to..." But then he snaps back into his posture, resting an elbow on the railing. "You know I never wanted you to be Duchess."

Doing my best to contain the kitten, my lip curls. "That makes two of us."

"But for this dinner... I need you to cooperate."

"You think I haven't been cooperating?" I twist my other arm back to still the kitten, and I don't miss it when Sy's eyes flick down to my tits. "I've been a goddamn ray of sunshine to you three for the last week."

He pushes his fingers through his hair, looking just as tired as I feel. "My parents aren't privy to the entirety of this situation."

"What part? The fights and parties? The gun running? Or do you just mean me? Your slave."

"They're not clueless. Our parents were Dukes. Both of our fathers and our mother... they opted out of challenging Saul to be King. They never wanted either of us involved in this lifestyle." He shakes his head, a frown creasing his brow. "But parents don't get to define who their children become." The statement hits hard, a gut punch, and Simon is too fucking clueless to even recognize it, because he continues rambling on. "Look, we need you to behave during dinner. Act like you wanted to be the

Duchess. Use your manners. Be polite to my mom and laugh at our dad's jokes."

"And why the hell should I do that?" I ask, chest flaring in outrage. "Are you going to threaten to rape me again? Gag me on your cock? Maybe set Remy loose on me during one of his episodes? Tell Nick he's free to punish me in the worst way possible? Is that the plan?"

Voice hard, he answers, "I don't need you scared. My mother will sniff that out in a heartbeat. I need you *believable*." He runs a palm down his face. "So, what do you want?"

"What the hell are you talking about?"

"I said, *what do you want*?! I know you and my brother do this tit-for-tat shit, bartering or whatever. Tell me what you want, and we can negotiate."

I stare at him for a long moment, determining if he's serious. I have to assume he is, because the only games Sy is keen on playing are the kinds with a trophy at the end.

I mull it over for a second, pretending to think about it, but I already know. I got Nick to promise to one unspecified thing for that kiss, but I know I'll need to get all three of them to agree.

"Let me keep the kitten."

He blinks. "What?"

I pull the kitten from behind my back, setting him in my lap. "Get me some supplies—food, litter, a box. Nothing extravagant. He won't be a prob—"

Snapping tall, he says, "Cats are nasty! They smell! They literally shit in a box." Looking rankled, he adds, "Can't I just swipe you a book, or some tools, or a candy bar or something?"

I give the kitten a pointed stroke. "That's what I want. Take it or leave it."

Sy chuffs a quiet laugh, arms crossing. "You're such a fucking pain in my ass."

I nod and offer my hand. "Do we have a deal, or what?"

He looks at it warily, like he's going to get herpes if he touches me, but I thrust it closer and he grimaces, taking it. His hand is rough, callused from all the fights. A jolt runs through me as we shake on it. I feel like I've just made a deal with the devil. It's one thing to negotiate back and forth over little shit in the house, but this feels different. Simon's not just negotiating to get me in his bed. He's firming up that I'll be good around his parents. This means he cares about what they think.

And that's just more information I plan on filing away for later.

25

Sy

I'm not sure where she got the dress, but it's perfect. The fabric is a pale floral print. No leather or sequins, straps or denim. The hem brushes against her knees and the top shows just a hint of her ample tits. It doesn't even matter that she's wearing those calf-high boots Verity gave her on Friday. She still looks... appropriate. Modest. It's exactly the kind of dress you'd wear to meet the parents.

The wave rolls over me—irritation. Anger. How dare she present herself to be anything so virtuous? A couple nights ago, she was swallowing Remy's load in front of an entire DKS victory party, and now she's crouching down in her pretty Sunday best to kiss that little white rat on its forehead.

"Be good while we're gone," she tells it, nudging his food bowl closer.

I'd taken Remy with me yesterday afternoon to a crummy pet store in South Side to get the creature the bare essentials, but the trip was more about checking where Remy's head was than anything else. Nick's no stranger to wet work, and to me, anatomy is just science. Clinically, bodies—gore, blood, muscle and bone—don't bother me. But Remy is unpredictable and can be swept off course by the smallest shit. I guess I shouldn't have worried. A dozen different shades of yellow will set him off, but dismembering a body?

I mostly had to stop him from cutting it up more than necessary. He was so excited to see what overly specific parts of someone's insides looked like. "Are all spinal cords this translucent?" he'd said, oohing and ahhing as he dug around in Felix like a candy dish. "Wicked, just wicked."

So the trip to the pet store was more about making sure Remy wasn't turning into a goddamn Baron or something, but it did result in this:

Lavinia Lucia, in the middle of my living room, shaking a toy mouse for our murder victim's cat.

"Jesus Christ," I mutter, rubbing my temples. "Let's fucking go!"

I round them all up and try not to think so hard about her looking like a Sunday school teacher. I asked her to do this. To pretend. To act like she isn't a cocksucker who has my brother pussy-whipped enough that he's burying bullets into motherfuckers.

At least he takes shotgun for once, leaving Remy to slide into the backseat with her. I wrap my hands around the steering wheel of the SUV and ignore her presence.

Of course, she makes it impossible. "Anyone want to clue me in on what to expect?"

Nick has been pretty blasé about what went down with Felix and it makes me look at him in a skewed light. If what he says is true about defecting to South Side out of some misplaced attempt to investigate Tate's suicide, then I'm not sure the explanation particularly matters. He's changed into someone I only halfway know—a guy who can lift a gun and pull the trigger without giving me the smallest indication of what he plans to do.

He answers, "If I had to guess? Mom will cook both meat and

something vegetarian, continuing her life's goal of pushing us to a plant-based diet." He twists to throw her a smirk. "She's convinced our inclination to trouble is due to inflammation from red meat." Turning back, he continues, "Dad will drink one scotch too many, pull us aside and regale us with stories from the 'good old days', and Pops will hound the three of us about our future plans, with a hard focus on 'outside of West End'."

Remy snorts. "He's wallpapering over the reality. You're in for a real show, Vinny. This is years of family drama coming to a head." I watch from the rearview as he leans his head toward hers. "Their mother—who is an absolute fucking MILF, by the way—"

"Watch it!" I snap.

Remy goes on, "She's going to tear Nicky here a new one for becoming a Duke. Some of that will bleed over to Sy, but Nick's her precious little baby. Their dads are going to get really weird about it, because they'll know Saul is the boss of us, and they're all possessive of their kids, for some reason." He and Lavinia share a baffled look. I guess Nick and I aren't allowed in the 'emotionally neglected children,' club.

Lavinia doesn't look comforted by any of this. Everyone with the slightest interest in psychology knows about 'Daddy Issues' and there's no question Lionel Lucia did a number on this one. Even if I didn't know he'd sold her, it's obvious in other ways. One is her hypersexuality—how she pretends she's not a whore, but the negotiations with my brother? Everything is a transaction, especially her pussy. Then there's the mothering: the tending to Remy's psychosis, the way she snapped so quickly into stitching up my eyebrow after the fight, her insistence on keeping that mangy feline. Lionel had her taking care of his soldiers from a young age. I'm not sure if she's realized it yet, but she was doing a Queen's job—the role of a Royal wife—while apparently fighting with her sister about who could do it best.

But the thing that I notice the most, probably because it's the most familiar, is the rage. It's deep and disruptive. Would she really turn on her father if given the chance, or would she fall right back into the position she's been trained for her whole life?

All I know is I don't trust this bitch for a second.

The bungalow comes into view, the big windows filled with warm light. I park in the driveway, and she peers at the house.

"This is where you grew up?" she asks.

Nick raises an eyebrow. "Are these fifteen-hundred square-feet of paradise not the sprawling estate you'd imagined?"

She looks taken aback. "I hadn't really thought of it at all, to be honest."

We all file out of the car, but I'm the one to open Lavinia's door. Child lock. Nick's idea. An irritated look crosses over her face as she slides off the leather seat, giving me a flash of her white panties in the process. Fuck me.

I inhale and exhale deeply, then adjust myself. It's going to be a long fucking night.

Grabbing her arm, I quietly remind her, "Remember our deal. Best behavior."

She narrows her eyes, tugging away from my grip. "I've programmed myself to perfect Duchess mode. Don't worry."

But even Nick looks uneasy. I doubt she notices, but I can see it in the way he keeps his eyes down as we march toward the door. This talk has been a long time coming, and his being a Duke is bad enough without the added unpleasantness of Lavinia being his illicit and unwilling South Side spoils.

Nick and I lead them to the side door out of habit, filtering into the mudroom with enough tension between us that it feels like an electric buzz. The feeling snaps when my mom meets us there, arms crossed, as she blocks our entry into the rest of the house.

"Simon," she greets me, turning her blue eyes to my brother. "Nicholas."

Nick and I share a quick glance.

Full names today.

That can't be good.

My mother is a short, slender woman with curly auburn hair.

Nick and I both share her distinctive, azure eyes, plus a little of her facial structure. These are the only things that really unite us, physically. I have Mom's curls and Dad's sepia complexion and broad stature. Nick has her fuller lips and Pops' straight hair and fair skin, and lean physique. When we were younger, people used to think one of us was adopted. That would have been an easier explanation than the truth, but having two fathers was all we ever knew. We used to talk sometimes about how weird it was that everyone else only had one, and some of them—like Remy's—weren't even good fathers.

Mom looks between us—her two miscreant Duke sons, despite her every effort. "You know the rules, boys. You're not coming in here until you unload." She points to the gun safe, which has been conveniently left open for us.

Guiltily, I reach for my piece, and Nick and Remy do the same, all of us placing our guns inside, one by one.

Remy clears his throat. "Knives, too, Sarah?" Mom dips her chin, giving him a significant look, and he grimaces, pulling his knife out and placing it beside his pistol.

Lavinia, who's been standing by the door and making herself as invisible as possible, shuffles forward, shooting me a wary look before she bends down and slides two fingers into her boot.

She emerges with a knife.

Cagily, she edges around us, avoiding our stunned stares as she gently places it in the safe. Nick and Remy look at each other, then at me, and the question is written on all our faces. Where the fuck did this bitch get a knife?

"Sorry." Lavinia looks up at my mom and gives her a rueful grin. "Just never know where these three are taking me."

Only one thing can penetrate the fury throbbing at my temples, and it's the sunny smile my mom bestows her with. "You must be the Duchess." Lavinia nods, hands linked behind her back, the picture of propriety. Mom stares at her for a long moment, lips quirking. "I used to carry a bat."

Lavinia blinks. *"Really?"*

She places a hand on Lavinia's shoulder, leading her through the door. "If I've said it once, I've said it a thousand times. Blunt force is far less messy."

Nick sends me a sidelong look. "Remind me to thank the Lady for the dress."

Ah, that's where it came from. Sighing, I stomp the dirt from my feet before entering. "We can send her a weapon to show our gratitude."

Remy agrees, "Bitches love weapons."

NICK CALLED IT, I think, wrinkling my nose at the plate of Brussels sprouts sitting on the counter. Mom is still on the vegetarian kick. This is a full dinner of zucchini in the shape of noodles and a variety of other vegetables.

We're going to have to stop on the way home for a burger.

The mood around the table is strained. Pops hasn't said one word to either of us—won't even look Nick in the eye—and Dad is sitting back, his shoulder-length black hair left to hang free as his dark eyes move between me and Nick. Neither of them looks happy, but at least Dad doesn't look so... fucking *haunted*.

His eyes flick to mine.

He just looks disappointed.

"So," Mom says, smiling across the table at Lavinia. "How's school going for you, Duchess? You're pre-med, I assume?"

Lavinia, who's been halfheartedly probing her pile of fraudulent spaghetti, looks at me, and then Nick. It's a lightning quick maneuver that's full of dread, because we haven't crafted a lie about this yet. Nick goes stiff beside me, and I try to convey a message to Lavinia with my tight jaw and wide eyes.

Lie through your fucking teeth.

Lavinia nods. "Yep! School's great."

Mom rests her elbows on the table, hands folded beneath her chin. "What's your favorite class?"

Lavinia stabs at a tomato. "Oh, I couldn't possibly say. I know which class is the worst, though." She flashes me an overly conspiratorial smile. "Organic chemistry, am I right?"

I give her a surprised blink. "Yeah, the pass-fail ratio in Sheff's class is abysmal."

"Not for me." She pops a cherry tomato into her mouth, explaining to Mom, "I'm doing a paper on carbonyl group modifications this week."

No, she isn't.

I am.

"Oh," Mom says, attention piqued. "Any particular method?"

Nick and I glance at each other, silently panicking.

Lavinia, however, just nods. "I'll be focusing on the mechanisms of hydrolysis thioacetals, but particularly oxidizing reagents." I just barely stop myself from snapping back in shock. *My* paper isn't even on that.

Shit.

Maybe it should be.

Mom studies her closely, and I feel sweat springing up on my forehead at the knowledge of what's happening here. This isn't a test. It's a thinly veiled interrogation. "Which reagent?"

"Hypervalent iodine compounds." Lavinia glances up, and fuck me. I'm sitting here sweating, but she looks cool as a cucumber. Butter wouldn't melt on this bitch. "Benzine, iodoxybenzoic acid— that sort of thing."

Nick slides me a questioning look, but I'm even more baffled than he is.

Where is she getting this?

And why is she so good at bullshitting?

Even Mom looks surprised, dropping her hands. "I don't think—"

Pops drops his fork, the clank piercing through the air like a knife. "Are we really doing this?" he asks, gaze fixed on Nick's ring. "Are we just going to sit here and pretend that our sons haven't willfully violated our wishes?" He finally looks up from his plate, staring at me. "You're one thing, Simon. I understand you need a physical outlet, and the gym has been a vital part of your therapy. I don't *like* it. But I understand it. You, on the other hand..." He slides his gaze, eyes sharp through his glasses, to Nick, who's sitting stiffly at my side. "You have the nerve to take the Bruin name—*my* name—back into that tower?" Pops has always been the most hot-tempered of the three of them. It flares up now, brows pinched angrily as he pitches forward, voice low and menacing. "How dare you."

My mom touches his hand, whispering, "Davis," but he isn't hearing it.

"I can count on one hand the number of times you've spoken to me in the last two years." Pops jerks a thumb at Dad. "Oh, you'll talk to your dad every weekend, but me and your mother? You've wanted nothing to do with us. And now you're using my name to... do what, exactly? What's so important about being a Duke that you'd lower yourself to associating with the Bruin name again? If I can't be your father for anything else but *this*, then you'd better fucking explain—"

"Stop," Nick says, sounding tired. "Me becoming a Duke... it doesn't have anything to do with you."

Pops' fist comes down on the table. "It has everything to do with me!"

Lavinia flinches so hard that the glass by her elbow flies off the table, crashing to the floor. The sound of it shattering is enough to douse the table in tense silence. Remy looks down at the pieces of glass, and Dad is already standing from his seat, saying, "I'll get the broom," but Lavinia...

She's gone white as a sheet, dropping to her knees to pluck up the shards. "I'm sorry—I didn't mean to. I'll pick it up myself."

The closer Dad gets, the faster her hands move, in such a hurry to clear the debris that she's going to slice her goddamn hand open.

Quickly, I move to intervene, noticing how nervous she's getting with Dad's approach. *Fucking daddy issues...*

"I've got it," I tell her, stilling her hand. She flashes me an anxious glare and I scowl back. "I've got it," I stress, shooing her back into her seat.

Dad clears his throat, hovering over me. "Well, if we've reached the 'dramatic outbursts' phase of dinner, then I think the three of us need to excuse ourselves and talk this out in private." He shoots Pops a disapproving look, and then one to Nick, who's rising from his seat like he'd rather be doing anything else.

"Fine," Nick says, dropping his napkin and following our father's upstairs to the study.

The second they're gone, Lavinia relaxes.

But Remy doesn't.

He reaches up to rub at his temple, eyes tight at the corners. He's really good at hiding his neurosis at times like these—times when he needs to. His dad never did do much for Remy, but at least he taught him that. To act normal. To pretend.

Unfortunately, nothing gets past my mother—especially when she needs a distraction from the yells currently coming from upstairs. "What is it, Remy?"

He freezes, dropping his hand into his lap. "Nothing."

But she frowns, observing him carefully. "It's okay if it's something." My mom was probably the only one who took him seriously when we were kids. She's the one who diagnosed him, back before any of us realized Remy wasn't just gone for large blocks of time on account of his dad being a prick. "There's nothing that can't be said under this roof. You remember the rules, don't you?"

But no one knows him better than I do, and I cast my eyes around the table, searching for—

Yep, there it is.

A bouquet of wildflowers fills the vase in the centerpiece of the table. I lean over my plate and pick it up, twisting to set it on the floor behind me. "He's sensitive to the yellow," I explain, and Mom gives me a long look.

"I didn't realize you were experiencing sensory issues," she says, slipping into her head-shrink posture. "When did that begin?"

"Mom," I warn.

Now that the yellow wildflowers are gone, Remy looks content to shovel food into his mouth, unbothered by her probing. "I don't think it's a sensory thing, Sarah. Yellow is just bad."

"Bad how?"

He shrugs. "Just is. Too bright. Wrong. Smells like brimstone."

Realizing that's not going to go anywhere, she turns her focus to me, eyes flicking up briefly when Nick's booming voice carries through the ceiling. "How are things going with your brother in the belfry?"

"Fine," I reply, beginning the clean up without being asked. I dump the remains of the sprouts down the disposal and flick on the switch, hoping the grinding will drown out whatever Nick is saying up there.

"No incidents?" she asks, the instant I turn it off. "It's been a long time since you two lived together."

"We're not sixteen anymore. We can co-exist."

Mom glances over at Lavinia, who's carrying a stack of plates from the table. "How do you think my boys are doing?"

"Me?" Lavinia asks, wobbling a little. A fork slides and I reach out and grab it before it hits the ground.

"*Mom*," I interject. She should know better than to bring this shit up. "I don't think—"

"I'd love to hear what *you* think, Duchess," Mom says, ignoring my interjection.

"Oh, there's definitely tension," Lavinia says, pushing the stack of dirty dishes toward me. "And I think at least one fistfight..."

That she caused. I shoot her a hard look and mouth the word, 'kitten.'

"But overall," she adds slowly, "they seem to get along. I mean, comparatively."

"Comparatively?" Mom tilts her head, and I suppress a groan. "Compared to what?"

Lavinia glances between us. "I just mean... well, I got into a lot of fights with my sister growing up. They're not as bad as that."

I watch my mom carefully, unsure if the rumors about the Lucias have penetrated this far outside of the territories. "I have a sister," Mom says, giving her a private grin. "There's nothing as merciless as a teenage girl whose favorite shirt has gone missing."

Lavinia responds with a fake little laugh that tells my mother more than words or I could have. I give her a threatening look before starting some dish water.

"But brothers can be brutal in their own way," mom says, standing to collect the glasses. "Things were complicated when Nick took off to go work for Daniel Payne. I was convinced we'd lost him for a while." My shoulders tense as my mother rambles on. I don't like Lavinia knowing our business, but from the somber cast in her eyes, I can see she's lost in facing down a difficult emotion. "It wasn't completely unexpected. Everyone was grieving, and poor Remy..."

Without really meaning to, we all turn to look at him, standing over the trashcan by the basement door. He goes still, a haunted expression frozen on his face as his arm hovers halfway over the bin.

The wildflowers are in his hand.

I fling my arms out haplessly. "*Dude.*"

Mom flicks a hand. "Oh, go ahead, Remy. I picked them this morning during a patient outing at the river. They're nothing special."

Looking relieved, he dumps them into the trashcan, closing it with a decisive slam. I knew I shouldn't have let him take all those stimulants from Cash the night before last. "Downstairs," I say, pointing a finger to the basement door. "Work it off on the pool table," and before he opens the door, "Don't mess with the yellow balls!"

"Grieving about Tate?" Lavinia asks, leaning her hip against the counter. The name brings me up short, which is why I've forgotten the discussion they were having before Remy decided to dispose of the floral arrangement.

"What?" I ask, voice sharp enough to make her visibly bristle.

She gestures to my mom. "She said everyone was grieving."

"That's right." Mom looks at me and back at Lav. "It was a difficult time for everyone, especially the boys. Suicide loss survivors internalize so much more guilt—"

"Okay," I say, dropping the fork I'd been cleaning in the soapy water, "that's enough."

My mother sighs. "How many times have I told you it's not okay to bottle everything up? You need to talk about her." She lifts the lid on a pot and stirs whatever is inside. "You should know this about my boys, Lavinia. They're like their fathers. It's easier for them to use their fists than to deal with their emotions. Lashing out is more fun."

My eyes meet Lavinia's and we hold contact for a moment. I don't know how she'll respond, but I don't expect her to ease up to my side and tuck herself under my arm.

"I don't know, Sarah. Simon has all kinds of ways he likes to express himself." She looks up at me, fluttering her eyelashes, "Isn't that right, babe?"

Every muscle in my body tenses. Not just from her touch, but her scent and the fact she's playing this game so well—a game I talked her into.

I swallow. "I'm working on it."

Mom's eyes light up. "I'm so glad to hear that. I knew one day you'd find the right woman to channel all that energy into." Mom leans toward Lavinia, winking. "It took me a few years, but now my husbands are also as good in bed as they were in the ring."

"That's it," I say, tightening my grip on Lavinia and pulling her from the room. When we're out of earshot, I mutter, "Jesus Christ."

"Nothing's off limits with that one, huh?" she says, and despite the heavy topics and clumsy subterfuge, there's a strange mirth in her eyes. I don't like it.

"She's a sex therapist. You have no fucking idea." My fingers clench around her upper arm, squeezing hard enough to bruise. "And I told you not to mention Tate. *Ever.*"

"You told me to be believable!" she hisses, trying to pull away.

The movement makes her tits jiggle, and I feel the ocean inside of me churn eagerly. Fuck, I want to hold those things in my hands. "Do you really think she'd believe I wouldn't ask?"

"I'll tell you what I think," I say, not realizing how hard I'm squeezing her arm until she winces, a pained sound escaping her throat. "I think you're getting a little too comfortable. Things were a lot easier when you were just some slut Nick kept ferreting away." Now she's in my home—my real home—with her tits and legs and plush, red lips, asking all these fucking questions.

She shoots a pointed look at where I'm grabbing her arm. "You think this is comfortable?! Why don't you just be honest with yourself for three seconds, Sy? Why are you actually so worked up?" She stares at me with a malevolent glint in her eye. "I did what you asked. I charmed your mother's pants off in there. You're mad," she steps closer, tits brushing my chest, "because of this."

Without warning, her hand cups my half-hard dick.

In a blink, I have her pressed into the couch, her wrist trapped in my hand. "Don't," I warn, my skin feeling spread too tight. "Do *not* fucking push me." It takes everything—every single morsel of my self-control—to not bend her over this couch, wrench her panties aside, and shove my cock into the nearest and able hole.

Her lip curls. "I'll stop pushing you when you face up to your own issues instead of taking them out on me."

I have a lot more to say, but we're interrupted by the footsteps on the stairs. Nick, Pops, and Dad descend, and I jerk away from Lavinia as if her skin is made of fire. I shove my hands into my pockets, hoping it hides the half-chub I'm packing as they enter the den. It looks like everyone's done being pissed off, even though Pops looks wrung out.

As we all go downstairs, I do what I always do; pretend everything is fine, that it's all under control, that Nick coming back hasn't both helped and hindered my life. That Remy's not teetering on the edge of a sharp knife and that Lavinia... I shoot her a dark look as she rests an elbow on Pop's prized bar he had installed right after I graduated.

Nick was still in high school then, finishing out his senior year, and I remember being jealous that he got a whole year with it. When I lived here, there wasn't anything in the basement but spider webs, a half-functional and possibly cursed chest freezer, and musty Christmas decorations.

Now, it's a total fucking *pad*.

I know the hatchet is buried when Nick and Pops begin a quiet game of pool. Whatever words were said up there, they seem to have eased some of the tension between them. Briefly, I wonder if Nick told him the same thing he told me and Remy about defecting to South Side to investigate Tate's death. We've talked about it a little bit over the last few days. The topic is usually brought up in the middle of doing something else, a conversation we keep picking up and putting down, like it's something none of us are confident enough to look in the eye.

Dad and Remy are sprawled out on the couch, watching the football game on the TV. Remy's flipping that marker through his fingers, eyes tracking the players on the field.

"How about I get everyone a drink?" Lavinia says, walking around the back of the bar. The ease in which she slips into playing the part of the doting Duchess is shocking.

I don't even understand why it pisses me off so much. It's a performance she's been ordered to do, but it's still a performance. *Fake.* God, I hate it when bitches are fake. And why do her tits have to look like that? All fucking grabbable. I keep tucking the hot feeling inside my chest away into the ocean, but it's hard to visualize my serenity when she's standing there in that dress.

All it'd take is one finger to lower a strap and expose her breast.

I resist the urge when she brings me a beer. Instead, I grab it and take an aggressive swallow.

My brother's eyes keep wandering to her, like a master who's eager for his puppy's affection. But he doesn't ask—doesn't manhandle her where he wants her. Not here, in front of our fathers, and especially not after having found a tentative peace.

During one of these overly intense stares, she finally strides right over to him, winding an arm around his waist. Nick looks shocked for a second, and then his mouth curves into this wicked little grin. "There's my Little Bird." I know what's coming before he even tips his face down to kiss her.

Sucking face.

Disgusting.

Ocean, ocean, ocean.

She accepts his kiss with minimal fuss, even going so far as to fist his shirt fabric, but the second his mouth releases her, her eyes flick to me.

Whore.

"Who's winning?" she asks, resting her hand on his stomach. Remy glances over, eyebrow raised. The Duchess' game must be more interesting than the one on TV.

"Pops is a shark," Nick says, sliding his hand down her ass and giving it a little squeeze. No way my brother isn't going to take advantage of this situation. "He'll take all your money if you don't watch out."

"I hope none of you bet on this game," Dad says from the armchair, cigar pinched between his fingers. "It's going to be a tough year for Forsyth without Payne playing." None of us care much about football, but Killian was a legend on the field. His decision to quit and focus on being King after his father was murdered was surprising—well, to anyone that didn't understand what was at stake. "But obligation to family is tough. We've tried our hardest not to put that kind of pressure on you boys."

Here we go. Nick and I share a resigned look. He might have already had his dressing down, but that doesn't mean they're going to support us being Dukes. I sit back in the recliner, fully prepared for a lecture about the pitfalls of West End.

It never comes.

But Lavinia does.

She steps back from Nick as he lines up his next shot and crosses in front of me, walking toward the empty seat next to Remy. Or I think she is, but suddenly she drops in my lap.

It feels like I suck in every bit of air in the room, pressing myself into the chair as if I could get away from her.

"Can I get you anything else?" she asks, batting those blonde eyelashes at me.

Through clenched teeth, I answer, "No."

"Alright, then." She doesn't remove herself, instead grinding down on my crotch with her ass. "I guess I'll stay here."

I grit my teeth, willing my boner to settle down. She slides her hand behind my neck and tugs at the hair at the nape of my neck. A shiver runs through me. Keeping my voice a low rumble, I ask, "What are you doing?"

She responds by pushing my hair off my forehead with her other hand. "Behaving. Isn't this what you wanted? A little Barbie doll that does whatever you want? A sweet little uncomplicated Verity?"

But she's not being sweet. She's wiggling her tight little ass against my cock. *Intentionally.* I dig my fingers into her hips in an attempt to force her to still, but it just crushes her closer. "You need to stop."

"Do I?"

Clack!

The cue hits the ball and I look over at my brother. One ball sinks in the pocket while the white ball bounces off the side. You'd think he'd be pissed about his pet flirting with me, but he just looks up at me through his lashes, lips curving into a dark smirk. He's enjoying my discomfort.

In the quietest, calmest voice I can muster, I say in her ear, "I know you think this is funny, but my cock is on a hair-trigger. I need you to *stop.* That's an order."

She stills, and I can almost breathe. It's taking every ounce of restraint to not buck up into her ass. If I can just count to ten like I normally do, I can get it under control. But this bitch, *this fucking cock-tease*, just can't leave well enough alone. She wiggles her ass discreetly, grinding down on me until white flashes in front of my eyes. I clamp my fingers down on her hips, but it's too late. I'm fully, *painfully* erect.

Suddenly, she stands and looks down at me with a grin that's sharp and full of venom. "I think I'll go see if your mother needs any help."

"Damn it," Nick shouts, focused on the board. Pops cackles, setting up his last shot. Remy and Dad are still absorbed in the football game, which gives me a chance to make a break for it. I grimace through the pain of standing, the friction of my pants, and head to the bathroom, balls aching. It won't be the first time I've jerked off down here.

I push open the door, my hand already on my fly, but as soon as I enter, I freeze.

Lavinia is bent over the sink, palms pressed to the counter as she peers into the mirror. Every shred of self-control vanishes and I step in, shutting and locking the door behind me.

"Jesus Christ!" She jumps. "What did I say about that bell, *Lurker*?"

I shove the flat of my palm into the center of her back and slam her down over the counter, vision going red. "You think you can do that?" I growl, frantically clawing at my pants' buttons. "You think you can fuck with me and just walk away?!"

I push my hips into her ass, seeking relief in that feral, mindless way I hate. Nick can make all the jokes he wants about me being a robot, but sometimes desperate appeals to my own inner logic are the only thing that keeps me from exploding like a goddamn H-bomb. It's never easy to force the urges back inside, but I can. It takes strength. Will. Determination.

So when I make the decision not to bother, it's done very deliberately.

Lavinia is the Duchess.

The Duchess exists to be used.

She shoots a hand out, struggling against my hold as I reach beneath her dress and wrench her panties down her thighs. Her eyes flash with panic and she presses her thighs together, gasping, "No, Sy—wait! Stop!"

I clamp over her mouth with my hand, curling over her back to hiss, "Shut up. Shut the fuck up!" I make sure she's looking at me in the reflection before I add, "If you don't, I'm going to shove my cock into your hole."

She goes quiet. Still.

"Did you like that?" I ask, seething. "Embarrassing me in front of my family? I specifically told you *not* to act like a whore, but you couldn't stop yourself, could you?" I shimmy my pants down to free my cock, not once taking my eyes off of hers in the mirror. "You don't get to rile me up like that, get me fucking hard and desperate, and just..."

I thrust against her ass, knowing that I can fuck her, tear her up, and ruin her for any other man. Ruin her for *Nick*, who gets her kisses and attention and fucking deference, while the rest of us get jack shit. I know my girth would do it, but then I'd have to look at the disgust on her face, hear her call me a monster.

Maybe I just want her to be humiliated, the same way she did to me.

"So you're going to stand here and take it, just like I did out there. You're not going to make a fucking sound." But I don't move my hand away until she nods, and if I thought her wriggling in my lap was the most arousing thing I've seen today, then I'm proven wrong at the sight of her eyes, bright with unshed tears.

I remove my hand from her mouth, hoping the tears spill over. My hands are shaking at the thought of it—seeing her cry. Seeing her sob. Seeing tears spring from those eyes as her face contorted with agony...

My cock is blistering hot, and I pull on it with a long, furious stroke. I flip the skirt of her dress up, getting a look at her smooth, bare ass. Her cheeks are clenched, and I let go of my cock long enough to force them apart, revealing the most hidden parts of her. I stare at the puckered hole, pristine. No one's taken her there yet. It could be *mine*. It'd be so easy to cave just this once and let go, let loose. I could do it. She has no choice but to let me.

But we're in my parent's house.

Someone would have to carry her out on a stretcher.

Instead, I reach over her and pump a thick dollop of lotion out of the bottle on the counter. I spread it all over, getting her good and greasy, then slot my cock between her cheeks. It spreads her wide and I see her bite her bottom lip as my thickness stretches her apart. I'm sure it's uncomfortable, but guess what? I've been in pain all day. All goddamn *week*. I hope she feels it. With both hands, I squeeze the fleshy sides together and rock my hips, sliding against the pressure.

"Jesus, *yes*." My voice sounds like sandpaper, rough and quiet. I've never had a girl like this. Never had a girl at all. And the ocean inside me is frothing, with the tempest of need settling at the base of my spine. It drives my hips forward, hypnotizing me with the sight of my cock nestled between her cheeks. One of her palms is still gripping the edge of the counter, elbow raised in the air, suspended in a failed attempt at getting away.

It's not a comfortable angle. Lavinia is too short and I have to bend my knees, but somehow, it's still the hottest fucking thing I've ever seen. I pull my shirt out of the way to watch every point of our skin connecting in hyper-detail. The slickness of the lotion, the muscles in her ass, shifting with every thrust I make into the crevice, the way the head of my cock looks, flushed dark and purple, against the paler complexion of her skin.

The last thing I want to do is go off in three strokes. It'd probably give her a false sense of her own appeal. Grabbing her thighs to pull her into the short, erratic punches of my hips, I manage to last fifteen.

Sparks explode behind my eyes and I grunt into the space between her shoulder blades, teeth gnashed as my orgasm rips through me. I watch as my cock jerks, surging cum against her lower back in thick, ropey spurts.

Lavinia remains frozen through all of it, suitably tolerant as her head hangs, blue hair veiling her face. My cock drains and then turns flaccid, dropping between my legs. I pull back to watch a large glob of my release slide down to the valley between her cheeks, spreading them to track its descent over her asshole, toward her pussy.

Still breathing heavily, an urge consumes me, and I run my finger down the sticky goo, traveling the same path, down her back to her crack, slipping lower, to between her legs. Her body betrays her, flinching when I toy with the puckered rosebud and then shuddering as I go lower, running my sticky fingers over her pussy. She jolts, hips rocking.

"God, you're such a dirty little whore," I tell her, feeling how slick she is. "I just dumped my cum all over you and you still want it." I scoop as much semen onto my fingers as I can and roll it around her folds. "Your pussy is soaked for it—dying to get a taste of my cum." I push my fingers inside, feeding her hungry cunt what it wants. My cock, exhausted and spent, twitches back to life. It's a never-ending cycle with this one. I fuck my fingers in and out, watching her in the mirror. She's too stubborn to look away, but I see the way her jaw relaxes and how her teeth fall away from her bottom lip. I bend over to whisper in her ear, "You're a filthy, horny little slut. You like feeling my cum in your pussy, don't you? You want to feel owned, like a bitch in heat."

Her walls clench around me and short bursts of air punch from her lungs. She curls around herself, knees wobbly and elbows collapsing. Her cries are soft, a contrast to the way her body reacts violently, the orgasm wracking through her. I hold her up as she falls apart and only remove my fingers when her cunt loosens.

There's no mistaking the smug feeling in my chest.

"Fuck with me again, Little Whore," I say, watching the emotions wash over her face. Anger, humiliation, want. "And I won't just come on your back. I'll tear your cunt apart, got it?"

She nods, and bites down on her bottom lip like she's forcing herself to stay quiet. Good.

I turn behind me and open a cabinet, pulling out two washcloths. I toss one at her while using the other to wipe off my dick. "Clean up," I tell her. "I'll tell them you have cramps, and we need to leave."

I exit the bathroom, leaving her there to clean up the mess. There's no mistaking the smug feeling in my chest. I may not be able to satisfy a woman the traditional way, but there's no doubt I gave Lavinia exactly what she wanted.

26

Lavinia

Deodorant, shaving cream, condoms…

I rummage through the bathroom medicine cabinet, but it's not here. *Fuck!*

Now I'm going to have to ask.

I swing the door closed and get a look at myself in the mirror. The dark rings under my eyes are a glaring reminder of how badly I slept the night before. After dinner with the parents and getting an assjob and a finger fuck, I opted for last night to be one of my solo nights. I realized it was a mistake as I tried to find a semi-comfortable position in my nest, but there was absolutely no fucking way I was going to knock on one of their doors, so I cuddled up with the kitten and feigned rest as well as I could.

Five days.

Time is running out, ticking away in an inevitable march, and I'm sitting here agonizing over the thought of Sy's semen swimming toward my eggs. I don't regret inciting him into it. I might not *really* know Sy, but I know enough to appreciate his hatred toward me.

"Nothing gets him prickly like a nice piece of ass."

Nick said it himself that first night, didn't he?

I've never met someone so sexually repressed in my life. I figured once he got a good one out of his system, he'd chill the fuck out and give me a break. It was a risk. Nothing was stopping him from going all the way and forcing that monster dick inside of me. But I just had to see him at his weakest—remind myself that these men are human. Flesh and bone. Bags of meat with hormones.

And now I'm staring down the barrel of his possible robot spawn.

I jerk open the bathroom door and walk toward the kitchen, scooping the kitten up on my way. His little claws clutch my shoulder, nose prodding into my neck, and for a moment, I'm so immensely grateful for him that it overwhelms me. His little purr is a calming vibration against my chest. I read in a book once that a cat's purr has medically therapeutic benefits, and that's how I feel when I press a kiss to his little head. Like he's healing me, his big blue eyes shining up at me curiously. He strains up to smell the tip of my nose and then rubs the side of his cheek against it.

"Two pussies in this house," Remy mutters, stabbing into his bowl of cornflakes, "and I'm still not getting laid."

Putting the kitten down at his food bowl, I pet his head. "Then I feel sorry for you, because the Archduke sleeps with me every night, and it's awesome."

Nick, who's still shirtless, hair wet from a shower, turns to me slowly. "The *Archduke*?"

"Yes." I give the kitten's chin a little scritch. "Archie, if you will."

"I definitely won't." Nick turns his chair just a smidge—just enough to make room for me in his lap—and stares at me expectantly.

Right.

There are two pets in this room.

How could I forget?

Gearing up for the coming request, I take a deep breath before clearing the distance between us. "We have a small problem," I say, perching on Nick's knee.

Naturally, he's not having it, his forearm like a vice grip as it drags me into the curve of his body. "Nothing about this problem is small," he says, grinding his half hard cock into my ass.

I clamp down on a shiver as his lips find my neck. "If you don't have any more of that Plan B stashed away around here, you're going to need to stop at the pharmacy before school today."

Nick goes rigid beneath me, mouth frozen against my throat.

"You finally nailed her? Oh, thank fucking god," Remy says, dropping his spoon into his bowl with a clatter. "I haven't been balls deep in a pussy in months." He stands, pulling off his shirt. His tongue prods the corner of his mouth as his eyes take in my bare legs. "I can miss my first class, and hey, if you're getting her an abortion pill, then I can nut inside her, right? That's, like, two-for-one on value."

Except Nick is grabbing my chin, wrenching me around to face him. "I didn't fuck her," he says, blue eyes blazing.

Remy scoffs, voice tinged with irritation. "Well, it wasn't me, and it obviously wasn't Sy, because she's... you know," he gestures to me, "*walking.*"

My face burns hot, but Nick won't let me look away, fingers digging into my jaw. "Yesterday, at your parents' house..." I swallow audibly. "Sy messed around with me."

"Be," Nick's fingers clamp tighter, "specific."

I set my jaw against the pain, meeting his glare with one of my own. "He fingered me with his cum."

Nick lets me go at once, brow furrowed in annoyance. "He dumped his nut in you and left it for me to clean it up?"

My nostrils flare as I snap, "It wouldn't have been a problem if you'd kept your end of our bargain. You said you'd take care of birth control."

Remy squeezes the bulge in his pants, dark eyes assessing me. "I'm still feeling pretty good about that value thing, Nicky. We should fill her up first. Sy's swimmers can't die alone. Those are your nieces and nephews in there."

My jaw drops in outrage when I realize he's not joking. "You're disgusting!"

Luckily, Nick and I have an agreement. I've been good, but he hasn't earned it yet, and Remy can't have me until Nick has. He wouldn't.

Would he?

So quick that I barely have time to process the movement, my back is slamming onto the tabletop, Nick's fingers hooking in my shorts and wrenching them down. Instinctively, I kick out, my foot glancing off his upper thigh, but Nick wrestles my ankles up high, and then shoves a forearm behind my knees and bends me in half, my pussy exposed that quickly.

"We have a deal!" I scream, trying to sound more incensed than panicked.

"*My* end of the bargain? What about yours?" Nick is already breathing in that tight, barely controlled way, the veins in his arm bulging as he restrains me. He speaks through gritted teeth. "If you want the Plan B, then this is the price." He only needs one hand to free his cock, reaching between our bodies to undo his jeans, pushing them down. "If you behave, then maybe I'll consider *just* stuffing you full of our cum."

Five days.

Nine days ago, the thought of this man kissing me sent me into a spiral of catastrophic hatred, but now my muscles are threatening to go lax at the realization he doesn't intend to fuck me. My stomach twists at the cost. I need the Plan B. Whatever happens five days from now, having a Duke's bastard growing in my belly isn't going to make it any easier.

My chin wobbles pathetically and I clench my teeth to hide it. I won't break over this. They can use me like a cheap toy, but their time is running out just as much as mine, and I *won't*.

I won't cry like the bitch they want me to be.

I let my arms go slack. "Fine." My agreement comes on an exhale that I almost hope he doesn't hear. It's one thing to have Sy crushing me against a bathroom sink and forcing me. It's another to say yes. To watch Nick stand to his full height, knowing I won't struggle. To feel Remy's hand pressing into the back of my thigh, keeping my knees tucked below my chin.

Both of their gazes drop to my center, and when I make a gap between my knees, I see it too, the most intimate parts of me obscenely exposed. Nick strokes his cock as Remy pulls his own from his boxers, tongue peeking out to wet his lips.

"Hold yourself open for us," Nick orders, grabbing my hand and replacing the palm he has jammed beneath my knee with it. Looking away, I fold my arms across my thighs, trying not to remember how I got so good at contorting like this.

"Fuck, she's got a pretty pussy," Remy murmurs, reaching out to touch me. His fingertips spread my lips and he dips lower, playing with the rim of my asshole. "But I've still got dibs on this. Right, Nicky? You promised."

Nick looks somehow both dazed and possessed, letting up a bit as he nudges forward to rub a sticky trail of pre-cum into my folds. "Her ass is yours. But this?" I watch numbly as he squeezes the head of his dick, collecting a surge of pre-cum on the tip of his finger. He looks me right in the eye as he forces the finger up my cunt, unconcerned with my wince. "This is mine."

They begin jerking off at the same time, styles different, goal the same. Remy's eyes are glued to my asshole as his fist flies over his cock. Nick nestles the tip of his right against my clit as he slowly strokes his shaft. He's going to relish every second of this, make me suffer through it. They stand hip to hip, neither looking particularly concerned when Remy slots the head of his dick up against Nick's, sandwiching my clit right between their cockheads.

I stare up at the ceiling and hope they're as quick as Sy. I wonder if it felt this way for Autumn. Did she ever open herself up like a vessel, riding out the sound of her Princes' flesh in their palms? Did she feel the lump in her throat as she realized what she's come to be? Did she fight this hard to avoid feeling anything? The sound of their short breaths is like static, and if I try hard enough, I can almost ignore the little electric storm that's brewing in the pit of my belly.

Almost.

"Oh, fuck," Remy breathes, dragging his cock down my slit. "She's getting wet. Check it out."

Nick ducks his head as Remy parts my lips, his fingertips spreading my growing slickness up to my clit. "Of course she's getting wet," Nick says, rubbing his cock through it. "This pussy knows who it belongs to. Isn't that right, Little Bird?"

I bite my tongue so hard, I taste the metallic tang of blood.

Remy is the first to come.

It builds in his movements, shoulder jerking faster and shorter as he edges closer. It's a little poetic—my ass and pussy are the only thing exposed. The only thing they want. An object in space. The first warm, sticky wave of his semen erupts right onto my slit. He makes a low, desperate sound, hand shooting out to clamp around my thigh as his cock surges, spurting a second rope onto the head of Nick's cock.

Remy flinches to catch it before it runs down onto the table, fingertips gathering it up, pushing it inside. I'm not sure why I don't expect what comes next, but I still stiffen when his slick fingertip breaches my asshole. "Goddamn you should feel this." He tilts his head to watch his finger disappear up to the knuckle. "It's so fucking tight, bro. Doesn't want to let me go."

I make a sound when he pulls the finger out, rushing to catch the rest of his load, packing it eagerly inside. Distantly, I'm struck with the notion that Sy would love this—a whole new level of humiliation as Remy painstakingly fills my ass with his seed. The thought is only drowned out by Nick's loud punches of breath, muscles flexing artfully. I'm so grateful that he's getting close. I don't even think to feel the familiar sense of dread when he pushes Remy out of the way and bends, brushing his lips over mine.

"Open," he growls, flicking his tongue against the seam of my lips. The head of his cock slots right up against my hole. "Give me your tongue or I'll push it inside."

My legs are crushed between our bodies, and I start feeling crowded—suffocated. So when I open my mouth on a gasp, it's only halfway in supplication, his tongue instantly invading. It just makes the wild panic in my chest grow, because he's *right there,* dick poised at my entrance, and I can't breathe, pinned by his weight and the threat of penetration.

The elevator might have been better. That I know I don't want. This? It's an eternal fight, my body on the precipice of betraying me. Inside the box, I know who my enemy is.

As his tongue moves greedily against mine, his hand begins pumping his cock faster, with shorter strokes, knuckles grazing my skin with every pass. And then he seizes, grunting into my mouth as he comes, the warmth of his release pumping right against my entrance. His hand drops between us and I suck in a breath when he pushes two cum-coated fingers inside.

Against my will, my toes curl.

This isn't about sex, it's about possession. I can tell from the way his mouth tries to consume me, how desperately he pushes his spunk into my body. There's no tenderness here, no passion. No consideration to my pleasure. It's Nick being Nick. Trapping me. Inflicting a punishment for what his brother did in that bathroom.

When he finally pulls away, I turn my head to the side, not wanting him to see the resignation in my eyes. I do hear the metallic tines of his zipper and the low laugh when he says, "Seeing your pussy covered in my cum—"

"*Our* cum—" Remy adds.

"Brings back memories." There's a long moment of silence after my legs fall, hanging limply over the edge of the table. "Hey," he whispers, tucking my hair behind my ear. I jerk away and he tisks. "Come on, Little Bird. Don't be like that."

I clench my thighs together. "You're such an asshole."

"Why?" He has the nerve to sound offended about it, brushing a knuckle against my jaw. "You know I'm just taking back what's mine. Or have you forgotten?"

I stare sightlessly into the kitchen. "As if you'd ever let me forget."

His fingers push between my legs like a compulsion—like he has to feel the mess he's made of me to make sure he doesn't forget, either. "Maybe if you stop sulking like a spoiled little princess, I can take you out with me today." He says this while fucking two fingers into me, a thoughtless, automatic gesture.

I glance at him, skeptical. "Where?"

The flush from his cheeks is fading, leaving him with an expression more stoic than his thrusting fingers suggest. "Pharmacy," he answers. "As much as I want to see you fat and filled up with a little Pretty Nick, now isn't the time. Plus," he adds, eyes growing foggy as they descend to my chest. "We can get you on the pill..."

I'm up in a flash, tugging up my shorts. "Fuck the pill. I want the implant." Those last up to three years. Sign me the fuck up.

Five days, I think.

For better or worse, things are going to change.

"Aren't you just a little beast?" I coo, shaking the toy mouse for the Archduke. I've felt bad for leaving him here alone for so long, having spent the morning and afternoon with Nick, but the Archduke doesn't seem to mind, humping his back menacingly at the little mouse.

At least I won't get pregnant.

I'm on the floor in Nick's room, legs folded beneath me as I zip the mouse across the floor. My arm is still a little sore from the implant, and I'm tired down to my very marrow. There are five days left. I can count that on one hand. In a few hours, I won't even need my thumb to do it.

So I try not to think about it, sinking my thoughts into Archie's little hops and wiggles. Father would have never let me have a pet. The closest we ever got was Amos, who was more like another sibling than something I could nurture or form a bond with.

The Archduke is full of gusto, so I'm trying to wear him out a bit before bed, not knowing how Nick will react to the thought of a kitten sleeping in his space. The whole day has been uncomfortable and tense, Nick dragging me from place to place as aggressively standoffish as possible. If someone had told me a year ago I'd walk out of a women's clinic to find Pretty Nick waiting impatiently for me in the lobby, I would have laughed in their face. The reality was a lot more awkward; Nick with his head tipped back, arms crossed, eyes closed, heel tapping restlessly against the floor. All the other women in the waiting room kept shooting him furtive, fearful glances, which was fair. I guess the last person you expect to share your pelvic exam experience with is a six-five thug with a tattoo on his temple.

Point being, we spent the whole day revolving around one simple absolute.

I am, at best, Nick's own tragic stray, rescued for the sake of having something entertaining to while away the hours with.

Archie darts behind Nick's gym bag, peeking around the side of it as he stalks the mouse, pupils dilating. He really gears up for the pounce, dropping low and wiggling his little butt.

The moment he finally springs out of the shadows, paws flying in the air spastically, I let out a delighted chuckle. He rolls onto his back to bat it with his back legs and I give his belly a scratch.

"You'll be a stone cold killer in no time, huh, Archduke?" I'm still grinning from ear to ear when I glance up, freezing at the sight of Nick in the doorway. My back goes ramrod straight and I drop the mouse, scooping Archie up into my lap. "I thought we could sleep in here tonight."

Best to get my obligations out of the way now.

Five days.

Nick is leaning against the jamb, body loose and half hidden—like maybe he's been standing there for a while, watching. Waiting. *Creeper.* There's a softness in his eyes that hardens the longer I stare at him. "You were laughing."

I duck my head, giving the Archduke a gentle stroke down his back. "He should settle down soon. Archie actually sleeps really well at night." Feeling defensive, I add, "He won't be any trouble."

Nick raises his palms. "Never said he would be." Slowly, he crosses the threshold, eyes locked on me as he gently closes the door. The only thing illuminating the room is the lamp by his bed, and it barely touches the angles of his face, casting his eyes in shadow as he begins undressing. "Wasn't expecting you to come."

I shrug. "Your bed's better than the floor."

My reply doesn't ease the crease in his forehead. If anything, it just carves it deeper. "So you're just here because you have to be." It's spoken in a bland, toneless rumble that falls as flat as the shirt he throws in the corner.

Archie squirms in my grip and I let him go, watching his tiny tail bob as he disappears beneath the bed.

I can't give Nick what he wants.

But I can give him this. "I could have gone to Remy's." I peer up at him as he approaches, the light moving across his features. It's impossible to know if my words have any effect—Nick would only let me see it if he wanted me to.

But he does reach out a hand.

An invitation.

Hesitantly, I take it, folding my hand into his larger one. He lifts me from the floor and then stands there for a moment. Assessing me. His eyes rove over my face, stopping on my mouth. I remain still as his palms frame my face, knowing that I won't stop him if he tries to kiss me. Ever since Remy stole that kiss in the ring, it's become an unspoken certainty that *this* is my real punishment for it. Nick has won my mouth, my tongue, my teeth.

But he doesn't kiss me.

He presses his thumbs into each corner of my lips and lifts them into a manipulated smile. He holds it there for a couple seconds, but as soon as he lets go, the artificial grin snaps away. Sighing, he shrugs, flopping onto the bed and patting the space beside him.

I try to take a deep breath, but my chest is constricted. The worry from last night, from the last few months, has built into something unavoidable.

"I need you to promise me something," I say.

"Another deal?" he says tiredly, rubbing a palm down his face. "Not tonight, Little Bird, I'm fucking beat, and I understand now I need to be clear-headed when I negotiate with you."

I glance at the kitten one more time, before shucking off my pants and climbing in the bed next to him. "It's nothing big," I insist. His eyes flutter shut, but he's still awake, running his hand idly up my thigh. I rest my hand on his, but I don't move it and I don't fight. "Nick," I whisper, intentionally using his name. His eyes open, finally meeting mine. "You have to promise me you'll take care of the Archduke if I can't."

He shifts, facing me. His cock is already half-mast between his legs, and when I feel it against me, I think this must be how he feels about the prospect of negotiating. *Not now.* "Is this some kind of Jedi mind trick to get me to commit to cleaning litter boxes or something? Because that's not happening. Ever. Not even for anal on the reg."

"I'm serious." I try to formulate the words I've been holding onto for so long. "If there's a time... when I'm not here, just please don't hurt him. Give him to Verity or one of the more responsible girls if you have to, okay?"

His eyes go flinty. "Sorry to break it to you, but as long as you're the Duchess, you're stuck with us. And I think you already know that if you try to run, I'll find you."

If the cards were stacked the way Nick thought, he'd be right. But they aren't. Before tonight, I didn't care how they felt about what was going to happen. In fact, they deserved to be blindsided. But now I'm the one responsible for something innocent and fragile, and I'm not Nick.

"Please?" I ask.

I don't hurt the things I claim to love.

"He made you laugh." Nick's eyes flick back and forth between mine, and then down to my mouth. "I'm not going to hurt him. He's yours."

I look at Nick. At his handsome face. At the tattoo beside his eye. Mayhem. He causes it. He brings it. Fuck, he *is* it.

I realize that I could tell him that I love him. He's said it to me before, so convicted. I could use that and play right into his hands, use his obsession with me against him. But the betrayal he'll feel when he realizes it's a lie, another manipulation, could bring this whole tower down to rubble. There's nothing left to do but tell the truth.

"There's something you don't know," I say, staring down at his hand on my thigh. "About me."

"There's *a lot* I don't know about you." His fingers dip under the hem of my shirt. "But I don't give a fuck—especially if you're about to tell me you killed your sister. I already know about that."

My head snaps up. "What?"

"That's the rumor going around about why your daddy sold you off." He rises up to a sitting position. "As punishment for getting rid of the chosen one."

I sit up with him, insisting, "I didn't kill my sister."

He shrugs as if he genuinely doesn't care, and he probably doesn't. Why would he? Nick's a murderer himself.

I force the truth out. "It's about the deal Daniel Payne made with my father."

His forehead furrows. "When Lionel sold you."

I wince, bringing my knees to my chest. It still stings to hear it said aloud. "That's the thing. He didn't exactly *sell* me. He made a deal for Daniel to hold on to me until one of two things happened. If—or when—Leticia is found, or," I curl my fingers over my toes, "on my twenty-first birthday."

Nick shakes his head. "I was there that night. I watched your father and Daniel shake hands. I put you in the car myself."

I remember that night. The bite of the asphalt on my sore knees. The noxious smell of car exhaust. The heat of Nick's hands as he bound my wrists. "You didn't hear the deal they made. They agreed on it before my father ever drove me to that parking lot."

A line furrows between his eyes. "But Daniel said—"

"Did you really think my father would just let an asset go like that?" I don't have to apologize or explain the word 'asset.' We both know what it means, and that's what I am. To the Counts. To the Lords. And now to the Dukes. "He needed me out of his way, but secure enough that he could collect me once he figured out his next move—the way to stay in control." Bitterly, I explain, "Marrying a daughter off to Perez is his ticket. He'd already had one daughter vanish. He couldn't risk another, and everyone knew Daniel Payne was the best person to keep a girl captive against her will. He had the resources. Anyone with tits could be hidden away in one of his whorehouses." I wrap my arms around my knees and pull them tight. "It didn't hurt to have the threat of becoming one of the brothel's girls over my head if something went wrong."

He hops up suddenly, jostling the mattress. "Are you telling me Killian gave me a Duchess I can't own?" Nick apprises me through slitted eyes. "Bullshit. That's playing Russian roulette, and he fucking knows it."

I scoff. "Please. You can't possibly believe Killian Payne knows all of his dad's dirty laundry. It's not like Daniel and my father were putting their temporary slavery agreement on paper. You were there, and you didn't even know about it. Also, I doubt Daniel was expecting to *die*."

Nick rubs his forehead, a strange flicker passing through his eyes. "No. You're right about that. He didn't have a fucking clue his days were numbered."

Talk about rumors. The Royal world was thick with speculation about what really happened the night of the fire at Daniel's office. If anyone would know, it's Pretty Nick Bruin. And he, suspiciously, isn't talking.

"On my twenty-first birthday, my father is going to collect me and give me to Perez. He's going to force me to marry him." I look up at him, and I know he sees what I'm *really* saying. My father is going to *try* to force me to marry him. Whatever is coming, it's not going to be a peaceful handover. It's going to be war. *My* war. "Perez could challenge my father for his title, but everyone knows he'd lose. My father could have Perez killed, but he's a loyal lap dog who does everything he wants. Why lose a soldier like that? This is the best of all worlds. Father keeps his throne, I get married off and tucked away, and Perez rises through the ranks. He can take over when my father is ready—maybe once I've popped out a kid or two, preserving the precious Lucia bloodline."

Nick paces the small room, two steps along the length of the bed, then back again. He walks over to his desk, pulls open the drawer and retrieves his gun, slides out the chamber, and snaps it back again. "So I'll kill him," he says, voice cold as ice.

"Perez?" I bark an empty laugh. "He'll just give me to the second best."

He whips around, fisting the gun. "So I'll kill your dad, too! I'll burn his whole fucking kingdom to the ground. Is that what you want to hear?"

I blink at him, mouth pressed into a tight, grim line. "You'd... do that?"

He gapes at me, spreading his arms. "No, I'm not a fucking idiot! All three of the other houses would come after me. I'd have to run away like a little bitch. I'd have to leave my goddamn family behind, *again*. Fuck!" He puts the gun back in the drawer, slamming it violently shut. He props his palms against the top of it, back contracting and expanding. "This doesn't make any sense. I *won* you."

"I wasn't free to be won."

"Why the fuck didn't you say something?" He whirls on me, fists clenching. "Why did you let me think this was real?"

I stare at him. God. I know he isn't dumb, but he sure as fuck *is* delusional. He let his obsession with possessing me cloud his judgment. "*You're* the one who broke into the Hideaway and raped me. *You're* the one who made the deal with Killian Payne. *You're* the bastard who got in the ring with Perez and demolished him." I stand up on the bed, and it puts us at a more even height. "*You* did all of this, Pretty Nick Bruin, because you were thinking with your dick and not your brain." I stab him in the forehead with my finger and he bats my hand away. "I kept my mouth shut because being your slave is better than being left at the mercy of my father. And for the record, that's not a compliment."

His fingers tighten around my wrist, closing in like a manacle—linking me to him. "I did it because I love you," he snaps. "When are you going to understand that?"

I don't flinch at the pain, his fingers pinching until the bones ache. "I don't know what love looks like," I admit, glancing down at his hand. Nick's inked knuckles are white with the pressure he's using to hold me. "But it doesn't look like this." I have to believe that. Anything else would just be too depressing.

Nick doesn't drop my wrist so much as he throws it. "You make me do that," he hisses, pointing at my red wrist. "If you'd just do what I ask and let me protect you—"

"They're coming for me, Nick! And there isn't anything you can do to stop them!" My chest heaves with the certainty of this, and *goddamn it*. I didn't want to think of this—not tonight. "So can you just *please* promise you'll take care of the kitten when I'm gone?!"

"When's your birthday?" he asks.

"September twenty-third."

I watch him calculate.

Five days.

"The day after the equinox," he says, expression morphing into something assured. "The Baron's party."

"Yeah, I guess."

He lifts his chin, eyes penetrating with a brutality that makes me bite down a shudder. Instinctively, I know that he wants to grab me again, force me closer. I can see it in the ripple of his muscles.

But he doesn't.

"I told you. The instant I claimed you in the Hideaway, you became *mine*. Nothing is going to change that. Not your father, and definitely not that nine-fingered fuck, Perez."

"Nick—" I start, because there is no stopping this. Absolutely no chance. Leticia left me to this fate when she disappeared.

But he presses his finger to my lips.

"Your father may be evil, and Perez might be desperate, but let me explain something to you, Little Bird. Daniel Payne wasn't taken out by his family. I'm the one who gave them the opportunity. I'm the one who planned it and planted the seed. *I'm* the one who took out a King." He presses his mouth to mine, kissing me long and deep, making me pay for those moments where he could have bruised, but didn't. When he pulls back, he rumbles, "And I have no fucking problem doing it again."

I KNOW the second I slam into awareness that Nick isn't beside me. He'd be touching me, if he were, with his constant tactile presence.

It's the first thought that flits through my mind.

The second is that I can't move.

This didn't happen last time—not with Nick and his quiet intensity shielding me from the world. There's a sliver of sight through my eyelids, but everything is indistinct beyond them, the room dark and empty.

Not empty.

There's a figure by the door, broad shouldered and looming, and my breath speeds. Hallucinations. I read it in one of Sy's textbooks, because he leaves them laying around the tower. It's how I knew enough about carbonyl group modifications to bluff my way through dinner with his parents. I recite the words in my head as the figure gets closer. Sleep paralysis. A disorder that occurs outside of REM sleep. Accompanied by hallucinations. That's what this is. It isn't real.

Except then the hallucination climbs onto the bed, making my body dip with the weight, and I know it's Nick, even though it doesn't make any sense.

He's dressed and wearing his jacket.

The scream stops before it starts, buried deep in my chest. The stillness, the pressure, the weight of a body against mine. It's not the hard, flat walls of the chest or the elevator. It's Nick's body, warm and muscular, rolling me on my back.

Safe? No.

Better than the alternative?

Fuck yes.

I take a deep, steadying breath. The memory of my conversation with Nick the night before flits through my mind. I was surprised at how relieved I felt about telling him the truth—about making sure Archie was okay.

A warm hand strokes down my throat and I fight to open my eyes fully—to make sense of the way he smells. Cigarette smoke and city air.

"I thought about it," he whispers, straddling me.

It takes a second to process, but his feet are pressed down on my calves, knees clenched against my thighs. I feel the crux of his legs against my lower belly. That, along with the wild look in his eye, is what makes my blood run cold. His cock isn't hard. His cock is *always* hard. I open my mouth to say something—*anything*—but the words lodge somewhere unreachable in my throat.

"I thought about it, and this is the way it has to be." In the faint light of the room, something metallic glimmers in his hand. I struggle through the fog of sleep to remember where I've seen it. He bends over me, his voice a soft rumble in my ear. "I won't let anyone take you away from me."

I'm frozen. Paralyzed in the bed. At his mercy.

He tilts my head to the side, the pads of his fingers touching the skin just behind my ear. Into the scant inch of darkness between us, he explains, "It's for your own good. I'll go insane otherwise. I'd have to lock you up here twenty-four-seven. I'd have to listen to you screaming in that elevator every night, and I can't." There's a plaintive note to his voice, as if it pains him to admit this. "Whatever it takes to keep you here. To keep you mine."

I try to remember what snapped me out of it the last time, when

Sy had me pinned in his bed. I struggle to pull air in my nose, sucking it and filling my lungs. It's not much, but it loosens my jaw and I grind out, "No—stop," because suddenly, I know what's in his hand. I manage to get a hand up, weakly slapping it against him. He grabs it, tucks it under his knee and presses down.

"This is happening, Lavinia," he says, my name cold on his lips. "No one is taking you away from me. *Ever.*"

His free hand comes down on the side of my head, twisting my neck. I feel the press of metal against my skin and the sharp, biting sting of the tracker as it digs into my flesh. I bite down on my bottom lip, absorbing the pain—the betrayal.

We had a deal.

He runs his thumb over the spot, and then brings it to his mouth. I see the red smear of blood before he licks it off with this tongue, blue eyes staring right into mine. A moment later, he releases me, lifting off the bed—off my body—and hovers at the foot of it. It's then that my arms and legs loosen, and I reach for the painful spot with my nails.

"You pull that out again, I'm just gonna put a new one in," he says, not looking up. "But it'll be somewhere you can't reach, and a hell of a lot more painful."

"You son of a bitch!" I shout, fully regaining the use of my body. I drag myself to my knees. "We made a fucking deal! You promised me you wouldn't put it back in!"

"You've broken the deal left and right. You broke it when you kissed Remy," he says simply, jaw hard.

"That was once! And he kissed *me.* And you already punished me for it!" I hate the shrill sound of my own voice. I hate what he does to me. I hate *him* and the way he's looking at me, so patronizing and calm...

"I want to believe you, Little Bird, but god knows what you let Sy do to you in that bathroom. You let him fill you with his cum. I can't trust that you didn't kiss him too."

"I didn't let him do anything, asshole!" I step off the bed and move until I'm right in front of him. "I haven't made one decision for myself in weeks—years! Stop pretending like any of this is my choice, like I have any autonomy or control over my life at all." Hot tears build in my eyes and *fuck, fucking, fuck!* I take a step closer. "I hate you so fucking much."

Nick warns, "Don't you fucking do it," and the door swings open just as I rear my head back and spit in his face. His expression hardens and there's no hesitation. It's as if his arm is connected to that spot on his cheek that's wet with my saliva. It's as if it's automatic.

He whips his arm back and strikes, his palm cracking against my cheek in an explosion of hot, teeth-rattling fire. The sheer, unforgiving force of the slap sends me stumbling sideways and I lose my footing, tumbling gracelessly to the floor. There's a ringing in my ears, an anguish in my chest, and I cradle my jaw, fighting back tears as I look up.

Remy is standing in the doorway, looking between me and Nick with an awed expression. "What the–"

"I told you what would happen," Nick snaps, brows pushed into a tight purse. "You made me do this. Why do you *always* make me do this?"

The anger and rage bubbles up in my chest. I may not be in the chest or the elevator or somewhere tight and confined, but the throb behind my ear proves one thing for sure.

I'm never going to be free.

27

Remy

In grade school, Nick took a liking to this girl in gym class.

He spent six weeks absolutely demolishing that bitch in dodgeball.

He'd follow her to lunch and steal her book bag, rifling through it right in front of her, like he had every right in the world. He'd drag her through the halls by her wrists, push her down when she struggled, rough her up for not being his in the very specific way he wanted. That's the thing a lot of people don't understand about Nick—that he's just as exacting as Sy, if not more so. The more intense he feels about something, the fussier he gets about it.

The girl's parents caused a huge stink—probably because their kid kept coming home all bruised up. Later on, I'd make him tell me about them. The marks. The purple and blue. The blood just underneath the skin. Even back then it excited me, the thought of Nick's fingertips making impressions on a girl's skin.

Poor girl never had a chance once Nick set his sights on her, but his parents got really aggressive about it and put him and Sy into a program for 'troubled youth'.

I'd been there since third grade.

Tate came a year later.

That's where it all started, the four of us instantly gravitating to one another. None of them were like me—there was nothing actually wrong with any of them on that deep, fundamental level. My brain has never been right, but theirs were fine. Sure, Sy got into a lot of fights, Tate had a problem with authority, and Nick only knew how to want someone homicidally, but none of those were the real problem. Sy's problem is that he never knew when to stop hitting. Tate's problem was that she didn't understand why she was different yet. And Nick's problem?

Nick's problem was a deep, internal belief that he could bully someone into loving him back.

Christ, some things never change.

The air tastes like lightning and hurt, and Nick is the ozone. Vinny's on the floor, clutching her cheek, eyes wide and wet with unshed tears.

Nick is just staring at her, still as stone. "I told you what would happen," he says, voice quiet and terrible. "You made me do this." More urgently, he asks, "*Why* do you always make me do this?"

She presses her wrist into her nose—a pathetic attempt at cloaking a sniffle. "Our deal is off." She tries to make her voice all hard and sharp, but it cracks halfway through.

Nick looks away, and *his* cracks are visible. The subtle fall of his shoulders, the flex of his jaw, the way he makes himself so unbelievably still. "If that's what it takes to keep you safe."

Vinny scrambles to her feet and charges toward the door, almost knocking me over as she shoves me out of the way. Something angry flares in Nick's eyes, but it shutters with the sound of the bathroom door slamming shut, rattling the walls.

Nick drops to the end of the bed and begins aggressively untying his shoelaces, attention a little too focused on the task. "She'll try to run away, so we'll have to stay with her. She's not to be left alone here again."

I fold my arms and watch him. "You're never going to win her like that."

His head snaps up, face contorted with rage. "I've already won her!" My feet take me back a step. Nick's better than anyone else in this tower at keeping his cool, but his fists are flexing like he's Sy all of a sudden.

"You did," I agree, watching him wrestle out of his shirt. "You won her. But you never won her *over*."

"Fuck winning her over," he sneers, chucking his shirt across the room. "I've been letting her toy with me since she walked up those stairs. I'm not her lap-boy. I'm her Duke. I own her." He jerks his chin toward the bathroom. "Let her win me over for once."

My lips pull back into a bleak approximation of a smile. "If she did that, you'd lose interest. That's why you have to chase the hard pussy. You don't want a girl—you want a project."

"What I want," he replies, fists curling, "is a little goddamn appreciation."

I give the jam a couple taps with my knuckle before turning away. "A bird is never going to appreciate its cage."

I CROSS MY ARMS, knee bouncing as I wait. The sound of my heel tapping against the floor must piss off the old guy sitting beside me, because he shoots me a glare before moving to the other side of the waiting room.

I don't want to be here.

Taking out my phone, I shoot off a text to my father.

I don't want to be here.

He doesn't answer, but I'm not surprised. My family has a single rule that predicates all others: no scandals. It's why my eldest uncle and his sons have law enforcement locked down, probably for generations. It's why my father owns every ritzy hotel in the state.

It's why I've been shuffled around to clinic after clinic, seen by doctors who are paid to keep me calm and as normal as possible.

But fuck, I really don't want to be here.

The dread builds in the pit of my chest like a fist around my lungs, and the longer I wait, the more restless I get, drumming a beat against the arm of the chair.

"Dr. Weatherby is ready to see you, Mr. Maddox." I look over at the lady in blue. She's behind a tall counter with a glass partition, nothing but a small slot open at the bottom. It always makes me want to duck my head down to make them deal with me. Are they afraid? Worried one of the clients is going to spread their crazy through the opening in the window? Terrified they'll be infected with it?

The woman's name is Doreen, and her smile never feels real. It's tight, false. I can't help but stare at her lips, how she paints them a shade between orange and red, making her smile seem even more false. Jokerish.

Staring at me expectantly, she adds, "You can head back to her office."

I stand and shake my arms out, cracking my back from sitting on the uncomfortable chairs. Nothing about this place is welcoming. Not the seating or the paintings of wildflowers or Doreen. But if I can get through it, it buys me a solid couple weeks of my dad's silence.

"Thanks, Doreen." As I walk past her, I tap my marker against the flat surface of the countertop and she narrows her eyes at it. Make one little mural of a crucifix fucking a pussy on the lobby wall and everyone's all suspicious.

Dr. Weatherby's office is the third door down, and the door is standing open. She's probably old enough to be my grandmother, but her shrewd eyes and ramrod posture are anything but maternal. The doctor sits in a gray chair, her back to a wall-sized window overlooking the city. I walk over to it and place my hand on the glass, peering down.

So many dangerous cliffs in Forsyth.

"Remy," she says, standing and closing the door with a soft click. "How are you?"

"Outstanding," I say, turning away from the window, from the cliff, orienting myself to the room. I drop to the couch, letting my body bounce on the soft cushions. This is the only comfortable seat in the place, I bet. Probably a trap. "I'm a Duke now."

"Oh," she says, looking at me over her glasses. She flips open her little notebook. "That's a big role. Congratulations."

I press my palm to my thigh, idly tracing the capped marker over the letters on my knuckles: D-U-K-E. Ever since last night, I've had these... flickers. Vinny's red cheek. Her big, wet eyes sparkling like a galaxy. Sulfur and panic. She didn't even look at me when I went to her this morning, climbing the staircase to her loft. She just kept glaring out of the dingy clock face as I worked her waistband down, counting the points on the star.

"How have things been going?" Her pen is poised over the paper, her eyes on me. "With school starting and all the changes a new semester brings, I wouldn't be surprised to hear you've had some trouble adjusting."

Dr. Weatherby asks the same questions, the same way, taking the same notes on the same blue pad every time I come. She tries to see me, but when I'm on the edge of that cliff, I'm invisible to everyone.

Except *her*.

"School is fine. Mostly art and the business admin class my father makes me take." That's the deal. I can be an art major as long as I minor in business. *'Something to fall back on.'* "I like my philosophy class."

She hums pensively. "And how have you been sleeping? New home, new room." Again, I get one of those flickers, clenching my eyes against it. "Remy? What's wrong?"

"Nothing."

She dips her chin, assessing me over the turquoise frame of her glasses. "You're doing drugs again."

"No, I'm not."

I totally am.

She sighs, jotting in the notebook. "Stimulants don't react well with your medication." She pauses. "You are taking your medication, aren't you? Your real medication."

"Consistently?" I ask, flashing a winning smile.

She shakes her head. "Yes, *consistently.*"

"I skipped my meds for a few days," I confess, tapping the marker on my knee. "It's fine, except..." My eyes stray to the window, considering the drop. This building isn't as high as the tower. I can see it in the distance, the clock frozen in time. I imagine Vinny is there right now behind the clouded glass, her stare piercing through the distance.

"Except?" she prods.

I rub my forehead. "I had a dream about the stars, and they said something."

Dr. Weatherby uncrosses her legs, sitting straight. "We've discussed this already. The stars aren't important. Have you drawn anything today?"

I look at her, eyes narrowing. "The stars *are* important. And don't distract me. I'm confused, not stupid."

"You know why we don't talk about the stars," she stresses, mouth pursing tightly. "You fixate, Remy. The stars are a metaphor for your dissociation. It's not helpful to think of them."

"Well, I disagree," I say, pushing to my feet. Dr. Weatherby watches coolly as I march to the coat closet, yanking it open. "What's *this* a metaphor for?"

Inside is a collection of items that have been collected from around her office. She puts them in here every time I visit and probably puts it all back once I leave.

Yellow coasters.

Yellow stationary.

Yellow pillows.

Among them is a painting of yellow flowers. It's a terrible piece —the kind of bland, lifeless bullshit that's probably churned out on a conveyor belt to be sold in bulk to healthcare facilities. And it's not quite right. Not the right flower.

"But I don't know why," I mutter, curling my lip at the sight of it.

She clears her throat. "Close the door, Remy. We're in the middle of a discussion."

"I used to like yellow just fine," I say, gesturing to the tableau. "Let's talk about that."

She crosses her legs again. "Sensory issues are—"

"It's not the fucking color!" I explode, hurling my marker at the window. It clinks against the glass and tumbles to the floor. Growling in frustration, I snatch up the painting and march it over to her, slamming it on the table at her side. I jab a finger into a painted yellow flower. "Tell me why looking at this makes me want to throw up. Tell me why my Duchess is always in the stars!"

She gives me an infuriatingly patient look. "Remy, these things mean nothing. You're abusing substances again. Have a seat and do your exercises."

I deflate. For some reason, I'd had this notion that Dr. Weatherby would have the answers, but I can't for the fucking life of me figure out why. These people never want to help. They just want me to be quiet and still—someone posed into an expression of normality, no matter how artificial. They want me to smile like Doreen.

I go back to the couch, pulling out my phone before landing heavily on the cushions. "The exercises never help." Turning the phone over in my hands, I quietly confess, "Sometimes when I see yellow, I think about... Tate." I don't realize why I say it so quietly at first—soft, like a secret. It's as if saying her name too loud will make something bad happen. I don't remember much about two years ago. I just remember a long stretch of hospital rooms and needles, fluorescent lights and cold floors, hard beds and bland food.

Mostly, I remember Dr. Weatherby and her stern face—a lot like she looks right now. "Let's start over, Remy. What have you drawn for me today?"

I raise my gaze to hers slowly. Something is occurring to me. It's difficult when all I have to count on are vague impressions of things. Yellow is bad. The stars have taken something. Vinny is older than we know. Flowers bring decay. But there's a reason I've always been so resistant about coming to see Dr. Weatherby, and it's because my head throbs when I think of her, like something has slithered in through my ear and bored a hole into my brain.

"You never let me talk about Tate," I realize. I've been seeing Dr. Weatherby since Tate died, and never once has she let me speak of her.

She clicks her pen. "Because I don't think it's healthy for you to—"

"You don't want me to." I look down at my phone, thumbing through my contacts until I find the one labeled 'Sarah'. Holding Dr. Weatherby's stare, I hit the call button, raising the phone to my ear.

The doctor frowns. "Who are you calling?"

I don't respond, waiting for an answer.

There's a click, and then her voice. "Remy? Well, what a treat. I just got off the phone with Simon and—"

"I need to ask you something," I say, cutting her off. Nick and Sy's mom isn't the kind of therapist I need, but I overheard something she said the other night at dinner, and it niggles at the back of my thoughts. "It's about my therapist."

Dr. Weatherby arches an eyebrow. "Who are you speaking to?"

Sarah answers, "Go on."

"She says I shouldn't think about stars or the yellow flowers," I say, eyes accusing. "And I can't talk about Tate. I can't fucking talk about anything! That's weird, right? You said at dinner... you told Sy he shouldn't bottle it up. You said he should talk about her."

There's a moment of silence from Sarah's end, but Dr. Weatherby fills it. "Remy, I'm the doctor who's treating you. I'm the only one who understands your condition and medical history. Your father wouldn't be happy to hear you're not following my—"

"She's never let me talk about it," I tell Sarah, speaking over the doctor. "Even when I was at Saint Mary's, she would..." I clutch my head, wincing at the memory.

"You're with the same doctor you saw at Saint Mary's?" Sarah asks. "Your father pays her?"

"Of course, he pays her. Probably a small fortune." Quieter, I admit, "When I think about Saint Mary's, it hurts."

Dr. Weatherby's eyes flash in alarm. "Mr. Maddox..."

Urgently, Sarah orders, "Leave. Get up and walk out that door, you hear me? You don't have to stay if you're uncomfortable."

I don't need to hear anymore.

"Remington!" Dr. Weatherby calls as I follow Sarah's orders, only stopping to pick my marker up off the floor before wrenching the door open. "Remy, I'm calling your father!"

I run away from her words just as much as I'm running toward home. I don't understand it—not completely—but I think I'm beginning to.

The flickers aren't flickers. They aren't metaphors or manifestations or hallucinations. They aren't unhealthy fixations.

They're memories.

WHEN SHE SHOWS up at midnight, as if I've summoned her with nothing but the power of thought, I'm in the middle of crushing up a pill. It annoys me at first, my attention being snatched away from the important things, and I whip the door open with an irritated grind of my teeth.

She's clutching the kitten to her chest, brows pulled into an agitated frown. "I'm sleeping here tonight."

I take a furtive glance over her shoulder, spotting Nick as he disappears into his own room. Reaching out, I touch her shoulder, urging her over the threshold. "I need you to come with me. I just need you to—in just a minute. Wait here. Right here..." I point to where she's standing and then return to my drafting table, cutting the pill powder into a tidy line. Dipping down, I snort it in one clean pull. *Bitter.* I shudder as it trickles into the back of my throat. It's faster this way, though. More potent.

I'm so close to remembering...

"Remy..." When I turn to Vinny, she's looking between me and the bed, body rigid. "What are you doing?"

I follow her gaze to the bed—or, more accurately, the paper covering it. It's not good—the flowers. They're drawn messily, the yellow not quite right, but if I squint, it's almost enough to bring back a flicker. "You need to come with me," I tell her, hurdling forward to pry the kitten from her grasp. At the panicked glint in her eyes, I rush out, "He's not a part of this; he'll be okay. Sometimes I watch him chase the moon and I think he'll probably outlive me." I set him down on my workbench, ducking down to get a good look into his eyes. "The Archduke has a big soul." Turning to her, I add, "You don't give him enough credit."

"Shit." Vinny's face falls. "You're having another episode, aren't you?"

"No." I gesture, coaxing her out of the room. "It'll only take a second."

But the moment we move toward the door leading up to the belfry, she wrenches out of my grip. "Absolutely not!" She shakes her head, edging back, and there's an explosion of alarm in her eyes that's bright enough to make its own flicker in my mind. "We're not going up there again. Not after—"

My hand shoots out, snatching her upper arm. "This isn't like before." When she struggles against my hold, I impatiently whisper, "Don't you trust me?!"

She barks a disbelieving laugh. "No! Not even a little bit. Not even with my kitten. Not even with yourself!" She turns on her heel. "I'm waking Sy up before—"

I open the door and grab her from behind, clamping my palm over her mouth as I drag her up the stairs.

She fights against me, but I'm too tall, too big, my arms like steel around her torso. "Shh," I tell her, and I might be bigger, but Vinny has a lot of fight in her. She thrashes and beats my forearm with her fists, feet kicking at the walls as I heave her higher and higher. Getting her up to the first room, the one with all the clock mechanics and the filing machine, is more work than I'm expecting. By the time I finally push through the door and slam it closed behind us, I'm actually a little out of breath.

She jerks her neck, freeing her mouth.

And then she clamps her teeth down on the soft tissue of my hand.

"Motherfuck!" I push her away, clenching my hand. Her wide, frightened eyes dart past me, back to the door, and it happens again. The flicker. "Vinny, would you listen? I'm not trying to hurt you!"

She backs away. "You're having an episode, and you're all hopped up on that shit Cash gave you. You're not thinking straight!"

I follow her deeper into the room, palms up. "I'm not crazy. The stars are real. I just need to see the way they touch you—" I pause.

Okay, that's not sounding less crazy.

Something flashes in her eyes and she yanks her hoodie up, hooking her thumb in the waist of her shorts. "You can just count the points, remember? Seven. You know it's seven."

"I don't need to," I insist, eyeing the ladder up to the belfry. "You're here, I get that. I know this isn't a dream. When I say the stars are real, I'm not talking about a thought or a fucking delusion." I look her in the eyes, making sure she understands that I'm here. I'm lucid. "It's a memory. It's something my dad paid the doctors to make me forget, but I'm remembering now."

If anything, she just looks even more discomfited. "That's paranoia, Remy. You're having some kind of reaction to the drugs. If you just let me wake Sy—"

"No!" The thought of him knowing about the stars makes me clutch at my hair, tugging hard at the roots. "Vinny, I need someone to listen—really listen—just for fucking once!" I hate the way she looks at me, all lost and pitying, as if she knows my mind is a salad of yellow and stars and red. "I won't jump. I just have to see you up there. I can't... I can't tell you why, because I don't know yet, and I know it sounds crazy, but it's important. It's *everything.*"

"Remy," she breathes, staring back at me. "I don't know how to help you."

"You can help me like *this*," I insist, holding out my hand. I'll make her if I have to, and I can tell from the dismay in her eyes that she knows it. But it has to mean something that I'm giving her the chance to do it on her own—that I'm not Nicky. Right?

Her shoulders slump. And then she lets out this long sigh that straightens her spine. "You have to stay away from the ledge."

"Yes!" I burst, wiggling my fingers. "I won't fuck around, I promise."

A hardness comes over her features. "And no fast moves or I'll go get Sy and I'll tell him everything." Her eyes narrow. "All of it, Remy."

If Sy knew about what happened before—about me almost jumping—about me almost ending up like Tate...

It'd fucking destroy him.

"Deal." I nod encouragingly and she finally reaches out, slipping her hand into mine. I lead her to the ladder, but I don't make her climb ahead of me. The hatch is too heavy for her, anyway. I brace my feet on the rungs and wrench it open, the rusty metal squealing in protest.

Up in the belfry, the air is crisp with the late September air, the coy tease of autumn looming in the clear night sky. The equinox is tomorrow night—twelve and twelve. Everything aligned. Harvest, death, rebirth. Fading yellow, orange and red.

When she slowly climbs out, I grab her hand, lifting her carefully around the enormous bell. She dusts a hand off on her thigh, but I don't let the other one go, pulling her toward the glow of the city. The light pollution from the other corners of Forsyth drives me to the back side of the tower—the one that faces west. From here, someone could almost pretend the other kingdoms don't exist.

That's where I drag Vinny, ignoring her protests—the spark of dread in her eyes—as I position her where I want her, right against the backdrop of night.

Overhead, a blanket of stars dots the sky.

"Here," I breathe, watching her glance nervously over her shoulder.

"W-what now?" she stammers, hands fisted in the pocket of her hoodie.

Now, I close my eyes and think of stars. Smoke. Black glass. Blonde hair. Red.

Yellow.

There's something soft in the memory that I can't quite put my finger on. It's a sadness, or maybe a regret. I know that it hurts. I know that it fucking kills me. I know that I want to turn away from it, because that's what I've been told to do—not to think of this place, this sadness, this horror, this pain.

I make myself face it, sinking into the tender places, forcing myself through the soreness of them.

And then I open my eyes.

A gust of air catches Vinny's hair, whipping it around her head in cold tendrils of pale blue. Behind her, the stars are beckoning, their distant light freckling the space around her. She never opens her mouth, but I hear her scream. I've seen that mouth, those lips gaping in terror. I've seen the gentle curve of her cheek as it hollows. I've seen the emptiness of oblivion in her watery eyes. I have, I realize, seen her skin beneath this sky, a yellow flower tucked behind an ear.

And I've seen her fall.

It doesn't slam into me like the wrecking ball I'd feared. The memory skulks toward me like a hidden thing that's stepping shyly from the shadows. It doesn't hurt me to know it. There's no catastrophe here.

There's only Vinny, looking at me curiously. "What?" she asks, fidgeting nervously.

I wonder how I must be looking at her, because when I step forward, it makes her flinch. "It's not you," I assure, cradling her face in my hands as I find what I'm looking for. Her eyes. Her cheeks. Her red lips. I rest my forehead against hers, so relieved that it brings a ghost of a smile. "It was never you."

The kiss is feather light, my mouth grazing hers so gently that her small tremor is enough to threaten it. I realize now why Vinny was never quite right. The dreams. The stampede in my chest that first night, in the Hideaway's basement. The way looking at her sometimes makes my temple throb with an urgency that galls me, as if I've forgotten to do something.

The memory unfurls like petals that are waking from a long slumber, and it's not complete. The flickers still dance in and out, and I might not understand what I'm seeing, but I know *who* I'm seeing, and that's...

The wrecking ball arrives on the crest of the kiss, slamming into me. I freeze, because the stars might have been sad, but the yellow...

"No." I stumble back, eyes wide. A sea of swaying yellow stretches out in my mind, and it's full of quiet, dead things. This is the source of the hurt. This is the flicker that carves a groan from my chest. This is the entropy and casual destruction I've been fearing all this time. "She was in the flowers," I realize.

Vinny watches me, forehead creasing. "Who was... what?" But I can't explain it to her. I can't even explain it to myself. Somehow, I just know.

"Remy, wait!" Her panicked voice chases me back to the hatch, and then down the ladder.

I don't know what it means.

But I know where to go.

28

Lavinia

Two days.

I walk out of the bathroom into the cool air of the tower with my hair still wrapped in a towel. The house is quiet, which puts me on edge. Nick's been insisting that someone be with me all the time. I should feel relief at the rare moment of privacy, although now that the tracker is back under my skin, I know that's untrue.

I peek through Remy's open bedroom door. The papers bearing yellow painted flowers are still covering the bed, which means he hasn't been home since he left me up in the belfry, eyes wild and body vibrating like he had an electrical current running through him. Part of me is grateful he took off. The last thing this tower needs right now is his instability. Plus, maybe the way Nick and Sy have been fretting over it all morning, heads bent as they discussed their friend, means we can skip the Barons' equinox party tonight.

I haven't told the others about what happened in the belfry. They just woke up this morning to find him gone. For one, I'm not on speaking terms with Nick. For two, telling Sy about our second belfry drama would probably necessitate telling him about the first one, and that's a bigger can of worms than I'm equipped to handle right now.

"Fuck them," I tell the Archduke as I scoop him up. I take the first step up the spiral staircase, whispering impossible words into his fur. "Maybe tonight we can leave." I can see it now, riding away from the harsh lights of Forsyth with Archie in my lap. My agreement with Nick is over. That means if he catches me, it'll be bad.

But if he doesn't?

"Oh good," I hear from behind me, "you're finished."

The scream almost escapes my throat and I clutch the kitten to my chest as I spin toward the voice. Sarah, Nick and Simon's mother, stands in the kitchen entryway with a pack of paper towels in her hand. Over on the counter is a pile of canvas bags filled with groceries.

"You scared me," I say, heart pounding. I look over at the locked door, eyes narrowing. "How did you get in?"

"I have a key," she says. "I made the boys make a copy for me when they first moved in."

"So you could be their housekeeper?" I nod at the towels.

Grinning, she answers, "Mother, housekeeper, therapist. Sometimes it's all the same thing." She doesn't look offended. I learned the other night that their mom is a kind, intelligent woman. It's hard to believe someone like her created two men like Nick and Sy, but what do I know? My father created me. After a moment of awkward silence, Sarah explains, "I've been helping them track down Remy. We're all very worried, but I worry less when I can do little things like this." She wiggles the paper towels. "I know it's not necessary. They'll survive on their own, but it's hard to stop." She gives me a sympathetic smile. "You'll understand one day."

God, I hope not.

"Also, I brought you something," she says, resting the towels next to the bags of food. She walks over to the couch, and I see a dress bag draped over the edge. A square box sits next to it, tied with an old-looking ribbon. She lifts the bag and offers it to me. "Something for the equinox. It's tonight, if I'm not mistaken? Admittedly, my Royal calendar is a bit dated."

I place the Archduke on the couch and he immediately springs on the ribbon, his little tail twitching excitedly as he clutches his kill. Although I take the hanger, I don't move to look at what's inside. There's something discomfiting about all of this. The mother of my captors having me over for dinner was one thing. There was a veil of deception there. But acknowledging the ins and outs of Royal life, what's asked and expected of me—both in and out of her sons' beds—is unnerving.

I wonder what she'd say if she knew what they've done to me.

She steps forward and unzips the bag herself, revealing a long dress. The fabric is completely sheer, dyed an earthy rust color. Felt leaves in the warm colors of fall cover the halter of the bodice. The bottom of the dress is breathtaking, a skirt that continues the theme of fallen leaves flowing to the ground. It looks like the embodiment of fire—yellow, orange, and red.

"This is amazing," I say, struck by the craftsmanship. "I'll have to find something nice to wear underneath it."

She slides me a slick look. "Oh, Duchess..."

My jaw drops. "Seriously?! Everything is going to show."

She flicks a hand. "Just wear some nice panties with it. The leaves will cover your breasts. This may even be one of the more conservative outfits." She smoothes out the leaves, a wistfulness taking over her features. "It was when I wore it."

"Wait." I look between her and the dress. "This was *yours*?"

She nods. "Oh, yes. The Barons' Equinox was a big deal, even back when I was Duchess."

I give her a quick look. The dress is sexy. Fantasy driven. It's designed to drive a man wild. Or in my case—*our* case—men. "I feel like Freud would have something to say about this."

She throws her head back and laughs. "I'm sure he would, but I assure you, neither of my boys knows this exists."

I don't know how you're supposed to discuss something like this with a mother. I didn't really have one, but I can't imagine her handing me a dress designed to seduce someone.

But in no world do the Royals operate like normal society.

"We didn't get an opportunity to speak privately the other night." Her smile dims to a tense line. "I was going to give this to you then, but you left so abruptly."

"Sorry about that," I say, although I have nothing to apologize for. Her son is the one who cut the evening short when he decided to assault me in the bathroom.

Her eyes grow solemn as they rise to take in the tower, roving over the guys' things. "Their fathers and I left this tower twenty-two years ago. It looked a lot like it does now, to be honest." She runs her fingers over the back of the couch, nodding toward the clock face. "It happened up there."

My head springs up to stare in horror. "What did?"

God, please don't tell me you conceived someone in the same spot I sleep at night.

Luckily, she doesn't. "Our agreement to leave the Royalty. It was easiest for Davis, because he'd lived under the expectations of being a Bruin his whole life. It'd lost its shine for him before he ever had the chance to experience it. It's one reason we chose not to raise our sons under that pressure. I think you can relate."

Swallowing, I zip the dress back into its bag. "Yeah, I know a thing or two about that."

"It was harder for me and Manny," she confesses, surveying the gallery of Dukes on the wall. "Perhaps by now you realize how seductive the Royalty can be—for men and women."

I don't answer, but the truth is, she's right. I glance at the Archduke, knowing that I'd chosen the name out of a misplaced sense of kinship, as if he and I fit snugly into this tower's vacant spaces. There for a moment, I'd seen myself as the Duchess of this Kingdom. I'd seen an army of fists behind me. I'd felt a part of something, and it didn't matter that it was incidental—that I wasn't chosen by anyone except Nick and his depraved entitlement. Briefly, I felt powerful. Important.

And *god*—I wanted it.

I doubt I could ever speak the words aloud, because they're shameful, dark things. But the plummet back to reality—the reminder that I'm helpless, an intruder, a pet—hurt as badly as Nick's palm. It stung as sharply as the betrayal, burned as hotly as the knowledge that Pretty Nick Bruin's tender touches would always be accompanied by hurt.

She turns, watching me closely. "My sons put on a good show the other night, but I've done my homework. I know a little about your circumstances, Lavinia. Enough to know you aren't here of your own free will."

Something inside of me unwinds at the declaration. I don't have the energy to pretend anymore. "Yeah, well...then you probably also know there isn't anything I can do about it." I can feel the tracker, like a bug burrowing under my skin.

Two days.

And then it might not even matter.

"I'm sorry," she says, and the odd thing is, she actually sounds genuine. "I'd like to think my sons have you here for chivalrous reasons, but I'm not stupid. Nick has grown restless and secretive. Simon has grown ambitious and powerful. And both of them have always been very physical creatures of habit." She perches on the couch, eyes beseeching. "They're far past a mother's influence, Lavinia. It's why Royal men need a woman to guide them, to help temper their need for domination—for bloodlust. They're chosen too young, before their prefrontal cortex is fully formed. They're impulsive and risky and aggressive. Fueled by hormones and the drive to conquer. It's all the stuff that makes a young man perfect for war, but stupid about life, and stupider about love." She gives me a look. "It's why my son thinks he can abuse you in my bathroom without me noticing."

I swallow, taken aback by this woman's bluntness.

She responds with a sad smile. "I know you were too young to remember your mother when she died, but I knew her. We weren't friends, but... equals of sorts. At least, in the way that Royal women have to work together to manage this system. She knew what she was getting into with your father. She thought she could control him, keep him balanced. And for the most part, I believe she did."

I flash back to the day she died. It's blurry and most of the lines have been filled in by Leticia, her memories becoming mine. But I remember feeling frightened, as if something inconceivably catastrophic had happened—and it wasn't just because she was gone. I didn't really understand the enormity of death yet—the permanence.

It was because I was alone.

"If she knew he needed controlling, then why did she kill herself and leave us alone with him?" I instantly regret the words, wishing I could absorb them back into the dark, secret place I've been hiding them all these years. This woman is psychoanalyzing me and I fell right into her trap.

Gently, she says, "No one can answer that, Lavinia. But I think your mother would have wanted me to tell you that it wasn't your fault."

"It'd be a lie." A hot tear builds in the corner of my eye, and I will it not to fall. "My father wanted a boy. An heir. Instead, she had me." She felt like a failure. Even Leticia said so. That's all Lionel knows how to do, tear down the women in his house and drive them away, by whatever means necessary. "Why are you here, Sarah?" I look at the dress, so well preserved, as if this woman had anticipated passing it on one day. "Why did you bring me this? So I'll control your bastard sons with my pussy? Keep them from becoming the next Daniel Payne or Saul Cartwright, or worse, Lionel Lucia? Trust me; I have less control over these three than any of the Royal women before me. I can't help them, and to be perfectly honest, I don't want to." I look her in the eye. "You seem like a nice woman, but you need to know this. Your sons are fucking terrible."

Her face falls in a slow, gradual way, but she nods, averting her eyes. "I was afraid you might say that." She touches the bag with the dress, frowning. "It's a strange thing, being Duchess to the fists of Forsyth. People expect you to be tough as nails the second you walk up those stairs. But that's not true of any of us." She lifts her gaze to me, setting her jaw. "We fight—every day. But unlike our Dukes, we don't win or lose. The hard truth is that the fight never ends. I walked out of this tower two decades ago, but I'm still fighting. It's why I'm here today. It's why I'm having this discussion with you. We don't get trophies, Lavinia. There aren't any spoils for us."

"Then why bother?" I ask.

She tilts her head, giving me a dark look. "What on earth would we do otherwise? Give up? Give in? Settle for something easy?" Standing, she straightens her pants suit. "Passion, Duchess. It's not all roses and orgasms. Sometimes it's pain and despair. I'd understand if that's not something you're looking for, but my sons? They're going to chase it to the ends of the earth. I don't know if it was nature or nurture, but that's just who they are now. I'd like to think they're doing it for someone who's willing to make them work for it." She dips her head, giving me a meaningful look. "If they're hurting you, then there's only one thing you can do about it. *Make them pay.*"

She grabs her handbag and leaves. I stare at the locked door long after she's left, flush with the realization. Sarah may have left the Royals and everything that comes with it, but deep inside, she's still a Duchess.

I guess that means I am, too.

I RIDE to the party with Nick, who's aggressively silent as he drives, the soft light of the dashboard barely enough to illuminate the hard lines of his face. He'd arrived back in the tower with a stony expression that just got stonier when he saw me in the dress.

He hasn't touched me.

Not once.

I'm wearing a pair of black lace panties beneath the sheer fabric, and it doesn't matter that their mother just basically gave me her implicit blessing to fuck their shit up. I'd rather be almost anywhere else than at his side.

The party is in a field, deep in the woods. Baron land, owned by their King. We meet in a clearing designated for parking. I haven't spoken to any of them all day, and I have no plans to start now, so Nick shuts the car off to a long moment of strained silence.

The new distance is both welcome and discomfiting. I suppose I should be grateful he hasn't chucked me into the elevator yet, and I've spent the better part of the last two days internally preparing myself for the eventuality that he will. Every time I've seen him on the couch, at the table, and not lowered myself dutifully into his lap, I've built another layer of armor around myself, anticipating.

I almost wish he'd just get it over with.

"You're pissed at me." His voice cleaves through the silence, fingers tightening pointlessly around the steering wheel. "But I want you to know that I tried."

I say nothing.

In my periphery, I can see his head turn. "I've been good to you, Lavinia. I was as good to you as you'd let me be. And you—" His whole body clenches angrily. After a second of his fuming silence, he quietly adds, "I've earned it. You know I have."

When I turn, I find him staring at my thighs through the sheer dress. "Earned *what*?" When he just raises his eyes to mine, face impassive, I squawk a disbelieving laugh. "You think you've earned *sex with me*? Are you fucking insane?! Your brother's more entitled to my pussy than you, and considering how much he openly despises me, that's saying a lot."

His low, chuffed laugh oozes ridicule. "You want my brother's monster cock? Good luck with that, Little Bird. Sy Perilini has never lost anything." Through the darkness of the car's interior, a distant pair of headlights catches the smirking curve of his cheek. "Virginity included."

Even though Nick is already climbing out of the SUV, I sputter, "You can't mean..."

His slammed door is the only response I get.

Outside, Nick and I stand in a pool of tense silence amongst the cars, waiting for his brother's arrival as I turn this piece of information over in my mind.

He can't be serious, can he?

A matte black, older model Camaro whips into the lot, loud music thudding against the windows, and it surprises me when Sy steps out, all grim faced and tense. I know before he says anything that he didn't find Remy.

"I don't have time for this," he says, walking over to us. It takes me a long beat to reconcile this new knowledge of him. Sy. *A virgin.* I suppose it shouldn't come as a surprise he's never found a willing hole for that beast. "I need to be out there—looking for him."

I break my silence with a bitter murmur. "Maybe you should have put the tracker in *him*."

Both of them ignore me.

"Did you call his dad?" Nick asks.

"Not yet, but if I don't find him by morning, I'll have no choice." He frowns toward the torches lighting the path through the trees. "Best case, he's here. Worst, he's just holed up with some cutslut fucking the pain away like usual." He looks over the top of the car at his brother. "You sure we can't get away with skipping this?"

It shouldn't bother me—the casual way he says it—the reality of Remy maybe being with someone else to ease his pain. Royal men aren't loyal to their women. God, it's part of the whole appeal. And maybe he left me up in the belfry with a gentle kiss and searing fingertips, but he's not mine. I don't even want him to be.

But something burns in my chest at the thought of Remy finding comfort in one of those girls. Shouldn't he have wanted to mark my skin? Shouldn't he have taken me into his room and made me strip bare for him? Shouldn't he have wanted to make art out of me?

Or have I already lost my shine?

Maybe I never had any at all.

Nick rakes his fingers through his hair. "Not if you don't want to offend the Barons. And after that shit with Felix, we can't afford to be on their bad side." There's a crevice in Nick's brow that's been present since I told him about the deal between Daniel and my father. It's a hardness that never leaves, and it makes him look oddly worn. "We need to curry some favor here."

Sy snaps back, "And whose fucking fault is that?"

Nick looks away, saying nothing.

And then he takes off his shirt.

The skin over his lean muscle and intricate tattoos shifts and pulls as he lifts it over his head, tossing it into the opened window of the car. On the other side of the SUV, Sy does the same thing and I quickly avert my eyes from the hard, curved lines of his biceps and forearms. *Royals and their stupid fucking dress codes.* I reach into the backseat and open the box Sarah left for me—the one with the ribbon. Inside is a crown made of thorny vines and antlers. I place it on my head just as Sy walks around the back of the car. His eyes fall on me and he pauses, Adam's apple bobbing in his throat.

He lifts his chin toward the field. "Let's get this over with."

Bonfires glow in the distance and I lift my skirt as I follow the shirtless men down the path. It's late and the nearly full harvest moon hangs brightly overhead. Without realizing it, my eyes rise to the sky, and not for the first time, I wonder what Remy saw last night that spooked him so badly.

Because that's what I saw in his eyes; naked, icy terror.

For the first time, I'm hit with an awareness that if what happened up in the belfry might help find him, I'd probably speak up.

Somehow, I just don't think it would.

I'm so lost in the realization I might actually *care* that I stumble over a tree root, my toe catching the bottom of my dress. I throw my palms out to catch myself on the leaf-littered ground below, but two strong hands grasp my waist, yanking me into a hard body.

"Careful," Sy tells me, his skin hot through the lacy fabric.

I'm caught in a strange mental loop of wanting to both apologize and thank him, and I bite down on it like a bone as he leads me the rest of the way. I think of his mother's words from earlier —*chivalrous reasons*—as Sy steers me around a downed tree limb, and I'm not sure what I want to do more: laugh or cry.

Maybe my father would have been easier to endure.

Far less confusing, certainly.

"Stay close," Nick says quietly as we approach the revelry. A shirtless man in a black mask approaches with a tray of drinks. Nick grabs two, and I don't even realize he was speaking the words to me until he hands me one of them, advising, "This is the perfect opportunity for Perez to make a move.

I reluctantly take the cup, completely aware of what he's doing. He's trying to convince me all of this is necessary—the tracker, the locked doors, the incessant hovering—all of it. It makes him feel justified. *Chivalrous*.

Well, he can call it what he wants, but it's all just an excuse to take away autonomy. He never wants anything more than to possess me, and the fact I could be at risk has only made him double his efforts. I never should have told him about my father's deadline.

"Do you see him?" Sy asks, searching for Remy. His movements are strained, bare shoulders filled with tension. He hoped that maybe Remy might have shown up here on his own, but this is the last place Remy would be. I could have told him that.

"No," Nick replies, frustration etched in his features. "I know you've got this whole mother chicken thing going on with him—"

Sy corrects, "You mean mother hen."

"I mean mother*fucker*," Nick snaps. "Remy is a grown ass man, and he's not our only obligation. It's our first inter-house event since becoming Dukes. It's bad enough Remy isn't with us. I'm not letting that fuck up our showing." When he flings out a hand, adding, "He's probably off getting high and defacing public property," I see the edge of desperation in his eyes and realize that he's trying to convince himself just as much as his brother.

Like Sy, I scan the small fire pits scattered about the field, each surrounded by plush seating. I'm not just looking for Remy, but trying to get a handle on what this whole event is about. There seems to be one area for each House, a metal icon burning in each pit: a viper for the Counts, a skull for the Lords, a crown for the Princes, the Duke's bruin, and in the middle...

It's more of an altar, the Baron's signature pentagram etched into the side, and thick pillared candles stacked across the top.

Thirty feet away, a half naked Prince is fucking his Princess, right up against a tree.

"Jesus, what is this?" I mutter aloud. Nick looks down at me, surprised to hear my voice.

Blandly, he answers, "Orgy."

"You brought me to an orgy?" I hiss, watching as another Prince strolls up and stands there. Waiting for his turn with the Princess. No wonder Nick was going off about him 'earning' the right to my cunt. This absolute son of a bitch was hoping he could bang me here, in front of the entire Royalty.

He replies, "The fall equinox is when the Barons unveil their Baroness. They like making a big show of—"

"I know what the Barons are," I say, sneering. "And I don't think the person who won their Duchess by cutting off his opponent's finger has any place to cast stones about big shows."

At least Sy seems to share my distaste, curling his lip at the debauchery. "Can we just make this quick?" He growls, looking across the field toward the bar. "Look, let's split up and do one sweep for Remy. If we don't find him, we'll meet up at our fire pit so we can play nice and get the fuck out of here as soon as possible."

"Fine with me," I say, lifting my dress so I don't trip over it again. I point to the opposite direction of the bar. "I'll be over there, checking that group."

I start toward them, realizing it's mostly women. *Royal* women. Fuck, not exactly the crowd I want to mingle with at the moment, but who knows, maybe they've seen a six-foot-four, devastatingly handsome, mentally fragile Duke roaming around. I steel myself and take a step toward them, but a hand grabs me by the elbow and pulls me back.

"I wouldn't bother with them," the female voice says. I spin and see a woman. Her dark hair falls in a cascade of big, shiny curls, bunched at the neck and hanging over a shoulder. Her dress is a gorgeous, pale tan, the color of a doe's skin, with fur lining the edges. It comes mid-thigh, revealing her long legs. The straps of her sandals wind around her calves like vines. She's striking, dark smudges of charcoal around her eyes giving her a wicked appeal.

"I'm Story," she says, thrusting her hand out. "The Lady."

She's more than that, I know. The Royalty has been abuzz about Daniel Payne's stepdaughter since the moment she returned to Forsyth. Her lover and *stepbrother*, Killian, is now a King. That makes her his Queen.

I take her in slowly. "So you're the reason I'm a Duchess."

She gives me an excited look, as if I've misunderstood this whole thing, and the reality is so much more appealing. "That honor belongs to Pretty Nick, actually. He's had his eye on you for a long time." I take a sip of my drink, trying to decide how to navigate this. The Lady isn't my equal. All I know about her is that she'd played a part in Nick's machinations. I suspect she's expecting gratitude, and from the way her smile slowly deflates, that's probably the long and short of it. "I know you've been through a lot," she begins, but I cut her off with a tense smile.

"Yeah, being imprisoned in the basement of your boyfriend's whorehouse was sure something. Not quite as impressive as him offering me up as damaged goods after being sullied on his watch." I reach out to pat her arm. "You must be so proud."

She frowns and looks over her shoulder, casting a glance at a handsome blond. Tristian Mercer. He gives her a smug smile and a wink. "It wasn't right for Daniel to hold you captive like that and…" A wince. "Maybe I should have pushed harder for them to release you, but—"

"It's complicated. I know." I take a sip from my glass. I can't fault Story for any of it—not now that I'm in the position she was once in. I understand now how little power there is in this. "Trust me, I get it."

"I wanted to get you out the second Rath told me about you," she insists, eyes beseeching. "But they said we had to be smart about it, because your dad—"

I shake my head. "There's no doubt Killian Payne is powerful, but up against the likes of my father?" I laugh. "My fate was sealed a long time before your Lord took possession of me." I look over to where Tristian is standing, warming his hands over the Lords' fire pit. The other two now stand next to him. Killian and Rath. They pretend they're not watching us, but if my Dukes are any indication, I doubt she's ever fully free of surveillance. "But I guess you get points for actually giving half a shit. That's a lot more than anyone else around here."

The hair on the back of my neck stands on end, and I don't need a device to know that Nick is nearby, keeping tabs.

Story notices my discomfort, following my gaze to where Nick is creeping on us from a cluster of trees in the distance. "How are they?" she asks. "I know it can be... challenging. At first."

"Well, I didn't have to sign a contract like you did." I give her a tight smile. "Or so the rumors say."

"Oh, I signed a contract," she admits. "I gave up my rights to everything. But I went into it knowing—well, *mostly* knowing— what I was getting into." She twists the cuff on her wrist, pushing the skull facing out. There's a daisy tattooed on her arm, and I realize it's Remy's work—one of the only other females he's ever relented to ink. The sight of it makes my stomach twist unpleasantly. "Don't get me wrong. It was hard—I had a lot of dark times. For a while there, I didn't know if I'd make it through."

"But what? Now you just comply?" I scoff disdainfully. "Give in to them? Be the perfect little pet?"

Looking unbothered by my judgment, she answers, "Someone who didn't understand the situation might see it that way. If I'm 'compliant'," she curls her fingers into air quotes, "then it's only because I have no reason not to be. And if I'm not compliant?" She grins. "Then they don't mind. The last thing they want is a mindless servant."

I narrow my eyes at Nick across the distance. "Can't relate."

"The Lords and I... we went through some crazy shit, but we stuck together. It's the only way any of us survived." She tilts her head. "They take care of me, and I take care of them."

Nodding, I surmise, "So that's the draw. They keep you safe."

To my surprise, she laughs. "Honey, if anyone looks sideways at one of my men, I will shoot them dead." She lifts up the hem of her skirt and I see the glint of a gun strapped to her upper thigh. "I love them and they love me, and I know it's not... conventional." She glances at them over her shoulder, a muted excitement sparking in her eyes. "It's not the easy love we're taught about in storybooks. It's so much better than that."

I know the look I give her is incredulous, but I can't help it. Falling for three abusive assholes... "They must be really good in bed," I finally say. We're at an orgy after all. "If they ever let you out of it."

She offers me a solemn nod. "When we get along, it's every day. When we're not getting along," she smirks, "it's every three hours." Before I can wrap my mind around that, she pushes her cup against mine in a subtle toast. "What about you? I hear Sy has a huge cock." At my blank stare, she clamps a hand over her mouth and laughs. "God, don't tell anyone I said that. I can't even look at another man without one of the Lords humping my leg. It's just all the other Royal women have been talking about for weeks." She leans forward and whispers, "But I am curious. How big is he?"

There's this tight ball in my chest, the one I carry around all day that expands and deflates whenever I think about sex with these guys. But Story is so casual about it, so earnest. And again, we're at a fucking orgy. Do I admit I haven't had consensual sex with any of them? Do I tell her about the negotiations Nick and I have—how he's easing away my boundaries, layer by layer? Do I explain how being with Remy is like riding a roller coaster in a lightning storm? Or do I tell her that Sy is hung like a horse, but has so many hang-ups about using it that it's terrifying to be around him? Finally I relent, "It's fucking huge, like..." I approximate length and girth with my hands and her jaw drops.

"Wow..." She gives me a long, impressed look. "Have you taken it?"

"No." I'm grateful for the dark and flickering firelight, because my cheeks are humiliatingly red. "He actually hasn't tried." Virgin, my mind screams. Sy is a virgin. No one's had that thing inside of them. Ever.

"Huh." She purses her lips. "Well, word to the wise, make sure he lubes it up good. My men are big—although not like that—but when they fuck me together, it's a lot. We had to work up to it."

I nod politely at her useless advice, trying to figure out how we got to this conversation—to this place. My stomach flutters anxiously. I have no interest in having Sy's cock inside of me, lubed or not, but I can tell that Story wouldn't understand. She's too fixated with the notion of having three dickheads lust after her.

I'm saved from responding when an arm snakes around her waist. When she tilts her head back, Tristian captures her mouth in a kiss, tongue licking out obscenely. His hand slides under her top, cupping her breast, and I clear my throat, averting my eyes. I'm wondering how long they'll go at it, and whether I can just walk away, when a loud gong clangs, vibrating through the field. Everyone looks toward the altar, including Story and Tristian. He wraps his arms around her and rests his head on her shoulder, saying, "*Finally.* You've been taunting me in that skirt long enough, sweetheart."

"Patience," she says, rolling her eyes at me, "this is the Barons' night."

"Well, the Barons need to hurry the fuck up before I pull that skirt up and get the orgy started without all their theatrics."

Story laughs, nodding toward the tree I'd passed earlier. "I think the Princes have already kicked things off."

But everyone's turning toward a path in the trees, and a hush falls over the party as a figure draws nearer. The three Barons, shirtless but hidden by their intricate bronze masks, stand at the mouth of the path. The branches hanging overhead rattle in a passing breeze as their Baroness appears. She's wearing a long, antique-looking black gown that's thin enough to show her dark areolas. A black veil covers her head and I find myself so curious to know what's underneath that I walk forward in anticipation.

A Baron stands behind her, folding her into the masculine curve of his shoulders as he fingers the bottom of the veil.

"Royals of Forsyth, be still!" he loudly begins. Everything seems to heed his order. The people around me grow impossibly more silent. Even the breeze seems to understand, the brittle leaves motionless on their branches, the flames in the pits standing rigid. Distantly, it reminds me of Sy's victory tattoo. The reverence. The respect. The ritual. "On this night," he says, the bronze of his mask reflecting the firelight, "we welcome our sinister sister. Daughter of death. Wife of the wicked path." There's a long, solemn beat of silence, before he yells, "Know her name!"

The other Barons announce, "Regina Thorn!"

"Know her face," the Baron behind her demands, lifting the veil, "and know what the shadows will show you."

Regina Thorn's dark eyes stare out over the clearing, and the sudden flicker of wind makes the reflection of fire dance in them. This is, I know, a face that will be seen before some men's last breath. So I suppose it's a plus that she is breathtaking. Regal. Sinister. Wicked.

And then she lets out a shrill whistle. "Let's get fucking wasted!"

"Daughter of death, indeed!" Tristian says, raising his cup to her.

As the crowd erupts in cheers, I take a step back, saying, "I need to... uh, go find my Dukes." I haven't even turned before Tristian's hands travel up her skirt.

I make my way through the crowd, heading over to the Duke's fire pit. I have to pass the other Royal women to get there, which is when I hear it.

"... probably can't even get it hard," someone is saying. It isn't until I get closer that I realize who. *Sutton.* "I don't even know why he came. He's never even fucked one of his cutsluts. Everyone knows Simon has two modes when it comes to pussy. Complete disinterest or hair-trigger."

Another girl I recognize as last year's Baroness laughs. "He's so dull. I bet that thing shoots out water."

Sutton snorts. "No, Simon is a robot. I bet it shoots out receipt paper with dirty talk printed on it." Her voice changes to a mocking monotone. "*Oh, Duchess, your bosom has stimulated the pleasure center of my brain.*"

My jaw clenches at their laughter, and I find myself searching for him. Sy is already at the Dukes' fire pit, sitting on the ground, back leaned against one of the intricately carved, aged wood logs. It's like as soon as the Baroness spoke, everyone started humping each other. Across from the Dukes' pit, the Princes are having another go at their Princess, and beside him, a couple of ex-Counts are already getting their dicks out for the ex-Countess Sutton was talking to earlier.

Perez is nowhere to be seen.

Sy studiously avoids all of this, keeping his eyes trained on the fire as he waits for Nick and me.

Nick, who's standing at the entrance to the parking path, blue eyes fixed to me. It's odd how being under someone's heel can make you so in-tuned to them. Right now, I know precisely the thought running through Nick's head.

"I've earned it. You know I have."

I tip my drink back, swallowing it in three long gulps, and then gather my skirt up, reaching beneath it to shimmy off my panties. The crispness of the air caresses my thighs through the dress, but when I march over to Sy, I don't feel the chill. He hears me coming, my feet rustling the dry leaves below, but he doesn't acknowledge me.

Not until I step over him and then drop, straddling his lap.

His head snaps back in shock, but his expression instantly morphs to confusion. "What are you—"

I grab him by the back of his hair. "Shut the fuck up," I say, and then crush my mouth to his.

The people around here need to learn a lesson about how things work between a Duke and Duchess.

Nick most of all.

29

Sy

I've been hiding a half-chub since I saw that Princess taking it from behind against that tree.

Fuck.

Who am I kidding?

I've been half hard since I saw Lavinia in that sheer dress.

I know there's a reason—a really fucking good one, too—I should knock this bitch right off my lap into the dirt. But it's hard to think with her tongue in my mouth and her body pressed up against mine. It's impossible to process anything but how she tastes like liquor, that her lips are both soft and firm. Intense. Deliberately teasing. I barely register anything other than the sharp scrape of her nails grazing down my chin. And for a hot moment, I don't think about how slutty she is, or what people are saying as they watch her grind against me. How they're probably laughing, mocking me. Whispering about my body as if they have a right.

It's when she pulls back that the sharp curve of her smile jolts me back to reality. I slam into the awareness of inadequacy that follows me around like a demon clawing at my soul.

I cinch my hands around her hips, digging my thumbs into the exposed skin, and force her to stop moving. "You're fucking laughing at me?" I hiss, looking around to see if anyone is watching my utter and absolute humiliation. They aren't, of course. Everyone is too wound up in their own pleasure to witness my Duchess' attempt at humbling me.

To my left, Tristian Mercer is sucking on his Lady's tits while Rathbone punches his cock into her ass with a steady rhythm. A few feet away, Killian watches, languidly stroking himself, waiting for his turn to strike. To the right, the Princes have their Princess surrounded, two of them inside her at the same time. Her tits bounce with the force, her jaw slack, until her third Prince stands above her and shoves his cock between her open lips.

These bitches—these absolute fucking whores—just take it, filled up with dick, begging for more. They all say they want a big cock, but then when they see a real one, they shut their legs and run.

"I'm not laughing at you, dumbass," Lavinia says quietly, leaning forward to whisper in my ear. Her pebbled nipples graze across my chest, eliciting a twinge in my balls. "I'm acting like a Duchess. Isn't that what you keep telling me to do?"

My teeth gnash as I dig my fingers into her flesh. "Not when you're trying to make me look like a chump." The monster in my pants leaps, begs, *throbs* with want. I never had a chance to invoke even a thought of my ocean, and now the need is writhing in the pit of my balls. Sex and debauchery are a Royal's bag, but I avoid it as much as I can. I fight. I study. I drink and hang out with my friends. I excel.

I *win*.

I win everywhere, except here.

When it comes to sex, I always lose.

"You know I can't—" She kisses me again, cutting off my words. I open to her like a man who's dying of thirst, and I hate it. God, I fucking loathe it—the desperate urge to feel her tongue against mine, slick and hot. I grab her tits and push her back. "If you're doing this to piss off my brother—"

"This is going to make you look good." She grinds down again and her lips part, letting out a soft sigh. "No one here needs to know what's really happening." She spreads the bundle of fabric that makes up the train of her skirt and gathers it around our hips like a shield. Her lips are so close to mine that I can hear her words when she whispers, "Just act like we're fucking, and you and I will be the only ones who know the truth."

The irony of my life slams into me all at once. The years I've spent suppressing the urges. Tucking my boner into the waistband of my pants, hiding all evidence with loose shirts. The non-stop workouts, the fighting, throwing myself into celibacy because it's easier than having a female look at me like *that*—like I'm deficient, abnormal. What I can't take is the rejection. It's just another form of losing, and Simon Perilini doesn't lose. I won the position of Duke, which led to this night, a spot at this insane pagan ritual of lust and depravity, and now Lavinia Lucia's forked tongue is coaxing me into her warmth. That's the biggest irony, and it cuts to the bone.

Her mouth twists wryly—bitterly. "I know you're not used to doing this with consent, so it'll be a little different for you. But don't worry. I'll walk you through it."

I bite down on a groan at the feel of her cunt pressing into my hard-on. "You're a bitch, you know that?"

"Then fuck me like one," she dares, surging against me, "Just act like it. Kiss me. Touch me. Put your hands under my skirt and pretend I'm riding you." She grinds down on me and drops her head back, arms hanging from my neck, her tits thrusting into my face. When I just sit here, rigid as a corpse, she adds, "Everyone is busy, but they'll notice if you just sit there like you've got a stick up your ass."

She's so fucking mouthy—bossy as hell—and I know if we were somewhere alone she'd never say this kind of thing to me. She wouldn't dare, because if I snapped, she'd be the first one to pay. Annoyingly, however, she's right that there's nothing to do but pretend. I can't actually take her in the middle of this thing. Not without bringing more attention to how much of a freak I am. All I can do is sit here and act like I have a thread of control.

I'm just not sure I do.

She reaches between us, grabbing my belt. "Here's what you're going to do, lover," she pushes the buckle loose and unzips my pants. I shift uneasily. There are rumors about my size—a few girls have seen it, and plenty of guys at the gym, but exposing myself in front of the majority of the Royal caste? I'd rather jam hot pokers into my eyeballs. Her hair brushes against my face as she leans toward my ear, intoxicating me with the scent of honey. "You're going to act like you want me. And—this is important—you're going to be rough about it. I'm going to whimper and moan and let these people think you're a motherfucking sex god."

"And then what?" I still her hand, even though my thighs are trembling with the strain of not fucking up into something. "Why are you doing this? You don't give a shit about what these people think." I look around for Nick, but he's vanished. That doesn't mean he's not around—watching. Fuming. I should be looking for Remy, not playing games.

"I made a deal," she says, lips grazing over my earlobe, "and despite what your brother thinks, I keep them."

I close my eyes, fingers flexing around her waist. "So this *is* about Nick."

"Does it really matter?" she asks, looking around. Sex sounds surround us. No one else is talking, and if they are, it's not about this. Every direction I look, I see tongues and cocks and tits. Right across the fire, I see the red puckered hole of the Countess' ass, and fuck, I don't even know what the Barons are doing on that altar. Wincing, I acknowledge that it looks painful.

I relent, watching Lavinia with heavy eyes as she slips her fingers into my waistband, working them over my hips. "No," I say, dropping my head back at the feel of her warm, soft hand on my painful erection. "No, you're right, it doesn't matter."

Lavinia touches my cock curiously at first. She can't see it because it's hidden by her skirt, but she can feel it, fingertips shyly roving the length of me. I wait for the flash of horror in her eyes. The fear. The disgust.

Instead, she lowers her warm cunt onto it.

I suck in a sharp gasp, toes curling at the heat of her. My fingers dig into her hips and I stare back at her, showing a restraint that I don't feel. "You're not wearing underwear!" I hiss.

She rolls her hips in a slow, agonizingly deliberate way. "Kiss my neck." When all I can do is breathe hard into the view of her cleavage, she grabs my hair again, yanking my face up. "Fucking *kiss me!*"

Lost in the fire of her against my cock, I can't think of anything to do but comply, burying my face into her neck and opening my mouth against the skin. The moan in her throat vibrates against my lips, and then her pussy stutters over the achingly sensitive head of my cock, making my teeth sink into the tendon.

Lavinia makes this shocked sound, her moan bitten off into a sharp cry. "Yeah, just like that," she says, voice tight as her fingers clench in my hair. "The Barons are watching." She keeps grinding against me and I keep tightening my grip on her hips, knowing that I have to be hurting her now.

If anything, it makes her hips rock with more intent.

They're these torturous little undulations that I can feel all the way down to my marrow, and it doesn't strike me at first that the feeling of it has changed—has grown warmer and... slicker—until my mind explodes with disquieting thoughts. Flipping her over and shoving my cock inside. Covering her mouth with my hand as I rip my way through her. Or not, even. Letting her scream reach the ears of everyone around us. Letting all of them see what my cock can do to a woman. She'd bleed and cry, and I'd come too fast, coating her insides with the enormity of me, pumping her so full and forcing it deeper.

My cum would mingle with her blood, dripping a grisly pink down her soft thighs.

"I can't," I say, not even recognizing the ragged sound of my own voice. "I won't be able to stop, I'll—"

I'll fucking destroy you.

Her nails dig painfully into the nape of my neck. "Don't come yet," she says, pussy sliding over my hard shaft. I realize she thinks I'm talking about my hair-trigger. But I'm not. I'm talking about the need, so deep and primal that my muscles pulse mindlessly with the urge to thrust and take and *have*. "Kiss me," she gasps, my dick slotting right between her slick folds.

My first thought is that I'd rather eat a handful of dirt, but then I'm turning my head and licking wetly into her waiting mouth. It's not me. It's this... *thing* inside of me. Craving is too weak a word for it. It's instinct, this drive to fist my hand into her pale blue hair and conquer her mouth as she rides me. It's an impulse so all-consuming that I don't even realize I'm ripping away the top of her dress until my palm is already cupping her tit, squeezing.

When I break away from her mouth, there's a flash of nervousness in her eyes that I pay zero mind to. It's gone as fast as it arrived, however, and she clutches me closer, directing my mouth to her tits.

"Suck me," she orders, breath hitching.

I lift the weight of her breast in my hand and open my mouth around the peak, tongue feeling the pebbled texture of her nipple. My teeth press into the soft flesh and it makes her grind down harder, a cry ripping from her throat.

I move instantly to the other, so eager to consume every inch of this soft, writhing body that I don't even notice all the eyes on us.

Lavinia does, though.

She ducks down, breath hot against the crown of my head, to whisper, "Everyone is looking, Sy. They all think you're inside of me."

I thought I'd reach the pinnacle of hatred when Lavinia became our Duchess. She was everything I despised about women. Entitled. Fake. Manipulative. Weak. But now I discover a well of loathing so deep that it makes my stomach roil. It's a black, wretched, ugly thing, because her words bring me such satisfaction that I growl around her breast. It's the knowledge that everyone here is accepting the lie, and I *like* it. The thought that, for these few brief moments beneath the void of night, people think I'm normal.

I'm winning.

I might hate my lizard-brain reaction to it, but I don't deny it. This is why I lift my mouth from her breast to pant against her mouth. "Faster."

Lavinia obeys, her hips working against me in a rhythm that makes my balls clench excitedly. I've been so focused on the heat of her against my dick that I'm only now noticing how heavy her eyes have become, her plush lips parted with her short breaths. Her cheeks are pink, but the tips of her ears burn a vivid red, and it jolts through me like a lightning bolt that she's *enjoying* this.

This tiny little crevice forms between her eyebrows, and she breathes. "Nipples. Play with my nipples." Instantly, I reach down to pluck one between my fingers, fascinated by the clench of her thighs around my hips. "Oh, fuck," she breathes, as if this is news to her as much as me.

I find my tongue licking out to taste the sigh that spills from her lips. I'm used to my dick eliciting gasps of shock. I've known girls who have gone stiff at the sight of it—the feel of it. I'm familiar with the wary looks and the whispers.

I've never had a girl moan like Lavinia does right then.

Her face pinches up, like she's angry or hurting, and when she buries her face into my shoulder, letting loose a soft, desperate-sounding cry, I know she has to be faking it. The way her body seizes, the rush of wetness against my sensitive shaft, the shudder that rocks her shoulders, the quiver in her thighs...

It's pure performance.

It has to be.

She goes limp, but my cock hasn't gotten the message that this act is over. I grab a handful of her ass, plant my feet, and buck into her senselessly, chasing the lure of my release. She's wet—*fuck*, so goddamn wet—and I've never had that before. A woman's slickness covering my cock. It's intoxicating, and I don't even notice the eyes on us, as if the only thing that exists is between our bodies.

I clutch her to me tightly, and she begins making these breathless, pained sounds as I punch my hips up, teeth clenched against the need to feel her velvety insides around my cock. I've been obsessed with the thought of it since I forced my fingers into her cunt at dinner the other night. It'd feel so tight and warm—constricting and soft. It isn't until I glance up into the eyes of a shocked Sutton, that I wonder how I must look, face contorted as I fuck up into my Duchess.

That's what she is, my brain reminds me. Mine by rights. Mine to fuck. Mine to claim. Mine to mark and fill and use.

As if hearing the path my thoughts have taken, Lavinia turns her head to speak coolly into my ear. "You can come now. That's what you want isn't it? It's what your body needs." Lips brushing against my earlobe, she breathes, "Show them all who I belong to. Make me your bitch, Sy."

A growl tears from my chest as I fist a handful of her hair, shoving her down into my thrust with a violence that makes her yelp. It could be the performance again. No one could possibly believe I'd fuck into her this hard without a few tears springing up in her eyes. But fuck, she's convincing.

So convincing that my brain doesn't care to note the difference between act and reality. It thinks of her crying out like that—baleful and plaintive—and it surges with pride at the thought of bringing her pain.

I come with a grunt into her hair, jaw clenched so hard my teeth ache. I feel it gush into her folds, and then against my belly, warm and sticky as my thighs burn with the effort of my mindlessly bucking hips. Until this very second, my best orgasm was had at three in the morning, half asleep in my bed as the woman below me lay paralyzed.

This one takes the top spot by fucking miles.

And Lavinia was both of them.

It's so good that I can feel it vibrating through my legs, my ears ringing from the force of it. But then I realize it's not the orgasm at all.

My phone's going off in my back pocket.

Lavinia makes a surprised sound when I lift her up enough to drag my pants back over my hips, grimacing as I tuck my dick back inside. My phone rings and rings, buzzing urgently, and I fumble to get it out of my pocket, only needing to see the flash of Remy's name before I'm dumping her out of my lap and answering.

"Remy?" His name comes out in a breathless bark. I glance over at Lavinia. She's sprawled against the chair, skirt still hiked against her hips, red-cheeked and with my sticky cum between her legs. "Remy?" I say again. "Where the fuck are you?"

30

Lavinia

ne day.

It's after midnight when Sy drops me off, idling at the curb. He watches me enter the tower, blue eyes glaring until the exterior door locks behind me. He's impatient to go. The phone call from Remy has made him tense and rushed, but not enough to give me an opportunity to make a run for it.

He doesn't speed off until he's sure the door has locked.

The climb up the tower takes longer than usual. It's dark and cold, and I shiver the whole way up, nearly sprinting at the prospect of a hot shower and the feel of Archie in my lap.

Upstairs, the living quarters are empty, and I stand there for a long time, gazing up at the silent clock face. I wonder if it used to whirr. Did the cables make sounds? Did the hands clank when they moved? Did the machinery fill this chamber with life and chaos, only to be replaced with a revolving door of three men who'd do the same?

Nick isn't here. The knowledge ricochets through me like a bullet in a barrel. There's nothing holding me here—not anymore.

I could take the Archduke and maybe break the lock, run on foot. I could slip underground. I've heard there are passageways down there, and even though it's probably no more than an urban myth, it's said that they can take someone right out of Forsyth.

I drop the thorn and antler crown on the couch, and after a long stretch of searching, finally spot Archie, curled up in a ball inside a shoe box one of the guys left on the coffee table. It brings me up short, the thought of waking him and ripping him away from the scant comforts that have finally been bestowed on him.

I press a finger to the top of his little head, wondering if Nick would still fulfill his promise if I disappeared. Would he hand the kitten over to one of the girls? Would he keep him here, in this quiet place with its broken machines and heartless inhabitants?

I need a shower more than anything. I can still feel Sy's cum between my legs. It's no longer warm, but sticky and cool. My cunt hurts from the pounding, my clit rubbed raw. For a flicker of a moment, I could see how good it could be, how good Sy could be, if we stopped fighting one another and he let go of all his insecurities and hatred.

I step into the bathroom and in the garishness of the overhead light; I see what a mess I am. The hem of my skirt is covered in dirt. The leaves around my breasts are now limp and stretched out from Sy yanking the top down. My makeup is smeared. My hair is a tangled nest from the crown and Sy's hands. The fantasy goddess from earlier in the night is gone. Now I just look like a used-up sorority girl after her walk of shame.

I take my time beneath the spray, even though I should be rushing like Sy had. I should be preparing, grabbing everything of use to me and bolting right down the staircase. Maybe I can't break the lock, but maybe I *can*.

For some reason, I just don't feel the urgency.

One day.

The inescapable march of time has caught up to me, but I don't feel the impending panic of an uncontrollable fate. In truth, I feel nothing. I'm numb from the surface of my skin to the marrow of my bones, like I've become Forsyth's perverse version of a baseball card that's been traded too many times, and now I'm faded, creased, worn.

I'm so fucking exhausted.

It's a curious feeling, the absence of dread that's made a home in the pit of my chest since Leticia disappeared. It's not better. It's not worse. It just *is*. But it's a sad realization to have this awareness that I have nothing to really fight for. I remember first walking into this tower and wishing time was like that clock—frozen and still. Impossible. Time will always tick away. But the people within it?

Without even intending to, I've become the clock. Inert hands and silent cables. Motionless gears, rusting away inside of dark rooms. A monument that's been hollowed out and occupied by ugly, twisted things. It was stupid to think I could fix it.

When I step out of the bathroom and see Nick, it's with a new understanding.

I'm not his pet—not really. I'm a structure he's laid siege to. I'm a tower of stone and mortar that he's always been desperate to conquer. He wants my flesh, but he won't be happy until he's captured all it contains—until he's swept the corners and made them his own.

"Where's Remy, Lavinia?" he asks. He's leaning against the back of the couch, looking as though he's just arrived, still wearing his jacket and shoes. His ankles are crossed, hands pressed casually against the couch's back. There's an eerie blankness in his eyes that might have startled me a couple weeks ago.

Now, it just makes me feel tired.

Feeling thrown by the question, I say, "What? How should I know?"

He observes me for a long moment, utterly still. "First your sister. Now Remy. Just think it's weird how people keep disappearing around you."

"Not enough of them," I bite back. "Anyway, Sy just got a call from Remy. Talk to him. Or would that mean you'd need to actually communicate with one another for a night?"

His eyes go tight at the corners. "Did you have fun with him?"

I answer, "Not particularly."

His gaze falls to my shoulders, my chest. I'm in nothing but a towel, hair still wet, and I watch as his eyes follow a drop of water from my jaw to my cleavage. "You looked like you did." He thumbs the corner of his mouth as he pushes off the couch. "I'm curious. Did you do it because you actually want him? Or was it all about me?"

My lip curls at the way he phrases it. Of course, he'd take a supposed show of rebellion as some kind of declaration. "I did it because I could," I say, honestly. "I did it because there's an increasingly small pool of things I *can* do, and that just so happened to be one of them. The Dukes are at the Duchess' disposal."

"Why?" He watches me for a long moment, blue eyes darkened in the dim light of the room. "No one will ever want you as much as I do. No one will ever love you like I do. No one will ever go to bat for you like I have." It's only then that I realize how bloodshot and glazed his eyes are. Alcohol, probably, but in this place, who knows? "Why isn't that enough for you?" He says the words with such bald desperation that it takes me aback.

It's a pathetic question with a simple answer. I give it to him earnestly. "Because you're an insidious asshole who embodies every sick thing about this place. Because you claim to love me one moment and then hurt me the next. Because you'll never see me as a person." Walking past him toward the stairs to my loft, I scathingly add, "Because you're *you*, Nick."

He grabs me by the arm, jerking me back, and I get a good, long look at the belligerence in his eyes. "I thought about taking you, you know." When I just stare unblinkingly back, he elaborates, "Back when you were in the motel. I thought about smuggling you out, taking you somewhere remote and just..." His fingers tighten around my arm, pinching the skin. "...ruining you. Making you mine. Proving to Daniel that you were too wild to cage up. Only one thing was stopping me, and it wasn't him or your dad," he says, using his other hand to finger at the bite mark his brother left on my shoulder. "It was the possibility I could make you love me back. And I knew I could. Even back then, I saw how dangerous you were. You were beautiful and sexy and forbidden—everything a foot soldier wants. But mostly?" He curls a finger, skating his inked knuckle along my collarbone. "Mostly you were just a sad, hurt, lonely girl."

I jerk away, nerves flaring. "Shut up."

Nick follows, his broad shoulders bearing down on me. "You tried so hard to keep up that bitchy front, but I saw the real you. You're not dangerous because you're tough. You're dangerous because you're not." He looks down his nose at me, eyes heavy with a sinister satisfaction. "You know it's true. You've been here for more than two weeks. You could have run, but you didn't. It's not because of our deal. It's not because you're afraid of being found. At the end of the day, you stay in your cage because it's all you know."

I shake my head, jaw clenched tightly. "That's not true."

"It is," he insists, and he just keeps coming, that ember in his eyes growing, glowing. "It's where you're most comfortable. You might not excel at anything else, but this?" His laugh is somehow both soft and harsh. "You're so good at being someone's bitch."

I strike out before I even realize my fist is flying up, knuckles slamming into the sharp ridge of his jaw. The pain explodes in my thumb first, and then radiates up into my arm, but it's worth it to see his head jerk to the side.

Even if he looks unfazed.

The flame inside of me—the one I thought I'd lost in the shower—bursts to life, and drives my fist back toward his face. It's a toxic thing, the urge to hit and scream and wound, and I don't care. I embrace it, barreling forward, and it feels endless, like I could destroy anything in my path with the heat of it.

But Nick catches my wrist before it makes contact, wrenching me into his body. His arms lock around my middle as I wrestle against it, teeth bared in fury as I shove at his chest, trying desperately to injure.

I can't hurt Nick, though.

Not physically.

"I'll never love you!" I snarl, hoping it cuts like razor blades. "Never! I'd rather die in that fucking elevator than be with you. I'd rather be with *Perez!*"

There's an ominous silence above me, and it's nearly a relief that he's finally going to do it. I'm ready, I think. Ready for the darkness and the suffocation. Ready for the panic. A small part of me worries that Nick is right. Maybe the only way I can feel comfortable anymore is within the small, malignant spaces I've grown used to.

I brace myself for it, feeling the elevator doors behind us like a tangible, looming presence.

Nick's chest expands with a hard inhale. "Then I guess there's nothing stopping me anymore."

Before I can wonder what that means, he's tightening his grip on me, lifting me off my feet. Instead of carrying me to the elevator, however, he drags me into his bedroom.

And then he pushes me back onto the bed, yanking my towel off as I fall.

Then it comes to me.

I thought about taking you...

Ruining you...

Making you mine...

Only one thing was stopping me...

The possibility I could make you love me back...

I watch him tear his shirt over his head, and his eyes hold none of the anger or misery I'd seen before. They're a bottomless pit of black desperation, pinning me with a sharpness that makes my stomach flop uneasily.

I scurry back, away from him, saying, "*No.*"

"Yes." He reaches out lightning-quick, those blue eyes searing as he snatches my ankles and yanks me down the bed. I strike out with my fists again, struggling to break my feet free, but he's already got something wound around one of my ankles. A cord—attached to the frame beneath the mattress. I realize too late that he's planned this, probably when I was in the shower. Maybe even earlier. I'm too slow to stop him from tethering the other ankle, his movements nimble and swift.

He's on me in a flash, pinioning me to the mattress with his hard body. One of his hands captures my wrists while his other winds a third cord around them, tying them off with an aggressive jerk. "Go ahead and fight," he says, voice eerily calm as he reaches down to palm my breast. "I always imagined this would be fast and hard. If you need it to hurt, that's fine with me." He rolls my nipple between forefinger and thumb.

I grunt with my struggle, ankles stinging from the tight stricture of the binds. His mouth brands my neck with a wet, open-mouthed kiss as his palm skates over my ribs, dipping between my legs. My pulse quickens into the same panic I felt that night at the Hideaway.

I could plead.

I could beg him not to do this.

I could scream.

And no one would hear me.

He pushes his fingers through my folds, prodding and invading, and then he forces a finger into me, pausing so briefly that I barely register it as a falter. "I knew you were just acting," he says, nipping over the sore bruise on my shoulder—the one his brother had made. "He wouldn't know what to do with one, even if you were throwing it at him like a slut. Did he even make you wet?"

"Yes. He also made me come," I sneer and buck up against him in an attempt to throw him off. "Everyone saw it." All it does is sink his finger deeper. He makes a gruff sound, licking downward toward my breast.

"No one could ever fuck you as well as I could, Little Bird." He glances up at me through angry brows and thick eyelashes. "I might share it, but this pussy belongs to me."

"Don't," I say, voice low and warning as he forces another painful finger inside.

My sharp wince just makes him glare back. "Your chance to

have a say in this went out the door when you broke our deal." Shoulders tensing, he slams his fingers into me, making me cry out in pain. Surging up, he snarls into my face, "When you *kissed my brother!*"

"Fuck!" I howl, the heel of his palm banging into my clit as he violently fucks his fingers into me.

"You're going to open for me," he seethes through clenched teeth. "You're going to take every fucking drop of my cum into this cunt you think so highly of." He grunts with the force he uses to batter his fingers into me and I know now that this is a punishment for me just as much as it's a gratification for him.

"It hurts," I keen, still sore from Sy.

"Good," he growls, slapping against me once more and then crushing his palm to me, fingers trapped inside my body. "You hurt me, I hurt you. How's that for a negotiation?"

It's painful when he rips his fingers out of me, but then he's crawling down my body and replacing them with his tongue. His hands shove my thighs apart and it pulls excruciatingly against my ankles, but it's hard to think of anything but the blazing point of his mouth, devouring me.

That's exactly what it is; the frenzied, overwhelming pursuit of someone who wants to consume. I clench against the sensation of it, but he makes a rough, irritated sound and wrenches my knees up, making my toes prickle with the loss of circulation.

He pulls back to peer at my hole, lips pursed tight as his cheeks shift.

And then he pitches forward and spits on me, right against my entrance.

My chest heaves up and down as Nick's fingers return, pushing his saliva inside, making me slick. Without the sting and stretch, I can feel myself responding to it on an involuntary level. It begins as an ache, deep within the pit of my belly, and it doesn't lessen any when his tongue flicks out to toy with my clit. There's a moment where I sink into it without meaning or wanting to. Nick eats pussy just like he kisses, so full of tongue and intensity that there isn't room for thought.

I know he can tell when the wetness slicking his fingers becomes less of him and more of me, because he begins frantically clawing at the button to his jeans with his other hand, shucking them down his hips sightlessly, lips still sucking wet kisses against my clit.

Then he dives down to lick between his digits, entering me with the eager tip of his tongue. He groans and takes his fingers away to make room, shoving his tongue as deep inside as he can.

My breath hitches painfully when he rears up, leaving my clit a throbbing mess of need.

I know I've lost when he notices the writhe of my hips, a viciousness falling over his features as he licks the taste of me from his lips. "The time for requests is over," he says, pulling his cock free. "But maybe if you're a good girl, I'll let you come on my dick."

I twist my wrists against the binds, feeling it pinch and chafe, but the knot is too secure. Frustrated, I rear up to sneer at him. "This is the only way you can get it from me," I say, panting from the struggle. "How does it feel to know you're so revolting, you have to tie me up and hold me down just to get your dick into me?"

Bending, he braces himself above me, fisting his cock against my entrance. There's a moment where he just...watches me, as if he's giving my question the consideration it deserves. The tattoo beside his eye twitches when his gaze narrows into a scowl. "It'll do."

He slams forward, forcefully plunging the entire length of his cock into me.

I throw my head back, crying out at the sudden intrusion, back arched as if I could get away from it. The noise that punches from his chest is animalistic and he fists a hand in my hair before driving his hips impossibly closer.

The stretch burns, but it's the sudden sense of fullness that takes my breath away. My body feels crowded and too tight, invaded and altered, and Nick's mouth is resting against my jaw, teeth dragging against the bone.

"God, you're so fucking tight," he grits out, and when he eases his hips back—the drag of his cock tearing a sob from my chest—it's only to slam right back into the cradle of my thighs, rocking every bone in my rigid body. "Won't be like last time," he pants, snapping forward again. "Gonna fuck you open until this pussy remembers me." The last words are growled into the skin of my throat and all I can see are the shifting muscles in his back as he surges into me like a hostile wave.

I clench against the pain of the violation, but it just makes him grunt, spurring him to push harder, deeper. This isn't sex. It's a fight our bodies are having. It's aggression and refusal, and the most awful part about it—the absolute fucking worst—is that my body is losing.

And it doesn't care.

"Fuck," he spits, lips dragging over the swell of my cheek. "Feel how wet you're getting for me? You say you don't want me, but look at you, trying so hard to hide the truth."

He's talking about the clench of my teeth, the stiff set of my thighs, the way my eyes are squinched, refusing to see all the raw power in his movements. "It's a lie," I bite out.

His fingers dig into my chin, forcing me to face his vehement gaze. "This is the only goddamn thing that *isn't* a lie, Lavinia. When are you going to get it?!" The words are spoken in a harsh tone, but the way he tips his forehead against mine is perversely gentle. His hips roll against mine, sending wild zings through my clit. "I fucking love you. You're it for me."

I can't explain the feeling that swells in the back of my throat like a boulder. It makes my vision swim with tears. It brings a tremble to my chin. It steals the breath from my lungs and hides it away somewhere inaccessible. "You don't know how to love, Nick." Even if he were being honest—even if this is the only love he's capable of feeling—it's corrupted and gnarled, and what I'm feeling must be heartbreak.

Because this is the closest I'll ever get to being loved. It comes to me in a certainty that makes the tears spill over, running down my temples in lazy rivulets. This is all I'll get. And for a moment, I can almost understand why Nick expected my gratitude. Out of everything in this town—my family, the girls at the Hideaway, the other Royals—Nick's the best there is for me.

"You're wrong," he insists, lips moving against mine as he fucks into me. "I know how to love better than anyone else in this town. Tell me you don't feel it." His lips pinch my own, tender but demanding.

I lay perfectly still, voice bland. "I don't feel anything."

"That's the lie," he says, levering himself up to watch my face. He reaches up to thumb a tear from the corner of my eye, twisting his hips. "Your pussy is so soaked for me, Little Bird. You're trying to push me out because you've already let me in." He tilts his head, kissing me, and it galls me to know he's right. I can't control the writhe of my hips or the curl of my toes. I can't stop the liquid-hot shot of lust that's settled into the pit of my stomach. I'm powerless to deny the throb between my legs, the instinct to meet him—to take from him.

My heels dig into the mattress as I lift my hips into him, driving his dick deeper. His mouth parts with a gasp and I use the distraction to jerk up, clamping my teeth over his bottom lip and piercing into soft flesh. Blood pools into my mouth and Nick lets out a loud, pained hiss.

But he doesn't stop.

His eyes roll back into his head and he punches forward, a long, gruff groan erupting from his throat. He clamps a hand over my tit but doesn't try to pry my teeth from his lip. He takes it, tongue licking out to run over one of my blood-stained incisors.

I finally give, wrenching my face to the side with a disgusted grunt. "Fuck!" His blood is bitter and tangy in my mouth, and maybe I'd spit it out if Nick weren't there to push it back between my lips with the artful twist of his tongue. He invades my mouth as he fucks me, harder and deeper, his fist tugging sharply at the crown of my hair.

It quickly becomes apparent that my body has fallen prey to the charade. It doesn't care that Nick's love is a fake, perverted thing. It feels the way he's crashing into me—these hard, ruthless jabs of his hips—and it sees the way he looks, some unholy marriage of desperation and resentment, and all it wants is release.

"Don't fight it," he growls, smearing his blood across my chin. "I can feel how bad your pussy wants it. Let it go. Give it to me."

I thrash my head to the side and battle to push back the storm building between my legs. "No."

He answers by wedging an arm between our bodies, his fingers finding my swollen clit. His voice emerges in a strained snarl. "I'll fuck this cunt all night if that's what it takes, but you're going to come for me." When I wrench my head to the other side in a sorry attempt at escape, he just presses his bloody lips to my ear. "I want you to feel what it's like to be owned."

I gnash my teeth against the rising tide, his fingers working tight, torturous circles into my clit. His dick pounds into me relentlessly, and there's no escape from it. Every nerve in my body has been distilled down to the point of his touch, shooting right to my center.

The orgasm gets ripped out of me like a tangled vine of roots, so piercing and abrupt that I lose control of my body, seizing forcefully beneath him—around him. My mouth opens in a strained scream and I can feel him watching me even if I can't see it, my eyes clenched tightly shut against the explosion of aching pleasure.

The sound he releases seems torn from his stomach—a deep, guttural groan that drags across my skin like sandpaper as the warmth of his release begins filling me.

"That's right," he grunts, following me with every turn of my head. "Every drop, Little Bird." He thrusts hard, cock jerking inside of me. His shoulders heave with the force of it, and I see him for what he is. A pulsing mass of muscle and ink, hardness and softness, obsession and contempt. Nick orgasms as if it's a weapon he's inflicting on me. I doubt he even lets himself enjoy it, he's so busy forcing me to feel his pleasure, emptying himself into me like it's the most vital part of the act.

And he just keeps going.

And going.

I can feel him deep inside, his cock pulsating as his cum rushes in. Nick does exactly as he promises, pinning me with blazing eyes as he wrings every drop into my hole, shoved as deep as he can go.

When it finally ends—when he finally lets out one last sharp grunt and tears himself out of my body—I find that I've lost control of everything.

A deep, pitiful sob erupts from my throat. I think it's been hiding there since that night in the basement—maybe even sooner than that. Maybe this sickness has been lurking dormant inside me since my father put me in that chest. Maybe I've been carrying it around with me like a lead weight, slowed by gravity and my own inability to carry it.

Maybe Nick's right.

Maybe I'm just weak.

My body strains with the release of it, chest constricted around an awful wail. I try to stave it off, wrestle it back, but it claws free, rending the air with loud, wracking sobs. Some part of me is so eager to let it go, to finally be free of its weight in my chest.

I cry.

I cry for my body, sore and discarded. I cry for the two years I've lost, trapped and helpless—and yes, Nick was right—sad, lonely, and hurt. I cry because I might be strong, but even steel bends under enough pressure. I cry for my mother, and for some reason, I cry for Leticia, too. For the fact that one thing bonds the three of us, and it's something as terrible as *this*: To belong to a Kingdom we never wanted, to be used, to be *Royal*.

It feels like I cry for hours, purging the grief from my system in gulps of air and deep, wet sobs, and maybe it was better that I never let myself expunge it, because now tucking it all back into myself feels like an impossible feat.

In the end, I'm just too exhausted to keep it up.

The cries fade out into hitched breaths, slow sniffles, and aching eyes. I don't feel my body anymore, just the tempting tug of oblivion dragging me under, covering me in its cold embrace.

The last thing I see before succumbing to sleep is Nick.

He's standing beside the bed, a shoulder propped against the wall. He's pulled his boxers on and his arms are crossed, the one solid-black forearm flexing and unflexing in some incomprehensible rhythm. He never unties me. He just stares out the window with this look on his face. *Creeping.*

He doesn't look happy. He doesn't look angry. He doesn't even look desperate anymore.

He doesn't look at me at all.

THE FIRST THOUGHT that comes to me when I wake is that I haven't slept nearly long enough. My eyes feel crusty and sore. But then, *everything* feels sore. My wrists, my ankles, my cunt. All of them throb and twinge.

It isn't until I turn, tucking a hand beneath my cheek, that I realize Nick's untied me.

I blink my eyes open to a pitch black room, and it's just like the other night when he put that tracker in me. Nick is standing at the end of his bed, fully dressed. Watching. Waiting.

But this time, he speaks. "Get up." There's no inflection to it— no clue as to what new hell awaits me—but it lacks bite. Perfectly flat. His silhouette shifts, and then something soft and cool lands against my side. Remy's hoodie. A pair of pants. Underwear. Socks. "Meet me out there in ten."

He turns and exits the room, and it all comes crashing back to me. The sex. The hurt. The invasion.

His cum is dried on my thigh.

I follow his orders mechanically, as if I've lost the will to ask questions or feel concern. My brain runs on autopilot because I'm thinking… anything that means leaving the malice of this bed must be worth it. The sheets are stained with our fluids; blood, semen, tears, saliva. I can't get away from it fast enough.

Walking hurts and I get this feeling that my sore ankles are holding me up because it's all they know how to do. They allow me to step into the panties, and then the pants. My wrists concede to the hoodie, letting me slip my arms into the sleeves. My muscles protest, but I put my head through it, feeling soiled and broken and confused.

Nick's waiting by the door to the stairwell when I emerge, holding my shoes in his hand. He's wearing his jacket and his boots, and a set of keys hangs limply from his hand. "Come."

I'd ask him where we're going, but I find that I don't care. I put on my shoes and follow him like a wraith, slow and trudging as we drop, step by step, down the tower. The descent must hurt—must be fucking agony—but I'm numb to it, my footfalls heavy and labored, but even and dogged.

Maybe he's going to kill me.

We reach the bottom before I'm expecting to, and I find myself feeling a nudge of surprise, wondering where I've just been. Trapped in my head, bound by my thoughts. But when he pushes the door open, it's all wiped away. It's still night, or more like early morning. There's something I should be worrying about, but I can't touch it in my mind. Nothing feels urgent anymore. I just walk with Nick to the SUV and climb into the passenger seat without having to be asked.

The drive is silent but void of the tension I'm used to. Nick keeps one hand draped over the steering wheel and the other against the center console, unmoving. Occasionally we pass by streetlights that flash over the sharp angles of his face, but mostly he's just a shadow, inert and looming.

I watch the West End pass by, distracting myself with the shape of it. It's different here at night: quieter, emptier, darker. It's as if somewhere between leaving Sy and waking up, the whole world has ended, everyone zapped from existence.

Finally, I speak, my voice harsh as gravel. "Are we going to find Remy? Did you hear from Sy?"

His eyes never leave the road, but the back muscle of his jaw pulses with a tic. He doesn't answer me, but swings the SUV into the parking lot of an abandoned warehouse. The headlights burst against the aged metal in front of us, nearly blinding my still hazy eyes. For some reason, my eyes stick to this tattoo on Nick's elbow as he shuts off the car. The design is a circle—red rays of sun, expanding outward. It reminds me of Remy's Lady of Sorrows, all those points stabbing inward.

If I had the motivation, I'd count the points on my star.

Maybe this is all a dream.

Nick gets out first and I follow him automatically, only distantly concerned about why he'd bring me to an abandoned warehouse at four in the morning. I can't shake this feeling, as if he couldn't do any worse to me than he has.

I know the second we walk through the rusted doors that I'm wrong.

"No." I take two steps back on instinct, but Nick's there behind me, pushing me forward. "No, no, no..." This isn't a dream. It's a goddamn nightmare.

Fifty feet away stands my father and Perez, waiting.

The air leaves my lungs in a painful squeeze of panic and I whirl around, gazing wide-eyed into blue eyes. "You gave me up?" My voice is rusty and torn, and it's his fault. As if that wasn't enough. As if he hadn't broken me to a satisfying degree...

He's staring straight ahead, dead-eyed and motionless. "It's what you wanted."

My breath comes quicker because I can feel him. I can feel my father, so close and malignant, and I can hear him crisp and clear when he speaks.

"Don't make a fuss, Lavinia."

I flinch at the sound, years of memories rushing back to me like a freight train of hurt and fury. "Nick..." I fist my hand in his shirt, and I'm not proud of the way my voice cracks, but I can't seem to care. I feel every bit of color leave my face. "Don't make me go with them."

He says nothing.

I've sunk to a lot of deep places in my life, but none so deep as the one I lower myself to when I ask this, "Please? I'll be better." The crest of his lip twitches in a ghost of a sneer and I fist his shirt, completely lost to any sense of shame when I spring up on my toes to kiss him.

He turns his head away.

My lips stutter over a stubble-rough jaw, close enough for me to see that there's nothing in his eyes anymore. No anger or want or frustration. I used to think being under the weight of his oppressive pining was the worst of Nick. His cockiness, his demanding nature, his need to dominate... they all rankle, but none so much as how gravely he wants me.

Only now I know better.

This is the worst of Nick. His aloof posture, the curve of arrogance in his brow, the complete disregard. It was bad when he wanted me, and it's petrifying now that he doesn't.

I fall to my knees. "*Please*. Please, Nick?" That boulder returns to my throat, making my eyes water as I begin fumbling for the buttons on his jeans. "I'll—I'll be good for you. I'll make you feel good, sleep in your bed, give you whatever you want. I'll let you love me, I'll—"

He wrenches himself away from me, leaving me there on the cold cement floor, and all I can do is stare up at him like a wretched, discarded plaything. Pretty Nick's broken toy, debasing myself in front of our enemies. Trash, just like everyone has always said of me.

He stares back at me with those cold, fathomless eyes, and inexplicably, I think of that moment in the gym. Standing under the heat of the spotlight. Looking out over a crowd of ruthless men and feeling a kinship I had no right to. The tears spring up, but they don't spill over. I take them into myself, tucking them back into their dark places, filling my crevices with the misery of them. A few days ago, I spent the evening with one of Remy's philosophy text-books, finding myself engrossed in a passage. It posited that the absence of time is the absence of life, and I spent hours staring up into the cables and gears, wondering if it could be fixed.

"You've killed me," I tell him, voice just as numb as Nick looks. "You might not have the guts to do it yourself, but it doesn't make it any less true." I believe the words just as firmly as I say them, and I stand, refusing to take this fate on my knees like a weak little bitch.

I turn to face my father.

Somewhere in Forsyth, a clock is ticking.

But not for me.

31

Nick

It's worse than hearing her in the elevator.

That's what I'm thinking about when she gets on her knees and begs, her eyes shining up at me with so much desperation that I have to curl my fists to stave off the impulse to snatch her up and take her away.

What's done is done.

It'd be a lie to say it doesn't give me a rush of satisfaction to see her looking at me like that. Helpless and so fucking willing. She'd blow me if I asked, and she'd do it right in front of her own father. She'd beg and scrape. She'd finally say the words I've been hungry to hear, all these years.

I love you, Nick.

But it'd be fake.

There was a time that wouldn't have even bothered me much. The words would have been enough—the curl of them on her lips, the shape of my name on her tongue. I would have been okay with the fantasy. But now, I know better. I'm chasing a figment, the wavy mirage never within reach.

Lavinia Lucia will never love me, and I hate her for it. I hate her for not unfurling. I hate her for keeping the deepest parts of herself away from me. I hate her for enjoying my dick enough to spasm in pleasure around it and then crying herself sick because of it. I hate her for never giving me a chance, but most of all, I hate her for only being able to see the mangled, deficient parts of me. I've taken lives, carved up bodies, dragged hookers from abusive John to abusive John, but none of them ever made me feel as fucking unworthy as her.

I can either spend the rest of my days striking out against that certainty, steadfast until she's black and blue beneath the burden of my hurt, or I can do this.

Perez steps forward, eyes zeroing in on the pale patch of skin below her jaw. I'd sucked a mark there as I fucked her into a sore, gasping mess, and from the flicker of disdain in his eyes, I can tell he realizes it. "So you took her for a spin, huh, Bruin? Must not have been all it was hyped up to be." He smirks, looking her up and down. "I get it. Great tits, but she's kind of bony. I'll fatten her up, though—chain her to the bed, put a couple babies in her. She'll do."

Lavinia stands rigidly between us, unwilling to move forward or back, and I have to clench down on the instinct to pull the gun from my waistband and bury a bullet into this piece of shit's head. The thought of him touching her, claiming her, using her up like his cum dumpster... it makes my insides writhe like they're on fire. The only saving grace to the rising tide of fury within is the knowledge that she won't be getting pregnant anytime soon. The implant I paid for is still nestled securely in her upper arm. It certainly helps that his right arm is in a cast, a bandage still concealing the sad stump of the finger I'd cut off.

He can only have her because I'm letting him.

He strides forward, casually noting, "Since you were so nice about returning her, I guess I'll let the fact you've soiled my property slide." But when he approaches her, reaching out to grab her arm, she rears her head back. I see it coming from a mile away—

can clearly remember the force she likes to use, and the stunning accuracy with which she uses it.

She spits right into his face.

There's a moment of stillness, Perez's eyes slamming shut with the wince of the impact. My lips twitch involuntarily, but then he balls a fist and slams it into her cheek, sending her stumbling back.

I've tried not to give much thought to slapping her the other night. I was worked up and on edge from meeting with the Lords' tracker guy, feeling like a string pulled too taut. It was going to snap—if not at her, then somewhere else. It didn't feel good to do it. There was no sense of satisfaction. No inner swell of pleasure.

I haven't gotten more than two hours of sleep since.

So when I pull my gun, some of the anger is pointed uselessly inward, still pissed at myself for being weak, for only showing Lavinia the most rotten parts of myself.

But Perez is who I point the barrel at.

"Drop it, Bruin." Lionel is standing back, his own pistol pulled. "No need to make this messy, son. Walk away."

"I'm not your fucking son," I grind out, watching Lavinia gain her bearings.

Perez doesn't give her time to fully reorient herself, thrusting out to grasp her by a handful of hair. "Don't worry," he snarls into her face. "I'll make a good little bitch out of you, eventually."

I flinch against the word, remembering the comment that set the whole night off.

"You're so good at being someone's bitch."

I don't walk away because Lionel orders me to. I walk away because I know if I don't, I'll kill one of them. It skitters beneath my skin like a livewire, the need to rend and destroy. *Mayhem.* That's the South Side way. Only it's the West End's way, too. The fists of Forsyth always strike back.

But my hands are tied.

I speed away from the warehouse like I'm being chased, fisting the steering wheel so tightly that my knuckles and tendons twinge.

The first stoplight I reach, I bash the heel of my palm against the wheel. "Fuck!" I do it again, wishing it were Perez beneath my fist. "Fucking fuck, fuck, *fuck!*"

I already wish I could take it back, but what would be the point? Keeping her chained to *my* bed? Putting my babies into her? Watching as the spark slowly fades from her eyes, turning her into a dead, empty thing? That's not the Lavinia I want.

I want the girl who kicks me in the face. I want the mouthy little shit who spits into the faces of men who can't have her. I want the bitch who'll slash a guy's stomach open for having the nerve to touch her. The irony isn't lost on me that all the things I love about her have been driven in one way or another by her hatred for me. But *goddamn it*, I'd wanted so badly to feel her softness. To drag her up against me at night and sink into the sweet scent of her. Foolishly, I'd imagined her affection. Fingers running through my hair. Kisses pressed into the skin of my neck. The weight of her body on top of mine as she took her pleasure from me.

I get the call when I'm halfway across town, putting as much mileage as possible between me and the warehouse. I get a glance at the screen and gnash my teeth, fumbling to answer. "What?!" I snap, not ready to deal with how my brother is going to react to my unilateral decision to dispose of the Duchess. The image of her on her knees like that *begging* me not to leave her is still burned into my retinas like a sick slideshow.

"Nick. I need you to come up to the cliffs," Sy says, voice low and full of a weight that brings me up short. "*Now*," he stresses, and I know that strain in his voice. I've heard it every night since Tate's death, my brother's voice over the phone, thick with something dreadful.

Not even giving it a second thought, I slam on the brakes and spin into a sharp U-turn, tires squealing off the pavement. The cliffs are outside of town, overlooking the river. I haven't been there in years, and I doubt either of them has either. "Is he...?"

"He's..." he pauses, voice rough. "He's not okay, Nicky. He needs... I need your help."

Sy hasn't called me by that name since before I left for South

Side, blind with grief and defiance and the impulse to hurt. Two years hasn't beat it out of me and I doubt it ever will, but it has taught me that my brother's been hurting just as much.

"Be there in ten," I say, hanging up as I stomp the gas pedal.

The ride is quiet and filled with the pervasive scent of Lavinia's shampoo, still lingering in the cabin. I try to put her out of my mind, focused on the task ahead as I reach the old dirt road. I turn down the path, going slower than I'd like over the potholes and rocks. It's just past four in the morning—too early for the outdoorsmen and too late for the rowdy high school kids who come up here to party. I know, because we *were* those kids.

When my headlights cut across the clearing, I stop the car next to Sy's, gravel spewing from the force. Remy's motorcycle is next to the narrow clearing in the trees, the trail leading up to the part of the cliffs called Widow's Rock. It's dark, but my eyes adjust easily, the large moon hanging by the horizon leading the way. The incline is steep, but levels off at the top, the ground turning to a craggy granite. I haven't been up here in ages, but it's not a surprise this is where Remy came to have a breakdown.

This is where it all started—or, I guess, ended. It's the before and after. The place that caused the fracture between us. It feels almost poetic that this is where I've been called after the hellish night I just went through with Lavinia.

Dead girls, all around.

These last few weeks have obviously been a buildup for Remy —the dreams, the benders, the nonsensical rambling. Maybe it's the transition to Duke, or maybe it's been *her*, another girl circling us, wary yet tenacious. Maybe he wasn't ready for that.

I sure as hell wasn't.

As I approach the figures in the distance, I notice Remy pacing back and forth along the edge of the cliff, backlit by the pale moonlight. The glowing ember of a cigarette burns between his fingertips, his eyes red and ringed in purplish smudges. His free hand is thrust in his hair, tugging it into wild peaks. I don't need to look him in the eye to understand what's happening here. I can feel the erratic current rolling off of him. My brother stands a few feet away, neck tense, his hands flat at his sides. He's trying to stay calm and in control, but Remy is a live-wire laying on the edge of a very deep pool.

"Hey," I say lightly, crossing over the rock, "what's going on?"

"Nicky," Remy says, eyes flashing when he sees me. "I've got it all figured out. I mean, mostly—it's *mostly* figured out. Things are still..." The ember of the cigarette bobs between his forefinger and thumb as he jabs his temple. "They're still fucking weird, but I think I've got it." Sy and I watch nervously as Remy paces toward the edge, pointing down. "Look at this. Look at it."

I shoot my brother a look, but he just presses his lips into a tense line. "He won't let me get any closer," he says, voice low.

But Remy hears him and he spins around, snapping, "Because you don't listen, Sy! I'm not crazy!" To me, he says, "I'll show you, Nicky. I'll show you, and then you'll understand."

Sy's eyes flick to mine and he's utterly silent, but I get the message he's sending me loud and clear. Do what I can to keep him calm—to keep him alive.

Squaring my shoulders, I march up the rock, spine rippling with the currents of energy Remy is putting out. He's restless as I approach, pacing away only to pace back, walking in tight, aborted circles. The closer I get, the tighter the circles become, until he's reaching out and grabbing my shoulder, shoving me toward the edge.

It's a steep drop into nothingness, the river below quiet and still, barely rippling. It's like the air around us is holding its breath, not even a breeze.

"Look," Remy says, breathless with some strange anticipation. "Look at it, down there."

I chance a better peek over the edge, shrugging. "It's the river, Remy."

He makes a sharp, frustrated sound. "Don't look at the river; look at what's on top of it."

I squint into the dark, trying to find a boat or a figure—something distinctive against the backdrop of the water's reflection of the night sky. But there's nothing. I look up at him, shaking my head in confusion. "There's nothing down there."

Huffing, he pinches the cigarette between his lips to reach into his back pocket, pulling out his phone. He begins thumbing through it, and when he turns the screen, thrusting it in my face, it's a photo of a row of canvases. They're the ones in his room—the half-finished paintings of a night sky. He's always talking about that now. Falling into the sky. Flying into the stars. Some such nonsense.

"The stars," he says, pushing the screen closer. "Don't you get it?" When I meet his gaze, his eyes are wide and hopeful. He must see the bewilderment on my face because he releases a tight, irritated growl and thrusts a finger toward the river. "I didn't fall into the stars! I was remembering the reflection, Nicky. I fell into the fucking *river*." His eyes follow the tip of his finger, something hard and haunted crossing his features. "I don't remember hitting the surface. I must have passed out or hit my head—I'm not sure." His fingers return to tugging at his hair, forehead creased.

I look over my shoulder at Sy, who's clearly struggling to hear. "When did this happen?"

This question just seems to inflame him more. "You're not listening!"

"I'm listening!" I bark, throwing my hands out wide. "But you need to start telling me something, Remy, because right now, you just look like a fucking lunatic who's standing on the edge of a cliff! Seriously, dude, take stock for a second!"

His fingers go still in his hair, and then begin rubbing. Morosely, he frowns. "Okay, that's fair."

"I believe you," I promise, because that's always been Remy's problem. "I know you talk in these winding fucking riddles and everyone writes you off, but not me." I make sure he's looking me in the eye when I add, "*Never* me. You just have to give me something to work with."

This seems to make some of the tension in his neck bleed away. "I can show you." Suddenly he's stalking away from the cliff, to the north side of the rock. I throw Sy a look and we follow him, but it's only to the boundary where the lush grasses meet the granite.

"There," he says, pointing his cigarette into the grass. He stares, voice going gruff. "The yellow flowers." There's a patch of wild-flowers scattered like weeds, and even in the dark, I recognize them as the ones my mom had on her table the other night. Remy's body vibrates with a shiver when he adds, "She was laying here."

Sy and I realize he's talking about Tate at precisely the same second, both of us sucking in a sharp burst of air. Without wanting to, I find myself imagining it. Her body. Lifeless and cold. I came here the day after she died, trying to find the blood—the evidence.

I figured she died on the rock.

And then Remy says, "I saw her." He tilts his head, looking pensive. "She looked so peaceful. Like she was just... stargazing."

"What?" Sy stares at him with a baffled expression. "You weren't here when they found her, Remy. You were in Saint Mary's being—"

"I wasn't here when they found her," he agrees, cutting in. Looking between us, he seems anything but crazy when he says, "I was here when they shot her."

My response comes instantly, every hair on my neck standing at attention. "Who?"

Remy shakes his head. "The red lights I kept seeing... I think they were taillights. I can remember the gun going off. I remember seeing her lying here. I remember the way the gunshot smelled, and the black glass of the lake, and then I remember falling into the river." He looks up at me, intense but perfectly lucid. "I think I was trying to get away, Nicky."

"Don't encourage this." Sy tells me, rubbing the bridge of his nose. "Tate killed herself, Remy. You know this. We've talked about this."

Before Remy can argue, I ask, "Why is this just coming out now?" I'd known from the start that the police were full of shit. That there was no way Tate did this to herself. It didn't track. Sy never believed it. Remy? He was gone—locked up. I spent two years in South Side searching for clues, digging up dirt. The only person from home I kept in contact with was my dad. Manny Perilini keeps secrets better than anyone I know, and he would only keep mine if I promised to keep him in the loop, checking in weekly. Sometimes I'd come to him with paper trails or rumors going around down on the Avenue and we'd talk it through like a puzzle, struggling to find some link.

But the Lords were clean.

Well... not clean. Daniel had so many skeletons in his closet, he was basically running a mausoleum. But nothing connected to Tate —nothing that would make me suspect any of them even gave half a shit about her, if they even knew she existed.

Remy gives me a grim look, replying. "My dad. What's his number one rule?"

Sy and I know this like the back of our hands and we recite it automatically. "No scandals."

The Maddox family is old money, with all the trappings. Reputation. Heritage. Tradition. Power. And none of them are as hard-assed about it as Remy's dad. Sy and I used to find this hilarious— Timothy Maddox running after his troubled son, always wrestling down any inkling of vulgarity. It was like watching someone attempt to make a fish breathe air.

Remy pulls something else out of his pocket—a folded piece of paper. He snaps it straight, thrusting it toward me and Sy. "This is a dispatch report made three hours before Tate's body was found. Someone saw a young male wandering along the road. Read it."

I take the paper and squint to make out the words, but Sy is already there with his phone, illuminating the page with the glow of his screen. The dispatch log describes a call reporting someone disoriented along the access road leading south. Injured. Wet. The person was picked up by...

"Your cousin?" I look up, and Remy's nodding.

"He picked me up and... I guess he took me to my dad once he realized something was wrong." His jaw goes tight when he looks away, back to the river. "You know the rest. My dad put me into

Saint Mary's, and I don't know what happened there, but they did... something." He cringes, digging a tattooed knuckle into his temple. "Some kind of mind control."

Sy finally speaks up, voice dry. "Mind control? Remy, you realize how ridiculous that sounds?"

But I don't think it sounds ridiculous at all.

I mean, yeah, the mind control thing does. But Timothy Maddox has more money than almost anyone in this town, and Remy's mind was fragile before he apparently witnessed his best friend being gunned down. Throw some trauma in his brain and get him all turned around? I can see Remy losing the threads of what's real.

I fold the paper back up, asking Remy, "Tell me what else you remember."

He gets this brightness in his eyes—a spark of elation and relief —and begins, "This is the best part. Because I jumped—I know I did—but here's the thing: I wasn't alone." He dashes back to the cliff, ignoring Sy's muttered curse, and glances over his shoulder to make sure I'm following. "The stars, right?" He sounds breathless and too alive as he glances down at the water. "I saw Vinny, and she reminded me of them, because she fell into the stars with me. It's the first thing I remembered. I dreamed about it."

Sy catches up, face twisting. "Wait, you're saying Lavinia was here?"

My stomach sinks at the sound of her name, and for a moment, I'm so caught up in wondering where she is now—is he touching her, hurting her, fucking her—that I almost miss Remy's reply.

"I wasn't seeing Lavinia," he says, a wild fervency in his eyes as he looks between us. "It was someone else. Someone who had Vinny's hair and lips and eyes."

Sy asks, "What does that even mean?" but it's already clicking in my brain.

Remy turns to look at the river over his shoulder, a ghost clouding his eyes. "It means I jumped from this cliff with Leticia Lucia."

WE ARRIVE BACK at the tower beneath the dim glow of dawn, tired and dragging. I unlock the door, all the while thinking how pointless that'll be now. Mostly, I'm fighting the impulse to run upstairs and tell Lavinia about her sister—even though I don't actually have much to tell. She'd want to hear it, though. Somehow, I just know that. I know it just like I know that wherever she is right now, she's hating me for what I've done.

We climb the stairs slowly, with heavy steps and ticking brains. If Leticia, Remy, and Tate were at Widow's Rock that night, then I can't for the fucking life of me figure out why. Leticia was North Side Royalty. Maybe she went there to kill one of them. Maybe Remy's got it wrong. Maybe she didn't jump with him, maybe he pushed her. Maybe she pushed *him*. Maybe Leticia killed Tate and Remy followed her over the edge of the cliff.

My mind whirrs with the possibilities, and the only thing that brings it to a halt is stepping through the last door to a quiet, dark, empty living room. I stand there for a moment as Remy and Sy walk inside, going about the rituals of dropping their keys, taking off their shoes and jackets, quiet as they wind down. It hangs around us ominously, these new morsels of knowledge we've gained.

Somehow, they've just raised more questions.

And then Remy starts up the spiral staircase to the loft.

I've noticed him doing that more lately—seeking her out to check the star inked beside her hip—so it doesn't surprise me. It does, however, make me tense when he comes back down. He doesn't even look concerned, detouring into my bedroom.

It's only when he steps out, taking a cursory peek into his own, that he turns to me. "You see Vinny anywhere?" His eyes flick to the door leading up to the belfry, and he doesn't even wait for an answer.

He just starts walking to it.

I drop my keys loudly into the bowl beside the door. I guess I can do that now. I suppose it's fine to take the gun out of my waist-band and leave it right on the table, pulling out the clip first.

"Lavinia's not here."

The announcement emerges in a muted, solemn voice, and I feel more than see the two of them turn to look at me.

There's a long beat of silence, and then Sy's defensive voice. "I dropped her off. I made sure she was locked in before I left."

"I bet you did," I mutter, remembering what she looked like, writhing on top of him.

But Remy's more perceptive and he lands heavily from the bottom step, eyes boring into me. "What did you do, Nicky?"

I shrug my jacket off, busying myself with the routine. "I cut a deal with the Counts."

When I finally raise my gaze to Remy's, I'm met with his tensed jaw, a look of comprehension stealing his features. "You gave her to them."

I don't say anything at first, annoyed that I have to explain myself. We all knew she was more mine than theirs, but now they're looking at me expectantly, waiting for an explanation. "Lionel was coming for her, anyway. There was some kind of deal that we didn't know about. Some bullshit between him and Daniel. I just saved him a trip."

Remy twitches.

And then he barrels at me, full speed.

I have no time to react, and neither does Sy, before Remy slams into me. His hands fist in my shirt, lips distorted in a snarl. "What did you do? What *the fuck* did you do?!"

I shove him off, barking, "Why do you care?! Neither of you even wanted her! We can get another Duchess." I look at Sy, hoping to find an ally. "You wanted Verity, didn't you? Now's your chance."

Hotly, Sy clarifies, "I never said I wanted Verity."

But Remy jabs a finger into my chest, eyes aflame. "She belongs to all of us. It's not your place to sell her out."

"Yes, it fucking is." I slap his hand away. "Lavinia was mine. She was always *mine!*" I look between them, Remy and Sy, and give them as much honesty as I can muster. "She didn't want us. She didn't want me, she didn't want either of you, and she sure as *fuck* didn't want to be trapped here. What was I going to do? Set her free to be gunned down in the street?" Breathing hard, I ignore the twinge in my chest and let the words bitterly spill from my mouth. "I gave her what she wanted."

Remy shakes his head, looking at me in that way I hate. As if I've betrayed him. As if he doesn't know me. "I need her."

My face screws up. "You *need* her? For fuck's sake, you didn't even know her!"

"She keeps me on the ground!" he argues, a thread of desperation in his voice. "Neither of you even know. You weren't here when I went up to the belfry, but—" He pauses, eyes flicking to Sy, and there's a wildness in them that confuses me. "I couldn't tell what was real. I was up there." He points to the ceiling. "I was up on the edge, and I would have jumped. If it meant waking up from the dream and having Tate again, I would have stepped right off."

Sy gapes at him, baffled. "What are you talking about?"

"The day I cut my arm." Remy thrusts his arm out, showing the two purple scars. "It happened in the belfry, and I was going to jump. Not," he stresses to Sy, "to kill myself. That's not what I wanted to do. But everything got so mixed up and it just seemed like the answer."

Sy steps back like he's been physically pushed, his expression morphing to horror. "You were going to jump off the fucking tower?"

Remy looks like he wants to argue, mouth twisting into several aborted denials. But he doesn't. He visibly clamps down on them, looking Sy in the eye as answers. "Yeah, I was. But she stopped me." He rushes forward, expression urgent. "I can't explain why. Maybe it's that my memory was all mixed up, confusing her for her sister. Or maybe it's because she understood what was happening when no one else bothered to ask. But when I look at her star—when I count the points..." He lifts his hands in a wide shrug and they land limply against his legs. "It helps. *She* helps."

"So tattoo the star on me," I try, mentally categorizing where my nearest patch of un-inked skin might be.

Remy slides me a wry look. "No offense, brother, but it's not the same. I need her skin. *Don't* give me that look," he says to Sy.

"You don't need her skin," Sy says, sneering. "You just want her pussy."

Remy snipes back, "Don't act like she's never gotten your dick hard."

Sy bursts, "Well, she's obviously not our problem anymore! And personally, good riddance. She was nothing but a complication. Find yourself a new set of skin, Remy."

Remy watches the two of us, jaw going taut, before he storms away, disappearing into his bedroom with a wall-shuddering slam of the door. Silently, Sy does the same thing, taking the path to his room in a slow, straight line.

Once they're gone, it's just me.

I stare up into the empty loft, imagining I can see the shape of her body beneath the nest of blankets she'd made. I wonder when it'll fade, this nagging question in the back of my head. Where is she? What are they doing to her? Is she kicking their asses? Is she breaking free?

My musings are interrupted by the appearance of a tiny white paw peeking through the bars. I approach the spiral staircase like I'm walking through a fog, taking each step like I'd rather be doing anything else. It's dark up here, but the second my head clears the height of the platform, I see him.

The Archduke—Archie—is pacing a circle around her blanket, sniffing, searching.

He was downstairs when I left, which means he somehow managed to clumsily climb his way up the staircase with those stubby little legs.

"She's not here," I tell him, knowing that he's looking for her. "She had to go away."

Archie turns to me and then lets out a raspy little kitten cry.

I'm drawn to the platform, taking a look over her space. It's clean, but cluttered. The tool box sits near the door that leads to the belfry. A stack of books about horology stacked next to it. I walk over to her nest and bend, lifting the pillows. Underneath is the box I stole from under Lionel's floorboards, the bands still securely in place. Next to me, Archie climbs my foot, butting his little head against my leg. I look down at him and watch as he rubs the side of his cheek against it, and I spend a second wondering if I'll ever feel as much like absolute shit as I do right now.

I pick both the kitten and the box up, tucking him into the crook of my arm, a warm reminder in the cold silent tower below. The three of us have been at odds for a long time. Lavinia was just another wedge between us and, apparently, so was her sister.

Somehow, I think on my way back to my room, Archie squirming against my side, North Side was involved with the murder of my best friend, and I'm more resolved than ever to figure out who the fuck killed her.

32

Lavinia

Perez and Lars, another Count, throw me at my father's feet. I make a small, pained sound that I wish I could suck back inside my lungs. I'm home now—for whatever that word may mean—and raise my head to come eye to eye with Amos. Appropriate. With the tracker under my ear, I might as well be a dog, too. For all my bravado and attempts at defiance, this is where I've landed. Right where my father wants me.

Weak and defeated and beneath his boot.

I already regret the crying. The pleading. The begging. I knew this day would come, but I didn't realize how demoralized I'd become in the face of it, degrading myself by appealing to Nick. The humiliation still lingers bitterly in the back of my throat, and even though I have no right to it, the betrayal stings just as sharply. He told me to trust him. He promised to take care of me, protect me. I knew it was false; I *knew* it, and yet...

A part of me believed. I know it did, because it's the only way I can possibly explain the hurt of it.

"They just handed her over?" Lars is asking Perez. He'd met us here, at my father's mansion, so he's clueless. "Why would they do that?" Lars is smart, I'll give him that. There's a hint of cynicism in his voice that says he doesn't quite trust this. Too easy. I could be a Trojan horse.

One glance up at my father confirms that he shares the skepticism.

"Bruin took her pussy for a spin," Perez says, the toe of his shoe prodding at my ass. "He got what he wanted from her, and then he threw her away. Are we surprised?" He says the last sentence dryly, and somehow it strikes me more as a condemnation of the Dukes than me. Not that Perez doesn't still get a jab in. "Must have been underwhelmed with the goods."

"Get her on her feet," my father says, dropping into his plush leather armchair. I can already hear the clink of ice in his glass, the scent of bourbon pervading the air. Strong, obedient hands lift me from the floor and my father orders, "Look at me."

There's no urge to lift my chin in defiance. No impulse to tell him to fuck off. What's the point? He always wins.

When I just keep my eyes fixed to the floor, Perez's harsh fingers grip my chin and force my eyes upward.

My father's face twists in disgust. "I shouldn't be surprised at the lengths you'll go to embarrass this family, but shacking up with the West End goons? You always manage to exceed expectations. My darling daughter, the cunt of Forsyth." His hand rests on Amos' massive skull, scoffing. "Well, I see you're still a disgrace. A pathetic representation of the Lucia name. I should—"

"You should what?" I jerk my chin from Perez's grip. "Get rid of me? Trade me? Sell me? You've done all of that, yet here I am. Back in this hellhole."

He taps his glass, the ring on his finger clicking noisily. "If I had another option, trust me, I'd take it. Perez is still willing to take you. I've spent too much time molding him into the kind of Count I want running the family business to spare him the burden of you."

He shoots me a look. "Family implies relation, and you, as distasteful as it may be, are that link."

I give a dark, humorless laugh. "All the talent and genius currently occupying the Forsyth Royalty," I jerk my head at Perez, "and this nine-fingered idiot is seriously the best you can do? The only one embarrassing this family is you."

"Don't you dare question my decisions!" he shouts, temper suddenly flaring. "All of this chaos started when Leticia went missing—"

"You think that's when this started?" I gape at him openly. "God, you're still blind as a fucking bat."

His eyes narrow and I bite down on my bottom lip, hard enough that I taste blood. "You were always such a jealous little brat, weren't you? Insecure and petty, just like your mother." He leans forward slightly and Amos shifts with him. "Your sister is worth fifty of you. She's strong, capable, and loyal to the Lucia name. I can't prove it, but I know you had something to do with her disappearance."

"Then, once again, you're wrong." Perez's hand clamps down on my neck in warning, but I just clench my teeth. "Leticia was spoiled and spiteful, just like you, but I didn't do anything to her. She ran away."

My father's mouth twitches. "Is that the angle you're going with? She ran away from a future of power, wealth, and influence, handed to her on a silver platter? I admit, I expected better. You might be trash, but you're still my flesh and blood. I'd hoped some of the Lucia proficiency at subterfuge might somehow trickle down to you." He sucks his teeth. "Pity."

"It's the truth." I don't bother telling him about the note, because even seeing it with my own two eyes, I have to agree with my father. It galls me to think it, but he has a point. No one would believe she ran like hell away from him and his empire, or god forbid, did something unspeakable. The running I can see, but after two years, I know the reach of my father's arm. There's no way she could have hidden for this long. "Maybe you can't handle the possibility that you drove your precious Tisha away, but I know better. You're not a viper; you're a constrictor. All venom, no fangs."

Perez's fingers dig painfully into my neck. "I'm his fangs," he sneers. "Show some respect."

"So what now?" I ask, gritting my teeth against the pain. "You won. I'm twenty-one. When's the wedding?"

"It'll happen," he says, leaning back in the chair. "Eventually."

The word clings to the air and paranoia creeps up my spine. My eyes dart around the room, to the fireplace, to my father's desk, calculating.

Even Perez says, "Wait—what?"

"You're not quite marriage material yet, Lavinia. I thought the Lords would've worked that defiant attitude out of you. Daniel surely would have, if he'd had more time," he muses, "but Killian doesn't have the same flair for suffering. And the Dukes," he features harden, "well, Nicholas Bruin thought he'd grandstand at the expense of my house. I didn't push back at the time because I figured the little thug would do the work the others hadn't." His eyes take me in, displeasure in the curl of his lip. "But no, you're still the same difficult girl you've always been. Look at you. You couldn't even keep the interest of a Duke—a bunch of bottom feeders." Shaking his head, he sets his glass on the table, concluding, "I believe a week should do it."

The color drains out of my face, all the air punching out of my lungs. "A *week*?"

But he nods, saying, "Yes, I think a week of timeout will do—for now. I'll reassess when you've had a little time to ponder your predicament."

My knees threaten to give. I've never done more than three days in the chest, and that was already impossible. A week in there will kill me.

But it'll kill me in the slowest, worst possible way.

Strangely, the voice that comes to me belongs to Sarah.

"We fight—every day. But unlike our Dukes, we don't win or lose. The hard truth is that the fight never ends."

I take a lunging leap at the fireplace, grabbing the iron poker propped against the stone. Amos instantly springs up, snarling at my sudden movement, and I feel Lars' hand closing around a fistful of my hair. But I don't plan on hurting anyone. Not the dog, not my father, not Lars, or even Perez.

Just myself.

I hold the stake high and plunge it toward my chest, hoping to finish this once and for all. There was a time I thought my mother cowardly for doing this—for taking her life. I see it now for what it is.

One last fight, and then we can finally be done.

Unfortunately, the moment the sharp point pierces my sternum —barely a couple centimeters—I'm being tackled to the ground by Perez, whose face contorts in fury as he pries the poker from my grip.

"Getting real tired," he growls, throwing the poker aside, "of people taking liberties with my things." He wrenches my head back to snap, "Your life isn't yours to take. You'll be dead when I want you dead, and no fucking sooner." He levers to his feet with one arm, the other wrapped in a hard plaster that's just smacked into the side of my head, making my ears ring.

"Take her upstairs," comes my father's voice, and I immediately struggle away, feet kicking out against everything and everything.

"No!" I yell, thrashing and snapping. "Just fucking kill me, you cowards!"

"You leave me with no choice, Lavinia." He nods at Lars, whose arms are fighting to keep me contained. "You know where to take her, son."

I don't make it easy for them, bashing my feet into the railing as Lars and Perez haul me up the winding staircase toward my room. I punch and batter and bash my head back into Lars' shoulder, eliciting an irritated grunt from him. For that brief span of distance between my father's study and my bedroom, I fight. I fight so hard that my bones ache with it—so hard that I'm blind to anything but the instinct to rend and hurt.

And then I'm in front of the chest, and it all just spills out of me in a wave of horror.

The chest belonged to my mother. That much, I know. I don't know where she got it, or how it became such a permanent fixture at the foot of my bed, but I know it's been here since as long as I can remember, an ominous, malevolent presence that I'd spend my days skirting around, avoiding at any cost.

Perez is the one to lift the top, wrenching it open with a jerk of his one working arm. Turning to me, he smiles, all teeth and viciousness. "Don't worry, baby. I'll get you a better one of these when we're finally together. Nothing but the best for my old lady."

Lars picks me up and shoves me inside, their arms pushing and thrusting all my limbs into the small space. In the ferocity of my resistance, all I manage to get is a finger free.

The lid slams on it, making the bone crack.

I howl, snatching it inside to clutch against my chest, but outside, I can hear Perez tapping on the chest, voice booming through the wood.

"That's for my arm, you fucking bitch!"

Once they're gone, even the dull, throbbing pain in my finger isn't enough to distract me from the sensation of being confined so tightly. It was better when I was younger. More space, more air. Now, my knees are crushed so close to my chest that it's hard to breathe. There's no logic to the feeling of being suffocated. Light slices through the meager slits between the wooden planks, which means air can get through, and even if it couldn't, it'd make more sense to conserve what's in here than to squander it by screaming and hyperventilating.

But my mind can never grasp logic when I'm in here.

I immediately begin gasping, my legs so desperate to unfurl that I think it might kill me if I don't. How can a person survive this? How can someone not just explode from their body's demand to break free? How is it possible? And through the rush of incredulity, my mind tells me that it's not. It's not possible. I will die here, screaming myself hoarse, curled into this wretched fetal position, and it'll be slow, torturous, agonizing.

It's how I know I've gotten rusty. I've gone too long without being exposed to this dread, this terror, this utter fucking certainty. At some point, I'd exorcized it from my mind, foolishly believing myself free *enough*. I'm sure of it, because suddenly, that elevator seems like the embodiment of paradise in comparison.

I doubt I last two minutes before the thrashing begins.

I kick and hit, throwing any part of my body against the wood as a scream claws its way up my throat. I think it must hurt to curl my fist and push with all my might against the front of the chest, but I can't really feel it. My mind is too full of desperation now, driving my feet and knees uselessly into the aged wood. Over and over, I pummel myself into a tender, sore mass of meat and misery, even though I can't get enough distance between my limbs and the walls to impart any useful abuse.

"...the fight never ends."

I don't know how long I'm engaged in this frantic battle, my muscles screaming in protest as I beat and beat and beat. Two hours? Three? Four? I just know that it's unstoppable, the urge to struggle and scream. My body becomes a vibration of pure, undistilled will, but it's futile.

"We don't get trophies, Lavinia..."

The light between the planks of wood grows brighter and sharper. It's the familiar sight of it that gradually eases the nuclear need inside my chest. It's replaced with the burn of my lungs, dragging in gulps of air like I've just resurfaced from drowning. I know this place. I recognize the slants of light. The intensity. The hue. The angle. This is late afternoon light, meaning I've been engaged in the war against the walls for something like twelve hours. I've never done a thrashing for so long before.

It seeps out of me in a shuddering exhale, allowing me to remember the routine. Time. I need to count the time. There's a beginning and an end, an alpha and omega, and it's the hands of a clock, ticking away.

"There aren't any spoils for us."

Panting into the darkness, I collect my thoughts around myself like a veil, flipping through my mind for a book—an escape.

And then I begin a new countdown.

Seven days.

IT'S NOT JUST the absolute darkness, the inability to know what is awake or asleep, that makes my mind go to such terrible places. It's the sporadic surges of energy that get me—the urges to punch against the resistance around me—because they're a reminder of what I am. Curled up, trapped, helpless.

If only it were silent and the *'buh-bump... buh-bump'* of my heart wasn't so determined to remind me that I'm alive. If only I could pretend, sinking into this oblivion. I breathe in and out, but never deep enough, my chest constricted in the same way my body is. There's not enough room, never enough space. And I'm alone—so fucking alone.

'Buh-bump... buh-bump'

I hum a tune to the rhythm of my pulse—something harsh and fast I recognize from one of Remy's sketching benders. I think back to his philosophy textbook and a passage I read on solipsism; the belief that one's self is the only thing that truly exists. I wonder what the opposite is. Simulation theory?

I distract myself with these little morsels in between the thrashings. My body's too tired and defeated to fight, but my mind still tries. My lungs still breathe for me. The sun keeps rising and setting.

Six days.

I SHIFT, triggering the pain that starts in the base of my spine, a tight burning like a searing ember. I try not to focus on it, to think of better things, but everything is so small, so dark, so hot...

Stop. Focus. Flex my toes. Curl my fingers. Twist my neck. The little things I can do. Count to ten. To twenty. To the space between here and there, where things just feel less hard and my thoughts tread lightly. My father is a genius. This punishment... there is nothing worse. Isolation from everything. Light, air, people, love, hate. I realize how much we need all of it to survive, as much as air and food.

That's the startling clarity that comes to me on the second day.

How much I need people. How much I hate that. How their hands felt, their tongues and skin. *No!* I slam my head against the side of the box. The Dukes aren't my people. They never were.

I suck in a deep breath and start to count.

Five days.

"PSST," I hear. A finger pokes me sharply. "Wake up."

I shake my head and burrow deeper under the covers. They're tucked tight, my legs unable to move. "Go back to sleep," I mutter.

"I have a secret," she whispers. "Don't you want to hear it?"

Leticia loves secrets, like her hidden spot under the floorboards. She loves hearing them, telling them, keeping them, hoarding them. They're her vanity, her currency.

"Not particularly." I attempt to push back the blanket, but it's stuck in place. I always have to see her eyes when she talks. It's the only way to know if she's telling the truth. Usually, she isn't. After a struggle I give up, saying, "What secret?"

"I'm leaving," she answers.

"Why?" I ask. "Where?"

"I can't tell you." Of course. "But I'll be gone soon."

"He'll find you," I say, even though we both already know it. There's no escaping.

"Not this time. I've made sure." I still can't see her, but I feel her breath on my forehead and it makes me squirm in anticipation of her strike. "But do me a favor." My eyes clench against the confusion, because Leticia knows better than to ask favors of me.

We're worse than enemies.

We're family.

"What?" I ask, wishing I could see her.

Her answer comes in a strange, intense voice. "Make him pay."

I push and pull at the blanket, this time getting it off, and now I can see her—I can just open my eyes and...

'Buh-bump... buh-bump'

Darkness. Absolute darkness. My breath catches and I'm frozen, paralyzed and unable to move, to breathe, to think. But I feel the tear, hot on my cheek, burning a path toward the bottom of the chest. The dream wasn't real, but the nightmare very much is.

Four days.

THIS IS ABOUT BREAKING ME, I think, fingers numb and raw from picking at the crease between the lid and the side. My father wants me broken. He always has. Back when Leticia and I were small, he'd pit us against one another, choosing a winner. It could be about anything. Who could hold their breath longest. Who had the better grade, the shinier shoes. It was never about who was best— that was already known to be Leticia. *Always* Leticia. Me? The object of the competition was to break me. Despite the outcome, no matter how low I went, it was never enough. He sent me to the Lords, pushed me into captivity. When my rape and assault wasn't enough, I was tossed to the dregs. The Dukes.

Even when I was on my knees, it wasn't enough, and look where I am. The only place he thinks does the job. That's all I think of when I hear faint footsteps on the hardwoods. How angry he'll be that I'm still here. Has the dehydration not gotten me yet? How will he try to break me next? Who will he pawn me off on? Or will he finally be fed up and lock me away forever?

I'm not optimistic enough to believe he'd put me out of this misery.

The sound of footsteps come and goes, crossing the room, passing over the creaky floorboard near my dresser. That's when I realize I must be hallucinating, caught in another dream. If it were my father or one of his soldiers, they'd yank this chest open and drag me out on wobbly legs that no longer wish to hold the weight of me. My eyes will cringe against the light, my lungs will burst with the promise of fresh air, and I'll cry. I always cry when I emerge from this place, weak and so discouraged—not a drop of hope left in me.

Coming out is somehow always more humiliating than going in.

It's how I know it's not real. Father wouldn't deny himself the pleasure if he really meant to end this.

Three days.

I slam my head against the side again, forcing myself awake.

'Buh-bump... buh-bump'

I start my routine: the stretch, the counting, reciting a passage in my head. But my ritual is cut short by the flash of a light over the keyhole. I hold my breath, bracing myself for the man on the other side.

The top wrenches open so suddenly that I foolishly flinch away from it, squinting painfully into the blinding glare of light.

"What the fuck?" a voice breathes, low and full of disgust.

This isn't my father, nor is it a soldier. The man is enormous, and when his hands reach into the chest, around my body, to lift me up, I find myself void of the instinct to fight against it, because his scent crashes into me.

Wood and coldness, an undertone of mint, and something aggressively masculine.

"Sy?" It comes out in a skeptical croak, my throat dry and brittle. He grunts, dragging me out of the chest, and my knees hit the floor with a thud that makes him stiffen.

But I can see his face now that the light is gone, and it's the oddest thing. This man used to make me shudder in revulsion. He used to make me shrink back against his hatred. He used to be the worst of the worst, something to be avoided and tiptoed around.

And now I'm flinging myself at him, arms locking around his neck as the crying begins. I don't mean for it to. In fact, my whole body hitches with the effort of holding it in, but it escapes in tight, high-pitched wheezes into the warmth of his neck, and I have no control. I feel more than see his hands flung out at his sides, body rigid and so solid that I have no problem leaning against it.

"He wouldn't kill me," I cry, trembling so violently that I hear it in my own voice. "He wouldn't let me die, he wouldn't—"

"Sh!" Sy hisses, pressing a palm to the middle of my back. "You have to be quiet!"

But I've spent days now letting it loose, and it's not about to be denied now. I gnash my teeth, but the dry sobs escape through them in shuddering squawks, and I keep clutching Sy tighter and tighter, as if I could disappear within his strength and resolve.

"Take a breath, you're hysterical!" he snaps, trying to pry me off him. "If you dad hears us, then at least one of us will definitely be fucking dead."

I shake my head, and when he wrenches me back, glaring into my eyes, I hope he understands what I can't open my jaw wide enough to say.

I can't stop.

Once again, I question the veracity of everything when it seems like he gets it, a somber comprehension filling his eyes. His mouth forms a tight, grim line. "Then I'll need to choke you out. I can't take you down the stairs like this."

He doesn't give me time to respond, darting around behind my back and wrapping a powerful arm around my neck. It's almost a relief to feel his forearm crushing my windpipe. To feel his other palm pressing against the back of my head, cutting off my air supply, making my vision go spotty and dark.

If he's expecting me to struggle, I don't.

Just before everything goes black, I think of time and how much of it I've borrowed. I think of the cost and wonder if I can pay it. I pass out thinking of that, but the panic sinks under the surface, too deep to reach.

I don't know how much time passes before I begin stirring. I just know that my body jostles against something firm but comfortable, and I rise from sleep like a frightened, wary thing. It isn't until my eyelids clumsily rise that I realize I'm in the backseat of a car, streetlights zipping by. My gaze swims in and out, but I manage to focus on the shape of the driver. The curve of Sy's cheek, the crouch of his bold eyebrow, the muscles shifting beneath his brown skin when he reaches out to flick the radio off.

I lay back here and watch him for a long time, quiet and still. It's the height of irony, but now that I can move, I find that I don't want to. Maybe it's a sense of security that I have no right to feel. Maybe I'm just defeated. Maybe this is what giving up feels like.

"You saved Remy." The low rumble of his voice doesn't startle me. It crests over me like a wave, tucking into the spaces beneath me. "Even after he fucked with you. Even after what he did at the Hideaway. Even after... everything." He stops at a red light, and the curve of his mouth is tense and pensive. "Verity couldn't have done that. It's not her fault. She just wouldn't know how to handle him. She would have freaked out—she would have bailed."

He turns to glance at me in the back seat, the shadows of the car blotting out his eyes. Even though I know he hates me—even though I know he's dangerous and full of hurtful things—I'm struck by the thought that I've never seen anything so soothing.

"But you stuck around and talked him down, even though you probably had every right not to. That's real loyalty." When the light turns green, he turns back to the road, easing the gas to accelerate. "You're our Duchess now, Lavinia. And that means we'll always come for you."

I wonder how Nick feels about that.

Through the windshield, I can see the tower in the distance, rising defiantly into the air. It's frozen hands look like someone who just took a breath one day and decided this was it—7:32 was as good as it could do—and now it's content to be inert, staring out over Forsyth with its hands so close to touching, suspended in the moment before a clap.

Silently, I close my eyes.

Zero days.

ACKNOWLEDGMENTS

Sam:

All our love goes out to our phenomenal beta team, Crystal P, Lisa, and Nikki. They're the mortar in this precariously tall tower of trauma. To the readers in Angel Antics: You glorious bitches make our clock tick. You'll never realize how often Angel and I are sitting here in chat going, "Oh, I hope they like this!" So yeah, we really hope you like this. And I'm sitting here so excited to pass this out to our ARC team, who for serious, is the best cheer team an author could possibly ask for. Thank you all so much for the help and kindness and encouragement. Additionally, big thanks to my cat, Crowley, for typing 300 words of this. Yeah, they were all the number '3' because he likes to roost on my num-pad, but still. He's made a vital creative contribution to this universe, and I appreciate that.

Angel:

Mine is about the same as Sam's! Thanks for being amazing, for all the awesome TT's and IG posts and edits, for the love of Sam's fictional cover models. The passion you carry for our terrible, evil, awful men we just can't stop creating. Hope you enjoyed this one as much as the last!

*If you're not in Angel's Antics on FB please give us a follow! Also, join our dark romance news letter sign up HERE!

AFTERWORD

The Dukes and Lavinia will return in book five of the Royals of Forsyth series, Dukes of Madness.

Two years of my life have been stolen by the Royals of Forsyth. Two years of captivity and hell. Two years at the whim of powerful men.
I spent that time seeking freedom.
Now I want nothing more than revenge.
It won't be easy. It'll be painful and humiliating, but in the end, taking down the thugs, thieves, and criminals terrorizing Forsyth will be worth it.
I just have to decide who to go after first.

The Dukes of Madness is book 5 in the contemporary, dark romance, *Royals of Forsyth U* series by best-selling authors, Angel Lawson and Samantha Rue.

Reading Order:

Lords of Pain
Lords of Wrath

Lords of Mercy
Dukes of Ruin
Dukes of Madness
Dukes of Peril

Continue for a sample of Devil Incarnate by Angel & Sam…

DEVIL INCARNATE

While you wait for Dukes of Madness here's a sample of Devil Incarnate, a m/f dark bully romance by Angel & Sam

Georgia
Freshman Year

I look into the camera, testing a crooked smile before clicking the button. I lower my phone to assess the picture, deciding that it's garbage. I try another, this one with my cleavage in the shot. Oh, yeah. That's definitely it.

I add a caption:

Getting ready to crush these lame PhysEd credits. Should I do swim, bball, or track?

#PrestonStrong #killmenow #whyaretheserequiredcredits #Swim-Devils #BallerDevils #RunningDevils

The bench in front of the gym is nice. It's a warm day for March —warm enough that I've abandoned my sweater in favor of undoing a few buttons on my uniform. I get a couple instant responses from people who don't even go here, so I'm scrolling down my ChattySnap when a group of people walk by.

I look up, realizing who it is.

It's *The Devils*, capital T, capital D.

They ignore me, of course. As they should. I'm just a freshman, and they're all juniors. Well, not just juniors. They're some of the most popular people in school. Athletic. Smart. Rich.

Just then, one of them makes eye contact with me. Heston Wilcox. *Oh, god.* He's so ridiculously handsome that my heart instantly starts pitter-pattering. It beats even harder when his steps falter, slowing.

"Hey, you're Georgia, right?" he asks.

I nod, holding back an inner, girlish squeal at the fact he knows my name. *My* name! "Uh, yeah. Hi!" I feel a little cringe at the excitement in my voice, but he just walks back a step, facing me.

Heston's lips tilt into a wry smirk. "You busy tonight?"

I feel a hot blush creep up my cheeks. "Er... me?" A couple of his friends wait nearby, and my eyes dart over. They're all Devils. Hamilton Bates, Ansel Davenport, Emory Hall. There's a girl tucked under Hamilton's arm. Her name is Campbell, but I'm not sure if that's a first or last name.

"Yes, you," he says with a little laugh, amusement dancing in this ocean blue eyes.

I push my shoulders back, trying to adopt a facade of perfect cool. "No, I'm not busy tonight."

He lifts his chin. "I'm having a party. You should come."

Holy shit! Heston Wilcox is inviting *me* to a party! I stammer out, "To your house?"

"Yep."

Blush deepening, I admit, "I don't have a ride."

He glances over at the guys, eyes zeroed in. "Campbell can give you a ride. Isn't that right, Cam?"

Campbell scowls, obviously not pleased at someone telling her what to do, but Hamilton leans down and whispers something into her ear. Whatever he says is enough to smooth her expression. She gives me a look and calls out, "Meet me by the parking lot at eight."

"S-sure," I stutter, trying to look casual as I cross my legs. "Yeah. Sounds great."

They walk off, just like that—as if Heston Wilcox hadn't just socially anointed me.

~

The ride with Campbell is awkward. I try to strike up a conversation three times, but it falls flat. She barely answers me. I give up, spending the rest of the drive staring at my phone, full of excited nerves. I've been to parties before, but nothing like one thrown by the Devils.

When we arrive, Campbell all but leaves me to scurry after her in my heels. About the only thing that makes me feel a little less like an out-of-place loser is the way Heston looks at me when his eyes find me.

He smiles. "Hey. You made it."

Breathlessly, I say, "Yeah. Hi."

His eyes have that little gloss to them, like maybe he's already a bit buzzed off something. I don't blink an eye when he hands me a beer, a hand landing on my lower back to lead me into a room with a billiard table.

We spend a long time like that; him leading me around the party, talking to people here and there—people I know *of*, but don't actually know. None of them really pay attention to me, but sometimes, Heston will bend down to say something into my ear, like, "You have nice legs," or, "See that guy over there? That's Carl. He can get you anything you want," or, "Want another drink?" Every time he does, I get a small shiver, and the hand resting on the small of my back rubs a little, like he knows.

I wasn't totally expecting it, so it's surprising to find that I'm definitely the girl on his arm for the night. The other girls seem surprised at the way he keeps me at his side too, throwing me the occasional confused or jealous glance. Even when he starts up a game of pool with his boys, he still returns to me, leaning in to talk some whispered smack about Ansel's form.

Never one to be bashful about these things, when the game winds to a close, I play it up, straining to give him a kiss on his cheek for good luck.

When he sinks the eight ball, his eyes find mine, mouth slanting into a wicked grin.

It's such a thrill. Heston isn't just good looking and popular. He's a *Devil*. He's one of the Four Horsemen of the school. He and the other guys have reputations beyond being smart and athletic. The Devils have impossible standards. Each one is rumored to have a 'test' girlfriends are supposed to pass to even be with them. Passing a test, getting 'marked' by one of them, is the fastest way to the top of the social ladder.

But that's not why I'm here. I don't really care about status. I've had my eye on him for a while—there's something magnetizing about him. Dangerous. Sexy. I've heard the rumors about his cock and I'm positively dying to give it a spin.

Sometimes you see the big, life-altering events barreling like a freight train down the track. Other times it happens in a blink, no warning sound, no flashing light, no barricades keeping you off the tracks.

I should know this is one of them, but it's hard to think when his lips are so warm, tasting bitter-sweet like beer when he kisses me, right in front of everyone. It's impossible when he whispers in my ear, "You're so pretty. Want to go upstairs?" And I'm too far gone by the time I'm up in his room, taking in the *boyness* of everything; the scent of his body spray, the box of condoms on his dresser, the grinning Devil on the flag hanging over his messy, unmade bed.

"Do you live out here by yourself?" I ask, chills running down my spine from the feel of his lips on my neck. "Not in the main house?"

"I like how it's quiet," he answers, voice deep and smooth. "Private."

It's not quiet now—well, not downstairs. Down there, the party is in full swing; alcohol, skinny dipping, loud music. The bass vibrates through the guest cottage walls, shaking the dresser mirror with every thump and thud. It's a crazy party, one made even crazier by the fact I was invited by Heston Wilcox himself.

He crosses the room and stops in front of his desk, fussing with a laptop. Music streams through the speakers, covering up the rowdy rap from downstairs. The curve of his shoulders, the way he moves—sure and masculine—makes something low in my belly spark.

I know how it is for guys. They have to flirt and put on a bunch of pretenses to get into a girl's pants. I've seen the games.

I'm not here to play.

I know what I want, and I know how to get it. No frills, no bull-shit. I want on Heston's dick, like ten minutes ago, and I'm not about to make him work for it.

I take off my sweater and take a quick glance in the mirror to adjust my purple lace bra. The bra makes my tits look fantastic, probably my best feature. Guys are super into them and I know it.

When Heston turns back to me, he blinks once, slow and long, as he takes me in.

My stomach flips at the intensity of his gaze. "It seems so grown-up to be out here alone. No parents, free to do whatever you want." I watch as his fingers tug at the zipper on his hoodie, and he shrugs it off, tossing it on the back of a chair. Next he removes his shirt and I'm treated to his lean and long body. The perfect swim-mer's physique. "It's cool that you can have parties like this, even though you're only a junior in high school, and no one cares. My dad is pretty strict—"

His mouth is on mine, cutting me off, tongue pushing through my lips. His fingers move quickly, confidently, under my bra strap. "Fuck, you're stacked," he says, eyeing my tits hungrily. He's right. My tits *are* big. He circles my nipple with his fingers, sending a tremor between my legs. He pinches it and grins. "You like that?"

Electricity zings through my body. Pain and pleasure. I arch back against it. "I do."

"I heard you like it dirty," he says, biting on my earlobe.

I'm distracted by his upper body. The hard lines of his chest and abs. I parse his words and look up, feeling dazed. "What?"

"I heard you like it dirty and *hard*," he says, kissing me, lips rough against mine. One hand circles my waist, thumb digging into my flesh while the other squeezes my breast.

"Who told you that?" I ask, reaching for the button on his jeans. I unzip his pants and pull his cock out. I just about die when I get my hands on him, a slow heat building between my legs. He's long and thick. Big like the rumors. Warm and ready.

His hips buck forward, pushing it into my palm. He shrugs at my question and gives me a smirk. "Think you can take that?"

I open my mouth to answer, to tell him I'm not a virgin and I'm ready to do this, but he kisses me again, harder this time, using his body to angle me to the bed. I try to keep up with his kisses, with his warm tongue, and when the back of my knees hit the mattress, I run my hands down his chest, hoping to slow him down. This isn't like Reilly from Spanish, or Trevor from The Nerd, or Lance from my parents' Christmas party. Being with a guy like Heston is something I want to savor.

"You're so sexy," I tell him, kissing along his shoulders.

He cups my face in his hands and grins down at me, a twinkle in his eye. In that moment, I feel like I'm the only girl he sees. The only one he wants. I feel special. His thumb runs down my cheek, and he bends to kiss me. Sparks ignite across my body, down my limbs, to my fingers and toes. His hand runs down to the hem of my skirt and then back up, fingers twisting tight in my panties. When the kiss breaks, I look at him once again.

"You want this, right?"

"Yes," I admit, but as I say it, something feels... *off*. It's the change in his expression. It's the feel of my panties digging into my sides. It's the dark glaze in his eye that tells me I'm not entirely sure what it is I'm agreeing to.

"Good." He moves faster than I can blink, using his size, power, and athleticism against me. He pushes me back on the bed and before I can bounce, he's on top of me, yanking my panties down my thighs in a sharp motion. His cock presses into me, hard and intimidating. He shifts and thrusts a finger inside, making me gasp. "Jesus, you're tight. Sure you're not a virgin? Is Halloway a liar?"

I blink, trying to follow his words while he fucks me with his finger. *John Halloway*? We'd hooked up a few times over the summer. I'd gone down on him behind the tennis courts at the club and let him fuck me at the Fourth of July party. Did he say something to Heston?

"I'm not a virgin," I gasp out, trying to get into the rhythm. Heston moves fast, hard. It's a challenge to keep up. I sit up to meet him, to find his mouth. He withdraws his finger and plants a hand right into the middle of my chest, shoving me back down flat. He waits for a beat, glancing over to the laptop. From this angle, he's like a magnificent animal, muscle stretched tight, corded and perfected. I reach for his cock, stroking it with my fingers. He looks down on me, his expression shuttered, and falls forward, both hands cinched roughly around my wrists. I grimace but spread my legs, giving him access.

This isn't quite like Reilly, or Lance, or Trevor, or even John, who fucked me hard in the coat closet. There's this spark in Heston's eye, a strange tightness at the corners of his jaw. He's just excited, I think—*by me*—but a dark shadow flickers across his face, and a chill settles in my belly. It intensifies when his grip grows tighter and I say, "Wait, can you—"

His hand loosens, but not to release me. It's just enough to gain leverage so that he can flip me on my stomach. The heavy weight of his hand presses on my lower back and I twist my head to the side. "Heston, I—" but the air stalls in my lungs, pushed out by the weight of his hand around my neck, curling around my throat. Over the music, I hear the tear of foil and the sound of him rolling the rubber down. My heartbeat is like thunder now, but I can't untangle the threads of fear and arousal long enough to decide which wins. I squirm against his hold, and the thing is, I've been with a few guys by now. I've been with the sweet ones and the rough ones. The clumsy ones and the experienced ones. Generally, I'm down to try every flavor.

Absolutely nothing has made me as wet as I am right this second.

A moment later, fingers dig into my hip, lifting me up, and he enters me fast and hard, the sound of our flesh coming together a deafening slap.

It strikes me then what that tight, dark shadow on his face reminds me of.

Like someone who wants to hurt me.

I close my eyes and let him.

Afterwards, when we're pulling on our clothes, he looks different again. Relaxed, calm. Like everything is normal, totally casual. I try my best to mirror this, taking my cues from the way he moves languorously around his room, pulling on a clean shirt, even though there's a lump wedged in the back of my throat.

He says goodbye with a two-fingered wave, goes back to join the party, and barely looks at me again the rest of the night.

An hour later, I'm back in Campbell's car. It's quiet again. I don't try to make small talk this time, instead staring out the window at the passing streetlights, wondering what this knot is that's taken residence in my chest.

It was just sex.

Truthfully, I don't even really mind that he blew me off after. That's what guys do. If they want some more, then they'll start being nice again, paying me attention. I'm used to it. Probably better off anyway, because boyfriends are just drama and a long stretch of same-same boring.

It was just... not the kind of sex I'm used to. Hot, but also cold. It felt good, but also hurt. It was nice, but also mean. Savage. Scary. Heston's a powerful guy—a lot stronger than me. Being at his mercy like that—being hurt like that—should have been repulsive and terrifying, and in some ways, it was.

Mostly, it was the best sex I've ever had.

My cheeks burn with shame, because I might be young, and

maybe I've only slept with a few guys, but I'm pretty sure that's not what sex is supposed to be—even casual hookups at parties with older guys. I already hear whispers behind my back at school, that I'm easy. What would people say if they knew I liked... that?

From beside me, Campbell lets out this long sigh. "Are you, like... okay, or whatever?"

I turn to her, blinking in surprise. "Yeah."

"Heston didn't do anything to you, did he?" Her gaze slides over to me. "Something you didn't want? You're not drunk or stoned?"

"I'm not drunk," I assure her. I had a beer, but it was gross and I ended up ditching it halfway through. "And Heston didn't..." I swallow, feeling a moment of panic that maybe she knows. Maybe she's looking at me like that because she's perfectly aware that I'm some kind of sexual freak. Meekly, I finish, "Everything's fine."

Everything's *fine*.

～

"Damn," Emory Hall says, leaning over Ansel's shoulder. They're sitting at their little lunch table, looking at Ansel's phone. I walk by, wedged between trying to catch Heston's eye and pretending like I don't care if he looks at me at all. It's been a month since the party, and although he hasn't outright rejected me, he also doesn't seem like he wants to come back for more.

In any case, I certainly never got an invitation to sit at the table or any of the perks the Playthings get. I'd nearly talked myself into believing it'd been his 'test', but if it had been, then I must have passed.

I *must* have.

"God, he's just drilling her," Carlton says, holding up his own phone. Hamilton glances over and then away with a bored look.

Xavier sits with his arm around Skylar Adams—*that's new*—who wrinkles her nose in distaste.

"Are those even real?" Ansel asks. "They're huge."

My eyes skim the room and see that almost everyone has their phone out. The reactions vary—wide-eyed, amused, impressed. I make my way over to a table with the other freshman girls that I know from soccer. Every one of them has their phones out, eyes glued to the screen.

"What's everyone looking at?" I ask, sliding into my seat and placing my tray on the table.

"You've got to see this," Amanda says.

Betsy frowns and puts her phone face down on the table. "This video that just went viral. It's... gross."

"Oh god, is it another video of some guy squirting milk from his nose?" I dig in my bag for my phone and see that I have a dozen notifications—maybe more. People are sharing the video like wildfire. I open up my phone, going to my ChattySnap account. The video is in the top ten spots. I click on one, and although it takes my brain a second to adjust to what I'm seeing, my body reacts differently, going fiery hot and ice cold, all at once. I know instantly, a ball of nausea building when I process what's happening on the screen.

It's a girl face down on the bed, a strong naked guy pounding into her while he holds her down. Neither of their faces are visible. Her hair covers her features, and he manages to stay just off screen. Bile runs up the back of my throat and I swallow it back.

The girl is me.

"Who—who is that?" I ask, pretending to narrow my eyes.

"No clue. Not even sure if it's from Preston. It just started popping up all over today." Amanda peers over at my phone. "Can you see anything identifiable? Like something that would tell whose room that is?"

I've spent all month trying to forget about hooking up with Heston. How off it was. How *bad* it felt afterward, when I was sore and spent, and wishing pathetically for one soft touch. How it was too hard, and too fast, and how despite all that, I've been alternately relieved and confusingly disappointed that he's not like those other guys who wanted to come back for more.

Looking at the video, small pieces click into place. The way he preened toward the laptop. How he kept me down and my face covered. How we didn't speak, how I *couldn't* speak with his fingers around my throat. How, when it was over, he wouldn't make eye contact. No, that's not right. His eyes were dark and emotionless. Cold.

Speculation flows around me, while all I can do is stare at the video, looking for anything that would identify it as me. Thank god my hair looks more brown than red. How long will it be before everyone finds out that it's me? That I let him do that to me? That I *liked* it? I finally shut it off, eyes stinging and every inch of my skin feeling the warm heat of humiliation. The rest of the table is still obsessed, eyes glued to their phones. I glance over at the table of Devils, and Heston's all grins, looking smug and proud.

For the first time in weeks, he meets my eyes.

And winks.

You can find the rest of Georgia and Heston's dark tale at Amazon.